Fallen Raven

(RAVEN DUET, BOOK 1)

DIANA A. HICKS

HMG, INC.

Copyright

This is a work of fiction. Names, characters, places, and incidents are either the product of the author's imagination or are used fictitiously, and any resemblance to actual persons living or dead, business establishments, events, or locales, is entirely coincidental.

Fallen Raven, Book One

COPYRIGHT © 2022 by Diana A. Hicks

All rights reserved. No part of this book may be used or reproduced in any manner whatsoever without written permission of the author or HMG, Inc. except in the case of brief quotations embodied in critical articles or reviews.

Publishing History

Digital ISBN 978-1-949760-50-7

Paperback ISBN 978-1-949760-49-1

Paperback ISBN 978-1-949760-63-7

Hardcover ISBN 978-1-949760-62-0

Credits

Photographer: Wander Aguiar

Cover Model: Andrew Biernat

Cover Designer: Veronica Larsen

Editor: Becky Barney

Recommended Reading Order

The Crime Society World

Beast Duet

Lost Raven - Novella

King of Beasts (Beast Duet #1)

King of Beasts (Beast Duet #2)

Wolf Duet

Wolf's Lair - Prequel

Big Bad Wolf (Wolf Duet #1)

Big Bad Wolf (Wolf Duet #2)

Once Upon A Christmas - Bonus Epilogue

Raven Duet

Dark Beauty - Prequel

Fallen Raven (Raven Duet, #1)

Fallen Raven (Raven Duet, #2)

Knight Duet

Wicked Knight (Knight Duet, #1)

Wicked Knight (Knight Duet, #2)

Cole Brothers World

Stolen Hearts Duet

Entangle You

Unravel You

Steal My Heart Series

Ignite You

Escape You

Escape My Love - Bonus Epilogue

Provoke You

Cole Twins Duet

Unleash You

Defy You

Praise for Diana A. Hicks

"Hicks' first installment of her Desert Monsoon series is confident and assured with strong storytelling, nuanced characters, and a dynamic blend of romance and suspense."

— KIRKUS REVIEWS

What makes any romance a great read isn't the fact that two hot people meet and fall in love. It is the episodes that bring about the falling in love and the unexpected places the experience takes the characters that make it an enjoyable read. Diana A. Hicks knows just how to make this happen.

— READERS' FAVORITE

About the Author

Diana A. Hicks is an award-winning author of dark mafia romance and steamy contemporary romance with a heavy dose of suspense.

When Diana is not writing, she enjoys kickboxing, hot yoga, traveling, and indulging in the simple joys of life like wine and chocolate. She lives in Atlanta and loves spending time with her two children and husband.

Check out my bookstore!

Don't forget to sign up to my newsletter to stay up to date on my latest releases, free content, and other news. Subscribe to my VIP List now!

Diana A. Hicks
SINFULLY DARK ROMANCE

Dear Readers,

I'm so excited to finally share Fallen Raven, Book One with you. This next installment in the Crime Society series features Enzo and Aurora. You met Enzo briefly in King of Beasts and Big Bad Wolf.

You don't need to read the previous duets to follow this new story. However, reading books one through four first will help you understand the mafia world and conflicts a bit better.

The reading order goes like this...

King of Beats Duet (books 1 and 2) - Rex and Caterina
Big Bad Wolf Duet (books 3 and 4) - Santino and Luce
Fallen Raven Duet (books 5 and 6) - Enzo and Aurora

So now it's Enzo's turn to find love. Though for him, the road to happiness is going to be long and bumpy. Enzo and Aurora's star-crossed lovers story begins in high school, where they both learn that in a mafia world of angels and demons, no one safe.

If you read the prequel **Dark Beauty** back in February, feel free to skip to Part II in this book.

One last note: Fallen Raven is a 120k-word bully romance in a high-school setting. It is book one in the Fallen Duet and is part of the Crime Society World. It contains explicit scenes with dubious situations some readers might find offensive and/or triggering. This is not a YA novel. Reader discretion is advised.

Welcome to Midtown High!
Xoxo,
Diana

PART ONE
Dark Beauty

RAVEN DUET, PREQUEL

Be Nice to the Dragon Lady

Aurora

Today my mother thought it would be a good idea to send me on a coffee run. She meant well. For whatever reason, she figured the more time I spent out and about in New York City, the sooner I would fall in love with it and give up on the idea of going home.

Home. I missed Las Vegas. I missed the hot summer nights. I missed Grandma.

I weaved my way through the crowded sidewalk, while people bumped into me like I was invisible. The fact that my brain was still on west coast time didn't help matters. Park Avenue was too awake and moved too fast for me.

"What will it be, Miss?" The barista behind the coffee shop counter pointed his chin at me. His tattoo sleeve peeked from under his long sleeve shirt as he reached behind him to grab an espresso mug and set it on the counter. "Clara," he called out.

"Um." I hesitated because there was no menu posted.

"You, Miss?" He moved on to the woman behind me.

The brunette with a Corgi in her arms stepped forward. Even though she was shorter than me, she managed to look down at me before she ordered. "Matcha cappuccino with oat milk, hold the sweetener, and add two scoops of protein."

"Large?" the barista asked.

I stood there like an idiot and watched them interact with each other. Another reminder that I was the outsider here. The city seemed hell-bent on reminding me of that fact.

"Miss? You ready now?" His deep voice brought me back.

"Two of what she said," I blurted out. Mainly, because I recognized the word cappuccino, and I didn't want to waste any more of his time.

"That'll be sixteen even."

Yikes. For two coffees?

I dug through my purse and handed him a twenty-dollar bill. When he didn't make an effort to give me change, I added, "Keep the change."

"Thanks." He motioned to the guy behind me.

Twenty minutes later, I found my way back to our new swanky apartment, still hoping my parents would change their minds and move us all back to Las Vegas. New York City wasn't for everyone. Not to mention, Dad's sudden luck in business seemed too good to be true. No one went from living from paycheck-to-paycheck to all of a sudden scoring a three-million-dollar apartment on Park Avenue.

What had Dad gotten us into this time?

Mom insisted everything was fine. That I was just missing home too much. But I knew better. I hadn't forgotten the last time Dad and "his business dealings" landed all five of us in a motel for a whole semester after we lost our house. I'd never been the proud type, but I had been so embarrassed when my friends saw me leaving the town's no-tell motel every morning to go to school. Needless to say, they weren't my friends for much longer after that.

With a sigh, I shouldered open the wide door to our new home.

"There she is." Mom rushed to me with the biggest smile and hugged me. "Be nice to the dragon lady," she whispered in my ear, took my tray of coffees, and set it on the side table.

Whenever she acted this bubbly and alert, it was because she wanted something badly.

"Three?" The dragon lady stood in the middle of the room, looking me up and down as if she could see into my soul. "I wasn't aware of any children."

Something about the timbre of her smoker's voice made the hair on the back of my neck stand on end. I didn't need to be a New Yorker to know the woman belonged in this world. She oozed wealth and power. When she finished her inspection of me, her features darkened like my mere presence was an insult to her. My two brothers weren't running up and down the stairs like they had been when I woke up this morning. No doubt the dragon lady scared them off.

"Signoria Vittoria." Mom placed her hand on my back and ushered me forward. "This is our daughter, Aurora."

"Nice to meet you." I offered her a nervous smile. My heart raced under her scrutiny. "And it's Rory."

"I suppose what's done is done." She waved her hand in dismissal. "How old are you?"

"Seventeen."

"She'll be eighteen in a few months." Mom stood taller next to me.

"Where are you going to school?"

"Midtown High," Mom answered for me. "Mr. Alfera was kind enough to give us a recommendation."

"Is that so?" Signoria Vittoria inhaled deeply. After a beat, she opened her clutch purse and retrieved a business card. "I cannot imagine you have discussed your husband's business dealings with your ten-year-olds."

The ten-year-olds. I supposed she meant my twin brothers.

"But Aurora is old enough to understand."

"She is, but of course we haven't said anything." Mom gripped my arm to warn me not to say a word. "She knows nothing."

"Well, if she's going to Midtown High, she needs to know." She shook her head. "She'll need to sign a non-disclosure agreement." At this point, she was talking mostly to herself as she dialed a number on her phone. "Charles. I need papers drawn for the Vitali family." She met my gaze. "They have a daughter." She waited another moment, then ended the call.

"Is there a problem?" I asked, and then winced, when Mom dug her fingernails into my arm.

And now I knew without a doubt that Dad was involved in something shady. I was somewhat okay with illegal. Dad sold used luxury cars back in Las Vegas. I always had a sense that not all of those vehicles were his to sell. But looking at Signoria Vittoria with her designer clothes and Prada shoes and all those diamonds around her neck, I could only assume Dad was in over his head on this one—way over.

"Michael Alfera personally asked me to introduce you to our circle. Children tend to complicate things. But I will handle things as we discussed." She handed Mom the business card clutched between her fingers. "Do call my interior designer to assist you with the apartment. I'll be at the Chanel store at four. Make sure you're there with your daughter."

I stepped back when Signoria Vittoria strode in our direction and headed toward the front door. The lock clicked behind her, and I practically spun around to face Mom. "What is going on, Mom? I mean, is she for real? She looks like she stepped out of one of those mafia movies, like the Sopranos. Omigod. What did Dad do?"

"Nothing." She shrugged. "I guess she didn't like our sectional. What do you think?"

In truth, the sofa with the chunky armrests and wooden legs and matching end tables clashed with the modern architecture and tall windows of the apartment. Our stuff belonged in a cheap motel, not in a high-rise in the Upper East Side. Not that I knew a lot about decor, but even the coffee shop two blocks down had nicer furniture than this.

"Don't change the subject, Mom."

"I will tell you everything. But you heard Signoria Vittoria. You need to sign the NDA first. I promise, it's nothing bad. Come on, Rory, this is a once in a lifetime opportunity. We finally get to have everything we want." She squealed and hugged me. "You get to go to an elite school that pretty much guarantees you'll get accepted to Columbia too. Isn't that what you always wanted?"

Yeah, Mom was right. Columbia had always been my dream. This move to the city could make all of that become a reality. But dreams were rarely what they seemed. I was old enough to know that. "The dragon lady scares me."

"Yeah, me too. But you heard what she said. She's here to help us get introduced into their circle. Now, go get ready, so we can meet her at four. I have a call to make." She wiggled the business card in front of me with the biggest smile I'd ever seen on her face.

Money did that to her. The promise of more money was how Dad always talked her into doing just about anything. Like being nice to rich people at the casinos so she could walk out of there with their car keys, the one time she slept with Dad's boss because Dad asked, or moving cross country to New York City.

"Mom, there's no way this thing can end well for us."

"You think too much." She kissed my cheek. "We're doing this for you and your brothers. So you can have a better life. Don't throw it away."

"Maybe it's not too late. Give Michael Alfera whatever money Dad took from him and let's go home. We don't belong here, Mom. This world isn't for us."

Mom blew out a breath and took both my hands in hers. "We promised your dad we would give this place a chance. Wear something nice, so we can sign Signoria Vittoria's papers, and then, after you hear all the details, you can decide if you want to stay."

"Wait. You're letting me choose?" I raised both eyebrows in surprise.

"Yes. Of course."

"Mom, I'm not leaving without you and the twins." I rubbed my temple as various scenarios flitted through my mind.

Dad wasn't a bad guy. He just had terrible business sense. Easy money was always his end game. And his friends were the worst. They knew just how to manipulate him into making bad deals on their behalf, which usually ended with him losing more money.

"There you go thinking the worst of your dad." Mom shook her head.

"Did Dad ask you to do it again?" I squirmed away from her.

I wouldn't put it past Dad to ask Mom to sleep with his current boss. Mainly because he'd done it before. I didn't know how many times Mom had had to save Dad. But I did know of at least one incident for sure. In the past year, I'd seen enough not to trust Dad when it came to his business ventures.

I thought of Signoria Vittoria asking about my age. Yeah, I was old enough to be sold to the highest bidder. I wished I could say Dad would never stoop so low, but I honestly couldn't. I glanced at the state-of-the-art kitchen and the shiny marble floors. What did Dad do to earn all this overnight?

"Rory, I'm sorry you had to see that. Walking in on me like that."

It had been only a second, but the scene was tattooed on my mind. Mom having sex with Dad's ex-boss in our motel room while Dad had a beer in the parking lot—as my brothers played soccer across the street.

I mostly saw the old man's balding head and saggy arms and butt. I didn't see her exactly, but I knew it was her. It was her hand on his right hip while he pinned her against the wall. I shook my head to chase the memory away.

Was this fancy apartment enough to make up for what she went through to get Dad back on his feet?

"Let's go home, Mom. Dad can stay. And do whatever he wants with this Michael Alfera."

"This is our time. I promise you're safe. And I'm about to become a socialite." She beamed at me. "Our old life in Las Vegas is over. A faded memory." She cupped my face. "You're so beautiful, Aurora, like an angel. I didn't want you there for another second."

Those words right there broke my heart because Mom meant every one of them. She loved her family. Everything she had ever done or sacrificed had been to save us. Back at the motel, it wasn't just Dad's livelihood on the line. It had been mine and my brothers' too. If Dad finally came up with a solution to repay her for all she'd gone through, I owed it to her to stick around and support her—even if the whole thing gave me the worst feeling. Mobsters had a reputation for reason.

"Okay. I'll go get ready." I grabbed my matcha cappuccino and headed upstairs.

Hours later, Mom dragged me out of the building at exactly thirty minutes past three. Even though we were a short cab ride away, she didn't want to risk being late. Fitting in with Signoria Vittoria's circle meant a great deal to her. I played along, though I had hopes she'd reconsider before I had to start school in the fall, which was only two weeks away.

"We're here." Mom paid the taxi driver in cash and climbed out. "Please do whatever she says. We're new here. And she knows what she's doing."

"I'm here. I'll be on my best behavior." I glanced up toward the Chanel sign and the beautiful clothes in the tall windows.

I had to admit, the allure of it all was hard to resist. Even now, knowing that nothing good could come out of Dad's dealings with these people, I couldn't help but be excited to be welcomed into a store like this one.

"Signoria Vittoria is waiting by the dressing rooms. I'm Alana." A woman greeted us at the door.

Mom quickly checked her watch before following Alana through the perfumed aisles of the latest designs.

In the back, Signoria Vittoria sat on a leather chair with a folder in front of her. "Right on time." She smiled. "I had Alana pull a few dresses for you to try on." She glanced at Mom, then turned to me, gesturing to the seat next to her. "Sit. Alana has something for you as well, but first, we must tend to our business."

Mom beamed at me and did a little wiggle with her shoulders before she disappeared into the first dressing room.

"You know? I'm no lawyer." I lowered myself onto the soft leather. "I'm seventeen. This document isn't legally binding."

"If you break our agreement, the police or the court will not be coming for you. It will be us. Do you understand?" She opened the folder and slid the papers over to me. "Take your time reading."

The NDA was basically a gag order. Whatever my parents discussed at home or whatever I heard at school, I was not allowed to discuss with anyone. In truth, the agreement wasn't asking for anything bad, like a kidney or sexual favors. I signed on the dotted line because even though Signoria Vittoria made it sound like a choice, it really wasn't. She wouldn't have threatened me just now if my silence wasn't important.

"Now what? Will you tell me what Dad got himself into?"

As soon as I put the pen down, a man came out of nowhere and took the folder from me. I furrowed my brows at him. Was he hiding behind the racks this whole time? I glared at his retreating form as he walked out of the store and climbed into a black limo waiting outside. The car didn't move after he shut the door. No doubt he was waiting for Signoria Vittoria to join him.

Alana returned and set three glasses of champagne in front

of us. "Let me know if you need different sizes." She motioned toward the second dressing room.

The bubbly was delicious. Back at home, the liquor store around the corner from our house never checked for my ID. I was used to drinking all kinds of booze, but this bubbly wine was like nothing I'd ever had. It sparkled and fizzled and made me feel so good.

"Would you give us a minute, dear?" Signoria Vittoria sipped from her glass. When Alana was out of earshot, Signoria Vittoria continued, "Have you ever heard of the five original crime families?"

Strangers at Tiffany's

Aurora

Crime families sounded too much like mafia stuff. It made me think of bloody weddings, severed appendages, and machine guns. I braced my elbows on my knees and let my gaze sweep across the way toward the shiny glass counter. The bright lights overhead made all the dresses sparkle a pretty blue and pink. I shifted my attention to the elegant woman sitting next to me. For all her perfect complexion and fancy clothes, her secrets were as dirty as my family's. She was mafia?

"No," I answered honestly, "are you? I mean, is that what you are?"

She nodded. "Your father made a deal with Don Michael Alfera. I don't know the details of their arrangement. All I know is that now Stefano Vitali is Michael's second-in-command. That's an important position within our organization, which is why I'm here to help with your transition."

"I've seen enough movies to know that getting in bed with the mob never ends well for the little people. Is it too late for Dad to walk away? I mean, we just got here." I should've fought harder when Dad announced we were moving to New York City for his big job promotion. But I had been too distracted by the idea of Columbia to protest too much.

But now that I thought about it. What job had Dad been talking about? He hadn't worked in months.

"I'm afraid so." She shot a glance behind her to the limo waiting for her at the curb. "That includes you. You signed the agreement and, as they say, now you know too much. You will attend Midtown High and remain under our supervision."

"You mean your control."

"They're the same word, dear. There isn't a place in the world where our organization won't find you or your family, if any one of you chooses to betray us." She stood and smoothed out her pencil skirt, looking all prim and proper, as if she hadn't just threatened my entire family.

A tiny voice in the back of my head told me to run, to get away from her. This woman wasn't just terrifying. She was lethal. I believed she would do us harm if we didn't comply. But it was as she had said, too late to get out.

I had a million questions. Like, was there a time limit on Dad's job promotion, or were we in it for life? What about my little brothers? They were too young to understand what happened, but in time, they would be old enough to notice things.

When she made to leave, I shot to my feet. "Is this like a forever thing?"

"Sweet girl." She touched her cold finger to my chin. "Like your parents, I promise, soon you won't want to leave. Everything you ever wanted is now yours. Including Columbia." She cocked her brow. "Your mother mentioned it this morning. I'd be happy to give you a recommendation. You're behind in the application process, but I can help."

"Rory, look at this dress." Mom practically pranced into the lounge area outside the dressing rooms. "You should see what Signoria Vittoria picked out for you."

The gleam in Mom's gaze melted my heart. She was happy. Maybe it was the perfect lighting or the expensive perfume in the air, but she seemed younger, so much younger than she looked last year when the five of us were crammed into that motel room.

Signoria Vittoria was right. Mom wanted this. All of it. Where did that leave me? "You look beautiful, Mom."

"Too bad I don't really have anywhere to go."

"That was the original reason for my visit earlier. That is, before I found you had children." Signoria Vittoria shook her head in disapproval. "Michael Alfera is hosting an end of summer cocktail party in the Hamptons. It's this Saturday. I'll send a car at two in the afternoon." She met my gaze. "Do join us. There will be kids your age there."

"Thank you." Mom closed the space between her and Signoria Vittoria. "I can't believe I finally get to meet Mr. Alfera. He's been so kind to my husband."

"Of course. Wear the gold rose dress. It suits you better." Signoria Vittoria pointed toward the dressing rooms. "I'll see you soon."

Mom wrapped her arm around my waist. Together, we watched our benefactor gracefully stride the length of the store and then climb into her waiting limo.

"I like this one better." She glanced down at the silky

fabric. "The blue makes my eyes bluer." She giggled. "I feel like we're in one of those eighties movies. You know the one? *Pretty Woman*. When she gets rejected by all the salespeople then she returns to rub it in their faces."

Who wouldn't want this level of acceptance? I had to agree with her on that one. Back home, the Vitali family had nothing. More than that, we weren't part of anything. Here, even if the circumstances were questionable, at best, we were welcomed.

I turned to face her. "Mom, they're mafia."

"Shh." She clasped her hand over my mouth. "Not here." Her face turned bright red, and suddenly, she looked like she couldn't breathe out of sheer panic.

"Okay." I reached for her hand and squeezed it. "We can talk when we get home."

"Rory. Be careful what you say." She freed herself from my grasp and ushered me toward the dressing room with my name on it. "You signed the papers, right?"

"Yes."

"Oh good. So that means you decided to stay?"

"I got the impression bad things would happen if I didn't sign. So yeah, I did. Some choice." I crossed my arms over my chest. Mom's nonchalant act scared the hell out of me because it was obvious she didn't understand how dangerous these people were. Or maybe she did, and she didn't care—too blinded by all the sparkling things. "Even if we wanted out, it's too late now. Do you realize that?"

"Why would we want to leave?" She grabbed my shoulders and turned me to face all the pretty clothes hanging along the wall—skirts, dresses, blazers, and fur coats. "Don't look a gift horse in the mouth, Rory. Come on." She flashed me the brightest smile.

"I've never seen you this happy."

"Your father finally did it. He can finally give us the life we deserve. Don't throw it back in his face."

I scoffed. "That's what I'm trying to tell you, Mom. I don't think I'm allowed to throw anything back."

"You think too much." She shook her head. "Get started. I'll get Alana to help you."

I did as she asked and tried every item the store attendant suggested for me. When I donned the last outfit, a short, pleated skirt with a matching blouse in a pink and green pattern, Mom came in with a pair of strappy sandals. I put those on too and turned to face the mirror. I didn't even flinch when Alana came in and added a belt that hugged my waist tight. Who didn't like to play dress up?

"This is my favorite for you." She added a headband in light pink, then proceeded to cut the tags off the skirt and blouse.

"Wait. I don't think we're taking all this home."

"Yes, we are." Mom picked up my jeans and old sweater off the leather bench. "You're keeping that, and I'm tossing these. Finish up, while I pay."

Alana made quick work of collecting everything out of the dressing room and escorting Mom to the counter. I filed behind them, but kept going toward the front of the store. Every step I took, the new shoes molded to my feet like butter. Signoria Vittoria knew what she was doing when she brought us here to get me to sign her agreement.

Outside, I found myself smiling back at strangers who nodded politely as they passed. They too agreed this was a better version of me.

When I glanced up, I recognized the jewelry store across

the way. Mom's favorite movie was *Breakfast at Tiffany's*. On a whim, I crossed the street and headed inside. Not that I could afford anything there, but the Chanel ensemble made me feel bold. It made me feel like I belonged inside Tiffany's.

The showroom was bigger than I expected with higher floors visible from the main area. Everything sparkled, even the housewares and the different trinkets designed for cats and dogs. I strolled around the different displays for a few minutes before I stopped in front of a glass case with a gorgeous sapphire necklace.

"Jesus," I said aloud, bracing my fingers on the panel.

"Would you like to see it?" A woman came out of nowhere. Her polite posture and smile told me she worked here.

"Oh no, thanks. I was just looking."

"She would love to try it."

I turned to face the deep voice on the other side of me, and my jaw dropped. Why was this gorgeous guy talking to me? He seemed about my age, maybe a little older. But his eyes showed all kinds of sinful thoughts. I attempted a smile, but really, I couldn't stop staring at his beautiful features.

"It's a velvety blue sapphire surrounded by brilliant round diamonds set in platinum." The saleswoman opened the case and removed the necklace. "I'm Chloe. Are you shopping for a special occasion?"

I glanced down at my clothes and then at the guy next to me. He wore a fitted suit and what looked to me like a very expensive watch. That a salesperson at Tiffany's would believe someone like him would be my boyfriend made my stomach flutter with butterflies. Guys like him didn't exist in my world.

"No," I answered. But before I could tell her I wasn't shopping for anything at all, the mystery boy stepped in.

"Let me help you." He nodded to Chloe and took the chain from her, handling it expertly.

I bet guys like him bought expensive jewelry all the time. On a normal day, I would've left already. On a normal day, I wouldn't even be inside this place. But my life wasn't normal anymore. Not two hours ago, I had signed and agreed to become a mafia teen. Whatever that meant. I was supposed to attend their exclusive prep school, wear their designer clothes, and keep all their secrets.

So when my mystery guy, with the deep hazel eyes, walked behind me and placed the necklace on my clavicle, I stood there and did the only thing that made sense to me in the moment. I moved my hair out of the way and let him get close. His fingers grazed the back of my neck. And then I realized, I'd never been touched by a boy before. And certainly not like this, with such skill and kindness.

"The color blue suits you." He arranged the sapphire, so it sat in the middle of my chest.

His gaze met mine. When it dropped to my lips, my heartbeat spiked. Did he like me? For some reason, just because my life lately had been so chaotic, I wanted him to like me, to find me pleasing. I wanted to get lost in the intense serenity of his energy.

I glanced down at his long fingers resting on the sapphire. If he dropped his hand a few inches down, he'd brush my breast. As soon as the thought crossed my mind, hot blood rushed to my cheeks. Could he feel the thumping in my chest?

I wasn't the sophisticated girl these new clothes made me seem. I had no idea how to play it cool, or how to stop my erratic breathing, or even how to talk to him. For crying out loud, he was still here. That meant he wanted to have a conversation with me, right?

"What do you think?" Chloe smiled at me, then looked at my mystery guy, silently asking if I was ready to buy.

I opened my mouth to say we weren't together, but he beat me to it. "I think she should have it."

"Oh no, I was just browsing." I reached behind me and removed the chain from around my neck, clumsily retuning the piece back to Chloe. "Thank you. No."

"Of course. Let me know if you'd like to see anything else." She arranged the necklace back inside the glass case.

With a polite nod, she left us. Alone.

"Um," I cleared my throat, "I should go."

"It was nice meeting you." He stepped back and gestured toward the door.

I wanted to ask his name. But if he hadn't bothered asking mine, that meant he didn't care. Right? What was the protocol for meeting strangers at Tiffany's? Smooth had never been one of my strong suits. I wasn't like him. I bet he met rich girls at designer stores all the time.

With a quick, awkward wave, I ambled away from him. Did he live nearby? He looked like he would own a penthouse in the city in some fancy building with a doorman. I ran a hand through my hair, thinking how my family and I also lived in a place like that now. Did that mean I could have a boyfriend like him?

I stopped to inhale. Gathering all the courage I could muster, I turned around to ask him his name, but he was gone. Of course he was. Just as well. Between the new school and Dad's new job, I didn't need any more complications. Rubbing the back of my neck, I made my way outside.

When my lungs filled with fresh air, I realized how hot I'd been inside and how sensitive my skin felt where he had touched me.

For the past several years, I had been so focused on helping Mom with the twins and Dad's bad business decisions that I didn't consider the idea of a boyfriend. I hadn't realized I longed for physical connection so much until now.

"There you are." Mom rushed toward me holding two big shopping bags. "Where did you go?"

"Oh, I went inside Tiffany's to take a look. I'm sorry I lost track of time."

"It's fine." She shrugged and handed me one of the bags. "Are you ready to go home?"

"Sure." I lost my balance as I took the clothes from her. I hadn't expected it to be so heavy.

When I glanced up, I saw him again. Though this time, he didn't notice me. The glass door to Tiffany's shut behind him as he strode across the way to a waiting limo. He had a small blue box with him. No doubt he had come to buy his girlfriend something pretty.

The limo drove away, and I couldn't stop thinking about his intense gaze and sexy voice.

"Earth to Rory." Mom stepped in my line of sight and blocked my view, so I didn't get to see which way the vehicle went.

"Yeah, let's get a cab." I raised my hand to hail a taxi, even though there were no yellow cars around.

What did it matter which way he went? Other than his affinity for jewelry, I didn't know anything else about him. The chances of him and I crossing paths again were exactly zero. Not to mention, that my life wasn't my own anymore.

We served at the pleasure of Don Michael Alfera and his organization.

House Alfera

Aurora

I laid in bed staring at the glittery chandelier in my new bedroom, surrounded by silky pillows and a velvet duvet. I'd been awake for almost two hours, but I didn't feel like getting up. Life on the other side of the door was getting too weird.

Yesterday, Mom and I came home with thousands of dollars' worth of clothes from a single shop. Then several other packages arrived with more clothes from different designers, shoes, handbags, cocktail dresses, and gowns—and yes, even a tiara with brilliant stones.

Was it worth our lives? The longer we stayed in New York, in this life of mobsters and tiaras, the harder it would be to eventually go back to what we were before. Or was that the point, to never return to Las Vegas?

I turned on my side and stared at my new closet filled with brand-new clothes. Mom insisted I get rid of everything I brought with me, which wasn't much if I were being honest. Maybe Mom was right. I shouldn't throw away this new life

Dad had worked so hard to get for us. All those deals that went wrong for him, all those times we ended up with nothing—it all had finally paid off for him. I couldn't stay on my high horse and pretend our previous life was any kind of perfect.

Signoria Vittoria with her wealth and power scared the crap out of me. But once school started, I would spend most of my time on homework. As for Mom, she didn't seem to mind Signora Vittoria's overbearing and condescending methods.

"Rory?" Mom knocked several times, then barged in. "Are you awake yet?"

"I am." I sat up.

She stood by the foot of the bed with her eyes red and puffy, like she'd been crying. I was familiar with the disappointment and hurt written all over her face. It showed up every time Dad screwed up. What did he do? Get fired on his third day? As much as it pained me to see her like this, at least now we were headed home.

"What happened? Where's Dad?"

"He's at work, not returning my calls. Rory, the boys are gone." She clasped a hand to her mouth and wept.

"Mom. What?" I jumped out of bed and rushed to hug her. "What do you mean they're gone? They love it here."

"Signoria Vittoria sent a car this morning. They're off to boarding school." She wiped her eyes. "I mean, she mentioned it yesterday, and I thought it would be a good idea, you know. For them to get a fancy education like that. But I didn't realize she'd take them away so soon."

"I didn't even get to say good-bye." I plopped down on the mattress.

Signoria Vittoria sent my kid brothers away because she didn't like that Mom and Dad had kids. Though I had to wonder, were they gone because she was annoyed with children or had my brothers become a colateral of sorts? To make sure Mom and I stuck to our end of the bargain and kept all their mafia secrets.

This was insane. I knew nothing about their dealings, illegal or otherwise.

"The house feels so quiet without the boys running around. I called for you, but you didn't come down. The driver said he was on a schedule and that he had to go."

"How did they take the news though? Were they okay with leaving?"

"Yes, they were. You should've seen them. They were sure they were on their way to Hogwarts." A smile pulled at her lips. "I know this is a good thing. I just thought I'd have more time with my babies to get used to the idea of boarding school."

"Do you know where they're going?"

"Yes, I have the packet downstairs. Some posh place in Cornwall."

This was all happening too fast. Last week, the twins and I were at Denny's for dinner, fighting over an order of fries. At the time, all I thought about was how I wouldn't have to put up with their roughhousing and overall crazy antics when I left for college. How was I supposed to know it would all change in a matter of days?

"Maybe we can try FaceTiming them tonight and see how they're getting on." I wrapped my arm around her. "I'm sorry. We'll figure it out, okay?"

"You're starting your senior year in a few days. You don't have to worry about me. Signoria Vittoria mentioned she had a few committees she wants me to join. You know, to stay busy?"

"There you go." I smiled at her. "You're going to make a great socialite."

I just hoped Dad didn't ruin this for her. The Italian mafia was serious business. They were all ruthless and deadly.

"Mom, do you think Dad is blackmailing Michael Alfera? Maybe he found out some dark secret. I mean, how else do you explain all this?" I gestured toward the apartment and the ridiculously gorgeous view outside my window.

"Of course not." She scoffed. "Dad has been working hard. Mr. Alfera noticed his efforts and decided to give him a job within his organization. That is all."

"What I did or didn't do to get us here is none of your business." Dad crowded the threshold. He lifted his phone and showed it to Mom. "I have ten panic messages from you. I call you and you don't answer?" He stepped into my bedroom and suddenly the room felt smaller.

At six feet, he towered over Mom's five-six frame. The lines across his forehead deepened as his dark gaze shifted between Mom and me. When Mom looked up at him with tears in her blue eyes, his features softened. For all of Dad's rough edges, Mom always knew how to calm him.

"What happened?"

"Dad, Signoria Vittoria sent the twins to some boarding school in Connecticut."

"Is that why you're crying?" He ran a hand through his hair, seemingly annoyed that the situation wasn't as dire as we made it sound.

But it was a big deal that Signoria Vittoria had that kind of say in our lives.

"We discussed this last night, Lia. You were okay with it."

"I just didn't know it would happen this fast. That's all." Mom snuffled a little.

"That's the point, Dad. Why the rush? All my old clothes are gone. The boys are gone."

"This is how these people work. They need us to be fully integrated."

"What did you do?" I asked again, since he wasn't as put out as he was when he first walked in. "How are we rich all of a sudden?"

"I saved Michael Alfera's life. Don't ask me how. But this is how he chose to reward me. By giving me a job as his right-hand man." He exhaled loudly, exchanging a meaningful look with Mom. "You're part of this family too, Rory. It's time you start acting like it. Don't go messing up what we've got just because you don't like my methods."

"That wasn't my intention." I rubbed the side of my arm, biting my lower lip.

"Your mother tells me you want to go back to Las Vegas. What for?" He braced his hands on his hips. "We have a chance to start over here. And get what's due to me."

I had clung to the idea of Las Vegas because that was my home. But I had to admit, Dad was right. There was nothing left for us there—the house was gone and so were my friends.

"I know. It's just that this whole mafia thing is a lot to process. I just want to know the truth."

"Now you have it." On his way out, he stopped with his hand on the doorknob and turned to meet Mom's gaze. "I'll go see if we can set up a call with the twins tonight, so we can see how they're doing."

"Thank you." She smiled at him. As soon as Dad was gone,

she shifted her attention to me. "All the furniture is gone too. We're getting a delivery tomorrow morning."

"Wow, Signoria Vittoria's interior designer works fast." I decided not to bother Mom with anymore of my conspiracy theories. "I'm sure she will do a beautiful job. Can't wait."

"I met with her this morning. She brought in some art that looks very expensive." She sighed and sat next to me. "Her designs are beautiful."

"Well, I'm all yours until school starts. What should we do today? How about lunch?" I figured a meal and a walk would cheer her up.

"I would love that, but Signoria Vittoria's driver left a message for you. A young lady is meeting with you today to help you with school stuff." She glanced down at her watch. "Omigod, it's almost noon. She'll be here soon. And look at you, you look like you just got out of bed."

"I did just get out of bed."

"How about you jump in the shower, and I'll go downstairs and wait for her?"

"Um. Okay." I rose to my feet as Mom rushed out the door. "Okay. I guess we jump when the dragon lady says jump," I said to the empty room.

I ambled over to my en-suite bathroom and stopped to read all the digital buttons on the control panel next to the door—there was one for each amenity—the heated floors, the towel rack, the steamers in the shower stall, and the jets on the whirlpool bath. I had to admit. I could get used to this.

I took a quick shower, wrapped a fluffy towel around my body, and strode over to my walk-in closet. Since I had no idea what Signoria Vittoria had planned for me today, I didn't know what to wear.

"Oh good, you're not a toad."

"What?" I spun around to face the stranger in my room.

"Hi, I'm Penny de Luca." She stepped forward with her hand out. "Signoria Vittoria sent me. She said you needed help. I thought the worst. But you look decent."

"I'm Rory." I shook her hand. "I'm not a toad."

"I'm glad." She walked past me and quickly went through all the items in the closet. "Signoria Vittoria has impeccable taste. How about this one?" She pulled out a sheath dress and a pair of pumps. When I didn't move, she furrowed her brows. "Come on. We have a lot to cover before school starts."

"Right." I took a pair of underwear and a bra from the chest of drawers at the far end of the closet and did my best to put them on without letting go of my towel. When I was ready, I turned, and she handed me the dress. "Where are we going?"

"First, lunch, so we can get to know each other. I've been assigned to be your student liaison."

"Like a babysitter?"

"Don't be put out. Signoria Vittoria doesn't trust anyone, especially teenagers." She laughed. "There's a way we do things around here. I'll walk you through it all, so you're not so lost on your first day."

"Okay."

"Lose that word."

I opened my mouth to say okay, but then closed it and moved to put on my shoes. She stood there the whole time, waiting patiently, but at the same time silently asking me to hurry. Surely, she learned that from Signoria Vittoria.

Penny's designer clothes and the way she carried herself reminded me of Signoria Vittoria. Though she wasn't as intimidating. Something about her friendly demeanor put me at ease.

"Signoria Vittoria. Is she your mom or...?"

"Oh no, she doesn't have children of her own. She's my godmother. Our parents are good friends. Well, there's more to it than that. But I'll explain as we go." She looked me up and down. "Are you ready?"

"I think so." I took in a deep breath.

As soon as we left the building, and I climbed into the back of her black SUV, she began with what she called my Midtown High indoctrination. Students used a car service to get to school. No school bus here. And public transportation was out of the question. For lunch, Adaline Hall offered excellent choices, but since I was a senior, going off campus was also an option. She also informed me that Signoria Vittoria and Mom had taken care of the school uniforms.

"I have a to wear a uniform?"

"Yes. You're in House Alfera, so your sweater and vest will be blue." She opened the door to a small restaurant that smelled of freshly baked pastries and coffee. "They have the best veggie quiche here." She beamed at me as the hostess escorted us to a table in the corner near the window.

"Can I get you anything to drink?" The server appeared as soon as Penny set her big designer purse on the floor next to her.

"We're not here long. Could you bring us a little bit of everything and a bottle of Champagne?"

"Of course." The server didn't even bat an eye at Penny's order.

"You do know I'm seventeen, right?"

"Yes, of course. Me too." She smiled.

"They serve minors here?" I raised my eyebrows in surprise.

"They serve the Society here. Did your parents not explain?" She scoffed. And for the first time since she arrived, she seemed impatient. "I'll show you around so they know who you are. But Aurora, you're part of the Society now."

"What is the Society?"

"Have you ever heard of the five original crime families?" She sat back and waited until the server had poured two glasses of champagne.

Signoria Vittoria had mentioned the five original crime families when she treated Mom and me to a day of shopping. But she hadn't really explained anything, other than confirm she was mafia.

"Not really. I know they were mafia."

"They are. Present tense." She sipped from her glass.

I did the same because I had a feeling this day was about to get weirder than a day of shopping with the dragon lady. "What are they really?"

"Over a century ago, the five original families formed an enclave to protect each other. Over time, it grew stronger and bigger. During Prohibition, they made a pact to go underground and manage all illicit activity from the shadows. Our families are the most powerful." She stopped to study my face. "You already know about the Alfera family. There's also Valentino, Buratti, Salvatore, and Gallo."

"My father works for Don Michael Alfera."

"I know. He's your sponsor at the school, which is why you'll be in House Alfera."

I laughed because what Penny was talking about was farfetched. Sure, I knew of organized crime. I sort of grew up around it in Las Vegas. But this level of organized crime? A secret society with its own mobster school.

"I thought I was going to high school. What do I do with a career in mafia?"

"I know you know that's not what we do. You'll learn the usual subjects. But for instance, the Alfera House also offers a pathway that caters to the automobile industry."

Dad sold luxury cars back at home. Was that his connection to Michael Alfera? Was that how they met and made this deal that changed our lives?

"What house are you?"

"I'm House Salvatore, which is why Signoria Vittoria asked me to show you around." She rolled her eyes. "Really, Mom volunteered me for the job. She's been trying to get back in Uncle Michael's good graces for a while now. She figured his new protégé's family might be the way in. I'm telling you this because I want you to understand that your success is tethered to my family's."

"Success in what?"

"Staying in line, upholding the Alfera name, and honestly just overall, not getting your parents killed."

"You're kidding, right?"

She arched her eyebrow and drank some more from her flute while she waited for me to consider my own question. I thought of the NDA papers I had signed, of how my brothers were sent away to boarding school, and how pretty much every small detail of our old lives had been wiped away.

Of course she wasn't joking. Who would go through these lengths to setup a family in a new city and a fancy boarding school, with designer clothes and a furnished apartment, just to be funny? "I have no plans to tell anyone what I know. I just want my family to be safe. I want to finish high school and go to Columbia."

"And you can have all that. As long as you adhere to the guidelines in the agreement you signed. And blend into the student body at Midtown High." She rubbed my upper arm. "Don't look so mortified. This is the best thing that could've happened to you. Very few people are allowed to join our ranks. Your father must've done something huge for Don Alfera."

She picked one of the bite-size quiches off the plate and bit into it with grace. I did the same. Then stopped to savor the explosion of exquisite flavors in my mouth when the pastry melted on my tongue. I'd never had something so delicious.

Everything about this world was intoxicating and addicting. Today was only my second day, and as much as I feared for my family's safety, I wanted to be part of it. I wanted to have a friend like Penny. I wanted everything.

"Are you ready to go? We have one more stop."

"Where are we going?"

"I'm giving you a private tour of our school. Finish your sweets and then we'll go." She beamed at me.

I tried to play it cool and not let a giggle escape my lips. Was I ready to see more of *her* world? Correction—this was my world now. Dad was right. There was no going back.

Who Are They?

Aurora

After spending a good part of the afternoon with Penny, I found myself in her black SUV, heading to Midtown and excited to see the school for myself. The buzz and bustle of the city on a Friday afternoon faded to the background as I considered everything Penny had said to me while we were eating brunch, doing a bit of shopping, and visiting the different hangout spots for Midtown High students.

The car pulled up to the curb in front of a tall gate. I leaned forward, mouth slightly open, to get a good look through the car window. Past the tall wrought-iron society crest and stone steps, stood what looked like an old church. On our way here, Penny had mentioned that the grounds used to have a church and a mansion that were repurposed to serve as a school, about ninety years ago.

Only families with ties to and in good standing with the five original crime families were invited to attend. This place was more than a private school. It was a status symbol, reserved for the most elite. I inhaled to ease the thumping in my chest. My heart beat fast with a mix of nerves and fear. This place could make or break me. As intrigued as I was by the opportunity to be here, I hadn't forgotten that I didn't belong. I was still an outsider.

Penny had made it very clear that one false move and my entire life would crumble like over-baked quiche. Her words, not mine.

The gates swung open, and Penny scooted over to my side. "Signoria Vittoria called ahead. We can go in." She motioned for me to get out then gave her driver a single nod. "We'll start with Adaline."

"With what?"

"The dining hall and general gathering place. Have you not been following the theme of our afternoon?" She rolled her eyes. "Come on. We only have access until six."

"Okay."

"Hmm." She leaned over me to open the car door. "Make sure you use bigger words when you speak to our professors."

"Right. I forgot." I wasn't sure what was wrong with the word 'okay,' but I supposed I had to trust her on this one.

I followed her through the gates, up the steps, and through the courtyard. The area had well-manicured hedges with blooming flowers, while maple trees provided plenty of shade. I could only assume reddish small flowers hanging from the limbs were the reason for the sweet scent in the air. As we made our way further in, I had to look back to make sure we were still in the city.

"Here we are." Penny strode ahead of me and opened the double doors.

We went under the tower and into a breezeway that led to

the great hall. The stain glass reminded me this place used to be a church. At my old school, we didn't have a dining hall. We had a cafeteria that served food that came out of huge plastic containers. Adaline had a kitchen with an executive chef, a sous chef, and a pastry chef.

"Like I said, the menu is farm-to-table, so it changes with the seasons. Sushi is always available, and it's to die for." She cocked her head to look at me then followed my line of sight upward. "Oh, the ceiling and windows. I was impressed the first time I saw them too. I believe it's called Didactic architecture." She pointed to either side of the building. "Through the stained glass, sculptures, and tapestries, the students can learn the history of the Society. That's how churches teach Bible studies."

"The Society?" I furrowed my brows. I probably should've been taking notes.

"The Society is comprised of the five original crime families. They first organized when Prohibition started as a way to protect our community." She scoffed. "I said all this before. Pay attention."

"Right. I remember." I sifted through all the information she'd crammed into my brain in the past four hours and thought of the different family names and the industries they controlled. The tapestries on the walls had those names embroidered on them, along with other symbols and animals.

"Your house mascot is a raven." Penny gestured toward the tapestry done in different shades of blue. The word wisdom was embroidered over a hand holding three floating gears of different sizes. "That's done in real gold, by the way."

"Why are you not House Alfera if Don Alfera is your uncle?" I asked to prove I had been paying attention.

"I was born into the Alfera family, on my mother's side. My parents and Don Alfera had a falling out several years ago. I almost didn't come to Midtown High my freshman year. Thankfully, Mom was able to procure a sponsorship from Don Salvatore. You met her."

"Signoria Vittoria is a Don?"

"Yes." She smiled. "Good, you're finally getting it." She ambled toward the tapestry done in deep golds with a panther as the mascot and the word guardian over a symbol that looked like a Greek temple.

I was surprised they hadn't chosen a dragon. I supposed all of these symbols and mascots were chosen a century ago, way before Signoria Vittoria's time.

"I can't imagine going to any other school. Can you? Oh, actually you can, because you have." She shook her hand in disbelief. As if the idea of public school was a real horror. She released a breath, then checked her watch. "If we're lucky, I bet we can still catch the varsity football tryouts. The seniors are putting the sophomores through the ringer today. Should be fun to watch."

Finally. A high school football team was something I understood. Last year, before I stopped going to school because we lost our home, I had made the cheerleading squad. The rumors about Mom turning tricks in a motel quickly spread. Even though she had only done it once, everyone assumed she'd become a prostitute. Within the week, the PTA moms found a way to kick me out of school for misconduct.

I was okay with it. After the motel incident, I had no friends and the boys assumed I was for sale too. They cornered me outside the cafeteria constantly, offering to double Mom's fee. Something they made up, of course. Mom's fee for sleeping with Dad's boss had been Dad's life. One guy even offered me five hundred dollars. That day I went home and cried myself to sleep. Not because I had been insulted by his assumption. I had been angry at myself for considering it.

I had nothing against sex workers. I just hated that my classmates had chosen that path for me because of something Dad brought onto himself—because Mom stepped in to save him.

"Hello?" Penny squeezed my upper arm and shook me a little. "Did you hear what I said? What do you think?"

I had followed her down a hallway and a set of steps, pretty much blindingly. I hadn't realized we were now outside facing the football field. I sighed. Even if my cheerleading career had been brief and painful, the deep green lawn and hint of sweat in the air felt like home.

"It's beautiful here. I can't even tell we're still in the city."

She ushered me toward the bleachers, where we sat to watch the boys run drills. The players wore practice jerseys and helmets so I couldn't really see their faces. Not that it mattered. I didn't know anybody anyway.

"So, are they any good?"

"Are you seriously asking that? They're state champs. We have the best coaches money can buy."

"Of course you do." I laughed, letting my gaze swipe back to the field, where Coach had moved on to organize the sophomores into three teams.

Football tryouts were definitely not for the faint-hearted. The guys looked pretty beat up and ready to throw in the towel. A handful of them joined their assigned teams, and then, dropped to the lawn in a heap of tired bones.

As soon as the varsity team charged onto the field, most of the underclassmen jumped to their feet, except for one. Penny raised her brows and sat up taller to get a better view. One of the varsity members broke away from the group. With long, assured strides, he made his way to the sophomore still on the ground and loomed over him.

Then my jaw dropped because I recognized that face. The buzzing in my ears made it impossible to hear what he said next. *"Blue looks good on you."* His words echoed in my head. My mystery guy from Tiffany's was here.

"Get up." His deep voice carried across the entire field. "Coach didn't say you could take a break." He kicked the younger boy's cleats. After a breath, he exchanged a glance with Coach, who simply shrugged. "On second thought. You're out. Grab your gear and go."

The sophomore jerked to his feet and puffed up his chest, all red-faced with his jaw clenched as if the words "go to hell" were on the tip of his tongue. His furrowed brows made it clear he didn't think anyone other than Coach could dismiss him—especially not like that, in front of everyone.

Two other seniors joined in and flanked their friend, glaring at the sophomore. It was overkill since they were all so much taller than the other guy. After a few beats of a standoff, the sophomore finally conceded and stormed off the field.

"Who are they?" I asked Penny. Though I really only cared about the stranger from Tiffany's. He was here. And I was fairly certain he was a student.

"The Royals. No one messes with them. I think that kid was too tired to realize who he was dealing with. I mean, that's our QB."

My mystery guy motioned for the first team of sophomores to huddle around him, while Coach paced the sideline with his arms over his chest. So he was a senior at Midtown High and the varsity quarterback. Of course he was.

The team listened intently as the QB ran them through the play. His voice carried a confident tone to it, like he'd done this run a thousand times.

Every one of his words pelted on my chest like raindrops on a tin roof. I found myself sitting on the edge of my seat, so I wouldn't miss what he'd say or do next. Back at Tiffany's, I didn't get a chance to look at him. I did now. His physique was impressive and exactly what a quarterback should look like—tall, broad shoulders, and a flat stomach that I was sure was all muscle. With every move he made, his tight pants stretched to reveal more planes and valleys over his thighs and butt.

Jeez, the guy was built like a Greek statue.

"What do you mean *the Royals*?" I couldn't stop looking at him. I couldn't stop thinking of those hazel eyes and the pull I felt when he grazed the nape of my neck.

"They're next-in-line to be Dons."

A don? My mystery guy was a future don?

"See something you like?" Penny leaned in and nudged my upper arm.

"What? No." I furrowed my brows and shook my head quickly.

She smirked then returned her attention to the field. All day she had been a wealth of information, inundating my brain with useless factoids on the colors of each family, the Society crest, and important dates. Why did she have to stop now? When she didn't offer any details, I decided I didn't care if Penny thought I was crushing on the QB.

"Who's the QB?" My cheeks heated. I wasn't here to flirt with boys. My whole future hinged on the opportunity to attend their prestigious school. I shouldn't care who our team's QB was, except I did. I wanted to know his name so badly.

"Ha! I knew it." She laughed.

"You knew what? Never mind. It doesn't matter."

"Don't be embarrassed. You're not the only one." Penny pointed her chin at the group of girls next to us. "Everyone agrees with you. Our QB is dreamy."

I hadn't realized that in the ten minutes since we arrived, more students, mainly girls, had gathered to watch.

"His name is Enzo Alfera. He's the son of your gracious sponsor, Michael Alfera." She turned to face me. "Hot QB who's also a prince of sorts. You can imagine the number of stalkers he has. That includes mothers looking for the best match for their daughters." She bit her lower lip as she studied my face. "Want my advice? Lose the starry eyes. And stay away from Enzo. He's all kinds of trouble you don't need. And he hates stalkers."

I met her gaze. Did Penny speak from experience? Someone as beautiful as her and with such pedigree would surely be able to date someone like Enzo. A future don wouldn't waste his time with someone like me—the daughter of a whore, I believed was the term my so-called friends used when they kicked me off the cheerleading team.

"Did you guys date or something?"

"Gosh no. My mom and his dad are first cousins. Gross."

I shifted my attention back to the field. Enzo and the varsity team had moved on to the next group of tryouts. Again, he huddled the boys around him and shouted out the play, pointing at each player as he went. They all scattered to find their assigned positions, while Enzo found his own behind them. Watching him execute the play with precision was such a rush. I'd always been into football. The blend of brute force and clever tactics was fascinating to me.

By the end of the hour, most of the sophomores had been sent home. The few that remained gathered around Coach near the bench, while Enzo and his friends stood several feet away. He had his arm around the two guys who flanked him earlier. His brows furrowed while he talked to them.

"That's Rex Valentino on his right and Santino Buratti on his left. Those three have been inseparable since birth."

I considered telling her that I had met Enzo yesterday. But what would be the point? Enzo and I were not friends. Yesterday, he hadn't bothered to ask my name, let alone offer me his. Even if we were going to the same school now, we were still worlds apart. He was the son of my dad's new boss, the one who now controlled our lives—a don.

"Anyway, maybe we'll get to see them tomorrow at the Alferas' End of Summer Soiree."

"Wait? The party tomorrow is hosted by the Alferas?"

"Yes, that's why Signoria Vittoria wants your family there. So she can bring you into the fold, so to speak." She patted my leg. "Come on. Let's go find you something to wear. I saw some great pieces in your closet earlier."

"Sure." I rose to my feet, and, like a magnet, my gaze flitted back to him.

He sat on the bench removing his shoulder pads, while laughing at something Santino had said. I smiled at his beautiful face, the thick eyebrows and full lips. This easy-going version of him was so enchanting. There was a chance I lingered too long, ogling him like a boy-crazy schoolgirl because he stopped pulling on his shoelaces and switched his gaze to me.

The way those intense, green eyes bore into mine told me he recognized me. Though I hadn't expected the other reaction I got from him. He pursed his lips as if he didn't like seeing me here, like my presence was an insult.

Everything Sparkles Here

Aurora

Signoria Vittoria's limo arrived exactly at two o'clock. Though Mom had us come to the lobby a whole half hour early to make sure we didn't miss our ride to the Hamptons. I wasn't sure what to expect from that place. I knew we were headed to the beach, but also, we were going to a party at a mansion hosted by Don Alfera.

Two weeks ago, I had no clue who the guy was. Now, he was everywhere. It seemed that no matter what, we couldn't escape him. He owned us, not just Dad, but all of us.

"She didn't need to send her limo," Mom complained half-heartedly as she climbed inside with a huge smile on her face.

"Yes, she did." Dad followed behind her. Then adjusted his suit jacket. "We're important now."

I settled in across from them, letting myself gape at the sheer size of the vehicle along with the soft leather of the seats. I'd never been in a limo before. Some kids in my junior class had rented one for prom. By then, I had already been kicked out for alleged misconduct, so I hadn't been invited. But I did see them as they drove by the Denny's restaurant.

My gaze shifted to the window and the early afternoon traffic. For no reason at all, I looked for Enzo on the busy streets, or whenever another limo pulled up next to us. Since Penny had told me the soirée was at his beach house, I hadn't stopped thinking about what I would do if I saw him again. After the evil look he shot my way last night after football practice, the best thing to do would be to avoid him as much as possible.

And just like that, I fell down the Enzo rabbit hole all over again. I had spent the entire night dissecting and overanalyzing his reaction to seeing me and his reasons for it. Did he think that after I met him at Tiffany's that I ran out to find out who he was, befriended his second cousin, and then proceeded to stalk him? That wasn't how it'd happened at all, but fuck, it sure did look like it. No wonder he was pissed when he spotted me in the crowd, surrounded by other girls who were also there to spy on him.

I closed my eyes and rested my head on the car window. In the sunny afternoon, surrounded by a luscious lawn, his eyes had looked so green— a contrast to how dark they'd seemed under the halogen lights in the jewelry store.

Jeez, I really needed to get out more if I was full-blown obsessed with a guy who talked to me once. He obviously hated me. Maybe if I explained how I wasn't at practice for him, he'd change his mind.

Stop it.

I had already gone through multiple scenarios last night, where I went up to him and explained, or had Penny explain on my behalf. Either way, the outcome was the same. Enzo couldn't be my friend, let alone my boyfriend. What I felt when he touched me at Tiffany's didn't matter. It wasn't real. Not to mention, he was the future don of House Alfera. He was a mobster. Or was going to be. That was a huge deal. His world was dangerous and most definitely bad for my health. And he hated stalkers.

So I had to stick to the original plan of keeping my head down and getting through senior year unnoticed. Next year, I'd be at Columbia, and Enzo and his mobster friends would be a thing of the past.

"I think that Rory is a smart girl." Mom's sweet voice filtered through the myriad of thoughts flitting through my mind and cutting through the last image I had of Enzo's angry face.

Her saccharine tone was the one she usually reserved for when she spoke to Dad. I had to guess they were talking about me, so I turned to face her to let her know she had my attention. Of course, she could see right through my blank expression. I had zoned out shortly after we reached the interstate and had no clue what they were talking about.

"Your father had a great idea." She arched her brow—her signature move to get me to pay attention. And also, to play along.

"Oh yeah?" I smiled at Dad.

"Tonight's party is a big deal. We're not here to have fun. We're here to make connections and see what opportunities come up."

Dad has had this same idea many times before. The last time, he conned his boss out of five thousand dollars. He was caught, of course. And then his boss retaliated by taking our house as repayment. And as a bonus for "hurting his feelings," the boss also asked for Mom—to humiliate Dad, no doubt. After the beating Dad took the night his boss found him hiding in a motel outside Vegas, he would've said yes to anything, including selling off his own children. Luckily, it hadn't come to that. Thanks to Mom.

Jesus, we'd come full circle. I didn't know much about Dad's new job, but I was one hundred percent sure that if Dad ever crossed Don Alfera and his organization, none of us would live to tell the tale. Don Alfera could make us disappear, and no one would bat an eye. He was far more powerful than Dad's old boss.

"You should do the same." He pointed at my dress. "You clean up nice. I'm sure they'll notice."

"What do you mean?"

He inhaled and slow blinked at the same time. "You'll be eighteen soon. Marriage to anyone within Don Alfera's circle would be a good match."

"I'm sure there are plenty of cute boys at school." Mom cut him off and reached over to squeeze my fingers.

"Boys? No, she needs someone who's already connected, not some stupid kid living off his folks' money." He clicked his teeth. "Your mother and I will find you someone suitable. The fancy Suits like them young. You'll do alright." He ducked to get a better view of the heavy traffic up ahead, then added, "You'll thank me later."

Mom squeezed my hand tighter, silently telling me she wouldn't let Dad go that far—that she wouldn't let him sell me off to some old man with, what he considered, appropriate mobster connections and money. Or maybe that was just wishful thinking. Either way, the whole idea made me sick to my stomach.

I wasn't sure what her reassuring gesture meant. Maybe she was just feeling sorry for me because if Dad really wanted to marry me off, she wouldn't be able to stop him. Mom loved this new world, where she was respected and included, and she wouldn't do anything that might cost her, her newly-established status.

I thought about how heartbroken she'd been yesterday, when she had to let the twins go to a school she'd never seen. But then she recovered quickly because she knew that if she put up too much of a fuss, Signoria Vittoria would find a way to ship us all back to Las Vegas.

Mom had mentioned she wanted to move on. Forget Vegas and start fresh in New York. In her eyes, all this glamour erased the time when we lost our house and she had to sleep with Dad's boss to repay his debt. Maybe she had already forgotten about those months, but I hadn't.

I could tell Dad that his plan sucked. But that would only make him angry. The best thing to do was to ignore him and bide my time until I turned eighteen and was able to go off on my own. I sure as hell didn't need a husband for that.

"I want to go to Columbia next year, Dad. Signoria Vittoria said she could get me in."

"We don't need her. Just do as I say, and we'll make it here." He smirked at me as if he knew something I didn't. "We'll make it big."

I let my head fall back and then roll to the side, so I could look out the window again. This right here was the problem with Dad. He was always looking for the next thing. Two weeks into his new job, and he already wanted something better.

"Stefano, we agreed." Mom rubbed his leg. "Our daughter

needs time to adjust to her new surroundings. You promised you would let her finish high school."

Gee, thanks, Mom!

"It doesn't hurt for her to think ahead." He snapped his fingers in the direction of the driver. "You, how much longer?"

"About an hour, sir."

Seventy-five minutes later, the driver pulled up to the Alfera mansion. It was like nothing I'd ever seen before. Not just because of its sheer size, but also because of its meticulously manicured lawn and garden on the side of the house. Las Vegas was a big desert. I still hadn't fully adjusted to the lush greenery on the East coast.

"Mr. and Mrs. Vitali, welcome." A guy dressed in a dark suit opened the door for Mom and Dad.

He ushered them toward the front entrance, and I followed close behind. When we reached the foyer, he gestured to one of the servers. Mom quickly stepped in and grabbed two flutes, one for her and one for me. I stood there with a glass of champagne in hand, ogling the chandelier overhead and the shimmering reflection on the marble floor.

"Everything sparkles here," I whispered in Mom's ear.

"I know." She giggled.

"You made it. Welcome." Signoria Vittoria kissed Mom hello. She turned to me for a moment, only to dismiss me quickly. "Go mingle." She escorted my parents into a room off the living area.

Great. I was in a house full of strangers, and all alone. I sipped from my glass and went looking for Penny. She had said she'd be here early, and the party was already in full swing. She had to be around here somewhere.

To my right, the grand stairwell had a red rope blocking

access, so I went left and ended up in the kitchen then another massive living area with plush furniture and a flat screen. Past the room's glass walls, the ocean water glinted under the dying sun.

"Wow." I finished my wine and grabbed another from a smiling server.

The alcohol had already gotten to my head, which made me not care that I had no friends here. I roamed the gardens for a while, still looking for Penny. Though every time a tall guy with dark hair turned the corner, my heart would jump up into my throat.

Sipping the last of the bubbles in my glass, I made my way back inside the house, hoping to find a quiet corner where I could spend the rest of the evening. I had only recently met Penny, but I was truly missing her tonight. She made me feel included, like I could belong here.

I was still trying to decide if I should hide in the bathroom or the small, upholstered bench tucked under the stairs, when I saw Enzo come in through the front door. His gaze fell on a group of girls hanging out in the living room. He glanced upward, stuffing his hands in the pockets of his jeans. I didn't know him at all, but he seemed put out by the party and the girls shooting furtive glances his way.

He scanned the room quickly, then headed upstairs, bypassing the red rope that was clearly meant to keep guests out. Right, Penny had said this was Don Alfera's beach house. That meant Enzo lived here too.

Maybe it was the Champagne. Or maybe I left my brain back in the limo. But the minute he reached the landing, I ducked under the rope and followed him. The irony wasn't lost on me. I was stalking the guy because I wanted to make it clear I wasn't actually stalking him.

As soon as I reached the top, he'd disappeared into one of the many suites. I slowed down my pace and stopped to listen to the first door on the right. When I didn't hear anything, I opened the door slowly to peek inside. The place was empty. Now I was in full spy-girl mode. I kept heading farther down the hall until the chattering from downstairs was no more than an excited buzz.

"Santino." A female voice with a raspy tone called from the room to my left.

The door had been left ajar. For a moment, I didn't know what to do, so I stood there frozen, listening to the woman moan and call for Santino. Mouthing a curse, I tiptoed toward the door to close it and give them some privacy.

As soon as they were within my line of sight, I realized my mistake. They were both naked. I'd never seen anything like that in real life. The girl, who was about my age, was spread eagle on the bed while Santino had his face buried between her legs. I sort of recognized her from football practice.

Hot blood rushed to my cheeks and ears. Suddenly, the image of the two of them was bright and sharp. I could see every detail—the hard muscles on his thighs and back, her tits softly bouncing as he fondled them, and her pink cheeks.

I hadn't realized sex could be like this. In truth, I'd never seen a couple have sex; Mom's incident didn't count. They had been fully dressed, and Mom never made a sound. This girl was enjoying herself. She couldn't get enough of Santino and whatever he was doing to her.

Santino stood, and in one swift movement, pushed her knees down into the mattress and then climbed on top of her.

She moaned louder, clawing at his back and touching him everywhere. I rubbed my own nipple to ease the itching there and gasped in surprise as ribbons of desire swelled through me.

"Every time." A deep voice boomed behind me.

I spun around and came face to face with Enzo's other friend, Rex Valentino. His blue eyes danced with amusement and something else I didn't recognize.

"It was open," I blurted out. "I didn't mean to—"

"To watch?" He chuckled. "That's alright. He likes it. It's why he always 'forgets' to lock up behind him." He leaned forward until his breath brushed my cheek then reached over to close the door. "I'm Rex." He offered me his hand.

"Oh. Um." I glanced down at his long fingers. Between the peep show and getting caught, my heart was racing out of control. "Sorry. I'm Rory." Great. Now I was speaking in rhyme.

"Well, Rory, guests are not allowed upstairs." He flashed me a knowing smile, still holding fast to my wrist. "Unless you'd like to join me in one of the suites."

"What?" I cleared my throat. His touch sent a rush of adrenaline through me. I didn't know Rex at all, but something told me he was trouble—that I was in trouble. "I gotta go."

I didn't wait for his response. I darted toward the landing and took the steps as fast as I could. Behind me, Rex chuckled, as if my reaction had been the funniest thing ever.

Downstairs, I ran into Penny. She was drunk and super happy to see me. "Rory! There you are. Have you tried the sangria?" She hugged me, then squinted at me. "Are you sick? You look like you've seen a ghost."

"Not a ghost. The Royals." I pointed my chin up toward

the landing where Enzo, Rex, and Santino stood, looming over us.

They were part of this world. They were devastatingly handsome. They sparkled with beauty and charm. But just like the rest of their circle, they were also just as lethal. Worst part was, they were looking straight at me.

"What did you do?" Penny pulled me toward her and out the front door. She didn't stop until we had reached one of the limos parked outside. Her cheeks were tinged with red, but she looked sober now. "I told you to stay out of their way. To keep a low profile. What happened?"

"Nothing. I went upstairs and ran into them. Then I found you." I omitted a few details from my trip to the second floor of the mansion. "It wasn't a big deal."

"Have you ever seen a cat play with a mouse?" She gestured toward the general direction of the Royals. "It never ends well for the tiny creature. Even if it's just a game."

PART TWO
Fallen Raven

RAVEN DUET, BOOK ONE

I Hope You Survive

Aurora

Best. Day. Ever.

My friend Penny stood next to a Lincoln Town car stretch limo parked in front of my building. As soon as she spotted me through the glass doors, she gestured toward the vehicle, doing her best impression of a model from *The Price is Right*. I beamed at her, shaking my head at how over the top all of this was. Showing up in a limo to my first day of school was the kind of thing that only happened in the Upper East Side.

We had moved to New York City almost a month ago. At first, I couldn't bring myself to trust our good fortune. But after spending hours and hours with Penny and learning all about the century-old enclave my family now belonged to, I couldn't help but fall in love with this world. Did that make me a mafia teen? Probably. And I was just fine with it.

Whatever doesn't kill you...or whoever as was the case in this mafia world.

The doorman pushed the door open for me and stood at

attention. I nodded to him once, then turned to Penny. "I can't believe you did this. A limo? Isn't it a bit much?"

"It's the first day of school. It's tradition." She gave me a one-shoulder shrug.

Her Salvatore uniform was the same as mine: pleated skirt, crisp white button-down shirt, vest, tie, and a coat with the emblem of the Society on her chest, just over her heart. The only difference was her sponsoring family colors—old gold and black—while mine displayed the Alfera colors—royal blue.

When Penny first told me about the family colors, I thought it was overkill. We were already in uniform, what did the colors matter? As it turned out, it was a huge deal. All the kids were loyal to their sponsoring families. At fifty thousand dollars a semester and a letter of recommendation from Don Alfera, I also felt I needed to do right by my benefactors. Only those with ties to the Crime Society, and in good standing with the Dons, were invited to attend Midtown High, a kingmaker school founded by the Society. Anyone attending the school pretty much had their futures secured.

"There's no way this is a thing." I climbed into the limo and scooted over to make room for her.

"After all these weeks with me, are you really that surprised? Signoria Vittoria insisted. She really wants you to make a good impression."

"I know. She's been a godmother of sorts to me and Mom. She's taken us under her wing. I don't know where we'd be without her." I let my gaze dart around the inside of the fancy vehicle.

"I know." She patted my hand. "I feel the same way about her. The way to repay her is to keep our heads down and get through our senior year without incident."

"I can do that. School is my priority. All I want is to graduate with top grades and make it to Columbia." That had always been the dream. Nothing wrong with serving drinks at the casino back in Vegas, but I wanted something different for myself—something different than what Mom had. Thanks to Dad's new job within the Society, I now had a real shot at it. "Um, question. Why is there a bottle of champagne in a bucket of ice?" I giggled, pointing to the bar nestled next to the long leather seat under the window.

"Oh, that." She bumped closer to me. Her gaze switched between me and the driver, as if she were about to tell me some big secret. "We have one more stop before we head to school."

"What do you mean?"

"We're sharing the limo with Signoria Vittoria's niece." Penny rubbed her temple as if trying to find the words to explain the newcomer. "She just got back from Paris. She's a royal. And also, a royal bitch. Don't worry. This is her aunt's limo, so she'll be on her best behavior. Just don't make eye contact."

I chuckled. "Are you serious? No eye contact?"

She shrugged as if saying, *"You'll see."*

The limo pulled to a stop. A few minutes later, the driver climbed out and opened the door on Penny's side. A blonde with long hair, perfect skin, and toned legs climbed inside. "Good morning, ladies." She sat on the seat along the window in front of us.

I didn't need Penny to explain this one to me. This was our school's Queen Bee—and a royal—which meant she was next in line to be a Don. A female Don didn't surprise me since her aunt was Don Salvatore. But this goddess across from me had an air of actual royalty—the way she sat with her back perfectly straight and moved with grace and confidence.

"Donata." Penny paused for a few beats until Donata finished pouring Champagne into a flute and turned to her. Penny cleared her throat and continued, "I'd like to introduce you to Aurora Vitali. Rory. She's, um, she's new."

"I can see that." Donata smiled regally as she braced her elbow on the back seat and sipped from her glass—because why not have a drink right before school.

She was dressed in the same school uniform as us, in the Salvatore colors, but somehow, she looked wealthier. I supposed that was the old money and her family pedigree.

"Aunt Vittoria told me about you. Welcome to Midtown High. I hope you survive." Her sentiment had a nice tone to it, as if she really wanted me to do well.

Or maybe I was imagining the whole thing—that a girl like that could be my friend. It was silly to even think about it. I had no reason to.

"Thank you." I swallowed, and for a moment I considered asking her for a glass of liquid courage. Twenty minutes ago, I had thought today was going to be the best ever. Now, I wasn't so sure. I was way out of my league here. I shifted my attention to Penny and mouthed a "Wow." To which, she mouthed, "I know."

Donata's phone rang. She glanced at the screen then beamed as she tapped it to put the call on speakerphone.

"Where are you?" A deep voice that sounded familiar boomed around us.

"Limo. We're almost there." She casually shifted her body to look at me. I got the sense that maybe we had made her late to meet up with her friends. "Save me a seat?"

"Always do."

The call ended.

I figured I should be nice to the niece of the person who had made all of this happen for my family. Don Alfera was our sponsor, but Signoria Vittoria had made it her mission to make sure we were welcomed into their circle. When I opened my mouth to ask Donata if she'd had a good time in Paris, I got a message from Penny.

Penny: That was Enzo Alfera.

Penny: She only hangs out with the other royals.

Penny: Obvi.

I furrowed my brows at her. Then my phone vibrated again with a new text.

Penny: Don't engage her.

"Oh." I nodded, staring at Enzo's name on my screen.

I met Enzo at the end of the summer. Our encounter was brief, but I had yet to stop thinking about the hot shot quarterback, who was also in line to be the next Don Alfera. He was the son of my sponsoring family. His dad was my dad's boss and the reason why our lives had done a one-eighty turn—from a motel in Las Vegas to a high-rise on Fifth Avenue. He was crazy hot, with dark hair, intense green eyes, and so, so, so, so out of my league.

We rode in silence the rest of the way. As soon as the limo pulled up to the front of the school, Penny put her hand on mine and gave me a meaningful look. Right, we should let the Queen Bee get out first.

"Have a good day, ladies." She climbed out and immediately let out a laugh. "Omigod, you guys. I missed you." She hugged Enzo, Santino, and then Rex.

"Let's wait another minute." Penny was the queen of

protocol. An old school such as Midtown High had a lot of traditions that made my head spin—too many things to keep in mind or mess up. "We're good. Let's go."

I followed her through the tall gates and into the gardens that led to Adaline, the dining hall. Over the summer, I visited the school and did a quick tour, but nothing prepared me for the madness that was the first day of school. I scanned the crowd for blue uniforms and made a point to smile at them. I figured anyone in House Alfera might be interested in being a friend. I quickly found out, not everyone was as friendly or as inviting as Penny.

Jeez, I bet they all could tell I wasn't one of them. And at that moment, I understood Penny's hesitation when she introduced me to Donata. She had said I was *new*. That was code for *outsider*. Everyone here knew each other because they all had grown up in the same mafia world. Their families were all friends. I was a nobody. I came from nothing.

If Signoria Vittoria told Donata about me, then it was safe to assume the other parents had talked to their kids about me and how the Vitali family had wormed their way into the good graces of Don Alfera.

"Hey." I pulled on Penny's sleeve.

She stopped in her tracks right outside the tall, wooden double-doors of the dining hall. "What is it?"

"Does everyone here know I'm..." I rolled my eyes because I couldn't bring myself to say outsider. "That this is my first year."

"I'd say yes."

"They don't seem to like me."

She puffed out a breath. "That's going to take time.

Newcomers aren't really a thing for us, if you know what I mean."

"Really? Like in the last one hundred years, no one new has been invited to the Society?"

"I'm sure that's happened, but you're the only one I know of." She shrugged. "Don't mind them. Just do your thing. You don't need friends to survive your senior year. You have me."

"Thank you." I ran a hand through my hair. "I just wasn't expecting this. You have been so nice to me."

She pursed her lips and shrugged again.

Then I remembered she wasn't exactly my friend. Signoria Vittoria had asked her to play student liaison for me. Penny's family had fallen from grace recently. She was sure that doing this favor for Signoria Vittoria might help her parents get back in with Don Alfera and be part of his inner circle again. It was as she had previously put it; her success this year was tethered to mine.

"I get it." I looked down at my phone to check my schedule. I didn't even know where Chem was. "Do we have any classes together? I meant to ask before."

"Oh, yes, we should have all classes together. I figured that would make things easier for us." She pulled up her schedule. "I have Math. Is that what you have right now?"

"No. I'm in Chemistry." I showed her my phone as proof.

"That's not gonna work." The lines between her brows deepened. "This new admin is not very bright. I knew she'd mess this up." She glanced around. "Why don't you head to class while I take care of this? I'll make sure they match our schedules."

"Yeah, of course." I must've made a face of sheer horror at

the thought of being left alone because she laughed and squeezed my arm.

"You'll be fine. How about this? Go inside." She pointed to the tall doors of Adaline. "And wait for me in the restroom. Use the time to collect yourself. I'll come get you in like ten minutes. Is that better?"

"Thank you, but don't worry about it." I had never been a chicken before. What the heck was wrong with me? I could maneuver through the school on my own. "I'll wait for you in class. I have a map." I wiggled my phone in front of her again.

"I'll see you in a bit then." She took off and quickly got lost in the sea of bodies.

I glanced around and suddenly it was hard to breathe. Maybe collecting myself in the safety of the restroom was a good idea. I let the throng carry me to the breezeway that led to the dining hall. The layout of the building looked different from what I remembered. The restrooms were not where I thought they'd be. When I was here before, the corridor hadn't been this congested and chaotic. People kept pushing me out of the way until I found an empty table near the entrance to what was the actual cafeteria.

At the end of the long, rectangular room, I spotted Donata sitting on one of the tables with her feet planted on a chair. She was deep in conversation with Santino, talking with her hands and laughing. Santino kept his attention on her as she told a story. She was lively and so beautiful.

I smoothed out the skirt of my uniform. In the next beat, Donata stopped talking to look in my direction. When Santino turned as well, I grabbed my bag and headed out. Somehow, I ended up in the locker area. I spun in place to try and get my bearings, but really, I was clueless.

"Hi." I stopped a girl who was headed my way while texting on her phone. She wore a royal-blue uniform, so I figured she was my best shot.

"Hey." She smiled at me.

Oh, good, someone friendly. "Could you show me where the restroom is?"

Her brows shot up in surprise. Then she chuckled. "Sure." She took about three steps and then pulled on a door and held it open for me. "Here you go, sweetie."

My cheeks and ears burned hot. The bathrooms were where I had thought; I just hadn't recognized the fancy doors.

"Thank you." I waved at her and walked inside.

I turned around just as the door shut behind me and muffled her peals of laughter. Confused, I pressed my hand to my forehead and leaned on the wall. What was so funny about not knowing my way around this massive campus? I hadn't realized how difficult it would be to start a new school. Though I should've known an elite school would be tricky to navigate. It was too late to turn back now. The time to leave had come and gone and now I had to make it work. In a few months, my senior year would be just a memory. And I would be where I was meant to be—Columbia.

With a deep inhale, I scanned the bathroom to make sure I was alone. When the urinal flushed, I froze. I stood there as Enzo Alfera glared at me, slowly tucking away his penis.

What Did You See?

Aurora

Before I could react, my gaze shifted down. Not once. But twice. This could not be happening right now. I glanced down one more time, hoping the floor beneath me had opened and was ready to swallow me whole. Forever.

"Not very original." He strode to the sink with a look on his face that said he was bored with me already.

"I..." I pointed toward the door as I tried to find the words to explain to him that I was tricked into barging in on him. Why me? "I'll leave."

"Stop." I gripped the door handle tightly. Out of fear or maybe curiosity, I did as he'd asked and slowly turned around. "I go here." I met his impossibly green eyes.

"I can see that." His gaze swept up and down my body. "You're in my house."

He meant House Alfera. "Yes. Don Alfera has been very generous. Thank you."

His gaze darkened at the mention of his dad. Why? Did he not like it when his dad helped others?

"Yes, my father, the magnanimous." He exhaled and inched closer. "Why are you here?"

"There was a girl." I pointed behind me. "She said this was the bathroom."

"And it is."

"Yes. I thought this was the girls' bathroom."

The smirk on his face couldn't mean anything good. Did he know I saw him? Did he care? He didn't seem as mortified as I was. My whole body screamed for me to run. But I couldn't move. I stood there and watched him prowl toward me with a curious look in his eyes—like a predator hunting its prey.

"What did you see?"

"What?"

"Earlier." He gestured toward the urinals.

"Nothing. I swear." My gaze dropped to his crotch and a wave of heat shot to my cheeks. What was wrong with me? So what if I'd never seen a penis before. So what if he was big? If he was beautiful, even down there.

"You saw my dick. Admit it." He braced a large hand on the side of my face. He smelled of clean laundry and mint.

I pressed my body to the wall and tried not to make eye contact. "I..."

"Don't lie, Aurora."

My gaze snapped up to meet his. He knew my name? How? I melted against the wall at the idea that Enzo Alfera thought of me enough to ask who I was. Not only that, but he also remembered my name. Of course, that couldn't be true. The more logical explanation was that Signoria Vittoria told her niece Donata about her charity case. And Donata, in turn, told her friends—as a joke, something funny she heard that day—not because she thought of me as anyone of consequence.

"How about we play a game of tit for tat?" He tapped his index finger to my sternum. The same way he had done at Tiffany's when he asked me to try on the sapphire pendant.

I glanced down at the spot where his touch seared my skin. What did he want from me? If I saw him, did that mean he wanted to see me? My heart pumped so hard against the pad of his finger, there was no way he hadn't noticed. The spot between my legs quivered, just thinking about letting him see me there. Or letting him touch me.

For a moment, I imagined him lifting my skirt slowly until I was exposed and pulling down my underwear to get a better view. What would I do if he decided to touch me? Or finger me? What would he do if he knew I was already wet? No, I couldn't let him see. That would be too embarrassing. Gosh, why was I even thinking about this?

"My friends tell me you like to watch." He leaned in until our noses were inches apart. "Tell me what you saw."

I shook my head. Though in my mind's eye, I had a clear picture of his cock. It seemed heavy to me, big and thick. I had no reference for it, but I would say it was nice. And I liked how manly he looked handling it when he tucked it inside his pants.

Wait. What? I couldn't let myself think about that.

"You're not leaving until you tell me."

"I have chem class. I can't be late." My chest lifted high with every labored inhale.

"First day of school. You should definitely be on time. Go on." He stared at me as if he were trying to read my thoughts.

"It looked big." Before I could stop myself, I looked down at his crotch again.

He licked his lips, then flashed me a sexy smile. "That's not what I meant. Rex told me you were spying on Santino when you came to my house in the Hamptons."

"I didn't see anything." I touched my cold hand to my burning cheek.

I turned around to leave, but before I opened the door, a boy barged in. He stood there frozen, staring at Enzo. I had a sense the boy would be in trouble later for interrupting Enzo's game, but I didn't care. With a quick "apologetic" look, I attempted a step, but Enzo gripped my upper arm.

"Not so fast, angel." He looked at the guy, who still hadn't moved a muscle, and pointed his chin toward the breezeway. "Give us a minute."

The guy shifted his attention to me then back to Enzo before he nodded and left.

Enzo leaned in and pushed the heavy door shut.

"Are you serious?" I peered at his hand, still holding me tight. "It was an accident. I told you. There was a girl who told me this was the bathroom. I didn't know you'd be here. I didn't come here to see your cock."

"Hmmm."

Oh, crap. The moment I said the word, the energy in the room shifted. It crackled and sizzled until it created a buzz right at the apex of my sex.

"You want to leave here? You know what you need to do." He braced his hand on the side of my head. "What did you see that night, Aurora? Tell me."

I squeezed my eyes shut because my name on his lips sounded so sensual. When I opened them again, I focused on the bow of his lips. Immediately, the memory from the end-of-summer party at his house came rushing back. My nipples tightened again, the way they had done that night when I found Santino naked and nestled between his girlfriend's legs.

From where I stood by the threshold, I couldn't really tell what he was doing. I didn't want to know. Enzo touched the tip of his tongue to his bottom lip and suddenly the scene in my head became something totally different.

I was the one sprawled on the bed and Enzo's mouth was on me.

"Well?"

"She was nude." I swallowed hard, ignoring the swell of desire in my core.

"What did she look like?" he whispered.

"Beautiful."

"Was he fondling her?"

"Yes." I sighed, biting my lower lip.

I stared at Enzo's handsome face and couldn't help but see him in that suite instead of Santino. With every inhale, the fabric of my blouse rubbed against my nipples. Why were they so achy? Why was this such a turn-on for me? I was embarrassed when I saw them. I didn't want to stay and watch. Whatever Enzo was thinking, he was wrong. I wasn't a peeping Tom—or a voyeur.

"Try using bigger words, Aurora." He inhaled deeply as if my words were affecting him too.

"He was kneading her breasts, making them bounce, making her moan with pleasure." I shook my head because now I couldn't stop the myriad of images in my head.

Several times in the past few weeks, I had thought of what I saw. But before the image was fully realized in my mind, I had sent it away. I didn't want to have those kinds of thoughts about anyone, let alone one of the royals. Enzo had managed to wrench that memory from me and now I couldn't stop the kaleidoscope of images flitting through my head. More than anything, I remembered how aroused I had been watching them.

"What else was he doing?" His gaze dropped to my chest.

This was literally the second time Enzo and I had spoken. How was this the topic of conversation? What kind of stuff were he and his friends into?

"I need to get to class. What more do you want me to say?"

"What was Santino doing to her?"

"I don't know," I answered honestly. "He had his face to her crotch. And she seemed to like it. He..." I lifted my hand to touch my breast, to give it some relief, but then I put it down. I didn't need to embarrass myself further.

"Go on."

"He lifted her and swiped his tongue along her...her." I inhaled.

"Along the seam of her pussy?"

I nodded as blood thrashed in my ears.

"Did he make her come?"

"I think so. She was calling his name. And then tensed up, pulling his hair."

The image of Santino's girlfriend coming hard exploded in my head. And I could almost feel it.

"I bet it was good for you."

I glanced up at him, eyes wide as the lights turned brighter. I dipped my head for a moment, feeling drained and oddly sedated.

He beamed and stepped closer to me. For a second, I

thought he was going to kiss me. I was so ready for it too. He reached for the hem of my skirt and pulled sideways on it. The fabric rubbed against me. That gentle stroke felt so good.

"That's a good girl." He kissed my cheek so softly I barely felt his mouth. "Such a good girl." When he stepped back, he reached into his coat and removed a bark of white chocolate. His eyes never left mine as he unwrapped it and broke off a small piece. "Your reward, angel." He parted my lips and placed the sweet treat on my tongue.

"Hmmm." A small hum escaped my lips.

I was still turned on, but somehow, I felt satisfied. Was it the dirty talk? Or his eyes, his voice? Or maybe the treat?

The candy immediately melted with a burst of delicious flavors of orange and cayenne pepper. It was spicy and so good. I wanted to say thank you. But this whole situation wasn't anything to be grateful for. Enzo was just being a bully to the new girl. I was sure he was going to go back to his friends later and have a good laugh.

Tears spilled down my cheeks. Now I understood why Penny wanted me to keep my head down and stay away from the royals.

They were cruel, spoiled, rich brats.

I pushed him out of the way and bolted.

Going against the flow of traffic, I bumped into several students before I reached the tall double doors that led to the courtyard. I wanted to look back and see if Enzo was following me, but I couldn't do it. My heart raced out of control and all I wanted to do was get fresh air and put a lot of distance between us.

"Rory." Someone called my name.

I kept going, even though I had no clue where I was headed.

After another beat, a hand gripped my arm and swung me around. "What happened to you?" Penny did a quick inspection of me. "You're crying."

"I'm fine. I just felt overwhelmed with all the people in there. It got stuffy."

"Right. Well, I got my schedule fixed." She waved a paper in front of me. "We're in chem together."

"Thank you." I hugged her. "For everything you've done for me."

I hadn't realized how much I needed a friend to survive this school.

"I'm not doing this for you, but you're welcome." She smiled at me. "Come on, we do *not* want to be late on our first day."

"Yes, please. Chemistry sounds lovely right about now." I rubbed my cheek where Enzo had brushed it with his lips. Suddenly, Enzo's words came back to me. *My friends tell me you like to watch.* Shame washed over me as I considered the implication of his words. If he knew about the incident in the Hamptons, who else knew?

"Hey, can I ask you something?"

"Sure. What is it?"

"You said before that people were probably talking about the new girl." My heart raced because a part of me didn't want to know. Though I had to know if people were saying things about me, calling me a peeping Tom. "Have you heard anything about what happened the night of the end-of-summer party? You know, at Enzo's house?"

Just saying his name out loud made my body shiver all

over. What exactly happened in the bathroom with him? Why did he make me say all those things? What the hell was his deal?

"I only know what you told me, which was nothing." She shrugged. "If they found you upstairs where you weren't supposed to be, they seem to have gotten over it. I don't think you need to worry about the royals. I think they'll let you be."

"Okay." I took in a big gulp of air.

"There's that word."

"Sorry." I ran my fingers through my hair to clear my thoughts and get ready for a day of classes. "Let's go."

Chemistry class was in the Salvatore building on the far end of campus, near the football field. The walk and the crisp autumn air helped me calm down. By the time we strolled into the classroom, I had already forgotten about the incident in the bathroom. Well, almost.

"Hey, I have to use the restroom." Penny pointed toward the classroom. "Save me a seat."

"Hurry. You have like a minute." I waved at her and then headed inside.

The classroom was set up like a lab, with two students per table. Only a few people had arrived, so I had plenty of options. I decided the front of the class was the best way to stay out of trouble and pay attention to the lessons. I set my backpack on the floor and placed my foot on the stool next to mine to save it for Penny.

I glanced out the window and smiled at the gorgeous view of the courtyard. Only the best for the spoiled brats, I supposed. I shifted my attention back to the lab and all the gadgets on the tables.

The royals.

I hoped Penny was right about them and that they had forgotten about the night in the Hamptons. The moment the thought popped into my head, all four of them appeared in my line of sight—Donata, hanging from Enzo's arm, with Rex and Santino right behind them. I couldn't hear what they were saying, but whatever it was, they seemed amused.

Did Enzo run back to tell them what he did to me? Or what he had me do?

I glanced down at my hands to pretend I hadn't seen them come in. But the body heat from Enzo was difficult to ignore. When I looked up, he was standing right in front of me and had his hand on Penny's stool, tapping on it gently with long fingers.

"Enzo." Donata pulled him toward her. "Leave the help alone."

In my peripheral vision, I watched them take the lab tables toward the back. This was bad. This was very, very bad. Now I had to see Enzo every single day until graduation.

"I'm so glad I switched," Penny whispered to me as she slid her seat toward her. "They're all here," she mouthed.

"Yeah, they're all here." I shot a glance over my shoulder and caught a glimpse of Enzo balancing on his stool while he leaned against the wall, looking incredibly hot and extremely dangerous.

His words echoed in my head. *What did you see that night, Aurora? Tell me.*

Pay Attention

Enzo

"What is it with you and the new girl?" Rex slapped my shoulder with the back of his hand then sat next to me with his lunch tray.

"Nothing." I shrugged as my gaze slowly veered back toward the far end of the dining hall where she sat alone not eating her food.

For the past ten minutes, I had been considering joining her to make sure she ate her lunch. What was it about her? This morning, I only meant to mess with her a little, make her squirm for barging in on me. Many women had seen my cock. And, yeah, they had made a big deal out of it, telling me how great it was. All stuff I'd heard before. While I knew it was true, most of the time, it all felt rehearsed to me. As if they had seen one bad porn clip and then decided to steal the cheesy lines.

But Aurora's reaction had been pure ecstasy. She ogled my

cock like it was the eighth wonder. For a long minute, I stood there with my dick in my hand, trying to decide if I should put it away or see if she would let me fuck her right then and there.

With Dad riding my ass to finish senior year without any incidents—and I was sure fucking the new girl on the first day of school would be considered an incident—I decided to opt for the sensible course of action. So I made myself calm down to lose the raging hard-on I had for Aurora and tucked it away.

What happened next, I didn't see coming. Never had one of my games gotten the best of me. I fell for it, just like she had. I thought I was going to lose my mind when she uttered the word cock. Her lips looked so plump. I imagined her little cunt would be as pretty as her mouth.

"What's the deal with her?" Santino's voice jerked me out of my reverie. He leaned forward and braced his arms on the table, openly staring in Aurora's direction. "I mean." He chuckled. "We already know what she's into. But really? Her dad is now your dad's right-hand man. How the fuck did that happen?"

"Hmm." I exhaled. "I don't know. Apparently, Stephano Vitali saved Dad's life."

"I didn't think Don Alfera was the grateful type."

"Me neither. The old man is planning something." My attention shifted back to Aurora.

"What did I tell you?" Donata hugged Rex from behind then set her tray of sushi on the table. "I think our Enzo has a crush on the new girl."

"I don't date the help." I glared at her as I stabbed a piece of Wagyu steak and popped it in my mouth.

I focused on chewing while I kept my attention on Donata's features and her blonde hair. Though I couldn't stop thinking about Aurora's reaction in the bathroom. The small sound of pleasure she had made when I fed her the chocolate echoed in my head. For the last three hours, that moan was all I could hear. All through chem class, I played the scene from the bathroom over and over again like a movie trailer.

A sharp pain on my shin brought me back to reality.

I lifted my gaze and met Donata's amused look. She smiled at me, shaking her head. "She rode in the limo with me this morning." She raised her eyebrow as if that sole statement made her point. "She's a mousy little thing, but Aunt Vittoria has taken an active interest in her. I'd stay away from that one, if I were you."

"Thanks for the advice." I rolled my eyes at her.

"Is our little Queen Bee going soft in her old age?" Santino pinched her cheek. "Paris was rough, huh?"

"Fuck off." She handled her chopsticks expertly as she dipped her tuna in the wasabi and soy sauce mix and placed it in her mouth.

One day, Donata would make a great Don for the Salvatore family. Her aunt regarded her as smart and capable. I only wished my own father thought of me like that. But nothing pleased the old man—especially not me. No matter how hard I tried, Dad would never see me as worthy of stepping into his shoes to become the king he wanted for the Society.

I adjusted my coat over the raw spot on my back and winced in pain. Sometimes I wondered if he even loved me. How could he? The great Don Alfera only loved himself and his empire.

"Is your back bothering you?" Rex bent down to rummage

through his computer bag. A cover so the others wouldn't hear him.

"It's fine." I mouthed and gestured for him to let it go.

"I thought maybe we had matured now that we're seniors." Donata sipped from her water, eyeing me with interest.

"Yeah, we're so mature." Rex pointed a finger at Santino. "Santino thought it would be a good idea to fuck a cheerleader at Enzo's house, in the middle of Don Alfera's big end-of-summer shindig." He laughed.

"Yeah, he told me. I need to have a talk with my girls." She shook her head at Santino, who only shrugged as if saying, *I can't help myself.* After a beat, she dipped her head toward Aurora and let out a laugh. "Was angel face really spying on Santino?"

"She was." Rex's eyes watered as the entire table burst into peals of laughter. "I was there. She was all flustered, and I'm fairly sure, turned on."

"She liked what she saw." Santino sat back and extended his arms out, placing his intertwined hands behind his head.

Across the way, Aurora rose to her feet and carried her tray to the conveyor belt near the kitchen. She hadn't touched her food. Why? Our chef was one of the best in the city. I highly doubted her food wasn't up to scratch. I glanced down at my perfectly cooked steak. No doubt her meal had been prepared with the same level of quality.

"Enzo?" Donata waved her hand in front of me. "Are you coming? Don't we have Italian together?"

"No, I have English Lit right now."

"Fine. Could you at least walk me to my class?" she asked with her hand firmly hooked around Santino's arm.

"Why do you need all three of us to walk you places?

Everyone is terrified of you. It's not like they're going to try and talk to you." I dropped my napkin on the tray and pushed it toward the center of the table for someone else to clear.

"I like your company. Is that so bad?" She flashed me a brilliant smile.

When I grabbed my backpack and slung it over my shoulder, I realized why she didn't want to be seen alone. Luca Gallo stood by the entrance, ushering students out. What the fuck? After the stunt he pulled last semester, I thought that asshole would be long gone. Why was he back? For Donata's sake, I played it cool.

"Ah, I see Mr. Gallo is back." I made a show of eyeing him up and down. "Has he lost weight?"

"What?" She casually scanned the room until she found him. "I hadn't noticed. Can we go? I don't want to be late."

I exchanged a meaningful look with Rex. Donata had had a crush on Luca for as long as I could remember. And just because everything always worked out her way, our junior year, Luca had come back to Midtown High after college to teach English Lit. Of course the creep couldn't keep his hands to himself.

"Let's go." I offered her my arm, and she took it.

When we reached the threshold, she gripped my sleeve tighter. "Mr. Gallo, welcome back."

"Ms. Salvatore." He nodded and gestured toward the exit.

Her chest expanded, then deflated like a balloon. I picked up the pace to quickly put space between them. Out in the courtyard, she released a breath but didn't loosen her hold on me. I had no doubt she was still hung up on Gallo.

"Smooth. Very smooth." Santino chuckled. "You know you're a minor, right?"

"Shut up." She let go of me and pushed Santino away from her. "I don't plan on staying a minor forever. I'll be eighteen soon."

"You do you." Santino put up his hands in mock surrender. "But I can tell you, he's not interested."

When the double doors opened again, she glanced over her shoulder. Gallo was still inside directing traffic. She sighed. "I'll see you guys later."

Santino raised his eyebrow as he watched Donata stomp across the lawn. "Should I have a talk with Gallo? I get the feeling he didn't learn his lesson last year."

"No. Just leave it." I slapped his arm and turned to Rex. "I talked to my father. We're all set for Friday night."

"First week of senior year. We gotta celebrate properly." Rex rubbed his hands together with a big grin on his face.

This was why Rex was one of my best friends. The guy worked hard. But he also knew how to party hard. I could always count on him. He was like a brother to me. He and Santino both were.

"Where are we meeting?" Santino asked.

"The Crucible." I beamed at them.

"Oh shit. You got us in?" Rex pulled me into a bear hug and kissed the top of my head. "About damn time. We're almost eighteen. It was bullshit that we weren't allowed in."

"I think Don Alfera wanted us to earn the right." Santino shrugged.

"Seems now we have." I nodded to both of them.

"Gotta get to class." Rex glanced down at his phone. "Hey, is Massimo racing tonight?"

Every Monday, for the last eighteen months, my younger brother had been running a lucrative street racing business outside of the city. Dad didn't approve of it because it put him in a tight spot with the cops. But Massimo was smart and knew how to handle trouble.

"Yeah, it's still on. You going?"

"I got my money on your little brother." Santino raised his brow. "I'll be there."

"Me too." Rex waved goodbye and strode across the courtyard to the adjacent building.

I waited until they were gone, then circled back to talk to Gallo. After the stunt he pulled last year, I didn't think he'd have the guts to show his face in our school again. If he wanted to fuck around with his students, fine. But Donata was one of us. She was a future Don. The mindfuck he did on her junior year couldn't happen again.

Just as I reached the entrance to Adaline, he opened the door and let more students out. I waited until we were alone, then rounded on him.

"What the fuck? I thought I was very clear last time we spoke. Donata isn't your meal ticket."

He glanced down, pursing his lips. "I explained what happened to the board. They all thought I was fit to return and teach. You can take it up with them."

"There's no way Dad agreed to it."

Dad knew I had seen Donata and Gallo making out in his classroom. He'd been the one to issue Gallo's suspension, pending an investigation. What happened? Did Donata deny the incident? Gallo was high up in the Society. But his dad was the youngest of five, which pretty much guaranteed Luca would never be Don.

Donata was a beautiful girl, but she was so much younger than him. I found it hard to believe his intentions were noble.

He wanted Donata to secure his rank within our organization.

A student-teacher relationship was gross. Also, for Gallo to go after Donata to secure a place at the Society table was something my father would never allow. It was why marriages between the five original families were forbidden.

Donata and Gallo could never be. Period.

"It was a unanimous decision by the school board. So, yes, he agreed." He fisted his hand. "Not that this is any of your business, Enzo. But I have no intention of letting Donata get close again." He swallowed. "You have my word."

I wished Dad had thought to mention that Luca Gallo had been reinstated. If anything, just so I could talk to Donata and make her see how wrong Gallo was for her. She was a smart woman. But she was different with him, and not in a good way.

"Just stay the fuck away from her."

I took long strides across the courtyard. According to the clock tower, I was already ten minutes late to class. *Shit.* I hated being late. I picked up the pace, going faster without breaking into a run. That bought me a few minutes. Though by the time I swung the classroom door open, class had already started.

"Mr. Alfera." Professor Reid stopped writing on the whiteboard to glare at me. "Good of you to join us."

"My apologies." I nodded once, then turned my attention to the rest of the room to see if there were any seats available in the back and immediately met Aurora's gaze.

My tense muscles relaxed. The anger that had pooled at the pit of my stomach when I first saw Gallo quickly dissipated.

She gave me the same "deer in the headlights" look from

this morning when I almost sat next to her in chem. Her lips formed an "O" that reminded me of our little storytelling session. With a quick glance around the classroom, I confirmed my choices. Front of the room or the seat next to Aurora.

I slow-blinked in annoyance because sitting next to her during English Lit would be too distracting. But since the lesson had already started, I couldn't exactly get someone else to give up their seat for me. Shaking my head, I made my way toward her. She ducked her head and started doodling on her notebook. When I plopped myself next to her, her head snapped up in my direction.

"As I was saying," Professor Reid continued, "you will have three research papers and a book report." He raised both hands when the whole class moaned in unison. "The book report is meant to show you Shakespeare can be fun."

She droned on about the syllabus, test dates, and finals. I managed to keep my attention on her words, but couldn't help but notice Aurora's excited energy, the warmth of her body so close to mine, and her floral perfume.

A smile pulled at my lips. I was surprised to find her presence so soothing. Of course, I couldn't say the same for her. She was a bundle of nerves, fidgeting and shooting furtive glances my way. At some point, she squirmed in her seat so much, she dropped one of her pencils. When she bent over to pick it up, the rest of her pencil pouch toppled over.

Her cheeks turned bright red as she stared at the mess on the floor.

I rolled my eyes at her, then leaned forward to scoop up her gel pens.

"Pay attention." I looked into her eyes, something I had

wanted to do again since she'd left the men's bathroom this morning.

"Thank you." She nodded.

The bell rang, and in ten seconds flat, she collected her things and bolted. I sat back and watched her leave.

God, I enjoyed watching her squirm.

The Virgin Place

Enzo

Our SUV pulled up to the curb in front of the Crucible. I glanced up and smiled at the oversized block letters looming over us, high above the midtown high-rise. The Crucible was Dad's by-invitation-only nightclub that catered to clientele with discerning tastes and unlimited resources. In short, the spot was a sex club, with three separate gambling floors, a VIP lounge, and private suites.

The lines to get in were always long. But every Friday and Saturday night, the front entrance became one big block party. Rex, Santino, and I were familiar with the scene. This had been our hangout spot for the last couple of years. But tonight, we got to go beyond the red rope.

Up until now, Dad had not allowed us to visit. For whatever reason, he had said yes when I asked if we could celebrate the start of our senior year at the Crucible. Maybe the old man felt guilty for his recent behavior. He'd never been much of a caring father, but lately his mood had turned darker than usual. He was on edge all the time. His temper got the best of him often.

"Mr. Alfera, welcome." The bouncer opened the car door and gestured toward the front of the line.

"Thank you." I adjusted my suit jacket.

"Ah, fuck," Rex said through gritted teeth. "Derek's here."

"Where?" Santino climbed out of the car, ready for a fight.

"By the DJ." Rex glared in Derek's direction on the other side of the street. "The asshole's still belly-aching over St. Francis Prep losing the state championship to us."

"I heard." I shifted my attention toward the crowd dancing to the techno beats in the middle of the street.

The laser lights rolled over the sidewalk and the sea of bodies, making them look like they were moving in slow motion. When our SUV peeled away, Derek and his friends were directly in our line of sight. My hands itched to punch that smug smile off his face. He'd been telling anyone who would listen that Midtown High paid off the referees to throw the game in our favor. The fucking asshole made that shit up. Our team won fair and square.

To the world, we were just another elite private school, just like St. Francis Prep. But we were more than that. We were an integral part of our century-old enclave. We lived by our code of honor. Cheating was beneath us.

And that was the part that pissed me off—that because of Derek's rumors, our school came off as just another cesspool of rich, spoiled kids. We were far from that. We were the future Dons. That meant something to the four of us.

"We should go say hi." Santino crossed his arms over his chest.

"No, we can't. Dad wants us to keep our heads down." I

wasn't ready for another go with Dad. I still hadn't recovered from the last time Dad thought he needed to teach me a lesson. "We'll get them some other night."

The bouncer removed the red rope for us to head in, then gestured toward the glass double doors. I'd been in the lobby before, the boardroom upstairs, and even the security room on the second floor. So I knew my way around.

We all did.

"This is gonna be fun." I pressed the call button. The doors opened immediately. I stepped in and ran my fingers down the panel. "Where should we start?"

"The Parthenon floor." Santino pressed the button.

"Do you even know what's there?" Rex leaned on the wall.

"Did you not pay attention in Greek Mythology? The Parthenon is the temple for the virgin goddess Athena. The word literally means the virgin place."

Rex chuckled. "What exactly do you think we're going to find in the Parthenon?"

"Maybe virgins?" He cocked his eyebrow.

"I'm gonna give you a minute on that one." I chuckled and stuffed my hands in the pockets of my trousers while I waited for Santino to do the math.

"I guess you're right. That would be a logistical nightmare." He shrugged. "I still think we start there. I mean it has to do with..."

The elevator door slid open, and for once, Santino was stunned mute. Truth be told, I didn't know what to say either. A quick glance over my shoulder showed me Rex was just as astounded. We stood there for so long, the gates tried to shut on us. I put my hand out and pushed them back.

"Do you think we can just join in?" Santino found his words again as he ogled a couple having sex on a velvet couch not too far from us.

As it turned out, the Parthenon floor was what made the Crucible a sex club. The large rectangular room was composed of groupings of chairs and settees—like intimate living rooms in a massive space. The lights were dimmed so low, I could barely make out the different body parts. One thing was for sure—there were plenty of naked people executing some fairly impressive maneuvers.

"I need a drink." I let out a breath.

"Me too." Santino nodded once.

But when I made to amble to the bar on the far left, he went in the opposite direction. I laughed. "You're going the wrong way."

"Am I?" He waved and disappeared into the darkest part of the room.

"I think we lost him." Rex chuckled, gripping my shoulder. "Come on, let's see what the bartender can do for us."

I took the barstool at the end of the bar and shifted my weight to face the main floor. I ordered a whiskey neat and kept my attention on the view in front of us. For some odd reason, I thought of Aurora. What would she think of this place? Would she be mortified, or would she stay and watch?

I smiled at the carpeted floor. Given the encounters we'd had this past week, I'd say she'd take a peek, while also being deliciously mortified. Since the first day of school, I hadn't had the opportunity to get her alone again. Penny had become Aurora's shadow. Everywhere she went, Penny quickly followed. And that had me wondering if maybe Dad had hired

Penny to be Aurora's keeper—make sure she stayed out of trouble.

Why would Dad care what Aurora did in school?

"How are you and your dad?" Rex leaned on the counter and sipped from his glass. "Is he still being an asshole?"

"Yep." I swallowed. "Turns out, it's an incurable disease."

"I'm sorry. I wish there was something I could do."

"Don't be. By this time next year, I'll be out from under his thumb. College will be a good reprieve." I raked a hand through my hair. "He's gotten worse lately."

"You know, you can always crash at my place."

"Don't worry about it." I thought of the penthouse and how serene it felt when Dad wasn't home, which lately was most of the time. "Mom refuses to leave Brooklyn, so..." I shrugged and took a long swig from my glass.

Mom was the only one who could weather Dad's temper. Unfortunately, she hated the city. Even though Dad's job as king of the Society required him to be here, she was resolute in her decision to live in Brooklyn with my little sister Caterina. That left my younger brother Massimo and me to fend for ourselves while we attended high school.

At first, I missed her, and couldn't understand why she would leave. Why she would split our family in two. Why my sister was more important to her than Massimo and me. It'd been two years now. I got over her absence a long time ago.

I spent another five minutes wallowing in self-pity when a pair of tits appeared in my peripheral vision. I lifted my gaze to meet hers and found a pair of blue eyes that, again, made me think of Aurora. Unlike Aurora, the friendly woman sitting next to me came with zero complications.

"Hi, I'm Alice." She smiled sweetly, then licked her lips.

"Is that your real name, Alice?"

"Hmm." She glanced upward. "Tonight, it is."

"Enzo." I chuckled and offered her my hand to shake.

She took it and pulled me toward her. "My friends and I have a suite." She gestured toward the middle of the main floor where two other women waved in our direction. "Want to join us?"

Time to let my cock do the thinking for me, so I could chill the fuck out. When I turned around to tell Rex I was taking Alice up on her offer, he was already leaving with some other woman—a pretty brunette with long legs.

"I'll be right back," he mouthed.

"Take your time." I saluted him as Alice tugged at my arm with more urgency.

From her suite, the bar area looked so far away, though the overall vibe of the place remained the same, bathed in shadows and sensual music. With her gaze fixed on my face, Alice nudged me down on the blue velvet sofa and climbed on top of me. As soon as she did, her two friends converged on me as well.

She slipped her hand inside the waistband of my pants, and I sat back and let it all go.

SOMETIME AROUND MIDNIGHT, I needed a break. I made my way back to the bar where Santino and Rex sat talking to Donata.

"He lives." She raised her glass. "We were wondering if we needed to come rescue you."

"I need a drink. I thought you weren't coming tonight."

"I changed my mind." She shrugged.

The minute I plopped myself down, Rex jerked to his feet. "Motherfucker."

"Who?" I slowly shifted my body weight, still tired from the hours I'd spent with Alice and her friends. "Oh, fuck me. How did he get in?"

"His dad has money."

I slipped down the barstool to stand next to Rex. Derek had already spotted us. By the smug look on his face, he was on his way over to start trouble. If I had to swallow my pride earlier and let it go, why couldn't he do the same now?

"I'm surprised to see you here all alone. Where's Daddy?" He leaned on the bar. The minute his gaze fell on Donata, he squared his shoulders as he shot a quick glance to the many couples having sex not too far from us. When he switched his attention to her, he was in total creep mode.

"I'm going to check out the gambling room. This place is not doing it for me." She smiled at Rex and me. "You guys coming?" When Derek practically jumped off his seat, she put up her hand, furrowing her brows. "Not you."

"Why not? My father has more money than these two combined."

I didn't think that was true. But given how I had promised Dad I would behave tonight, I decided to let it go. Again. I smirked at him and braced my arm around Donata's waist.

"Maybe I should ask Father to buy me a state championship. I would bet you'd find me pretty then."

I pinched the bridge of my nose. Derek just had a way of putting me on edge. The bliss from the last few hours wore off quickly and left me with the powerful urge to punch him in the mouth.

"Let's go." I tilted my head toward the elevators, holding Donata tighter than I should. She let me because she realized I was really struggling to keep it together. If I started something with Derek here, Dad would not take kindly to it. I wasn't about to lose my access to the Crucible simply because Derek was a sore loser.

Dad would never stoop so low. Yeah, he liked to win. More than that, he liked to see us win. But cheating wasn't how we did things in the Society. Even if our entire way of life was steeped in crime and violence, honor was everything.

"What is he talking about?" Donata turned to face me.

"Stupid lies he started up over the summer," I said.

"What? You didn't know about that?" he spoke directly to Donata. "I have it on record that Daddy Alfera paid off not one, but all of the referees, to throw the game in their favor."

"If you have proof, how come the referees haven't come forward? As far as I know, Midtown High is still the reigning champ." Rex stepped forward.

"Because for whatever reason, the officials are afraid of Michael Alfera. But I know they cheated. It was the only way they could beat my—"

My fist connected with his nose before I realized I had thrown the punch. It made a cracking sound as blood splattered all over the bar. Just fucking great. But now, I had to finish it. I couldn't have Derek spewing lies about my family. I hovered over him where he lay sprawled on the floor, then gripped the front of his button-down shirt.

"You lost. You know why? Your defense sucks. You have a decent arm, man. But you don't have a team to back you up. Mainly they don't want to, because you're an asshole." I let out a breath and shoved him to the marble tile. "So how about you and I settle this once and for all?"

He swiped blood off his nose with the back of his hand. "What do you have in mind?"

The terror in his eyes told me he thought I meant to challenge him to a fight. I couldn't do that without risking Dad's wrath. "You have a car, right?"

Long ago, the five original families that made up the Society were assigned key industries to infiltrate. The Valentino family had a handle on politics, IT, and secrets. If we needed a favor, Don Valentino was our guy. The Salvatore family was in finance and investments. At the lowest level, they controlled the loan sharks. At our level, they handled hostile takeovers, acquisitions, and risky investments.

The Gallos ran the guns. The illegal kind. The ones needed to win a war. The Buratti family had their hooks in so deep in the real estate market, Uncle Sam relied on them to get people to pay their property taxes. It wouldn't look pretty for government officials to kick people out of their homes for failing to pay property taxes. Someone had to take out the trash —the Buratti family were always more than willing. The Alfera family had their hands in the automotive industry— from manufacturing and exporting, to the world of racing and gambling. This was the one thing Dad and I had in common.

We loved cars.

Like my father, but at a much lesser scale, Derek's dad was also in the automotive business.

"A drag race?" He stood as his hungry gaze shifted to Donata. "Winner takes all?"

"Don't be gross." Donata rolled her eyes at him. "You race for pinks, as usual."

"What she said." I dipped my head toward Donata.

His face lit up because he'd seen my spruced-up Toyota Supra. "You're on, Alfera. Just say when."

"When."

Fast Cars, Booze, and Cocky Drivers

Enzo

Maybe drag racing wasn't the best solution to shut Derek up. It was certainly better than beating his ass at my father's club with a bunch of cameras recording every punch. At least this way, there was a slight chance Dad wouldn't find out. I had the perfect guy for the job too—my brother Massimo. He was two years younger than me, but already a damn good driver with a knack for setting up drag races. His record was impeccable. He'd never been caught.

"It's two in the morning. Is he even awake?" Donata leaned her hip on the back wall of the penthouse elevator car as she typed fast into her phone. "I mean, I want to put that Derek guy in his place too, but we have to be smart about this."

"That's why we're here. Massimo can make this happen." I winked at her.

"Would your maid call your mom or dad?" Santino asked.

"She goes home after dinner."

The elevator door slid open. I stepped out and headed

straight upstairs to my brother's bedroom. Dad bought this penthouse years ago when he first married Mom. It was the epitome of a Fifth Avenue, Upper East Side apartment—tall windows, marble floors, lavish decor.

Too bad Mom hated it. So much so that she rarely set foot in it, which left my brother and me to fend for ourselves most of the time. Every now and then, Dad would stop by to play the father figure. Those were the times when I wished Mom hadn't left.

I knocked on the door once, then pushed it open. "Got a minute?" I asked when Massimo removed his headset to look at me.

"I'm in the middle of a campaign here."

"I need your help." I stepped inside. "Remember that asshole telling everyone Midtown High cheated last year during the championship?"

"Yeah, just yesterday he was outside our school gates telling his ridiculous story. Why is Dad letting that go on?"

"No idea, but I intend to shut him up tonight. He's agreed to race me."

A low rumble of a chuckle escaped his lips. "Hell yeah."

"Can you arrange that?" I raised both eyebrows. I was asking for too much. But if the race didn't happen right now, Derek's surge of bravado would fizzle out. I had no doubt he'd back out come morning. "Tonight?"

"Fuck, Enzo." He rubbed the side of his face as his gaze veered toward his monitor, then back to me. "Fine. Give me an hour." He swiveled around to face his screen, where the game was still going on. "Guys, I need to drop. And I need a favor."

"Thanks, man," I said to the back of his head, then headed out and down the hallway to my own suite.

I ambled to my closet as I undid my tie and removed my suit jacket. When I removed my button-down shirt, I heard the door open and close. I didn't need to look to know it was Rex. Rex was that friend who always made me see reason. He had been quiet the whole way here, which could only mean he'd been waiting for the right moment to talk me out of doing this highly illegal thing.

That moment was now.

He appeared in the mirror as he leaned on the doorframe of my closet. His gaze didn't meet mine in our reflection. Instead, he examined my back and the myriad of scars jumbled with new cuts. Dad had a temper that he hid from everyone except me. He claimed that he wanted me to be the best version of myself, a better king for the Society. I wanted that too. Even if his methods had me at the end of my rope most days.

One day I would become the king of a century old Society. The Dons of the other four original crime families would answer to me. I understood my role and my place. I only wished Dad found me capable of leading.

"You know how this ends, Enzo." He pointed at my back. "Even if you're doing this for him, Don Alfera won't appreciate this coming from you."

"He doesn't have to know." I pulled a T-shirt over my head and tucked it into my jeans.

"If you get caught—"

"I won't."

"But if you do..." He released a breath. "Let me take your place. I can beat that asshole."

"You're not a performance racer."

"Neither are you."

"I got this." I squeezed his shoulder. "Don't worry about me, brother. I can handle my father's wrath."

He clicked his tongue. "Tell that to your back."

My phone buzzed in my back pocket. I grabbed it and read Massimo's text. "He's got us a street and a diversion. We're on in an hour." I grabbed my lucky leather jacket off the back of my closet door. "You coming?"

"You know I am." He shook his head in both disapproval and concession.

Forty-five minutes later, the rumble of engines, loud cheers, and techno beats drowned the voice in my head, telling me that racing at three in the morning on a Saturday could end poorly. I strode toward Massimo, who was standing next to my car. He had the hood popped open and was in the process of letting Derek peek under our skirts. I didn't like seeing him drool all over my ride, but these were the rules.

I looked around the dim-lit street and found many familiar faces. Was the whole school here? How did they even know? I spotted Donata in the crowd. She had spent her time sending out a blast to get everyone here. I shook my head at her, smiling. I did appreciate the support.

"What do you think?" Massimo slapped my arm, looking all smug. He should be proud for putting this race together in record time.

"Nice turn out." I put my arm around him, then lifted my chin toward the engine. "Did he agree? No NOS."

"What's the point of racing if the stakes are low?" Derek raised his voice, so everyone would hear.

More classmates gathered around the cars. They all quieted down with excitement shining in their eyes. Derek puffed up his chest when he noticed he had an audience. He smirked at me as his gaze swept over the sea of faces again.

I did the same. When I met a pair of familiar blue eyes in the crowd, my cock jerked. Aurora was here. Her presence sent a jolt of raw energy through me. If I had doubts about this race before, they were gone now.

"Anyone can drive a car," Derek continued, and I had to peel my gaze away from Aurora. "The NOS boost is what makes it interesting. Can you handle your car or not, Alfera?"

Fuck, he was right.

NOS—Nitrous Oxide System—was used to enhance the performance of our already jacked-up cars. The nitrous had two main functions. One, to cool off the fuel and air mix to create a more violent explosion in the combustion chamber. And two, it fooled the car computer into adding more fuel to the chamber. Fuel plus nitrous meant an extreme increase in performance.

The NOS qualified us as performance racers. It was also the reason street racing was illegal—fast cars, cheap booze, and cocky drivers made for a lethal combination.

"Fine, you're on. Where's your pink slip?"

"I got it right here." Donata stepped forward with a sheet of paper in her hand and a stack of cash in the other.

When I turned to Massimo, he shrugged. "I had to cancel Monday's race. I gotta get paid."

"I'm in too." I turned to Donata. "Put me down for five thousand."

"You got it." She smiled sweetly as she tapped on her phone.

"I win." I glared at Derek. "You stop spewing lies about my team, and I get your car."

"You're on, Alfera. I win, maybe you'll find the balls to talk to your dad. I'm also keeping your ride."

The hate in his eyes made me wonder if maybe this was about something other than football.

Hell if I cared.

He couldn't go on disrespecting Dad. The old man was a lot of things, but he was still our king.

"Get in your cars." Massimo strode to the finish line spray-painted on the asphalt.

The intersection was quiet with rundown buildings on either side of the street. We were somewhere in Harlem, far away from Fifth Avenue, but not exactly out of Dad's dominion. I hopped inside my racer and fired up the laptop hooked to the system. Adrenaline surged through me as I double-checked every gage. I pumped up the volume and let the music inundate my nerves until I felt cool and ready.

"Just remember, eyes on the road, light feet, firm grip." Santino leaned into the car window. His gaze darted between the different gauges. "You've got this."

"Thanks, man."

My attention shifted over to Massimo, while he paced the starting line with his phone glued to his ear. To my right, Derek sat in his racer, a decent souped-up Honda. He glared at me as if he knew something I didn't. I knew better than to fall for it. Between losing the championship because he choked, and then spewing lies about Dad, he'd already proven he was all talk. In the next beat, Massimo stopped between the cars with a big grin on his face.

"It's time. Gentlemen. Get set. Ready." He paused for effect, egging the crowd on.

"Go."

I dropped to second gear and slowly let out the clutch. The startup could make or break a race. From there on, it was smooth sailing as I eased the car through the gears. At the top of the odometer, I tapped on the computer to make sure I was still in the green. A quarter a mile wasn't a big distance, but the NOS boost didn't last long.

This race was all about pride. I wanted Derek and everyone else to know that I was the better driver—and the better football player. Images of Aurora waiting for me at the finish line rolled through my head. What a beautiful trophy she'd make.

The tires gripped the road and made me in full control. This was the part I liked best. A deathly machine going one hundred and sixty miles an hour with me at the wheel, in charge of where it went and how it got there.

The idea that I could control chaos was addicting. I craved it. And now, here it was. The engine roared with a loud zoom as I dropped to the next gear. To my left, Derek inched into my line of sight. The smug smile on his face had set-in permanently, it seemed.

"Enjoy it, fucker." I tapped on the screen and let it rip. The dark night turned green in my rearview mirror. "Here comes the drag."

The car propelled forward, sinking my body into the seat. I inhaled and held my breath a couple of seconds before letting it out. The lurch in my stomach made me grip the steering wheel tighter. My whole body felt tightly wound, like a rubber band stretched to its limits.

When the finish line came into view, Derek's car was no longer on my side. The adrenaline kicked in. My heart thumped so hard, everything else slowed down as the wheels careened past the red paint on the asphalt. The car fishtailed to the left, but I didn't fight it. I simply let the car roll and slow down at its own pace.

I'd won.

And now Derek could go fuck himself—and his lies.

The low rumble of the engines fell around me. We both sat in our cars facing each other for several minutes while the crowd made their way to us. He nodded once, just before we got surrounded by cars. Well, mostly me. Derek had lost the race. So they'd lost interest in him.

"Nicely done, brother." Massimo opened the car door and dragged me out to pull me into a hug.

I quickly scanned the faces for Aurora, but it was hard to make anything out with so many people shoving their way toward me.

In the next breath, police sirens blared in the distance and hell broke loose. But Massimo had an exit plan. By the time the cop car's psychedelic lights flashed on the abandoned buildings and the street, the throng had dispersed.

"Get in the car." Massimo shoved me into the driver's seat and hopped over the hood. "Drive."

I waited another second until people had cleared the way and then floored it. "Motherfucker called the cops."

"You know, for someone who loses to you often, he should be used to it by now." Massimo gripped the driver's seat headrest. "Turn here. There's a garage up ahead. They're expecting us."

Sure enough. When I made the turn, I spotted a rundown

mechanic shop with its doors wide open. I slid inside and followed the guy's instructions. As soon as I killed the engine and climbed out, he and his buddy came in with a tarp and covered the car.

"Thanks, man." Massimo gave him a stack of money then shook his hand. "I'll be back tomorrow."

"You got it." The guy in the greasy pants shut off the lights and hit the button to close the rolling door.

I ran for it and ducked to clear the steel coming at me. "What now? Train?"

"Yep." Massimo gestured toward the sidewalk.

Now that the commotion had died down and my heart wasn't pumping a hundred and sixty beats a minute, Harlem seemed eerily quiet. I stuffed my hands in the pockets of my jeans and picked up the pace. The last time I raced and won, I had two cheerleaders waiting for me at the finish line. They both helped me celebrate my victory that night.

For no reason at all, Aurora's angel face flashed in my mind's eye.

Fucking Derek. The sore loser had to call the police and ruin my fun.

When we reached the end of the block, a cop car flashed its lights twice. No sirens blaring, but he was here for us.

I spun around to run the other way, but another car pulled up just in time.

"Fuck. Do we run for it?" Massimo asked under his breath.

"What's the point? Their guns are still holstered. They know who we are."

Both policemen sauntered toward us, as if we had planned to meet in a deserted street in Harlem exactly at this time.

"What's this about?" I asked when they were within earshot.

The officer flashed his flashlight in my face and then Massimo's. He relaxed his stance and spoke into his shoulder. "I got them, sir."

I met Massimo's gaze. If the cop wasn't in a hurry to take us in for illegal street racing, it could only mean one thing. He was on Dad's payroll.

That was really, really bad news.

I hit Massimo's arm with the back of my hand. When he looked at me, I raised both eyebrows and pursed my lips. "Run."

Did I Hurt You?

Enzo

He didn't run.

By now, I was sure Dad knew about the race, and that the cops had to get involved. Dad wasn't worried about the authorities. He cared more about aesthetics, and the fact that his son got caught. Whatever Dad was planning for me, I had to make sure Massimo wasn't part of it. This wasn't his fight, or his idea.

"I said go," I mouthed, keeping my gaze on the cops, who had now trudged back to their cars and were deep in conversation with each other, as if they couldn't agree on what to do next.

"I'm not leaving without you." Massimo crossed his arms over his chest. "We can take those fuckers."

"We're not taking them on." I put emphasis on the *not*. "They're government officials. We can't touch them. Even you and I are not above that rule."

"What now?"

We could not come home in a cop car.

Even if Mom didn't live there anymore, she was still in contact with people from our building. Mostly because it was the only way she could keep tabs on us. The Upper East Side wives were more than willing to oblige. If Mom found out, Dad would blow a fucking gasket. Containing the situation was all we could do at this point.

First, we needed to shake the police. And then, Massimo had to go stay with Mom, far away from Dad.

"We run."

I waited for the span of three breaths. When one cop shoved the other, still arguing about who knew what, I fisted my brother's sleeve and pulled him toward me. "Now."

We both bolted toward the dark alley.

"Motherfucker," one of the cops blustered out. "What the fuck are you standing around for? Go grab them."

I didn't exactly have a getaway plan. But I figured if I kept running, I'd eventually stumble into a way out. Several options flitted through my mind. The train station was several blocks away. Hiding in a dumpster or on a rooftop felt like a cowardly thing to do. Plus, I wasn't the type to sit around and wait for shit to happen.

At the end of the street, I hung a right. And fuck my luck, if this part of Harlem wasn't extremely well lit. Going back the way we came wasn't an option. The guy chasing us was slow, but he wasn't far behind us.

I headed toward the next building. As much as I hated the idea, hiding was now the official plan. But before we reached the back entrance, an SUV came to a screeching halt next to us. The tinted window on the passenger side slid down, and Rex's friendly face appeared.

"Get in," he called out.

Massimo didn't miss a step as he quickly jumped off the curb and climbed in the back seat. I followed close behind him. Before I even had a chance to close the door, Rex careened out of there.

I melted into the seat and let the pent-up adrenaline rush through me in unrelenting waves. "Derek will answer for this."

"He got picked up." Rex leaned on the steering wheel and shot me a glance over his shoulder, smiling.

"How? He had already left when the cops showed up."

"I picked it up on the scanner. The asshole was trying to flee in a race car. He didn't think to drop it off." He chuckled.

"Well, fuck." Massimo threw his hands up in the air. "That was our car."

"Who cares?"

"I do." Massimo slammed his fist on the door in frustration.

To him, this was business. I was an asshole for getting him involved in my vendetta against Derek. "I'll get you your car back. But now, you gotta lay low in Brooklyn."

"What the hell are you talking about? I'm not going to Mom's."

"Dad's going to be pissed about this. I don't want you there for that." I exchanged a meaningful glance with Rex. He knew how bad things were with Dad. And how much worse they could get. Up until now, Massimo had been spared. But something like this, I had no doubt Dad would take it out on Massimo too. "Let me handle it."

"I'm not leaving you alone." He glared at me. "You think I don't know? We all know."

"How about you come crash at my place?" Rex met Massimo's gaze in the rearview mirror.

"No. I knew what I was getting into. I'm not leaving my brother alone with Dad."

Rex pursed his lips and nodded in my direction. As if saying, *he's right*.

"Fine. But you stay in your room. No matter what you hear. You stay away." I gripped his shoulder, cocking my head to look him in the eye.

He nodded, but I knew he had no intention to hide like a coward.

"I'll be out here too."

"Nah, go home." I checked the clock on the dashboard. "It's almost four in the morning."

"I'll wait."

For the next half hour, we rode in silence. Normally, I'd have a plan to handle the situation. But when it came to Dad, there wasn't much I could do. So I sat in the back of Rex's SUV and didn't think at all.

After a few minutes, I let images of Aurora biting her lower lip linger in my mind. I thought of her and her blue eyes as she recounted what she had seen in the Hamptons when she spied on Santino. That put a smile on my face, and the pressure in my chest lifted.

Had she made it home? I realized I had no way to check up on her. And also no reason to. She was the new girl. No one of consequence as far as I was concerned.

I glanced out the window, just as Rex turned onto Fifth Avenue. In no time at all, he pulled up in front of my building. I slapped his shoulder as a thank you for picking us up and climbed out of the car.

When we reached the penthouse, the place was empty and completely silent. Maybe Mom had been with Dad when he got the news about the race. Maybe she got him to calm down and let us be until tomorrow. Or maybe he understood that I couldn't let Derek continue to bad mouth our family.

I released a breath and turned to face Massimo. "I guess we didn't need to worry."

"Guess not." He shrugged and headed upstairs, taking two steps at a time.

I made my way to the kitchen and filled a glass with water. I sipped from it. Between the racing and running from the cops, I hadn't realized I was a little hungover from all the drinks I had at the Crucible. Jeez, that part of the night seemed like it happened months ago instead of just a few hours.

The hairs on the nape of my neck stood on end. In the next breath, the elevator door dinged as it slid open and then closed. I stood frozen, facing the sink and listened for Dad's light steps on the marble floors. He stopped right behind me on the other side of the counter in the middle of the kitchen.

His suit jacket made a shuffling sound as he removed it and placed it over the counter stool. "When are you going to get it through your head? You're the future king of the Society. That Irish boy? He's beneath you."

"He's been telling lies about you. It was time somebody shut him up."

"The doorman has a dog. The little bitch doesn't like me. Do you think I give a shit?" He ambled around the counter. The next sound was all too familiar. He undid his buckle and pulled his leather belt through the loops of his pants. "You elevated that boy tonight. Made it look like his words meant something to you. To me. Now people will wonder if what he was blabbering about was true all along."

I shifted my weight slightly toward him, ready to ask if it

was true. If he had really paid off the officials to throw the game in our favor. My team and I won fair and square. We busted our asses to make it happen. We didn't need to cheat.

Dad struck without preamble, and I didn't get to say any of it. His belt cut the side of my cheek and my shoulder. I winced and gripped the lip of the sink as he delivered another blow. And another, and another.

He never appeared to be out of control. His rage was methodical. He knew what it did for him. He knew how to use it to his advantage. I had no doubt he believed he was teaching me an important lesson. But I had also seen enough of this to know that inflicting this kind of pain, on me in particular, brought him pleasure.

Mom had rejected his mafia world. I had seen how that pissed him off. He hated that she wasn't here, same as us. But he couldn't strike Mom. Good for him. So that left me. He got his first taste my freshman year in high school, the night Mom left for good. He beat me with his belt until my back was soaked in blood and his fury had been appeased.

Now every time he needed an outlet, he'd come looking for me. Better me than Mom, my little sister Caterina, or Massimo, I supposed.

His belt licked my back again. The sharp crack pared the existing scabs off my back. The wet on my T-shirt was his cue. He puffed out a breath as he stepped away from me and raked a hand through his disheveled hair.

A hot drop of blood trickled down my spine. Normally, it would take longer to bleed, but the wounds from our last encounter hadn't healed all the way yet.

"Are you done?" I faced him.

His chest rose and fell with every breath as he glared at his hands and then at me. He wanted to keep going. I could tell by the way his shoulders trembled. First blood was where he drew the line.

After a dozen heartbeats, his features relaxed, and he met my gaze. The regret I found in his green eyes made my stomach churn with anger. Now he would play the loving father and try to pretend that his insane outburst didn't happen. Or worse, that he did it all for me, and our family.

"I won't tell your mother about your run-in with the police. It would kill her if she found out you're going around acting like a thug." He tossed his belt on the counter, then wiped his mouth with the back of his hand.

A thug? If I weren't in so much pain, I'd chuckle at that.

We were mobsters because of him. We lived in a world of beasts, and he was the king of it all. Dad was the ruthless monster everyone feared. But he pretended to be a good man, a good father, a good husband because of Mom. Because in spite of all the terrible things he was, he actually cared what she thought of him. It was why he made us lie to her—why we had to hide the fact that Dad was mafia. That he never quit being a mobster like he told her he would.

It'd been years. At first, I couldn't believe Mom would be naive enough to think that Dad could leave the Society, his mafia family. But it didn't take long to realize that Mom wanted to believe Dad's lies. They both wanted to live in this pretend world where he was a regular guy—a family man—and she was a doting wife.

"Did I hurt you?" He cocked his head.

"I'm going upstairs."

"One day you will be king." He stepped toward me. When

I shuffled back, he stopped. "One day you'll understand this is all for you."

Fuck off, I wanted to say. But no one told the great Michael Alfera to go to hell. That he was demented. And wrong. More than once, Rex had offered to tell his dad. Don Valentino was Dad's friend. Dad listened to him. But that didn't mean Dad would appreciate me airing our dirty laundry. I had one more year of school. And then I'd be out of here and away from Dad. For a little while, anyway.

I fisted my hands and turned my back on him. A risky move, given that his belt was still within reach. But with a bit of luck, he'd let me walk away from him tonight. He seemed tired and content with the punishment he'd already imparted.

My back tingled with anticipation. I kept waiting to feel another blow on my skin, but it never came. I made it all the way to the top of the stairs before I found the courage to look back. The elevator door chimed again. Dad was gone.

On my way to my bedroom, I stopped in front of Massimo's door. I pushed it open and found him at his computer with his headphones on. He'd come home to finish his game. I didn't blame him. As tired as I was, I didn't think I could go to sleep either.

I strode straight to my en-suite bathroom and peeled off my T-shirt. I was on automatic now—grabbing the first-aid kit from under the sink, a towel to protect the floors, and a handheld mirror to inspect the damage. I stood in front of the vanity and twisted my torso to take a good look.

"Fuck."

The skin looked mangled and bloody. Sitting on the edge of the claw-foot bathtub, I thought about what I had to do next. This part would hurt more than the actual licks of my father's belt, but I couldn't risk an infection that could possibly land me in the hospital. They would call Mom for sure. And I couldn't let that happen.

"Fuck it."

Starting at my shoulders, I squirted my back with hydrogen peroxide. The liquid scurried down with a quiet sizzle that burned everything it touched. I kept at it until I was sure it was all clean. There really wasn't much else I could do. The strikes drew blood, but I wouldn't need stitches. Dad knew what he was doing. Except for the one time when he went too far, he always made sure I didn't need a doctor.

I wrapped a bandage around my midsection, then hooked it over one shoulder then the other, making sure it was on tight. The pressure felt good and eased some of the pain. It also helped to stop the bleeding.

I popped three Advil in my mouth then drank water from the faucet. Suddenly, all I wanted to do was sleep. On my way to the bed, I removed my shoes, socks, and jeans. I fished my phone from the back pocket and tossed it on the bed. When I finally lay down on my stomach and closed my eyes, the screen lit up with a new message.

Mom: Good morning. I'm on my way to the city. Did your father tell you about the charity brunch tomorrow?

Mom: I feel like I haven't seen you in forever. I miss you. See you in a few hours.

Now I had to spend the day with Mom and Dad and pretend our lives were peachy. My thumbs hovered over the screen. What could I say to her to make her see who Dad really was? What could she possibly do?

Fuck my life.

You Kiss by the Book

Aurora

"Sit up straight, Rory," Mom whispered under her breath as she dabbed her lips with a napkin, quickly scanning the many round tables around the ballroom.

The place was beautifully decorated with white linens, oversized floral arrangements, and even an ice sculpture. As with everything related to our newly-acquired mobster life, the charity brunch hosted by the Alfera family was over the top: the food, a work of art, with booze everywhere.

"And smile. You look like you're at a funeral."

"It's pretty depressing, Mom." I inched up in my seat and did my best to square my shoulders to satisfy her.

For the past hour, though it might as well have been all morning, I had been listening to the charity chairperson drone on and on about her cause. She assured us our hefty donations would save lives. It wasn't that I didn't care to help. But she could've delivered her message in ten minutes without all the sad pictures. My parents had already given a sizable amount, on top of the ten grand to reserve the table. Not that Dad cared about the children. Philanthropy made him look good and important. I knew this because he said so twice on the way here.

The chairperson called another family to the stage. On the floor, most people had already scattered to help themselves to more crepes and mimosas. To my left, the line to the dessert table had dwindled down, and the pastry chef was setting out more tartelettes. I made to get up when Dad came up behind me and pressed his hand to my shoulder. I gave in under the weight and sat.

"Aurora, let me introduce you to my good friend, Angelo." Dad gestured to the guy sitting next to me.

I hadn't even noticed him come in. "Nice to meet you." I dipped my head.

I didn't bother with a smile. Dad had been parading me around to several of his newfound friends for the last month. He was dead serious when he'd said he wanted me to marry sooner rather than later. It seemed he was letting me choose. Though his pool of candidates was not what I wanted at all.

"Angelo Soprano." He took my hand in his as his hungry gaze swept up and down my body.

The guy had to be in his thirties. Maybe a little younger than Dad, but definitely closer to my parents' age than mine. More than a love match, Dad wanted an alliance for himself. At this point, playing along was easier, though I had no intention of marrying any time soon. I wanted to go to college. I wanted Columbia, not this creep. Yeah, creep was the word for him. He had to know I was underage. Yet he looked at me like I was one of those lemon tarts from the dessert table.

"Your father has told me a lot about you." He sat back and unbuttoned his suit jacket.

With those deep blue eyes and set jaw, I'd bet women his age found him attractive. What did he get out of this arrangement with Dad? Surely, he didn't have a problem getting women. So why me? It wasn't like my family had any pull with the Alferas.

"Your father tells me you have a good head on your shoulders. I like that in a woman." He smiled, cocking his head to catch my eyes.

Was that supposed to be a compliment? I glanced down at my hands and rolled my eyes. The chair scraped quietly in my direction, and suddenly, his cologne was all I could smell. I glanced over my shoulder, looking for my parents, but they were gone.

Just freaking great.

He exhaled. Before I realized what he meant to do, the back of his fingers brushed my bare thigh. The gesture shocked me out of my chair.

"I need to pee. I'll be right back." I spun around and headed toward the ballroom exit.

The fancy hotel in Midtown wasn't any bigger than the casinos in Las Vegas. Though this place looked more expensive and refined. I made a right when I reached the grand staircase in the main lobby, then followed the signs to the restrooms. Several times I looked back to make sure Angelo wasn't behind me.

Of course, he wasn't. He didn't need to chase me. Dad had already served me up on a silver platter.

I picked up the pace, walking mostly off my tippy toes, so I wouldn't make a big clanking noise on the shiny floors. When I turned the corner, I spotted Enzo talking to an older woman. He had his usual broody stare, but he seemed engaged in the conversation.

The restrooms were a few steps away, just past the thick column that ran from the first floor up to the third floor above us. When I tiptoed toward the door, Enzo glanced my way. No idea why I decided to hide behind the marble structure rather than continue on my way. His intense gaze always made me jumpy like that.

This morning when we drove in, I was nervous to see him outside of school. His family was hosting the event, so I'd assumed he'd make an appearance. But when the other royals showed up and the presentation started, I realized he had decided to skip the event.

"I'm just saying, it wouldn't kill you to come see me in Brooklyn." The woman spoke again.

"I have school, Mom."

Mom? Now I was really intrigued. I poked my head around to get a better look. Enzo's mom was beautiful with dark hair, smooth skin, and bright brown eyes. She looked elegant, but not overly done in designer clothes and big diamonds. She seemed down to earth.

"So, would you stay the weekend? You haven't been to the penthouse in months." He stuffed his hands in the pockets of his trousers.

Dressed in a tailored suit and donning a sad smile on his handsome face, he looked tragically beautiful—like a character in some Shakespearean play. I peeled my gaze away from him and rushed to the bathroom. With a little luck, he wouldn't see me. What was wrong with me? Enzo was cruel. He liked torturing me just for the fun of it. A light current of adrenaline rushed through me when I thought of all the things he made me say the first day of school. He'd done it to humiliate me, to punish me for barging in on him while he was using the urinal.

Every time I thought of that moment, shame washed over me. Not because of what he did to me, but because of how I felt when he did it. He turned me on. He made me want to touch him and kiss him.

I stomped to the sink and washed my hands. I considered splashing my face with water, but Mom would have a heart attack if I returned with my mascara running and my makeup smeared. The door squeaked open, then shut with a light thud. When I glanced up, I met Enzo's green gaze. And of course, he seemed angry at me. What did I do this time? I checked quickly for urinals, making sure he was the one barging in on me, not the other way around.

Wait. Did he know I had been eavesdropping on the conversation with his mom? Crap. I spun around to face him. "I didn't hear anything."

He smirked. "I didn't hear anything, she says." He prowled toward me. "Why is it that every time I turn around, there you are, spying on me."

"I wasn't."

He raised both eyebrows, and I forgot my words.

Okay, sure, technically speaking, I was spying on him right outside the bathroom. But it wasn't like I was stalking him. He just happened to be here when I showed up. And the car race didn't count. Everyone from school was there. Penny got me out of bed because she didn't want to go alone. Apparently, Donata herself texted Penny to invite her. She couldn't skip it.

"I wasn't," I repeated. Jeez, I couldn't even string a sentence together. "I'm going."

I pushed past him and headed for the door. When I pulled the handle, nothing happened.

"What?" I glared at his hand next to my head. When I turned around, his body heat engulfed me, and I melted against the wall.

His nose brushed mine, and for a heartbeat, I thought he was going to kiss me. This wasn't the first time he'd leaned in close like that. I puffed out a breath. He inhaled deeply, ducking his head. We stood like this for a whole minute—his hand on the side of my face while an invisible force kept me glued to the wall.

"Enzo." I reached under his lifted arm and touched my fingers to his shoulder blade.

He winced in pain, or maybe it was disgust. In the next breath, he gripped both my wrists and pinned them over my head. Okay, so touching the royals was not allowed. My breath became erratic, matching the thumping in my chest. Was he mad at me now?

He scowled at me with so much intensity in his eyes, I stopped breathing all together. Then, he took a half step, pressed his body to mine, and kissed my mouth—hard. So hard, I didn't know how to keep up or what to do with what he was offering. My eyes fluttered as I stared at the blur that were his features.

An exhale-like groan escaped his lips. He pulled away but didn't release my hands. The staring was unnerving. It was as if he could see into my soul. When he spoke again, he loosened his hold, just enough for me to remember to fill my lungs with air again.

"You've never been kissed before, have you?"

Technically, I'd never been touched before. I'd never had anyone look at me like this before, let alone kiss me.

"What's it to you?"

He furrowed his brows and dropped his hands to his sides. He watched me with curiosity as I brought my arms around my belly. Tears stung my eyes because I knew he'd say something cruel again. I knew I was going to have to deal with the fallout come Monday morning. I made to leave, but he blocked me, caging me in again.

"Let me show you how."

What? As in, teach me? "Why?"

"Because I want to."

He wanted to kiss me? Or teach me? "Why?"

"Tell me to go to hell." He unraveled my arms from around my body and brought my palm to his face. "Say the words. *Enzo. Go. To. Hell.*" He enunciated every word.

The raspy quality of his voice was so sexy and hypnotizing; I wasn't going anywhere.

"What happens if I do?" I moved my fingers ever so slightly. I was afraid if I did more, he'd shut me out again like before.

"Then you're free to go."

I shook my head as my mouth fell slack. His face was warm and smooth. When I didn't speak, he held my lower lip between his index finger and thumb. The dour look in his eyes that I had come to associate with Enzo vanished and was replaced by curiosity.

"Give me your tongue."

"What?"

He flashed me a smile that effectively turned my legs to

Jell-O. He clicked his teeth. "Do it now. Or say the magic words."

I had a choice—stay in a public bathroom, pinned to the wall by one of the royals, and learn how to kiss, or leave to go sit at a table with some old guy.

Where my brain refused to let me use my words, it was totally fine letting me move closer to him. I felt ridiculous as I slid my hand from his cheek down to his neck and touched the tip of my tongue to his lips. I waited for him to say something mean, to laugh and leave me hanging. But instead, he captured my mouth again. Slower this time, as if breaking down the kiss for me. His tongue swirled around mine as he deepened the connection, retreating ever so slightly. I copied his movements, pulling away when he did, coming in closer when he resumed the kiss.

I sucked on his bottom lip. Then I let my tongue mimic the same dance as his—exactly as he had shown me. I found myself wanting to be a good student. He smiled, and that gave me a surge of confidence. I stood on my tiptoes and sunk deeper into him. He tasted like a crisp autumn night, one of hopes and dreams, and all the things I could never have or be.

Yeah, Enzo and I lived in the same mafia world. But we were far from being equals.

He was a royal.

And I was the new girl. Nothing. No one.

Hell if I cared, though. Right now, all I cared about was how soft his full lips felt, and how good he was at teaching me what to do. In this moment, we were the same. He wasn't some tragic character trapped in a book. And I wasn't a nobody.

He applied more pressure, fusing our mouths together.

Every time he switched gears like that, the spot between my legs quivered with anticipation.

"You kiss by the book," I mumbled and sighed. Why did my brain decide to speak now? "I'm sorry. I mean."

"Don't be." He chuckled. "I get it. Shakespeare, right?"

"I was reading it for class. I don't know. It stuck with me." I wanted to keep kissing him.

In this moment, he wasn't the untouchable mobster, the unattainable royal, or the mean bully. He was just Enzo. The first boy to ever kiss me. And, wow, it was everything I had thought it would be. Not that I sat at home thinking of kissing him. I never dared make it that far. But I had imagined myself kissing someone one day. Never in a million years would I have guessed that *someone* would be Enzo Alfera.

"I like kissing you." He cupped my face. "Give me my sin again."

He stole Romeo's line.

And omigod, when he pressed his lips to mine a second time, he started doing the twirly thing again. This time, his efforts were more urgent. I got the sense we had skipped a bunch of steps in the middle. He pushed his hips to mine. He was hard. Like, his actual cock was hard. Through his pants and my dress, that small pressure brought me a bit of relief, but also made me want more.

The avalanche of emotions that was his kiss, the adrenaline rushing through me, and this thing building at my core was too much—it was sensory overload. I pushed him away because I didn't know what else to do.

He glared at me in confusion. As if I had done some big kissing faux pas. "What's wrong?" He reached for me again.

"Enzo, go to hell," I blurted out.

He froze and pursed his lips.

I glanced around me to collect my things. Then I realized we weren't in school. I hadn't brought anything with me. With my heart thrashing in my ears, I spun around and swung the door open. A gush of cold air hit me square in the face and sobered me up.

Penny had warned me to stay away from Enzo. I ignored her warning and now here I was—running away from him in a fancy hotel, running as if my life depended on it, running as if he were the devil himself.

I kissed Enzo Alfera.

What had I done?

Winner Takes All

ENZO

The door closed, and I pressed my forehead to it. What the hell just happened? I came into the bathroom to mess with Aurora. And, once again, she unknowingly turned the tables on me.

She'd never been kissed? How was that possible?

That small fact awoke an untamed instinct in me. I'd never been the possessive type. Hell, Rex, Santino, and I had no problem sharing women. But showing Aurora how to kiss unleashed something feral in my chest. And now I had no idea how to reel it back in.

I raked a hand through my hair, glaring at the door. I wanted to kiss her again. I wanted to do way more than just kiss. Why had she run off? She'd been into it.

My eyebrows shot up in surprise as the realization washed over me. Fuck me. Aurora was a virgin. At my school, most everyone turned in their V-card freshman year. The thing about virgins was that things got complicated fast with them, which was why I avoided them one hundred percent of the time.

Shit. Now what?

I couldn't stop thinking about how much I wanted to do that again.

Goddammit, the best thing to do would be to let her be. I had way too much shit going on at home to get involved with someone like her. Images of Aurora's pink cheeks on my pillow flitted through my head, but I pushed them away.

Aurora Vitali was no one of consequence. And I had no interest in a bad lay.

With a loud exhale, I swung the door open. Mom and Dad wanted me at the stupid brunch until at least two in the afternoon, playing the gracious host. Showing up late bought me some time, but I still had another two hours before the whole thing was over.

I strode down the hallway, making my way to the ballroom where the presentation was still in progress. The cause Mom had chosen to sponsor was near and dear to her heart. She had a friend who'd lost a child to leukemia a few years ago.

For weeks, she went on and on about how dreadful it would be to lose a child. The irony was that later that year, she moved to Brooklyn and more or less lost Massimo and me. These days we only saw her for charity events, or whenever I got my head out of my ass and went to visit her. Admittedly, that was a rare occurrence. I could be as stubborn as she was.

As soon as I turned the corner, Aurora came into my line of sight. She sat at one of the front row tables with her parents and one of Dad's new crew bosses, Angelo. He was an up and comer, someone Dad had recently invited to his inner circle. I personally didn't think he was that clever or that good. But Dad couldn't care less about my opinion.

I let my gaze settle on her face. She squirmed in her seat, and her cheeks turned a pretty pink again. And that right there got me going once more. I craved seeing her like that—all nervous and fragile. I kept my gaze on her until she found the courage to turn in my direction. When she did, I shifted my attention to the other guests.

On the other side of the ballroom, near the bar, I found my friends. I sauntered toward them and sat next to Rex.

"You look like that cat that drank the milk." Donata sprung from her chair and came to sit beside me.

I chuckled. "What does that mean?"

"It means you did something." She cocked her head and exchanged a knowing look with Rex. "Something bad. Come on. Spill."

"There's nothing to spill. Milk or otherwise." I shrugged.

Rex put his index finger on my shoulder and pushed on it. I jerked out of his reach. My heart raced at the sudden assault. He hadn't hurt me, but I didn't need anyone touching my back today. And I certainly didn't need or want Santino and Donata to know what'd happened. Seeing pity in Donata's eyes always made my stomach lurch. I glared at Rex and mouthed, "What the fuck?"

"For a minute there, I thought maybe Don Alfera had let you off the hook."

"Not a chance, man."

"Then Donata is right. A shitty night like last night should not have put that big of a smile on your face." He scanned the room, furrowing his brows. "What did you do? Or who?"

"I see it too." Santino leaned on the table and slid a glass of champagne my way. "It was a quickie in the bathroom, wasn't it? Nice." He dipped his head in my direction.

"Fuck off." I drank from the glass he'd offered and downed most of it in one gulp. I needed to wipe Aurora's kiss off my lips. Being close to her was messing with my head. I couldn't have that. "Can't I have one good day?"

"We're stuck here for at least another hour. Give us something to do?" Donata put her hands together to form a steeple.

I shook my head. Before I could stop it, reels of my seven minutes in heaven with Aurora swam in my head, in and out of focus—her tongue as it searched mine so tentatively, her warm hands on my cheek, and the little moans that escaped her every time she came up for air. To those details, my mind added a few improvements—like Aurora naked in my bed.

No, fuck. What was I thinking? Just no. I couldn't be her first. As delicious as her first kiss had been. Sex with a virgin, with Aurora, would be a complication of epic proportions. I had to stick to my plan and let her be. My gaze flitted toward her table.

Was that Angelo guy still there? And by himself? What could they possibly be talking about? He scooted his chair closer to her, and a lump churned in the pit of my stomach. He was too old for her. And all wrong.

Now that I thought about it, I hadn't welcomed him to the brunch. What if I went over there and...

"Don't think I'm letting it go. We will talk about this later." Donata pointed her index finger at me and beamed. "We were waiting for you, so we could discuss our annual bet. This is our senior year. It has to be epic. And it has to last more than a week. So I came up with a few new rules to make it more interesting." She fished her phone out of her clutch.

I squinted at her. "What are you talking about?"

"What am...?" She stopped scrolling on her phone to glare at me. "You guys catch him up."

Santino ambled to the bar, got four flutes, and set them on the table. "Welcome to this year's pop a cherry contest." He raised a glass to me. "I came up with the name."

"Yeah, very original." Donata sipped from her glass. "We need rules."

"They're upping the stakes this year." Rex braced an elbow on the table, pointing at Santino and Donata, who were always the ones most involved in the game. "We all go for the same girl, instead of just earning points."

I chuckled, crossing my arms over my chest. "That game has lost its luster, really."

The royal's bet started our freshman year. It was mostly a bet to see who would lose their virginity first. We were the fucking royals. The game ended in a tie that same weekend. Since then, we'd been trying to up the ante. But it never worked. Donata had that whole demi-goddess look going for her. No guy or girl ever said no to her. Santino had a way with words. And everyone loved Rex's broody stare.

"You say that because you lost last year." Santino cocked his brow.

"I got tired of getting head and getting laid." I ran both hands through my hair and laughed. "For a seventeen-year-old to say that, that should tell you something."

"I didn't get tired." He shrugged. "Which is why I won. Some of those participants got really good at giving head. Honestly, the time I spent mentoring those young women should've counted toward my community service hours."

"Yeah, you're quite the inspiration, Santi." I shook my head at him.

"I'm with Enzo on this one." Rex let out a breath. "It's hardly a bet."

"Exactly." I gestured toward Rex.

Santino opened his mouth to retaliate, but Donata beat him to it.

"That is why I'm revising the rules this year." Donata put both her arms up to get us to quit our bickering. "This year, you have to sleep with a virgin. Winner takes all."

"Oh, come on." Rex rolled his eyes. "So the new rule is let's see who gets the worst lay?"

"Would you let me finish?" She pressed a hand to her chest. "I will pick the girl. Someone I have confirmed is a virgin."

"How exactly does one do that?" Santino asked. "I mean without actually...you know."

"Trust me. She's a virgin. I've done my homework. Once you agree, I will give you all the deets on her. Guys, trust me. I found us the perfect girl."

"This is gonna be fun. I can tell." Santino beamed at her. "So how do we earn points this time?"

Last year, we had a very elaborate point system. Basic services like blow jobs, fingering, anal play, vibrators, etc., were fifty points. We had the opportunity to earn extra points for the completion of a task if a kink was involved—a blow job in public was a whopping one hundred points, a blow job while someone else watched, one hundred and fifty points.

A blow job while the boyfriend watched, that was five hundred points. Permanent marks of any kind added another hundred points. Sex was five hundred points, and it went on from there—multiple partners at the same time, number of times in a single night, location. Exotic locations like the girl's house or school earned the most points.

But that wasn't how Santino took the cake last year. I was way ahead of him, until he banged a St. Francis teacher in her classroom with her boyfriend watching. The woman even let him carve the letter S on her wrist. Donata awarded House Buratti a thousand points for that one. He got bonus points for dedication and commitment to the game, as she put it. All the people, staff and students, at St. Francis Prep School were complete assholes. I didn't know how Santino managed a whole night in their company.

The list Donata and Santino came up with last year was twenty pages long and had very specific tasks that needed to be completed to earn points. Some activities were borderline ridiculous, while others were kind of kinky and fun. I glanced over at Aurora, who was still entertaining that asshole. Would she be game for any of it? No, not Angel Face. Aurora was a good girl.

If my life wasn't on this side of fucked-up, I wouldn't mind spending the semester corrupting her—a blow job at her parents' house would earn House Alfera two hundred points.

"You don't." Donata shoved my shoulder to get my attention.

"What?"

"New rules. No point system this year." She sat up straighter in her chair, looking like the cat that drank the milk. "Winner takes all. Whoever pops her cherry wins the whole thing."

"That's too easy."

"Full consent. She has to beg you for it." She glanced down at her hands and smiled. "She has to fall in love with one of you."

We all chuckled in unison.

I'd never been in love in my life, and I liked it that way. My future, my entire life, belonged to the Society. I had a duty to uphold. One day I would have to marry to ensure I had a successor. That piece was required. After seeing Dad and Mom lie to each other on a daily basis just to keep what they have, I'd come to the conclusion that love wasn't for me—that falling in love would be the dumbest thing I could do.

Who in his right mind would want to make a woman fall in love with him anyway? That shit was for fools. I'd seen enough of that at home. I'd seen Dad become the worst version of himself for love. Love conquered all. True. But I'd seen the devastation it left in its wake. I had zero interest in it.

"Sounds like a lot of work. Now that I think about it, it was more fun when I was getting laid every day last year and racking up points." I sat back in my chair.

"What part of epic did you not understand?" The V between her eyebrows deepened. "This will be fun too."

"Well, half the girls in school are already in love with the dark prince." Rex pointed in my direction. "That's not that big of a challenge."

"Oh, sure. Who doesn't love Enzo?" Donata pinched my cheek until I slapped her hand away. "Everyone loves his handsome face and the fact that one day he'll be king. But I'm talking about the real thing. The kind of love that would make a real good girl turn in her V-card."

The lines around her mouth hardened as if the idea of sex

for love reminded her of someone. I bet she was thinking of our revered English teacher. If he was an ounce of the man she thought him to be, he wouldn't be sleeping with minors. When would she understand that Luca Gallo wasn't for her?

"I like it." Santino rubbed his hands together. "Three dicks, one girl."

"I like those odds." Rex cackled. "It might be less work to focus all our efforts on a single person."

"Fine. I'll bite." I wouldn't mind a distraction, not just from all the shit with Dad and Mom, but also from Aurora. Focusing my energy on someone else might get my mind to stop thinking about her. I swiped my fingers across my lips where her kiss still burned.

"Yes." Donata bounced in her seat. "So, I thought about also participating."

"Oh." Santino grunted. "I would award House Salvatore two thousand points if you let me watch."

"Don't get cute." She rolled her eyes. "I'm not playing this year. Instead, I'm going to make sure none of you win."

"What?" I laughed. "Now you're just making shit up."

"I said I wanted epic. This is how I'm going to make it happen. She has to fall in love with one of you, in spite of me."

"You already have something planned. Don't you?" I shook my head at her.

"Have you met me?"

"Who's the girl?" I met her gaze. Donata loved a challenge. But no more than me. I needed this diversion.

"My aunt's sweet protégée, of course. Aurora Vitali." She waved her fingers behind her toward Aurora.

Fuck.

"Are you fucking kidding me?" Santino knocked back the

rest of his champagne. "She's already seen what I can do. This bet is in the bag. Are you sure this is the girl you want?"

"I am sure. Sex is not love, Santi." She turned to face me. "You still in, your highness?"

"No." I rose to my feet. "I'm out."

Could've Fooled Me

Aurora

Three tables down on my left, Enzo shot to his feet and headed for the door. My whole body tensed because all I wanted to do was chase after him. I wanted to talk to him about what happened. Most of all, I wanted to know what had almost happened in the bathroom. I glanced down at my hands as heat rushed to my cheeks. Why did he kiss me?

Next to me, Angelo chuckled quietly. He found my blushing adorable, which pissed me off. He was so condescending. If he thought I was such a child, why stick around. The whole thing was just too weird.

"I'll get us some desserts." He stood and walked off.

I glared at the intricate flower designs on the carpet as his Italian leather shoes disappeared from my view. My head swam with a myriad of emotions that I had no idea what to do with. On the one hand, I was mad at Dad for inviting Angelo to our table. Disappointed at Mom for letting it happen, for thinking Dad would, in the end, do the right thing. My entire life was proof that Dad only did what was best for him.

On top of everything else, Enzo decided to kiss me, which totally turned my world upside down. An hour ago, I had a plan to get me through until graduation. I was going to do whatever Dad asked of me—smile politely at his chosen suitors and do my best not to stab them with a butter knife. Come next summer, I'd disappear for good. And then, Dad would have no say over my life.

I was heavily banking on the fact that Signoria Vittoria had offered to help. If she could get me into Columbia, I would be free—to be my own person and make my own choices. I still had to figure out how to pay for it, but one problem at a time.

My gaze swept across the room to where Enzo and Don Alfera stood by the entrance. Right, first things first. How in the world was I going to survive senior year, knowing Enzo liked kissing me? And I had so many questions for him. Like, did he get hard every time he was with a girl? Or if I had let him, would he have gone all the way?

Omigod, I hadn't thought about sex.

Well, I had. I just hadn't thought Enzo would be an option. Was he? Did he want me? He was a royal—an ungettable get. I was a nobody. The new girl who wormed her way into his mafia world. But if he wanted me...did I want him like that? Was I willing to go that far with him, knowing we could never be an actual couple? The questions swirled in my head until it was all a jumble of incoherent thoughts.

In the end, it all boiled down to one thing—Enzo and I were an impossibility of epic proportions, no matter how I looked at it. He was meant to be king. And I was headed for

Columbia. I couldn't mess that up. I couldn't let him mess with my head or my plans. Period.

"Hi."

"What?" My head snapped up. Donata's bright blue eyes met mine. Gosh, she was beautiful, dazzling even. "I mean, hi."

"Do you mind?" She gestured toward the chair.

I nodded. Out of habit—yeah, now it was a habit—I scanned the room for Enzo. When I found him by the bar talking to Angelo, he shifted his weight to look in my direction. He was back to hating me again. His broody stare quickly dissolved all the sexy, bad ideas in my head. And now only one question remained—did he regret kissing me?

"Is anyone home?"

"What?" I met Donata's gaze again.

She sat on Angelo's chair. "I said, how are you enjoying the brunch?" She placed a mimosa in front of me. "It helps. Trust me."

"Thank you." I sipped from the glass. Penny had warned me not to strike up a conversation with a royal unless they asked a direct question. I rubbed my forehead. All these rules were driving me a little crazy. I decided to just be myself and forget about protocol. After all, Donata came to my table. "Are these events always this painful?"

"Yes, unfortunately." She laughed. "It'll be over soon."

"Could've fooled me." I shot a glance over to the MC. She sure liked to talk. "Did you need something? You never talk to me."

"Never is such an ugly word." She winked. "But yes, I did have a reason for coming over. Penny mentioned you were interested in cheerleading."

"Yes." I sat a little straighter, ignoring Enzo's glares. He was alone now. And not happy that I was talking to Donata.

"That's great, because I wanted to personally invite you to try out for the team." She picked up her clutch purse, pulled out her phone, and gave it to me. "Here, put your number in and I'll text you the details."

I held the device carefully as I typed my full name and number in her contacts. When I gave it back to her, she typed fast. My phone pinged next to my champagne glass. My first text from Donata Salvatore. What was happening right now?

"Thank you. I'll be there. This is amazing. I didn't even know there were tryouts."

"Now you do." As she put her phone away, she glanced in Enzo's direction. She didn't seem affected by his scolding glare. "Enjoy the rest of your weekend. I'll see you tomorrow after school."

"Yes. Thank you." I waved at her retreating form.

Apart from Penny, I didn't have any friends at Midtown High. And even she wasn't really my friend. Signoria Vittoria had enlisted her to help me with school and to stay out of trouble. As she had put it, my success was tethered to hers because she was sure helping Don Alfera's right-hand man would put her family back in his good graces. From day one, Penny didn't hide the fact that our relationship was more business than pleasure. We weren't exactly friends.

But now I had the opportunity to really be part of the fold. A spot on the cheerleading team would do that for me. I really wanted to believe that.

Monday morning, I showed up to first period with my heart in my throat. I had spent the rest of Sunday dreading coming to school and facing Enzo and his many moods. I hugged my chemistry book to my chest and forced myself to enter the classroom.

Penny was already sitting at our table. Enzo and the other royals hadn't arrived yet. I released a breath and made my way to my seat.

"Morning." Penny greeted me with a smile. "How was the brunch? I can't believe we weren't invited."

"Oh, I didn't realize." I dropped my backpack on the floor next to the lab stool. "You could've come with us. There were plenty of chairs at our table. No one wanted to sit with us." I shrugged.

"Thanks." She patted my shoulder. "But that's not how these things work. If Don Alfera didn't invite us, that's the same as being banished."

"That's harsh."

"You have no idea. I heard you had a nice time."

"You did?" I instinctively glanced over my shoulder to Enzo's table in the back. Had people seen me or him leave the ladies' bathroom? "What, um, what did you hear exactly?"

"That Donata invited you to the cheer squad."

"Oh, yes, she did." I beamed at her. "That's a good thing, right?"

"Hmm, it's hard to say. She has invited girls in the past. But mostly, the tryouts are a fun time for the royals. They all just sit there and make fun of the hopefuls."

"Wait, what? You mean Enzo..." When she cocked her head to the side, I added, "Rex and Santino will be there too? Why? What do they know about cheerleading?"

"Do they need a reason, really? They don't need to know about cheer. They do it because they find it entertaining. Some girls see it as an opportunity to try and catch their attention. We've had broken arms before, nasty falls, wardrobe malfunctions. Everyone tries so hard. The competition can get intense." She braced her elbow on the table and shifted her body, so she was facing me. "Are you sure you want to try out? I mean, can you even do a cartwheel?"

"I can. I'm surprisingly well-coordinated, believe it or not." I laughed. "I used to cheer at my other school. I want to give it a shot."

Cheerleading had been the reason I woke up early this morning. As embarrassed as I was to face Enzo again, I was truly excited for the tryouts tonight. But if it was all just a big production for the royals' personal entertainment, maybe I should sit this one out.

"Do you think I should skip it?"

"No, it's not that. Donata did invite you. And now you pretty much have to go. I just want to make sure you're not making a fool of yourself. We're in this together, remember?" she said matter-of-factly.

"I want to do it. Would you go with me?"

"Give Donata a chance to tell me exactly what's wrong with me? No, thank you." She furrowed her brows as if considering her options. "I'll watch from the bleachers. That's the best I can do."

"I'll take it." I leaned in to squeeze her hand. "Thank you."

She froze. When I turned to apologize for touching her without asking, she wasn't even looking at me.

"Good morning, girls." Donata stepped out of the aisle and

into our space. "Penny, I don't know if Rory told you, but I've asked her to join our cheer team. Would you join us too?"

"Of course. I would love to," Penny said without skipping a beat.

"Great. I'll see you both tonight." She waved as she walked toward the back of the room.

"Oh no. Are you going to be able to do it?" I huddled toward Penny to ask.

"Crap. I mean, I can do a few moves, but I'm not a cheerleader. Fuck." She turned to face the front of the class.

"We can practice together, if you want." I rubbed her arm when she hugged her book and nestled her head between her crossed arms.

The hairs on the back of my neck prickled. My reaction was to look for Enzo by the door. He was deep in conversation with Rex. But the minute he saw me, he pursed his lips and inhaled deeply. If I had doubts before, I didn't now. He regretted kissing me.

He walked past our table, and his scent engulfed me like a cocoon. I didn't fight it. I breathed it in until the air cleared, and he was all the way in the back.

Why did I kiss him back?

"Give me your tongue." His words from that day in the bathroom made my lips tingle again. My body heated and then there was nothing I could do to stop myself from going down the Enzo rabbit hole. His mouth on mine, his tongue, his hands.

"That's you." Penny elbowed me in the ribs.

"What?" I mouthed to her.

She pointed to my right. I looked up and met Mr. Taylor's

gaze. "Ms. Vitali, would you pass these for me, please? Make sure each person gets one of each color. The copier was hell this morning."

"Why?"

"Excuse me?" The teacher leaned in to catch my words.

"I mean, sure." I grabbed the two stacks of papers because it was easier than asking why he'd chosen me for this task.

I started with our table, pulling one peach sheet from the bottom and one white one from the top, then moved on to the next row. For the most part, no one paid me much attention. They simply took the pages from me and started reading. By the time I had finished distributing packets to the first two rows of tables, I had a good system going. Though as I started working my way toward the back, my fingers stiffened. Luckily, Enzo had switched from shooting daggers at me for existing to pretending I was invisible. That soothed my nerves a little.

This was the moment Rex and Santino decided to give me their full attention. I hadn't noticed it before, but they were as bad as Enzo when it came to putting out intense vibes. I could feel their gazes on me—like long fingers caressing my overly sensitive skin.

Rex's deep blue eyes were pools of serenity. Though the energy I got from him was far from serene. He was dangerous. No idea how I knew that. It was something like a gut feeling. He leaned back and watched me with keen interest as I placed the pieces of paper in front of him. I had met him before. Once, under extremely embarrassing circumstances, so he had to remember who I was. But right now, he was looking at me like he was seeing me for the first time.

"Thank you." He smiled, a sexy, blinding gesture that made me step back.

My heart picked up its pace because I wasn't sure how to act around the royals. I wasn't supposed to talk to them, but what was the protocol when they looked at me or said thank you?

"You're welcome." I moved on without making eye contact.

"Can I get two copies?" Santino put out his hand. For a moment, I thought he was going to touch my hand, but he simply hovered his fingers close to mine. His body heat hit me square in the chest. I looked up out of sheer curiosity. His hazel gaze was hypnotizing. For a good five seconds, I couldn't move. Then he grinned at me like he knew something I didn't.

These guys had to be toying with me.

"Of course." I stood there and went through my little process twice, while Donata tittered one table over.

So this was how it was going to be tonight at cheer tryouts —me performing like a circus monkey while the royals watched me trip over my feet. I bet Donata thought I'd be a mess, so she invited me to ensure they had solid entertainment tonight.

"Don't mind them." Donata took the stacks from me. "They think they're being funny."

Funny? I didn't find their scrutiny amusing—more like unnerving and mortifying.

"How many copies do you need?" I asked.

"Just one each." She smiled politely and handed back the leftover papers. She had taken a set for herself and one for Enzo.

At least now I didn't have to interact with him. Not that he even noticed me while he typed something on his phone. I took in a breath and returned to my table.

"Tonight is going to be a shitshow," Penny said under her breath and opened her chem book with a huff.

"I think you're right."

Sex and Murder Qualify as Epic

Enzo

"I'm here for the tryouts. Not the bet." I walked around the judges' table and plopped myself on it.

Cheer tryouts was a royals' tradition. We got to choose who we wanted on the sidelines with us. This year, I had no doubt Aurora would make the team. If only because it suited Donata's plan for this year's Pop a Cherry contest. I had no interest in the bet, but I was still the QB. I needed to make sure my team was happy with the new cheerleading squad.

"Of course." Donata shrugged and sat next to me. When Santino and Rex stood at the threshold, she gestured for them to join us. "We only have ten minutes before the girls show up."

"So he's in?" Santino pulled up a chair in front of us and turned it around. "I knew he'd come around."

"No, he's out." Donata rolled her eyes. "But he can listen in if he wants. It's not like the intel I have on Rory is confidential."

I sat back and stretched out my legs in front of me. Since Sunday, when Donata announced her pick for this year's bet, I had not stopped thinking about Aurora—about this year's prize.

The more I tried not to think about Rex or Santino winning, the more my mind conjured images of the three of them together. For reasons unknown to me, I couldn't stomach the idea of my friends touching her. But participating in this bet would put me in a situation I wasn't ready for. I couldn't spend all my free time with Aurora. Making her fall in love with me would require time and effort. I would have to actually get to know her. This was the sadistic part of Donata's game.

We could have sex with anyone we wanted by simply asking.

With Aurora, we'd have to come up with a plan to get her alone, learn what she was about, and find common ground.

"Coward." Rex stepped toward us and crossed his arms over his chest.

"You know that's not true." I released a breath. "She seems like she'd be a bad lay."

"Well, that's the challenge, isn't it?" Santino smirked. "I plan to use my time making sure she learns a few things first."

The anger that reared its ugly head every time I thought of Santino and Rex with Aurora crept up into my chest and threatened to bust it open. I shifted my weight and glanced at him. "What makes you think she wants to learn?"

"A hunch." He wiggled his brows, smiling.

He wasn't wrong. Aurora was eager to know more. I thought of her first kiss. How passive she had been at first. But after I guided her, she improved by a mile. I touched my thumb to my lips. Yeah, Aurora most certainly wanted to learn.

"Oh, they're here. We'll talk afterward." Donata grabbed the clipboard and greeted the first girls to arrive.

In a matter of minutes, the line ran the length of the gym. I counted roughly fifty participants. Not a bad turnout. This was our third year running the tryouts. I had a few drills planned that had mostly to do with stamina. I liked to see girls do stunts and a well-choreographed routine. Rex preferred the interview part. Anyone who couldn't handle his and Donata's cross-examination had no business being on the team. Santino's rating was solely based on how good they looked in a wet T-shirt.

The last part of the tryouts was a fundraiser led by Santino. The participants who made the first round of cuts were assigned to a stop light in Harlem, where they would wash cars for an hour. The trick was to get the vehicles clean in the time it took for the light to turn green. Things got wet and messy fast—and that was the whole point of it.

Aurora ambled into the gym and walked across the mat to find Penny sitting against the wall. I almost got up and left. I didn't like how her mere presence messed with my head. I didn't like how Santino and Rex were looking at her now because of Donata's bet.

I rose to my feet. We needed to get these tryouts over with quickly. "Athletes." I projected my voice, so the girls chatting in the back could hear me. When they looked up with terrified faces, I continued, "Let's start with a quick warm up."

Donata walked to the middle of the panel and guided them through her routine. My gaze swept past all the girls until it landed on Aurora. When Donata invited her to join the team,

I felt sorry for her. Competition amongst the hopefuls was so fierce; it sometimes bordered on cruel.

But the minute we started, Aurora's face and overall demeanor changed. She didn't look shy or intimidated. For the first time since I'd met her, she seemed confident—at home. A smile pulled at my lips, which was my cue to busy myself with something else.

"Wrap it up," I called out to them again. Time to see what they could do. "Line up against the wall. Five rows. Let's see those cartwheels."

"Feet together when you land, ladies," Donata shouted out after me, clapping her hands. When the first line reached the opposite wall, she pointed at Aurora. "Come on. We don't have all night."

Aurora turned to say something to Penny, which prompted Donata to yell at her again. "Keep the line moving. You do know how to do a cartwheel, don't you?"

Aurora nodded but quickly turned her focus back to Penny. What the hell was going on? She was holding up the line. The girls behind them were not happy.

"I thought they'd make it through the first round, at least." Donata rolled her eyes.

"Give them a second. It's her first time." I crossed my arms over my chest. A jittery energy fluttered through me. For whatever reason, I wanted her to do well.

After another beat, Aurora finally looked ahead of her and inhaled deeply. And then she let it go. She tumbled across the mat in three consecutive flips, finishing with a double twist. She even stuck the landing.

"How about that? The girl can jump." Donata beamed at me. "This is gonna be fun."

I shot a glance over my shoulder. Both Rex and Santino stood in front of the judges' table with their mouths slightly open. And there it was again, that feral instinct to kick their asses for looking at her that way. I glared at her while she high-fived Penny, who apparently had also made it across the gym.

Donata called corners, and all the athletes quickly found their spots. It was obvious now that this wasn't Aurora's first tryouts. I stood back as Donata put them all through the wringer, with back flips, splits, and wide-legged jumps.

The last fifteen minutes, she put them in groups of five and had them do a few stunts they'd learned during the cheer clinic last week. The one Aurora and Penny had not been invited to because last week Donata hadn't decided yet that Aurora would be part of her little game this year.

"What did you think was going to happen?" I asked Donata when she joined me on the sideline.

"I thought it would be fun for you to see her fall on her face." She shrugged. "She's done this before."

"Yeah, she has. You're really going to let her on the team?"

"She was going to stay no matter what." She winked and walked off, reading names off her clipboard.

I should've known that was Donata's end game. She wanted Aurora close by, so she could influence her and make sure she wasn't easily persuaded by Rex or Santino. I was with Donata on this one. Aurora needed a lot of help in that department. Rex and Santino could be very charming when they wanted to be.

"So Donata is taking Aurora's sweet cherry under her wing." Rex stood next to me, watching Aurora like a hawk. "I was worried this was going to be too easy."

"Me too." Santino joined us. "Either way, this will be over in two weeks, tops."

Rex chuckled. "The interview round should be fun."

"I'm personally looking forward to the fundraiser." Santino exhaled loudly.

I stood there like an idiot and let my asshole friends talk shit about how easy a task Aurora would be. A month from now, Aurora would lose more than her virginity. A broken heart would make her bitter and hopeless. It would destroy all the things that made her who she was, sweet and innocent.

The interviews dragged on, even when each participant only had to answer Rex's favorite question: "If you could go on a date with any historical figure, dead or alive, who would it be and what would you do?"

When it was Aurora's turn, she stood in front of the judges' table, not meeting my gaze. She focused mostly on Donata. Donata had that effect on women. They trusted her for some reason. Even with her mean-girl energy, they all confided in her.

"Hi, I'm Aurora Vitali. Um." She cleared her throat as if what she had to say next was some big secret. "I'm in House Alfera."

A calm washed over me when she said my family name. It felt as if she somehow belonged to me, as if we had an unbreakable bond.

"And who's your date?" Donata asked.

"Maya Angelou." Aurora squirmed in place. The confidence she wore earlier when she was tumbling across the room was gone.

"And what would you do with her?" I asked before I realized my mouth was even moving.

She looked at me with big doe eyes, shaking her head a little. "I don't know. She could read her poems to me, I guess. And explain them. I think there's a lot there I don't fully understand."

By now, I knew enough about Aurora that her answer didn't surprise me. Poetry. I thought of Angelou's most famous works and what little I remembered of them. Aurora liked poetry, the heart-wrenching kind.

"You can go. We'll let you know our decision next week." Donata dismissed her and called the next person in line.

I sat there for another hour, not paying attention to anyone else's answers. Aurora's words kept bouncing around in my head. Then I remembered Donata had something she had wanted to say to us before tryouts started. Whatever it was, it had to be something big. Big enough to pique Donata's interest, enough to make Aurora our target this year.

The gym door shut behind the last participant. I let out a heavy sigh and dropped my clipboard on the table, rubbing my eyes with my thumb and index finger. "Some of those answers were just wow."

"Lunch with Kim Kardashian? That was hysterical." Rex barked out a laugh. "How is she a historical figure, again?"

"Do we vote now?" I asked. "The choices are pretty clear to me."

"No, we still have the fundraiser this weekend." Santino shot to his feet. "I can't make a decision without that valuable information."

Did I want to see Aurora all slippery and wet while washing cars? "We'll decide on Saturday then." I made to get up, but Donata gripped my shoulder.

"I still need to tell you something about Rory." She waited until I settled back into my folding chair.

"So what do you have on her? Any boyfriends we should know about?" Rex asked. This was his territory. Rex knew secrets made the world go round.

I turned my attention to Donata. All this time, I hadn't considered the idea that Aurora might already be in love with someone else.

"No boyfriend." She beamed, thoroughly pleased with herself. "A fiancé."

"What the fuck?" I stood. "She's getting married?"

"She is." Donata nodded.

"Oh, you're good." Santino chuckled, pointing a finger at Donata.

"Thank you."

"What's the deal there?" I could tell them that I knew for a fact Aurora wasn't in love. And that the reason I knew that was because I was her first kiss. If Aurora had a fiancé, it couldn't possibly be a love match. "There has to be more to that story."

"Here's what I know from a little recon I did."

"You overheard one of your aunt's conversations, didn't you?" I shook my head at her.

"Yes." She put up her hands. "But you have to admit, the plan is solid. We stick it to her pompous dad while having a little fun ourselves."

"What did you hear?"

"Her dad has arranged a marriage between her and Angelo Soprano. Pretty much as soon as she turns eighteen in December. My aunt believes that Stephano, Rory's dad, is under the impression that he needs family ties to make sure his place within the Society is secured." She pursed her lips and swallowed. "I've met that guy before. He's a total creep. Puke." She fake-gagged.

So that was her angle. Deep down, Donata lived up to her family's name and ideals. The Salvatores' mascot was the panther—the fierce guardian—for a reason.

"Has she agreed to this marriage?" No sense anymore in pretending I didn't care. Technically speaking, I didn't, though I was intrigued.

"I don't know if she knows. Her birthday is in three months." She shrugged. "By then, she'll know for sure. Think of it this way, thanks to us, she'll go into the marriage knowing what it's like to do it for love."

"Donata, the romantic." I leaned in to pinch her cheek, but she slapped my hand away.

Even if her intentions were weirdly noble, this bet was going to mess with Aurora's head in a major way. Fuck. So not only did I have to put up with Rex and Santino having a go at her, she was going to be Angelo's wife. As in, forever, only fucking him.

"Are you guys still in? Because according to Aunt Vittoria, Angelo was in the market for a virgin bride. If he gets to his wedding night and finds out he was duped, he'll retaliate against her father. Possibly her family." Donata didn't seem that concerned with Aurora's dad's well-being.

"I'm in." Rex spoke first. "You wanted epic. I'd say sex and murder qualify as epic."

"So let me get this straight. We have to pop her cherry before she gets married." Santino rubbed his jaw.

"Clock's ticking." Donata tapped her watch twice.

"Fuck it. I'm still in."

"And you, Enzo?" Donata turned to me. "Have you

changed your mind? Is the bet challenging enough for you now?"

"You're kind of sick. You know that?" I raked both hands through my hair.

"That's why you love me." She beamed.

At first, I'd said no to the bet because I didn't want a reason to be near Aurora or talk to her. She had a certain influence over me, and I didn't like it. That was before I knew she belonged to someone else—before I knew I couldn't have her. I was no knight in shining armor. I wasn't here to save Aurora from a creep ten years her senior. No, I wanted Aurora for myself.

"Yes, I'm in."

Have You Ever Seen a Cat Play with a Mouse?

Aurora

"You're late again, Ms. Vitali." Mr. Taylor glanced at me over the rim of his glasses with his hand hovering over the whiteboard. "That's the third time this week."

"I know. I'm sorry. Traffic has been…um…I don't know. Difficult." I ambled to my seat while the entire class glared at me.

"Your fellow classmates had to endure the same traffic conditions. And yet they managed to get here on time."

I wanted to tell him that it wasn't my fault. Our driver took longer than usual to get me to school. On Wednesday, he decided to take a different route. Yesterday, he simply didn't show up at the scheduled time. And today, he drove super-slow. I had considered that maybe he was doing it on purpose. But what would he get out of making me tardy?

"Page seventy-two." Mr. Taylor gestured toward my Chem book. "Ms. Conti can help you catch up."

I nodded and dropped my bag next to my seat. "I'm sorry."

"Start measuring." Penny slid the scale toward me. "We have to finish this lab today. Or my mom won't let me do the fundraiser tomorrow."

"Don't worry. We'll get it done." I set up the beaker on the scale and zeroed out the display.

"You can finish during detention." Mr. Taylor placed a pink sheet on the table. "Enjoy."

Crap. Now I had detention? I grabbed the paper and stuffed it in my bookbag. When I glanced toward the tables in the back, Enzo met my gaze. For once, he didn't glare at me. His eyes even had a hint of a smile in them. I swore his mood swings had me all dazed and confused.

As the day wore on, I found that Enzo wasn't the only one being nice to me at school. Or maybe not nice, but at least, not hostile like the first day of school. The friendly faces put me in a better mood. Even if I still had to do my first ever detention in the afternoon. I was planning to use that time to do homework, so I could meet up with the cheer squad in the morning.

According to Penny, the fundraiser was just an excuse for the royals and the football team to see the cheerleaders all wet and soapy. I didn't care. It wasn't like we'd be washing cars naked. Though I did hear some participants discussing bikini options. The thought of parading in front of Enzo in a skimpy outfit made me smile. I shouldn't be thinking of him like that. Our kiss from last weekend didn't mean anything. But I couldn't help myself. He was hard to forget.

"I see you're minding your Ps and Qs now and getting to class on time." Santino fell into step next to me in the middle of the breezeway.

For a beat, I wasn't sure if he was talking to me. I glanced behind me, expecting to see a group of girls laughing at me over some joke I didn't know about. Why was Santino even in the same space as me? In the last few weeks, since school started, I hadn't seen him in the Salvatore building after lunch. I was sure he didn't have a class on this floor.

He waited for me to get my bearings then smiled. "You have detention tonight?"

"Oh. That. Yeah, I got detention for being late to class."

"Thrice." He put up three fingers. "Such a rebel."

I laughed. When Santino wasn't smirking or looking me up and down, he could be so charismatic, even pleasant. I lifted my gaze to meet his. He was being nice to me for real. Why? Because there was a good chance I'd make the cheer team? The lump I'd had in my throat since the first day of school slowly began to dissolve as I got lost in his hazel eyes.

"Are you ready for the fundraiser tomorrow? We changed venues. Did you get the text?" He shifted his attention to a girl staring at us with her mouth slightly opened, then winked. "It's here at the school now. Front courtyard."

"I did." I looked behind me and recognized the girl fuming a few feet away from us. "Isn't she your girlfriend?"

She was the redhead from Enzo's beach house. My cheeks burned hot as the memory of Santino nestled between her legs flashed in my eyes. My heart raced when the image quickly morphed into something else—Enzo kissing me, Enzo asking me what I saw, Enzo feeding me spicy chocolate.

"Who? Hanna? Nah, more like friends with benefits." He stopped in front of my classroom door. "Here you are. Safe and sound."

"Thank you. I didn't need you to walk me to class. I know my way around now." I smiled at him.

"It was a pleasure." He leaned in, but his eyes were focused on something behind me. "I'll see you after school."

"You will?"

"Yeah, I have detention too." He beamed at me. "Enjoy English Lit."

I stood there and watched him take long strides as people moved out of the way to let him through. He turned the corner at the end of the hallway, and the spell broke. Whatever his reasons for being nice to me, I didn't care. All I cared about was that, now, I wasn't so much the outsider anymore.

The bell rang, and I rushed past the threshold, so I wouldn't be marked tardy. Though I didn't need to hurry since Dr. Reid hadn't arrived yet.

"Hi." Enzo smiled at me when I sat at my desk, next to his.

"Hi?" I didn't mean for it to come out as a question. This day kept getting weirder and weirder. First, everyone at lunch was nice to me. Then, Santino walked me to class. Now Enzo was saying hi to me?

"I didn't realize you were friends with Santino."

"I'm not," I blurted out.

Even if Enzo had spent a whole month pretending I didn't exist in school, I still didn't want him to think I was interested in Santino. Wait. Did I want him to think I was interested in him? That ship sailed a long time ago. More specifically, it sailed the day I let him teach me how to kiss in the women's bathroom of a luxury hotel. This sort of thing would never happen in Las Vegas. That place felt so far away now. Like the time I had spent there happened to someone else.

"But you let him walk you to class." He crossed his arms and braced them on his desk, turning his head to look at me.

The sexy smile that pulled at his lips made me feel all

bubbly inside. "He didn't exactly ask. What about you? Are you talking to me now? Last weekend, I thought you were mad at me for..." I cleared my throat, and my cheeks burned again. I'd bet they were bright red. "You know."

"For kissing me."

I shot a glance behind me to see if anyone had heard him. But all the other students were busy with their own conversations.

"I didn't..." I started to say I didn't kiss him, but that wasn't true. Sure, he started the whole thing, but I was a willing participant. I hadn't forgotten how soft his lips felt against mine.

"I could never be mad at you." He raked a hand through his hair as he surveyed my face. "I want to show you something."

"What is it?"

"Not here." He furrowed his brows. "Meet me after school. In the courtyard." He pointed to the window, where the clock tower was visible. "Past the maple trees."

"I have detention after school."

"It won't take long." He leaned in and whispered, as if our rendezvous was some sort of clandestine meeting. "I promise."

A secret meeting with Enzo Alfera? My chest expanded like a balloon. "I can do that."

I somehow made it through social studies and world languages that afternoon. When our last period ended, I told Penny I had to get to detention and bolted. In the back of my mind, a small voice told me I shouldn't be alone with Enzo. But an even louder one screamed, *"Why not?"*

The images of the first time we met flitted through my mind, followed by memories of him going up the stairs in his house in the Hamptons, the bathroom, and finally the hotel. Enzo was the fire on the stove. Every time I put my hand over it, I got burned. A normal person would have learned the lesson by now and not reached out anymore. But it seemed that when it came to Enzo, reason went out the window.

I followed the path to the clock tower, then veered off it when I reached the maple trees. Just as Enzo had said, there was a courtyard behind the building. At this time of year, the leaves had already changed to a pretty, crimson red. I stepped closer to the water fountain in the center. From here, I was out of sight from the students heading to the front of the school to get picked up.

The wind blew and showered me with what looked like pieces of colorful paper. I glanced up and smiled at the foliage. As I sat at the edge of the fountain, Penny's words, from the beginning of the year, flooded my mind. *Have you ever seen a cat play with a mouse?*

Was that what this was? A game?

I rubbed my forehead and tried to put it all into perspective, and quickly came to the conclusion that I couldn't be here, meeting with Enzo like this. Before I lost my resolve to leave, I shot to my feet. But when I turned to find the path that led back to the clock tower, I found myself face to face with Santino's non-girlfriend. I hadn't forgotten her seething face when she saw me with Santino earlier today.

"There she is." She smiled at me. It was a chilling gesture that made my heart race. "Students are not allowed back here. The courtyard is for faculty only."

"I didn't know that. Um, I was just leaving."

"Oh no, stay."

As soon as she said the words, two guys strode into the

courtyard. Had they been hiding just beyond the trees, waiting for their cue to enter? One of them had a football tucked under his arm. And the other one had a gym bag over his shoulder, like they were headed for practice.

"It's Rory, right?" The tall boy with blond hair and intense blue eyes stepped toward me. "I saw you at cheer tryouts. Not bad."

"Thanks." I lowered my head. Something about the way they looked at me didn't feel right.

"I'm Brody. This is Ian." He gestured toward his friend, who was now looking at me like I was some odd thing.

"Good meeting you." I picked up my bag and made to leave.

"Not so fast." Brody gripped my upper arm. "Hanna says Santino has taken an interest in you. We were curious."

"I don't know what you mean." Was this really about Santino walking me to class earlier? "I'm late for detention."

"I bet she gives good head." Ian tittered, elbowing Hanna. "Why else would Santino hang around?"

Hanna laughed along with him and stepped back to let him through. The look in their eyes should've been a warning. I should've run out the minute Hanna showed up. In a blur of arms and bodies, Brody shoved me against his friend's chest. When I turned around to get away from them, Ian wrapped his arms around my whole body and dragged me down to my knees. I sank into the wet grass while he held me in a bear hug. My head snapped up, just as Brody's crotch moved into view.

They couldn't possibly be thinking about making me do this. I searched for Hanna, but she was gone. Or at least, not where I could see her. I watched in horror as Brody unzipped his pants and freed his erection.

"Stop it." I struggled against Ian's hard body. He tightened his hold until I thought my ribs would crack under the pressure. Tears streamed down my cheeks. Why would they do this to me? Because of Santino? Because Hanna thought she had some sort of claim on him?

"Open up, sweetie?" Ian whispered against my ear, then spread his knees apart to press his hard-on against my back.

Where the hell was Enzo?

I sobbed when I realized that this was what he had meant to show me. Enzo sent me here so his buddies could get a quick blow job. This was a game to him. Like all the other times, he only wanted to toy with me and watch me make a fool of myself. I was an idiot for thinking he wanted to hang out with me.

What was I thinking? Why would a royal want to spend any amount of time with me? He'd said it before—*I don't date the help*. This whole day had been a joke. Something they started just for fun—Donata being nice to me at lunch in front of everyone. Santino walking me to class. And Enzo talking to me like we were friends. It was all a cruel game. Because that was what they did. No doubt they were bored this morning and decided it would be amusing to serve me up to the football team.

I was the mouse they'd chosen to play with today.

Brody gripped his cock and pumped a few times. The eagerness in his face made my stomach churn. He didn't care that I was shaking my head no or that I was struggling against his friend. He seemed confident that he could get me to do this. That he could force me into sucking him off.

"Be a good girl now. You wouldn't want to disappoint the royals, would you?" He made a lewd sound that was a half chuckle, half groan, then he grabbed my jaw and squeezed it tight until my lips fell open. "Such a pretty mouth. We'll train you up. Show you how to give Santino the best head."

"No." I tried to form the word, but only managed a stifled sound. Ian's steel grip cut off all the circulation and air supply. I couldn't speak or move. The tears and the lack of air made the trees, the water fountain, and even Brody's figure, just a bunch of blurry shadows. Suddenly, the woodsy scent of the maple trees was replaced by a stench I could only qualify as sex—his arousal. "No." I clung to that one word, even though I couldn't say it aloud anymore.

I didn't want this. I had done nothing to deserve it. I repeated the mantra in my head while Brody made my jaw open wider for him. He kept pumping with his other hand, as if he wanted to enjoy this moment, making me cringe and cry, before he plunged into my mouth.

In the next beat, my lungs filled with cool air. I blinked away tears as I tried to catch my breath. When the scene in front of me finally came into focus, I saw Brody on the ground, and there was blood everywhere. I shook my head and then Enzo's form appeared, hovering over Brody, gripping the front of his jersey.

The hate in his eyes made me crawl away from them.

"Did you not hear her, you fucking asshole? She said no." Enzo punched him again and again.

I covered my ears to muffle the sound of Enzo's fist pounding on flesh. Was he really here to save me? Or was this another one of his games?

You and me both, Angel

Enzo

"Answer." I fisted the front of Brody's jersey tighter.

I meant to wait for him to tell me that he had heard Aurora say no. She clearly had no interest in him. But after another heartbeat, I punched him again. Every time an image of him taunting Aurora with his erect cock flashed in my mind, I saw red. And all I wanted to do was beat him to a pulp.

"She asked me to meet her here."

That was a lie. The only reason they found Aurora behind the clock tower was because I asked her to come. She was in a place where no one could see or hear her because of me. But what the hell gave Brody the right to assault her just because she was alone?

"You're lying."

"I swear. Hanna said she'd be into it." He sputtered blood, holding on to my wrists with both hands.

I scanned the courtyard, but only found Ian a few feet away. At least he hadn't decided to bolt. He knew there wasn't a place in the school, or the city for that matter, where I wouldn't find him.

"You both disgust me." I shoved Brody to the ground. His head hit it and made a satisfying thud. Though I knew that wasn't enough to erase Aurora's memory and make her feel better. If I could still see him clearly looming over her, I had no doubt she could too. I pointed at Ian. "Get him out of here. You're both off the team."

"What?" Ian stepped forward with his brows raised in surprise. "Why?"

"Are you kidding me? You assaulted a student on school grounds, you fucking asshole." I advanced toward him. My knuckles raw and bleeding, but I didn't care. I wanted to see him hurt too.

He backed down and put his arms up in surrender. "She asked us to meet her here. You can't kick us off the team because of her."

"I can't?" I pinched the bridge of my nose. "How about this? You're no longer on the team. The rules state that only students in good standing are allowed to play. Given how you're no longer a student here, I don't see how I can keep you on."

"The fuck?" Brody shot to his feet and joined his friend. "You can't do this to us. We're not even in your house."

"Right." I nodded at the gym bag on the wet grass with the Salvatore crest on it. "I will personally have a conversation with Signoria Vittoria. Once I tell her how you treated her protégée, she'll agree with me. You don't belong here."

"Her protégée?" Ian furrowed his brows and shot a glance toward Brody.

"You need us on the team." Brody met my gaze. "You're

gonna throw away the chance to win the championship your senior year for some nobody?"

"That's right." I glared at him. "Grab your junk and get the fuck out of my sight."

Did I have enough pull with the school board to get these fuckers expelled? Possibly not. But I was banking on the fact that Signoria Vittoria's protection of Aurora extended to her physical well-being. Donata would have to help me set this right. If Aurora had become a target to everyone else at school, it was because of us, our sudden interest in her, and the fucking bet.

I stood my ground, hands braced on my hips, daring them to have a go at me. Brody puffed out a breath. After several beats, he conceded. He hoisted his gym bag over his shoulder and started down the gravel path back to the main entrance. As soon as they were out of sight, I turned my attention to the far end of the courtyard.

When I'd come in earlier, I saw Aurora run in that direction, which was a dead end. There was only one way in and out of this place. I raked a hand through my hair, trying to find the words to make her feel better—to make her understand she was safe.

I ambled toward her. She seemed so alone. I made to touch her upper arm. "Hey, they're gone."

"Don't touch me." She jumped out of reach. Tears streamed down her red cheeks as her gaze darted across the courtyard, looking for an exit. "Was that your idea of a funny joke? What did I ever do to you?"

"You didn't do anything." I put out my hand, and she recoiled. "Wait. Do you think I sent those guys here?"

"Who else? You asked me to meet you here." She raised her voice and fisted her hands, as if she wanted to hit me.

I couldn't blame her. She was angry, and possibly hurt. So I gave her the only relief I could. I placed my hands behind my back and met her gaze. An invitation to let it all go.

She slammed her fist on my chest. "I trusted you." She struck me again. I swayed backward but stayed in place, right where she needed me. "I trusted you," she repeated.

She trusted me? Why in the world would she do that? I let her throw a few more punches, then I wrapped my arms around hers to get her to stop and listen to me. "I swear. I didn't know those guys would follow you here."

"Well, they did." She winced.

"Did they hurt you?" When she glared at me, I rephrased, "I mean, physically?"

"I don't know." She shook her head. "The one guy held me so tight, my ribs feel achy now."

I glanced up and counted to ten. All I wanted to do right now was find Brody and Ian and show them what real pain felt like. I exhaled and reached inside the pocket of my suit jacket. I had brought her more of that chocolate she'd liked the first day of school. I had no idea our day would end on such a fucked-up note.

Since last night, I had thought of nothing else but meeting Aurora here and kissing her again. The spicy treat was going to be her reward.

"Here. Eat this." I broke off a piece of chocolate and touched it to her lips. "I promise it'll help."

Her eyes went wide, like big saucers. I thought she was about to tell me to go to hell, but instead, she opened her mouth and accepted my peace offering.

"You never have to see those assholes again. I swear." I cocked my head to look her in the eyes. When she didn't move away, I cupped her cheek and pulled her toward me to rest her head on my chest. "I'm sorry."

She shivered. "I didn't ask them to come here."

"I know."

I held her in my arms for a good ten minutes. For the life of me, I couldn't remember the last time I felt whole like this. Or the last time I felt like I mattered to someone. The bell above us chimed four times. I was late to practice. And she was late to detention. But I didn't want this moment to end. Why did I think that I could spend more time with Aurora and not be affected by it? By her? Maybe that was it. I wasn't thinking.

"Why did you ask me to come here?" She glanced up at me.

"I wanted to show you something. It doesn't matter now." I pressed my lips to her temple. "It was a silly idea."

"What?" She pulled away from me. Her cheeks were pink again, and her eyes were tear-free. "Tell me."

I quickly scanned the courtyard. "Well, I think all the yelling and punching scared him off."

"Scared who off?" She furrowed her brows at me, then smiled.

The genuinely happy gesture melted the lump in my chest. If the chocolate was working, maybe the other part of my plan could work too. It was stupid, but I really wanted her to meet my buddy. Since pretty much my first day of school at Midtown High, I'd been coming to this courtyard to find some peace and quiet. Last semester, I found a scruffy kitten that looked like he had been hurt—probably chased by some predator looking for a meal the night before.

I couldn't take him home, but I also couldn't leave him out here to die. So I made him a place to sleep inside the clock tower and fed him some blueberries I had in my backpack. To my surprise, the little guy hung around. He lived here now.

"Wait here." I went to fetch the lunch bag I had brought for him.

Earlier, I had dropped it by the fountain when I saw Brody looming over Aurora. As soon as I reached the water fountain, my cat decided to show his grumpy face. I turned to Aurora to tell her to stay put and not scare him off, but she was already on her haunches, trying to get his attention.

"Omigod. What is it?"

"It's a cat."

"Are you sure?"

"He meows like a cat. I'm sure." I chuckled. "I think he's some sort of mix. He's tripled in size since I started feeding him." I gave her the container with chicken and peas in it. "Go ahead."

She opened it and laid it on the ground. Fluffy was a total scaredy cat. But his belly did most of the thinking for him. He didn't care at all that Aurora was a stranger. He prowled to her and started munching on his dinner.

"He's so soft." She petted his head. "Why is he here?"

"He lives in the tower. I couldn't take him home." I sat on my ankles next to her. If I knew for sure Dad would never come home, I would've brought Fluffy home. But the old man wasn't done with me just yet. I didn't even want to think about what he would do if he found out I had a pet. "Dad doesn't like animals."

"That's a shame. Mom is allergic to cats. Otherwise, I would ask her if we could adopt him."

"No need. He's happy here. He's got a bed in there. Toys. And Ms. Molly spoils him rotten. She's one of the cafeteria cooks. I hired her to keep an eye on him and feed him. Last week, she made him rabbit and peas because she read somewhere it would be good for his coat."

"I don't think I've ever met Ms. Molly."

"She's a grumpy old lady who works in the back. She's good at what she does, but Chef likes to keep her away from the students." I shrugged. "Apparently, parents complained about her customer service. She can't stand spoiled brats."

"I bet." She laughed. "Well, she was right. His coat is beautiful." She scratched him softly on the chest, where his fur was big and full. "What's his name?"

"Fluffy." I winced. "I know, not very clever. I called him Scruffy the first few days. But then he got bigger. The name didn't fit anymore." I smiled at her.

"Fluffy's good." She met my gaze.

The charge in the air switched to something electrifying and raw. The same happened when I met her at Tiffany's before; I knew she was a student at Midtown High. I felt it again when she barged into the bathroom the first day of school. And then at brunch when we kissed.

That kiss.

I gripped her elbow and helped her to her feet. I'd never had this much trouble trying to decide what to do next with a girl—if I should do what I want, or what I thought was right. Normally, I would go for it. Things were different with Aurora. Probably because before I met her I didn't give a shit. But I did now.

"Tell me to go to hell."

She shook her head.

I glanced down at my fingers, where I held her elbow firmly. I loosened my grip and slid my hand up her arm. Make her fall in love—that was the challenge. But at what cost? I leaned closer until our noses touched. I wanted to see her surrender to me. Now that the idea had taken hold in the deepest recess of my soul, I couldn't let it go. The thought of someone else holding her this close made me mad with jealousy. Because that was what I felt when I saw Brody and Ian touching her like they had some kind of claim on her.

The kind of claim Angelo Soprano had bought.

I brushed her lips with mine. She tasted salty. I hated that she now had such a bad memory of this place. If I could erase what happened from her mind, I would. I kissed her cheek and the corner of her eyes to soothe them. Her giggle and the way she clung to me stirred all kinds of bad ideas in my head.

I gripped her waist and brought her closer to me. She didn't tell me to leave her alone, and that made my desire take a deeper hold on me.

"Fuck, Angel. Why do you have to be such a good girl?" I whispered in her ear, then captured her mouth.

She responded by giving me her tongue. Just like before, she let me explore her mouth while she tunneled her fingers through my hair.

"Good girl."

I walked her back toward the wall. When my hand touched the cool bricks, I gripped her thigh and wrapped it around my waist. Her legs and ass were toned, her skin so soft. I bent down to kiss her neck, and she rewarded me by pressing her pussy to my erection. This full-on make-out session had not been my plan at all. But I couldn't stop thinking about how the only thing separating us right now was her wet underwear and my pants. If I freed my cock now, I was one hundred percent sure she'd let me fuck her.

Jesus, I wanted nothing more than to bury myself inside her and ride her until she forgot about everything and everyone. I reached for my belt and undid the buckle.

"Enzo." She panted in my ear.

My name on her lips was pure ecstasy. I unfastened the button on my pants and pressed her against the wall.

"Stop," she mumbled.

Fuck.

I pulled back, laboring to catch my breath. "Why?" I knew why, but my brain wasn't quite working yet.

"It's too fast. I..." She touched her fingers to her lips. "I've never done this before. I mean. Not the kiss. The other thing." She pointed at my cock peeking through my boxer briefs.

Aurora was a virgin.

"I wasn't sure," I lied because I couldn't exactly tell her that Donata had already told us she was. And that I had spent a great deal of time thinking about what it would be like to be her first, and what I would do to make it good for her. Jesus, if I was going to get my cock to calm down, I needed to stop thinking about all the sex Aurora hadn't had yet. "I got carried away."

"Yeah, me too."

It took another minute to let the fire sweeping through me die down. "How about I walk you to detention?" I glanced down at my watch. "If we hurry, I can still make the second half of practice."

"Yeah." She nodded with those big blue eyes full of disappointment.

You and me both, Angel. You and me both.

She Was with Me

AURORA

Enzo brushed the pad of his thumb over the inside of my wrist. I was sure he could feel my pulse beating hard and fast. I was also one hundred percent sure he wanted to have sex with me. A smile pulled at my lips. I wanted him to be my first, but I had no idea where to even begin with him. Enzo didn't seem the type who did the whole boyfriend-girlfriend thing. And who was I to ask for any kind of commitment from him when Dad was still bringing suitors home? Dad had made it clear that he wanted me to marry as soon as I turned eighteen, which was in just a couple of months.

I met Enzo's serene gaze. If Dad didn't give up on the idea of marriage, I'd have to leave before the year was over. Either way, whether I stayed or left, I couldn't have Enzo—not even in the way he wanted me—because I was sure that sex with him would change my life forever. I knew that if I went down this path with him, I'd fall head over heels for him.

"Don't look so disappointed." He kissed my cheek.

My belly did a somersault, and the usual rush of adrenaline invaded all my senses. It was like standing in the middle of a field with the rain falling on me, pelting my face, my arms, and legs. All of me was affected by his touch, and I couldn't stop it.

"This thing you feel right here—" he pressed a hand to my chest and smiled, "—I can make you feel so good. If you let me."

I believed him. "I have detention."

"Of course you do. I have no doubt Santino had something to do with it." He chuckled.

"What do you mean?"

"Don't worry about it. Are you ready to go?" He pointed at the top buttons of my blouse.

I quickly fastened them and smoothed out my skirt. My underwear were uncomfortably wet, but there was nothing I could do about that. Heat rushed to my cheeks. Now I had to sit in class with this ache between my legs, thinking about how Enzo could've made it go away. I squeezed my eyes shut and waited for the wave of desire that stormed through me, yet again, to pass.

"I want to kiss you again."

My head snapped up at him. "Kissing seems to make it worse."

"Or better. It depends on perspective." He cocked his head and leaned in.

A puff of warm breath lingered between us. He was as turned on as I was. None of this made sense to me, but when he was this close, I didn't care to understand. I cupped his cheek, feeling the slight stubble there. "Why are you wasting your time with me?"

He furrowed his brows. After a beat, he reached for my wrist and pulled it off his face. "You're not a waste of time, Aurora."

He picked up my backpack and slung it over my shoulder. After he cleaned up Fluffy's dinner and said good-bye to his cat, he gestured for me to go ahead. I did, deeply regretting not asking him for one more kiss. Why was it always like this with us? Every time I walked away from him, I felt like something was missing. And worse, I felt like whatever it was, we wouldn't get it back. I wanted to ask him if we could meet again, but what was the point if he couldn't be my boyfriend?

We strolled across the lawn with the Buratti building in sight. I still had another twenty minutes of detention. At this point, I was only going in to apologize for missing it and to accept my punishment. But what would I say to the teacher? That I was tardy because I was assaulted behind the clock tower? Or that I stayed even later because I was making out with Enzo Alfera?

Enzo opened the door to the building. The distress on my face had to be obvious because he seemed to know exactly what I was thinking. "Do you want to tell anyone?"

I shook my head as the image of Brody with his penis out flashed through my head. I winced in disgust. "Would they even believe me? You heard what Brody said. He'll tell everyone I egged him on then changed my mind."

"Nothing wrong with changing your mind. But I understand what you mean. I won't tell anyone. And I'll make sure Ian and Brody keep their mouths shut about it too." He raked a hand through his hair. "But I don't want those assholes in my school. And the only way to get them expelled is to tell Donata and her aunt."

I thought about the implications of Signoria Vittoria finding out. Would she tell Mom and Dad? Dad would be pissed. Not because of the assault. But because the men on Dad's list of suitors might not want to marry me if they found out about it—if they found out my virginity was in question. I wasn't an idiot. I knew those guys were only after one thing. They liked the idea of marrying a virgin. Something I had no doubt Dad had mentioned to them. I knew this because Angelo alluded to it more than once at the brunch.

The creep had asked me if I was being a good girl at school and staying away from boys. No, I couldn't tell my parents about what happened. They would, no doubt, accelerate their plans to marry me off. I needed a little more time to finish school and make a solid plan to bolt as soon as I had a diploma and a full ride to Columbia in hand.

"My parents can't know about this. Please." My eyes watered.

"They won't, I promise." He ushered me inside the building and let the door shut. "But those assholes can't get away with this. Do you trust me?"

I nodded before I fully considered his question. For whatever reason, I did trust him, wholeheartedly.

"Let's call her now." He offered me a kind smile as he fished his phone from the inside pocket of his coat.

To my surprise, he put Donata on speakerphone, so I could hear. I glanced around the empty hallway with my heart beating fast. Telling people made the incident real. When Donata answered, Enzo pulled me into one of the classrooms.

"Donata, I have Aurora with me."

"Shouldn't you be at practice?" Donata laughed.

"I need your help with something. It can't wait."

"Shoot."

"I need Brody, Ian, and Hanna expelled. They're in your house."

"I know that." She clicked her teeth, then let the silence linger. "You want me to talk to my aunt?"

"Yes."

"What did they do?"

Enzo lifted his gaze, silently asking if I was ready. Tears stung my eyes as the same crude scene played in my head. I inhaled and shook my head. Though Donata didn't need things spelled out for her.

"Fuckers." Donata released a breath on the phone and static noise filled the room. "How are you doing, girl?"

"I'm fine."

"Let me talk to her." She paused. "If she needs details, can I call you, Rory?"

"Yes." I stepped toward the phone. I wasn't alone in this after all. Though I had to admit, Donata was the last person I thought would help me. Though, technically, she was helping Enzo because he felt guilty. A part of me wanted to think he was protecting me because he cared.

"She doesn't want her parents to know."

"Why? You don't think they'll get it?" she asked.

"Um." I rubbed my arm. Where would I even begin to explain the shitshow going on at home? Would they even understand? Sure, we lived in a mafia world, but arranged marriages were such an archaic idea, even for mobsters. "No, they wouldn't. We're new. You know?"

"Right. Shocker." She blew out a breath. "Don't worry. Leave it to me."

"Thanks. I owe you one." Enzo braced his hip on the

teacher's desk. "I would've gone to Dad, but you know how it is."

"Yeah, no shocker there. He wants his team to win."

"Exactly. I'll see you tomorrow."

He slowly put his phone back in its place, then removed the bark of chocolate from his pocket. My mouth watered because I knew what was coming. The sweet and spicy treat melting on my tongue was so soothing. I had no idea why. But that was the thing about being around Enzo. His mere presence was comforting to me.

He sat on the table and pulled me between his legs. Before I could protest, he placed the chocolate against my lips. I opened for him and bit into the bark. The cayenne and orange flavors exploded in my mouth. On instinct, I sucked on it harder to make it melt faster.

"That's a good girl." He kissed my cheek.

"Why do you carry chocolate in your pocket?"

"For you." He winked.

I glanced down as I placed my hands on his muscular thighs. The guy was so freaking hot. And sweet. And kind. "I've never tasted anything like it."

"Hmmm." He wrapped his hand around my throat, squeezing ever so slightly. "There's so much you haven't tasted."

His lips brushed mine, and I got lost in his kiss all over again. As soon as I started to melt into him, he pulled away just enough, so our mouths weren't touching anymore. The soft strands of his hair skimmed my temple, and I moved closer. I didn't want him to let me go just yet.

"Let's get you to detention."

"Are they even going to let me in?"

"We'll find out." He gripped my waist and walked me back until he had room to jump off the desk.

The classroom was only a few doors down. We made it there in less than a minute, even though I took half-steps the whole way there because I still couldn't get over the fact that Enzo Alfera was walking me to detention. How did we get here? First, he acted like he didn't know me. Then he hated me. Then he showed me how to kiss. And now, he was doing things only boyfriends would do.

"Here you are." He gestured toward the classroom. When Santino lifted his head to look our way, Enzo placed his hand on my lower back. "Like I said."

"What is it?" I turned to him.

"Nothing. Looks like you'll be in good company." He glared at Santino, who sat back in his chair looking thoroughly satisfied.

I didn't have time to figure out what was going on between them. Now that I was here, I had to talk to Mr. Gallo and smooth things over with him. With an awkward gesture that was half a wave, smile, and a shrug, I said good-bye to Enzo and headed toward the teacher.

"Ah, Ms. Vitali. Good of you to join us." He was annoyed to say the least.

I had Mr. Gallo for Calculus. In class, he always seemed so proper, dressed in his expensive slacks, cashmere sweater, and suit jacket. He was one of the younger teachers, but the students didn't dare cross him. He was imposing and kind of scary. Though he was hot enough that the girls were willing to let go of that fact and flirt with him just the same.

"I'm sorry. I..." I had been so distracted by Enzo that I

didn't even think to come up with a good lie. Telling him the truth was out of the question.

"She was with me." Enzo stepped back in. "I needed her for something."

Hot blood rushed to my face. And just because I'd become a total glutton for punishment, I turned to face the classroom. Every seat was taken, which made sense, given how Mr. Gallo was in charge of detention this semester. The girls glared at me in shock, while Santino simply rolled his eyes. The smug smile he'd had on his face when we trudged in was long gone.

I rubbed my temple and inhaled deeply. Shit.

I believed Enzo when he said he had nothing to do with the incident in the courtyard. So that only left Hanna. I had no doubt she and those guys had come after me because she saw me talking to Santino. But what about Enzo? Did he have a girlfriend I didn't know about? Was she one of the girls scowling at me right now because he stuck up for me?

This was not good.

"It's okay." I put up my hand, hoping Enzo would get the hint that I didn't need his help, especially not in front of everyone.

"Ms. Vitali, why don't you take a seat?" Mr. Gallo motioned toward the only empty seat in the class—right next to Santino and Hanna.

Why?

I ran a hand through my hair. I wanted Enzo to leave, but also, I wanted this whole thing to be over already. With a quick nod, I slowly shifted in the opposite direction and ambled toward Santino. I plopped myself in the chair and scooted down. In my peripheral vision, I could see heads turning in my direction, as if they were waiting for me to do something else.

"I have my money on Gallo, you?" Santino leaned on his desk, facing me.

"What?"

Were we placing bets now?

"Enzo can be persuasive. And Gallo has no leg to stand on these days. But much to my disgust, he's still a teacher." In this light, Santino's eyes had a golden hue to them. He looked handsome, friendly.

"Oh, I don't know."

He stuck out his hand, and I almost jumped out of my seat. "I don't think we've been properly introduced. I'm Santino Buratti."

"I know." I stared at his long fingers. Behind him, Hanna had the biggest pout. "Um. Rory. I'm Rory."

"I know." He raised a brow. "You're the new girl."

I turned my attention to the front of the classroom, where Mr. Gallo and Enzo were deep in conversation. Was Enzo negotiating on my behalf? Why would a teacher listen to him? Because he was the dark prince? The one next in line to be the king of a secret crime society? I supposed that kind of title *would* carry a lot of weight in a school such as this one. Then it hit me. The Gallo family was one of the five original crime families. That meant that when Mr. Gallo attended Midtown High five years ago, he would've also been a royal.

I was so out of my league.

After a few more minutes, Enzo patted Mr. Gallo on his shoulder, then made his way toward me. What now?

"Santino will make sure you get home." Enzo smiled at me then shifted his attention to Santino. "I'm sure you'll have no trouble making arrangements with her driver."

Santino chuckled. "I can do that. But what's going on?"

"I'll tell you later. Right now, I have to deal with the team." Enzo shot a glance toward Hanna. "We're meeting at Donata's place."

Santino leaned forward, rubbing his jaw. "Bring her?"

Her—he meant me.

Enzo met my gaze and studied my face for what felt like hours. My cheeks burned—not just because of Enzo's proximity, but because I was sure this meeting at Donata's place had to do with the Hanna incident, which meant now all the royals knew about what happened. Or they were about to find out. Crap. So much for keeping it a secret.

"No. Just us this time."

No More Than Me

Aurora

By the time Enzo left and everyone went back to working on their assignments, the dismissal bell rang. I had literally only done ten minutes of detention. Since I'd yet to know my punishment for being late, I decided to stay behind and wait until the other students had left before approaching Mr. Gallo. I busied myself with my schedule for the week and all the homework I still had to do.

Santino stayed in his seat. He had agreed to take me home, and now it seemed, he meant to do exactly that. Next to him, Hanna took her time re-arranging her books and neatly putting away the sheet she'd been working on in her folder. It was obvious she didn't want to leave him alone with me.

"Ms. Vitali, can I see you for a moment?" Mr. Gallo's voice boomed in the now empty room.

"Sure." I shot to my feet and ambled over to him. He glanced up from his laptop, and I used the opportunity to make my case. "I'm sorry. I ran into trouble earlier and Enzo was kind enough to help. And, um..."

"Enough." He raised an eyebrow.

Oh, shit. I'd never thought of myself as a coward, but Mr. Gallo was scary. "I'm sorry," I mumbled one more time.

"Enzo explained. Cryptically. But I got the gist of it. However, I can't let you off the hook. You understand?"

I nodded.

"Good. You're in detention all next week. Try to be on time from here on out. Yes?" He did the eyebrow thing again.

"Thank you."

"You may go."

"Thank you." I backed away. By some miracle, I managed not to do a curtsy for him. I spun around and went to grab my things.

Santino and Hanna sat at their desks waiting for me. What did Hanna want? To rub it in? Seeing the two of them together, alone like this, my stupid brain decided to show me a few memories of them. Crap. I squeezed my eyes shut as I pretended to look for something in my backpack. But it only made it worse. The images of Hanna sprawled out on the bed with Santino between her legs was so vivid in my head—and so was Enzo's voice in my ear.

"What did you see, Aurora?"

Wait. Did she know that I saw them?

Rex and Enzo knew for sure. So that meant Santino knew. I was sure they told him about it. If anything, to share a good laugh. Did Santino tell Hanna? When I lifted my gaze, I met hers. She was pissed. So what did that mean? Was she mad about Santino walking me to class, that I spied on them, or that I told Enzo she was involved in the courtyard incident?

"You don't have to escort me home. My driver will be here soon." I showed him my phone.

All I had to do was text the driver and meet him out front. So I really didn't need a chaperone home. It wasn't like my life was in danger. Enzo made sure Brody and Ian understood they couldn't mess with me again.

"Except I do." He shifted his attention to Hanna. "What did you do?"

"I didn't do anything." She furrowed her brows.

"You're hovering. And you have guilt written all over your face." He crossed his arms over his chest. "Did you two get into a fight?"

"It was nothing." I shrugged it off.

"It was a joke." Hanna grabbed her backpack. "Those guys took it too far, so I left."

"What?" Santino slowly rose to his feet.

I shot a glance toward the teacher's desk, but Mr. Gallo had already gone. At least this conversation was private. Jesus, this was the longest day ever. Why were we still on this?

"Describe too far." He narrowed his eyes at her.

"You left me waiting for you after class." She practically spat the words. "Then I ran into you while you were walking her. I was pissed. When I told the boys about her, they said they could teach her a lesson. I thought they were only going to ruffle her feathers a little. You know, make fun of her, something." Her eyes watered.

Was she sorry? Did she not think that those guys meant to hurt me for real?

"Ruffle her feathers? Are you kidding me?" He ran a hand through his hair then turned and asked me. "What happened?"

When I shook my head, Hanna answered for me. "Brody whipped it out. He wanted a blow job."

I decided to leave it at that and not go into the details of how Ian shoved me down to my knees and held me in place so tight, I almost passed out from lack of oxygen. I simply nodded again. And that was enough to make Santino rage.

"You're a fucking bitch."

"I didn't mean it like that. And it's not like she doesn't like to watch." She pointed at me.

Oh, shit. I glanced down, wishing the floor would open up and swallow me whole. Hanna knew. She knew I'd seen her naked with Santino. I opened my mouth to apologize, but what could I say? *Sorry I walked in on you. Sorry I stayed and watched. Sorry I got turned on by it.*

"I didn't see anything."

"Oh please." She crossed her arms under her boobs, which made me look down at them.

She rolled her eyes at me as if saying, *I know a peeping Tom when I see one.*

I wasn't a creep. Enzo put ideas in my head, and now I couldn't shake them.

"Please tell me you didn't tell those guys," Santino said through gritted teeth, rubbing the creases on his forehead. "I only told you about Rory because I thought you should know. You promised you wouldn't say anything."

"And I didn't. I swear. The guys only know you're suddenly into her. Why is that, by the way? We were having so much fun."

"I'm." He cleared his throat, scratching the light stubble on his chin. "That's not the point here. Donata texted. You're in serious trouble. Do you understand what you did?"

"I didn't mean for it to go that far." She turned to me. "I'm sorry. Okay? It was a stupid joke."

"It was cruel." I pursed my lips to keep the tears at bay. I didn't want Hanna to see me cry. "I don't know what they would've done if Enzo hadn't shown up. Two big football players holding me down isn't funny, Hanna. I was terrified."

"Fuck." Santino put his arm around me and brought me in for a hug. "I'm sorry."

Santino was a complete stranger. But his genuine sympathy brought me comfort. Why were they acting like they were my friends? Not that I was complaining. I didn't want to be alone in this. I was willing to take whatever they could give—fake friendship included. Or were they concerned for real? It would be the humane thing to do.

"Thanks." I pushed away from him.

"What happens now?" Hanna asked. "You can't tell my parents."

"I believe it's gonna be worse than that. Enzo is on a war path. And you're on it."

Tears streamed down her cheeks as her features softened. The switch in her demeanor made her look more beautiful, innocent. She clung to Santino's neck, playing the damsel in distress. Or maybe it wasn't pretend. She was truly in trouble. Enzo had asked Donata to get them all expelled.

The three of them were in House Salvatore, which meant Signoria Vittoria was their sponsor. If she wanted to rescind her invitation to their families, they'd no longer be able to attend Midtown High. This went beyond expulsion. Losing the favor of one of the Dons was a huge deal. Penny's family was a prime example of what could happen when a Don turned his back on a family. The Contis were practically castoffs.

Hanna pressed her chest to Santino's. His hands immediately circled her waist. The sobbing was totally working on him. And I had to admit, it was working on me too. She looked desolate—something I understood well. She blinked at him with big, wet eyes. "Talk to him for me. Tell him I'm sorry. Tell him I made a mistake. It was a lame joke. I won't do it again." She pressed her lips to his. "I'll leave her alone."

"Jesus, Hanna." He held her tighter. He really did like her. "I'll see what I can do."

"Thank you." She hugged him then planted a loud kiss on his mouth. "I'll go now. You go do your thing."

He waited until she had left to clear his throat and then turned to me. "Maybe she didn't mean it."

"Yeah. Maybe." I nodded.

"I'm really sorry you got scared."

"No more than me." I hugged my belly.

"Still." He braced his butt on the desk and stretched his long legs out in front of him. "Is there anything I can do to make you feel better?"

I met his gaze. As much as I appreciated Enzo going through all this trouble to help me, I wanted to be an active participant. I wanted a say in what happened to those guys. Maybe I was asking for too much, but suddenly, I felt entitled. Plus, Santino was asking.

"Take me with you."

"I'm sorry, what?"

"Enzo said you were meeting at Donata's house tonight. I'm pretty sure he means to talk to Signoria Vittoria on my behalf. I want to be there and, um..." Flutters coated my stomach. Signoria Vittoria was a force of nature, way more terrifying than two self-entitled football players and a hundred Mr. Gallos. "I'd like to talk to her too."

"Ballsy." He glanced up at me through his long eyelashes. He was truly handsome when he wasn't smirking. "Fine. Get your things."

I had no idea what I had gotten myself into, but this felt like the only viable next step. Revenge never got anyone anything. I knew that. But this wasn't about that. All I wanted was for Signoria Vittoria to make this go away. I wanted a guarantee that Dad wouldn't find out. Because if he thought that his plans to marry me off were in jeopardy, I was sure he'd move everything up, and finish the deed before the end of the month. I needed more time. And I needed a better plan than to wait around until I turned eighteen to make my escape.

I fell in step next to Santino. At this hour, the hallway was completely empty. He had been in a rush to leave before, but now his steps were languid, like he wanted to spend more time with me. Was Hanna right when she'd said he was into me? That couldn't be. He was most definitely into her. When she pressed her body against him, his eyes changed. They looked like they had the day I saw them having sex.

A smile pulled at my lips because I'd seen that same look in Enzo's eyes—in the courtyard and later in the classroom.

"You don't need to be embarrassed." His deep voice startled me out of my reverie.

I had already gone down the usual Enzo rabbit hole of unfulfilled fantasies.

"I didn't do anything wrong. They followed me to the courtyard."

"I don't mean that." He slanted a glance at me with a slight smirk on his lips. "I meant about you watching us. I didn't mind it. It was hot." He winked.

I stopped in my tracks and covered my face with both hands. "You saw me?"

"Hey, no worries at all. I promise." He peeled my hands away. "It's fine."

"You knew I was standing there, and you kept going." My cheeks burned so hot. I thought my skin would melt right off. It was impossible to feel any more embarrassed or mortified.

"Well, I had two options. Stop to shut the door or finish. She was so close. I did what any gentleman would've done in my predicament." He gave me an innocent look.

"Wow. Just wow." I rubbed my temple. "I'm sorry. I didn't see anything."

"I think we're past silly lies, don't you think?"

Yeah, between the peep show, the courtyard, and this favor he was doing for me, we were past pretenses. I saw him and his girlfriend naked and having sex—worse, I saw her come. And then him. Crap. I had to stop thinking about that. Every time I thought of that night, I ended up with the same movie playing in my head—Enzo and I together in a big bed like that. Hadn't I already decided that giving into Enzo was a terrible idea? Sex with Enzo would ruin all my plans to get out from under Dad's thumb. Because how could I get so close and not fall hard for him?

I'd like to think I was smarter than that.

"Okay. You're right." I glanced up then resumed our walk. "Would you ever be able to forget that happened?"

"Not a chance." He chuckled.

I groaned. Then laughed. Santino was funny? I'd seen him in the dining hall with Donata many times, always laughing like they were having a good time. Now I understood why.

By the time we reached the football field, Enzo and Rex were alone. The tension in the air was palpable. Something had happened after he left Mr. Gallo's classroom earlier.

"What's going on?" Santino asked.

Enzo turned in my direction and threw his hands up in the air. "This isn't what we talked about, Santino."

"Nope. But Rory and I had a nice chat. She thinks she should come along. And I agree."

Rex didn't react to Santino's words, which meant Enzo had already told him everything. I hadn't realized how close they were. They told each other everything. They had each other's backs. For a moment, I yearned for a family like that. Mom, Dad, the twins, and I had gone through a lot together. But none of it brought us closer. Instead, I became Dad's pawn. The twins were gone. And I couldn't count on Mom. When we left Las Vegas, she figured she'd suffered enough. She was here only to get what was owed to her. She wasn't wrong. Dad did owe her a better life. But that didn't change the fact that I was alone. Now more than ever.

"He's right, Enzo." Rex stepped toward me.

"What happened?" I asked.

"Enzo told Brody and Ian they were off the team. They didn't take kindly to it." Rex pointed at Enzo's bloody knuckles.

"I'm sorry." I brushed Enzo's upper arm.

"Not your fault." Rex smiled at me—a blinding gesture that left me speechless.

I still couldn't get used to the royals being nice to me. Enzo got into another fight because of me? I wanted to hug him and thank him. But we weren't girlfriend and boyfriend. And I didn't think I should be touching him in front of Rex and Santino.

"You've done enough, Enzo." I attempted a smile, but the most I could do was not frown.

"I'm not done yet." The intensity in his eyes told me this wasn't the time to try and calm him down. "You want to come see Don Salvatore? Let's go." He motioned toward the front entrance of the school.

The Dragon's Lair

Aurora

If anyone had told me that by Friday night, I'd end up in the back of a limo with Santino and Rex flanking me and Enzo watching me like a hawk from across the way, I would've said they were high on bad weed.

"Do you ride a limo everywhere you go?" I asked, mostly to break the awkward silence.

Every time the car hit a pothole on the street, both Santino's and Rex's thighs would brush against mine. Luckily, the ride to Donata's penthouse wasn't that long. Though, the last twenty minutes seemed like an eternity.

"Only when I need the extra room." Enzo smiled at me with a wicked glint in his eyes.

Seriously, I didn't think I was ever going to get used to him looking at me like that—like he wanted me. Which by now, I was sure he totally did. Why else would he bother talking to Signoria Vittoria on my behalf? I smiled at my hands and worked hard to keep my head clear of Enzo fantasies. That would be weird to get all hot and bothered over him with Santino and Rex so close to me.

"Don't be nervous." Santino tapped his knee to mine. "Signoria Vittoria can be a real dragon lady, but she seems to have a soft spot for you."

I laughed because I knew exactly what he meant. The first time I met Signoria Vittoria, I got dragon lady vibes from her. The woman was terrifying—the fact that she pretty much threatened to kill my whole family if I didn't comply with her mafia rules, didn't help matters.

"Here." Enzo leaned forward and grabbed the bottle of champagne from the chiller.

I could only imagine the kind of texts he exchanged with his driver.

Enzo: Hey, need a pickup from school. Bring the champs.

Of course, Enzo would use bigger words and sound way cooler. They all did. As if they'd been specifically groomed to be superior to the rest of us—top-notch education, fast cars, designer clothes. Of course, I had that now too. But to me, it was still all so new. For one, I had never asked my driver to bring booze when he drove me to school.

"Liquid courage." He offered me a glass of champagne.

"Thanks." I took the flute and took a long sip.

The limo finally pulled into a private garage, and I released a breath. I didn't know how much of these guys I could handle. It was like the air was filled with testosterone—as if we were in the wild and they were competing for the only female around. I drank some more from my glass, suppressing a smile. The royals fighting over me? As if. This limo ride was going to my head. I had only one job to do tonight: convince Signoria Vittoria to make my courtyard incident go away. Get those guys and Hanna to keep quiet. And most of all, make sure Dad and the suitors he'd picked for me never found out. They kept Dad busy. And I needed more time. So far, this plan to make a plan was getting me nowhere.

Santino climbed out first and held the door for me. I did my best to scoot over and get out while holding my skirt in place, so I wouldn't flash the guys behind me.

"There she is." Santino greeted the woman waiting for us by the glass doors. He took two long strides then hugged her. "Giuseppina, let me introduce you to Rory." He gestured toward me.

I smiled at the middle-aged woman with the pink cheeks and her hair up in a bun. "Nice to meet you."

"She's Donata's maid," Enzo whispered in my ear. "She guards the dragon's lair."

When I turned to face him, he winked at me.

"What does that make her?" I asked

"A trained assassin." Rex ushered me toward the curb.

"You guys are messing with me." I shook my head, smiling.

"Or are we?" Santino pushed open the door and held it.

"Ms. Donata wants you to use the service door." Giuseppina said with a heavy Italian accent. "Don Salvatore has visitors."

The three of them exchanged a meaningful look, then nodded almost in perfect unison. That was Giuseppina's cue to escort us through a side door that led to another set of elevators that weren't as shiny as the ones in the private lobby. We rode the elevator car in silence all the way to the top floor. Of course, Donata lived in a penthouse in one of the most expensive buildings on Fifth Avenue.

The elevator door opened to a huge kitchen with a marble

island in the middle, done in white with gray cabinets. Giuseppina strolled in and found her place next to the sink, then waited until we were all gathered around the counter. "You wait here."

"Thank you," Enzo called after her.

From across the way, I felt Rex's gaze on me. Something about him unnerved me. He seemed to know what I was thinking. It was creepy. I ignored him and slid my hands across the marble, feeling the cool stone under my touch. He watched me intently for another beat, then walked over to the cupboard. He'd obviously been here before because he knew exactly where to find the first-aid kit.

To my surprise, he brought it to me. "He might let you help him. If I ask, he'll start throwing punches again." He dipped his head toward Enzo's bloody knuckles.

"Oh. Yeah." I nodded and took the plastic container from him. Enzo was bleeding because of me. He had to, at least, let me clean out the cuts. By the time I turned to him, he was already waiting for me to ask. "May I?"

"Fine." He offered me his hand.

I knew some basic first-aid stuff. The twins were always bouncing off the walls. That meant daily cuts and bruises. I rummaged through the box and got some gauze and oxygen peroxide. It was old school stuff, but I knew it would work. With a big smile on his face, Rex tossed me a tea towel. I placed it on the counter and held Enzo's hand over it.

"This part is going to hurt."

"I know." He kept his gaze on mine. "Just do it."

He meant the cleaning solution, but my mind went in a completely different direction. What if we did just do it? We both wanted to. I could see it in his eyes, and the way he stayed close to me. I inhaled when he did. And then we both exhaled. The warm air hovered between us, and an electric charge surged through the air. It would be so easy to fall for him. And so terrible.

"Hmm." Santino cleared his throat behind me.

I snapped out of it and got to work. When I tilted the bottle, Enzo winced, but didn't yank his hand away, like the twins used to do. Out of habit, I held his fingers a little tighter. "Sorry." I added some more hydrogen peroxide and watched the bubbles do their thing.

"Don't be."

"Is it always like this?" I gestured toward Santino and Rex on the other end of the kitchen. "So cloak and dagger?"

"No." Enzo shook his head. "I think Dad's here."

"What makes you say that?" I liked that my brain didn't trip over words around him anymore. After today, talking to Enzo and his friends felt easier.

"Signoria Vittoria doesn't care who visits her niece. If Donata is making us wait in the kitchen, it's because whoever is here could ruin our plans." He pointed at Rex and Santino. "Their parents don't care about what happened today."

"And your dad would?"

"He likes his football team to win. So yeah, he would care that I kicked off two key team players." He shrugged. I opened my mouth to apologize, but he raised his hand to stop me. "We're doing this whether he likes it or not."

"Thank you." The school would feel safer if I didn't have to see those guys again. I glanced up and smiled. "Um, I didn't know Donata lived with her aunt."

"Yeah, since her parents died."

"Oh, I'm so sorry."

"It's been a while." Santino furrowed his brows. "And she's probably better off."

I wanted to ask about Donata and her family, but in the next beat, she barged into the kitchen with the biggest smile that lit up the entire room. I had no reason to think of her as a friend, but her presence here made me feel like we suddenly had a solid plan to finish what Enzo started.

"Hey boys." She sat on one of the barstools, then dipped her head in my direction. When she raised both eyebrows in surprise, I let go of Enzo's hand. She continued, "And new girl. So, Enzo, your dad's here. From the looks of it, it's getting pretty intense. God, that guy never lets up, does he?"

"Nope." Enzo leaned his hip on the counter, facing me.

"I almost told you not to come, but this was too juicy. Never hurts to stay informed. You know?"

"We're here to eavesdrop on the Dons?" Rex braced his forearms on the counter. In this light, his blue eyes looked so bright—a striking contrast to his dark hair and chiseled features. "I thought you had a plan."

"We can't talk to my aunt right now. I figured we might as well listen in." She winked at me. "The adults never tell us anything. This is how we stay informed."

"I can relate to that." I beamed at her.

The twins and I were eight years apart, which meant I grew up as an only child. So any recon missions I did when I was younger, I had to do alone. Spying with the royals was a nice change. The last time I heard my parents fighting, I snuck out of my room in the middle of the night, in my pajamas and fluffy corgi slippers. I tiptoed to their room and sat there for a good half hour, listening to them argue.

Mostly Mom cried while Dad tried to explain how he lost

so much money and how we had to sleep in the car for a night or two until he had enough cash to get a room in a motel.

The bad news was devastating to me because I didn't know if I'd have to switch schools or stop going altogether. But in the end, it had been a blessing that I sat through their conversation because they never thought to tell me what was going on. A whole week went by before Dad announced we had to pack what we could because the house wasn't ours anymore. I'd been ready for it. And even made sure the twins had their stuff together.

I glanced around the kitchen at the friendly faces. Money, in the end, didn't matter. For all their fancy clothes and cars, the royals didn't have it that much different than me. Enzo, for sure, had zero regard for his dad. It was written all over his face every time someone mentioned Don Alfera.

"I'm in." I met Donata's gaze. "I can go over there and check it out."

I pictured myself in my corgi slippers, following Donata down the hallway to eavesdrop on the adults. The image made me smile because I'd never had a partner in crime before.

Donata laughed. "You're so cute."

"What?"

"We're not your regular teenagers here." Santino smirked, shaking his head.

"We're mobsters, love." Rex nodded at Donata. "Is it still there?"

"No. My aunt sweeps the room every day. But I went in there shortly before you arrived and planted a new bug." She fished her phone from the back pocket of her jeans. "Pina." She called over her shoulder. When Giuseppina rushed in, Donata swiveled around in her seat. "You're on watch duty.

This time, signal the minute they end the meeting and not after they walk out of the library. Last time we were almost caught."

"Of course. I apologize."

"Don't apologize. Go keep watch." Donata gestured toward the door.

As soon as Giuseppina left, Donata tapped on app on her phone. "Here we go. You're gonna have to get closer."

I stepped toward Donata and stopped the minute her perfume filled the air. To my right, Enzo did the same. For a second, we did this subtle dance where he leaned in, then I leaned back. Back and forth, inch by inch, until our bodies were touching. His body heat made my stomach flutter.

"I think it's still connecting." Santino tapped on the screen.

Static filled the room. But nothing came through. Donata gripped her phone and turned up the volume. Then a loud clap, like a hand slamming on a table came loud and clear.

"Oh shit." She lowered the volume.

The intensity in the other room dripped through the speakerphone and crept around us like smog. Don Alfera spoke first, which led me to believe he had been the one to hit the table. I could only guess it was him because he wasn't getting his way. Why did Mom think he was such a good guy? Because he gave us all this money, and a position within his social circle?

"We've known each other for a long time, Vittoria. You should know by now that I don't give a fuck if people live or die. What I need is more important. The longevity of the Society is at stake here. It must be done."

Donata peeked up from her screen. "Like I said, the man never lets up."

I thought Dad was bad. Don Alfera took the cake. Did I hear that right? He wanted someone killed. Or maybe someone had to do something dangerous for him.

"They're children, Michael." Signoria Vittoria's smoker voice boomed in my chest. "Have you thought about what their mother, your wife, will say?"

"She's the reason I'm doing this. She will never find out."

"What about Rex? Does he get a say in this? Kill a mobster. I don't care. But we should draw the line at innocent children. I get that you crossed that line a long time ago. But your choices have nothing to do with mine. I won't go there."

"That's where you're wrong, Vittoria. I'm still your king. And you will do as I say."

"I don't care what Vittoria says. I'm keeping the girl."

Shit. That sounded like Angelo Soprano. The guy Dad had made me have dinner with twice after I met him at the charity brunch.

"That's Don Salvatore to you." Signoria Vittoria raised her voice. "Why is he even here?"

"He was your idea. Someone must take out the trash." Don Alfera let out a breath. It created static on the phone and that made all of us look up. Was he close to the device Donata had planted in her aunt's library?

"Oh crap." Donata covered her mouth, then grabbed the phone and shut it off.

We all stood around the counter. After Donata turned off the angry voices, the kitchen seemed eerily quiet. I exhaled and the words came out of my mouth before I realized I was talking. "It's never good news, is it?"

Revenge is a Dish Best Served Cold

Enzo

"Well, it was nice to see you, Rory." Donata put her arm around Aurora and ushered her to the service door. "My driver is downstairs. He'll take you home."

"What? No. I haven't talked to Signoria Vittoria." Aurora sidestepped Donata to look at me.

Aurora wasn't here because I decided to bring her. She was here because Donata thought it would be a good idea. After hearing that asshole Angelo on the speakerphone talk about Aurora like she was some sort of an Arabian horse, I had a pretty good idea as to why Donata wanted Aurora here.

Before, when we made the bet, we had all agreed not to tell Aurora about the arranged marriage to Angelo. Of course, the minute Donata saw me making progress with Aurora, she decided it was time to let her in on that dirty little secret. What did she think Aurora would do when she found she was engaged to some old dude? Did Donata think Aurora would lock herself in her room and save her v-card for him? That she would stop seeing me?

The last thought sent a cold shiver down my spine. Whatever this thing with Aurora was—I didn't want it to stop. That was exactly what Donata was going for. As part of the bet, she had said she would do everything in her power to keep Aurora from me—from us.

Fuck Donata and her epic bet.

I'd never liked Donata's games. Though tonight, I had to admit, her scheming brought me some valuable information. Dad was planning something. Something bad. Something big enough to get Signoria Vittoria to play his bitch. I didn't think that would be possible. She was a queen in our world. In her own way, she always found a way to get what she wanted. I hadn't been around the Society and its board members a long time. But I'd seen enough to know that much. Signoria Vittoria bowed to no one. But tonight, she let Dad play his king card with her.

Why?

Whatever it was. It involved Aurora's fiancé and me—well, my siblings and me. I understood Massimo would be a valuable asset when the time came. But what could my little sister Caterina possibly do? She couldn't become Don. That spot was my birthright. Nothing could take that away from me. Unless, of course, I was dead.

But even Dad wouldn't attempt something like that. Would he? What line had he already crossed? What was so terrible that even Signoria Vittoria didn't want to get near it?

"This is Society business, Aurora. You can't be here." Donata blocked Aurora's path back to me. "When I saw Angelo, I thought the conversation would be about something else. Not this. I mean." She turned around to face me. "Did your dad just put a hit on someone?"

"What did you think our parents did for a living?" Rex raised an eyebrow. "Play with kittens all day?"

"No." She rolled her eyes. "This felt different. I didn't know there was a line my aunt wasn't willing to cross. I mean, we can all agree that's bad, like really bad. Right?"

"Wait? What did you mean by that?" Aurora stepped back into the kitchen, meeting my gaze then Donata's. "What does Angelo have to do with me?"

I glared at Donata. I had no idea what Aurora's reaction to the marriage contract was going to be, but it couldn't be good. And I was sure that whatever she decided about it, it would not include me. She was a good daughter. She would want to do whatever her parents asked. Fuck.

"You're right. She should go home." I nodded to Donata.

"Well, not so fast." Donata beamed at me. "I had hoped she'd found out the truth tonight. It didn't exactly work out. But there's no reason why we can't tell her. She deserves to know."

"Well, not all of it." Santino raised his eyebrows and gave us a meaningful look.

Fucker. He wasn't ready for the bet to end either. A knot in my stomach churned. By now, I knew what it was. I knew it had a name—jealousy. I didn't want anyone touching Aurora.

I turned to Donata. The look on her face said it all. This was part of her game. Get us to go at each other. And then, let Aurora have the last word.

"Don't." I pursed my lips, glaring at her.

"Tell me." Aurora reached for her arm. "What did you want me to hear?"

"My aunt has become very protective of you. Earlier, when Don Alfera and Angelo showed up, I thought they were here to get her permission. So to speak."

"Permission for what?" Aurora let out a small nervous chuckle. Did she know?

"For your betrothal." The smile on Donata's face was one of pure satisfaction...and evil.

"My what?"

"Your engagement."

"Betrothal sounds so archaic." Rex leaned back on the sink counter, crossing his arms over his chest. He was loving this. He always did love her games.

"Which is what this is." Donata winked at him, then switched her attention to Aurora. "Your dad signed a marriage contract with Angelo." Aurora's features remained frozen, which wasn't what Donata had hoped. She wanted big drama and fat tears from Aurora. But she wasn't getting it. After another beat, she added, "He wants you to marry Angelo. Like super soon."

Rex's laugh boomed in my chest—like something drumming hard and fast, waiting to get out. He pushed away from the counter and braced his hands on the marble in front of him, facing Aurora. "She already knew."

"What a good girl." Santino tittered. "You're really cool with that?"

I thought of our time in the courtyard earlier. When our kiss almost turned into something else. She wanted me. More specifically, she wanted sex with me, but something was stopping her. If she wanted to take things slow, I was happy to wait for her. But all this time, she had been saving herself for some guy her dad picked for her. In my head, I saw her kissing him. I saw them touching. And then I saw red.

I glowered at her. And focused on her features before my thoughts went down a path I didn't understand.

"So much for your dramatic reveal." I smirked at Donata before I glared at Aurora. "I wished I'd known your v-card was up for sale."

"It isn't like that." Her eyes watered as she hugged her belly. "And I don't expect any of you to understand."

She seemed so lost when she did that.

"You're really doing this, huh?" Donata touched her shoulder. "I did some digging on Angelo. He's a pompous ass. But as far as choices go, he's a decent one."

"Donata, just fucking stop." I couldn't stand the thought of those two together.

Why was she talking about this as if it were some sort of inevitability? It wasn't. Aurora had a choice in this.

"Why? She has to deal with it. It's not like she's your girlfriend. You stop." She furrowed her brows at me.

"Enough." Rex put up his hands.

"Well, this puts a wrench in a lot of things." Santino plopped himself on the barstool. He was still thinking about the bet.

So was I. Was I ready to give up on her? Did I want to make her change her mind and choose me instead? Yeah, I so fucking did. To hell with her dad and Angelo.

"Nothing has changed," I muttered.

"That's the spirit." Donata smiled at me, placing her arm around Aurora. "How about some tea?"

The door burst open, and Giuseppina barged in. She panted a breath then spoke. "The meeting is over."

"We know. Omigod. Why is this so hard?" She glanced up then froze. "Crap," she mumbled.

"Yes, the meeting is over." Signoria Vittoria strolled into the kitchen. "Pina, where is my tea?"

"Right away, ma'am." Giuseppina busied herself with a kettle, filling it with water before she placed it on the stove.

For someone who had just had a tete-a-tete with the king of a century-old enclave, Signoria Vittoria didn't seem perturbed at all. Dad could be an asshole most of the time. But he was right about one thing: I had so much to learn before I could begin to consider the idea of filling his shoes as king. Signoria Vittoria would be a much better choice.

"To what do I owe this pleasure? A study group? I hope." She offered Aurora a kind smile.

"She wanted to talk to you." Donata placed both her hands on Aurora's shoulders and ushered her toward Signoria Vittoria.

Giuseppina placed a saucer and a cup in front of Signoria Vittoria. When she lingered for another beat, Donata rolled her eyes then gestured toward the door. "You may eavesdrop behind the door."

"My apologies." Giuseppina placed a napkin on the counter then left.

"Don't encourage her." Signoria Vittoria steeped a bag of tea in the hot water, then glanced up at Aurora. "You have four minutes. Talk fast."

Aurora opened her mouth, but no words came out. For all her bravado when she asked us to bring her here, she couldn't talk about what had happened with Brody and Ian. It was too soon. Tears brimmed her eyes, then she shook her head. "I didn't ask them to meet me there."

Signoria Vittoria's gaze darted from Donata, to Rex, to Santino, and then to me. She released a breath and waited. I had a feeling she knew what Aurora would say next.

"She means Brody and Ian." Donata gripped the back of the barstool.

"The Thomas boy?"

"That's the one."

"What did he do?" Signoria Vittoria asked Aurora.

"He whipped it out. Tried to her get her to suck him off." Santino gestured toward Aurora, who only nodded.

Signoria Vittoria slow-blinked. I couldn't tell if it was because of Santino's blunt words or Brody's fucked-up behavior. "I see. And you're here, why?"

"I want them off the team," I added. "I want them expelled."

She glanced down at my hands. "A beating wasn't revenge enough for you?"

"Not even close." I stepped closer to her. "You're their sponsor. You can rescind your invitation."

She exhaled loudly, dipping the tea bag in the hot water several times. "Revenge is a dish best served cold, dear one." She studied Aurora's sad face. "Unfortunately, my hands are tied."

"What?" Donata's voice went up a few octaves. "Are you serious? You're the dragon lady."

"Excuse me?"

"That's what they call you." She shrugged.

"What happened was horrific. I understand. Believe me when I say that. But right now, the Society is going through a pivotal moment." She shook her head as if considering something. "The Thomases are an integral part of it. I need them on my side."

"Politics. That's your excuse?" Donata glared at her aunt.

"We're all about to get everything we ever wanted. I can't do what you ask. Not right now."

"I don't want revenge." Aurora's voice cracked. She swallowed then continued, "I just want to make sure no one finds out. Especially not my parents."

Her reasons for it now made sense to me. If her dad found about what Brody did, no doubt he would assume things went farther than they did. And so would Angelo. If all he wanted was a virgin wife, would he want her if he thought she had sex with those guys? Would he want her if everyone knew about it? An asshole like that—my guess would be no.

I shouldn't care that she wanted this contract. But I did. Aurora didn't want her reputation tarnished because she wanted to marry Angelo Soprano. I fisted my hands and stuffed them in the pockets of my trousers. Why did that make me want to punch a wall?

Donata gripped my arm, then slipped her hand around the nook of my elbow. Her touch stopped the avalanche of images invading my mind. I glanced at her, and she mouthed, *Calm down.*

"I agree with you on that." Signoria Vittoria sipped from her tea. "I can help you there. I'll speak with Amanda. She will ensure her son does the right thing. And his friend."

"I can handle Hanna," Santino added.

"That's all I wanted." Aurora offered both Signoria Vittoria and Santino a meek smile. "Thank you."

I hated that I couldn't do this for her. That now, she'd have to return to school on Monday and see those assholes. She'd have to cheer for them during games. All because the adults had bigger fish to fry.

"Go home, Aurora. Your family needs you." Signora Vittoria picked up her napkin and teacup and walked out.

Donata released a breath, running both hands through her hair. "I'm sorry, Rory. That's all you get."

"It's fine. That is enough. Thank you."

"Stop saying that word. No one here has done anything for you. Trust me on that." She cocked an eyebrow. "Enough about Brody and Ian, what are we going to do about this pivotal moment my aunt was talking about?"

"What do you mean?" Aurora asked.

"Was I the only one paying attention?" She put up a finger. "One, there's a mobster with a target on his or her back." She lifted another finger. "Two, it involves you and your fiancé. And three?" She gripped my shoulder. "The great Don Alfera, your dad, is planning something with Massimo, Caterina, and you."

"Forget revenge." The furrows between Rex's brows deepened. He loved a good puzzle. "I want to know what they're up to."

"I want to know what they want." Santino walked around the counter and put his arm around Aurora. "Maybe Vittoria is right. Revenge is a dish best served cold."

"New game." Donata brought her hands together. Her unruly blond ponytail, the uniform skirt and sweater tied around her waist made her look like a teenage rebel without a cause. Though I'd seen enough of Donata to know that she always had a cause. "Let's find out what they're up to."

"What was the old game?" Aurora squinted at Donata.

"Don't worry about it." She beamed at her. "If you help us,

maybe we can figure out a way to get rid of your Angelo problem."

"How could I possibly help you?" Aurora met Rex's gaze and then Santino's.

For the last ten minutes, she'd gone back to avoiding eye contact with me. Maybe she could sense how pissed off I was. And I was. But this was different. Whatever was going on with the Society, it involved all of us.

"Obviously, Angelo has a thing for you, like a real thing for you. Contract aside." Donata brushed a strand of hair away from Aurora's face. "You can be our spy."

"Oh fuck no." I'd no reason to object to this plan, other than I didn't like the idea of Aurora using her charms to get information out of Angelo. Because I had no doubt that was exactly the help Donata wanted from Aurora.

"Why not?" She shrugged, giving me an innocent look that I didn't buy for a second. "She has access to him. And we don't."

"Is my family safe?" Aurora asked.

"I don't think so, Angel," I answered honestly.

The Wet T-Shirt Contest

Aurora

The next day, I sat at the breakfast table eating my Greek yogurt while Mom and Dad ate in silence too. Was Enzo right in thinking my entire family was in danger? Why? Because of the marriage contract with Angelo? What did Dad get us into this time? This whole situation was starting to feel too much like that time in Las Vegas, when Dad made one bad deal after another until we had nothing left and Mom had to basically prostitute herself to save his ass.

Of course now, it wouldn't have to be Mom. It would be me. The worst part was, Angelo wasn't asking for a quickie in a motel. He wanted marriage, as in forever. Though that still didn't add up to me. Why would someone like Angelo want to tether himself to someone like me? I was ten years younger than him.

"I have a school thing later this morning." I sipped some of my coffee.

"That's sounds like fun." Mom beamed at me. "I'm going shopping with Signoria Vittoria today. We're really becoming fast friends."

"What school thing?" Dad rumbled.

"It's a literacy fundraiser." I cleared my throat. "We're washing cars to raise funds to buy books for two local libraries. All the cheerleaders are doing it. I get to find out if I made the team today too."

"You think I'm an idiot?" Dad glared at me. "We had those 'fundraisers' when we were in high school too." He pointed at Mom then himself. "It's just an excuse to see the girls."

I was grateful that Dad chose not to finish his thought. But I knew what he meant. Santino told me he was very much looking forward to this one segment of the cheer tryouts. The wet T-shirt contest was what he'd called it. Even when Donata insisted it was a fundraiser.

"It isn't like that, Dad. Midtown High isn't your high school."

"She's right." Mom placed her palm on his forearm. "These are classy people."

"I want her to remember that she's not like those girls. She has value."

I did my best not to roll my eyes. By value, he meant my V-card. He was assuming I was the only virgin in school. I took a big gulp of coffee and mentally crossed off months on the calendar. Soon, I wouldn't have to hear his nonsense.

"He means the marriage, Rory. When we find you a nice boy, you'll see we're doing this for you. You'll have a future with a beautiful home like this one and a driver." She gave me the biggest grin.

Mom truly believed this was for my own good. What if I told them that Angelo was plotting something evil with Don Alfera, something that had to do with us. Would they believe me?

"I met so many men, Mom. I'm not sure which one Dad likes best." I shifted my gaze to Dad, doing my best to appear clueless.

"As soon as I make a decision, we'll talk." He forked a lump of eggs and stuffed it in his mouth.

"I need to go get ready."

"Of course, honey. Go on. I can drop you off on my way to meet Signoria Vittoria."

"Yeah, sure." I got up and strode back to my room.

When was Dad planning to tell me about Angelo? Or was Donata wrong about that? I shook my hands to forget about marriage and evil plans. I needed to get ready. Donata wanted all the girls in a white T-shirt and shorts. As much as she told Santino this was a fundraiser, she also knew this was the best way to make the most money.

I donned a pair of jean shorts, a top, and slid my feet into a pair of designer flip flops. I laughed as I looked at my pedicured feet and thought about what Mom had said earlier. "These are classy people." How clueless could she be? Or maybe she was pretending, the same way I was.

I tinkered with my makeup for a few minutes, then headed downstairs. The fundraiser wouldn't start for another hour, but I wanted to get there early and maybe help with the setup and earn more brownie points with the judges. The judges being the royals. I would need all the help I could get with Rex, Santino, and Donata. Enzo was a lost cause. After our talk at

Donata's place yesterday, he went back to hating me. I'd hoped he'd give me a ride home at the end of the night. But he didn't offer. I left alone, feeling, as always, dazed and confused.

"Rory, look who stopped by." Mom chimed from the bottom of the stairs.

Oh, just freaking great.

"Hello, Mr. Soprano." I liked that he cringed every time I called him that.

He didn't do that though. Instead, his gaze swept up and down my body, then up to my boobs. Yeah, super classy.

"Angelo says he can give you a ride. Isn't that nice?" Mom patted his shoulder as if he were some hero.

What did she think? That if she treated him like he was much younger than her, the marriage contract wouldn't be so creepy?

"My car needs washing. It's a win, win."

"I'm running late. I have to go now."

"I was just leaving too." He gestured toward the door.

I glanced around the apartment, but Dad was nowhere to be found. He always let Mom do the dirty work for him. But I supposed a quick ride to school couldn't hurt. Though I hated the idea of being alone in a car with Angelo.

"Okay. Thanks."

Angelo placed his hand on my lower back and ushered me out of the house. This part was awkward for me since I met him—the way he acted like he owned me. Now I understood why. He thought he owned me because he did. I let it go this time because getting to the car wash was more important today. Not just because I wanted to see Enzo again, but because I wanted to know if I had made the team.

We stepped out onto the curb and a limo pulled up. Really? I rolled my eyes as his driver swung the door open. I climbed in quickly and sat on the bench below the window. I dropped my backpack on my left side, and then set my water bottle on my right, leaving him no choice but to sit across from me. My chest hurt when I realized that if he wanted to, he could whip out his cock right now and make me suck him off. No one, not even Dad, would bat an eye.

He was a decent choice as Donata had put it.

"I didn't know you were a cheerleader." His gaze lingered on my legs.

"Yeah. It's fun." I pressed my lips together and smiled.

The next fifteen minutes, I kept my attention on the road while he ogled me from his seat. He didn't try polite conversation like before. Maybe he had finally gotten tired of my yes-no answers.

When we pulled up to the front of the school, I made to get up, but he reached over and grabbed my wrist. "I want you to wash my car."

"Yeah, okay. That's why I'm here."

"Just you though."

"You'll have to talk to Donata about that. She's in charge."

The driver opened the door. I grabbed my things and bolted. My lungs filled up with air as soon as my feet hit the sidewalk. I hadn't realized how stifling the limo had been. I couldn't let Angelo's surprise visit ruin this day though. I missed cheerleading and being part of a team. If all went well today, I was getting that part of my life back.

Donata had really gone all out with the event. The entire front courtyard was set up as a fancy car wash with white tents and snack stations for our patrons. On the right, the first tent was the rinse station with water buckets and a hose that ran all the way back to Adeline Hall. The next tent had sponges and containers full of cleaning solutions. At the far end, the final tent had a table with cloths for drying off cars and vacuums hooked up to a super loud generator.

"Oh good. You made it." Donata greeted me, while she checked her clipboard. "You're in tent two."

"Thanks." I nodded.

"Try to stay dry." She winked.

Summer days were long gone. But even though there was a chill in the air, the bright sun made it comfortable to be in short shorts. Still, I had a feeling getting wet in this weather would not be fun. I followed the driveway into the school until I found a bigger tent meant for only the royals. Enzo sat on one of the tables with his feet on the chair. Suddenly, I felt warmer inside. We had been apart for all of sixteen hours, and I missed him. I had missed him since the minute I left Donata's building.

As if he could feel me staring, he lifted his head. Adrenaline rushed through me while he held my gaze. He was still angry at me. I had no idea why. But we were here now. I had all day to find out.

"Hey." Hanna bumped my shoulder with hers, then smiled.

"Hi."

"Looks like we'll have a good haul today. Look at all those cars waiting." She pointed outside the gates.

"Yeah. It'll be a good one." I stuffed my hands in the pockets of my shorts.

I got that she was sorry and wanted to make friends now. But I wasn't ready to let go. I hadn't even had time to process everything that happened yesterday.

"Oh wait. Everyone, make room, Your Highness has arrived." Brody shoved people off the lawn and onto the asphalt, pretending to make way for me.

"Grow up." Hanna pulled me to her side. "And do as you're told."

Brody glared at me, gritting his teeth. His lip trembled with rage, and he swallowed as if the words he wanted to say to me were stuck in his vocal cords—held there by some magical force. There was no magic here. Signoria Vittoria was the reason he couldn't say anything to me—anything related to the incident in the courtyard anyway.

The gag order was enough for me. At least I could still show my face at school and not have to deal with Brody's lies. I had no doubt that if Signoria Vittoria hadn't done her thing, he would be telling everyone that I lured him to the clock tower and gave him a bad blow job—or something to that effect, something nasty to make me feel small.

When rumors about Mom spread through my old high school in Las Vegas, I had to deal with the same thing. The girls and their moms called me a cheap whore, while the boys cornered me in the hallways to offer me money to sleep with them. I blew out a breath, trying to chase the memories. That time was over. I repeated those words in my head.

I lifted my gaze and met Enzo's across the lawn. His scowl was back. Though, this time, it was directed at Brody. Brody fisted his hands, looking at me then Enzo, while he decided if this fight was worth the consequences. After a beat, he leaned in and whispered, "You're not worth it."

"I think that was the worst of it." Hanna watched Brody storm off toward the school entrance.

"I hope so."

"It's starting." Hanna pulled on my sleeve, beaming at Santino, who had come out of the judge's tent.

"Morning, ladies." He addressed the girls who had gathered around him.

The whole team had shown up to participate in the last round of cheer tryouts. Out of the thirty girls remaining, only fifteen would be chosen. I had no idea how they were judging this final round, since we were just washing cars. The task required zero cheer skills.

"Welcome to this year's wet T-shirt contest." Santino beamed. When Donata hit him on the arm with her clipboard, he corrected, "Sorry. We're not calling it that anymore. Welcome to this year's Literacy Fundraiser. The more money we collect today, the more books we'll be able to donate to a local library of your choice. So, start scrubbing. Have fun. And don't be afraid to get wet." He gestured toward the school gates.

The huge wrought iron doors kicked into gear and slowly opened to the cars lined up outside. First in line was Angelo's limo. It rolled into the half-moon driveway and stopped in front of the first tent that was set up as the rinse station. Then it moved on to mine for scrubbing.

Angelo ogled me from the other side of the driveway while I grabbed a bucket and a sponge to start washing his car. I did my best to get suds all over, making sure there were no smudges left anywhere. The limo wasn't even that dirty. I would bet Dad called him this morning after breakfast to get him to join me at the school.

A part of me, the naive part, wanted to believe Mom had asked Dad to wait until I was eighteen to tell me about the marriage contract. She was sweet for wanting to give me time to get to know Angelo and maybe fall in love with him. But that only proved my parents didn't know me at all. Spending time with Angelo only showed me how big of a creep he was.

"Hey, Rory," Hanna called from her station. "You missed a spot."

When I faced her, she sprayed me with the water hose. She started on my chest, then moved up when I shifted away from her. Great, just great. If I thought Angelo was staring before, now he looked like he was ready to jump me. Something that, for whatever reason, made Enzo's face turn bright red. If looks could kill...

I shot a glare at Hanna, but she and the other girls had already moved on to their next victim. Their laughs were contagious, and I was reminded that this was the whole purpose of this event. The royals wanted to have fun. Shaking my head, I chuckled as I peeled the wet fabric off my boobs.

"Rory." Donata called from behind me, keeping her distance so she wouldn't get wet. "I need to see you in the judges' tent?"

"I'm not finished." I had only done one side of the limo.

"Hanna can take over." She gestured toward the other tent where Hanna and her friends were still chasing each other with the water hose. "We need to talk."

Yesterday, after our talk with Signoria Vittoria, we didn't have time to discuss her plan to figure out what Don Alfera was up to. I should've known she'd use this time to hash out the details and give me my first assignment. I wasn't a spy. Just thinking about getting closer to Angelo made my skin crawl.

I couldn't do this for her, but then it wasn't just about the royals. Whatever Don Alfera was planning, it involved my family too. When I glanced at Angelo, he was a few feet away, openly staring at my chest. No way in hell Donata's plan could work.

Love and Duty Don't Mix

Aurora

The minute I stepped into the judges' tent, Enzo left through the back access. A hint of his scent lingered in the air, and I walked straight into it. With my heart beating fast, I stayed there until I realized that whatever I thought I could smell wasn't real.

To my right, Donata blew out a breath. "I need him here. Where did he go?"

"Sorry." I shrugged. It wasn't like I had the power to make Enzo stay.

"Here. Change out of those wet clothes." She tossed me a jersey.

When I pulled it up in front of me, my belly did a somersault. It was a top with the school crest and a cheer squad emblem on it. "Does this mean I'm in?"

"You're in. Congratulations." She waved a hand in dismissal and crossed off a few things on her clipboard. "Santino, help me get Enzo back."

"Do we have to do this now?" he asked while he kept his attention on Hanna. "This is supposed to be for fun, not work."

"We can do both." Donata turned to Rex for support.

He slow-blinked and ambled over to Santino. "She's trouble. You know that, right?"

"Trouble can be fun." Santino smirked at him, stepped off the curb, and headed straight for Hanna.

When he reached Hanna, he gripped her waist from behind and whispered something in her ear. She glanced up toward the sky and mouthed something before she spun to throw her arms around his neck. So what if he wanted to hang out with her?

"Is there like a rule where royals can't date commoners?" I winced because I hadn't meant to say that aloud.

"Royals?" Rex raised both eyebrows, but somehow still managed to look down on me. "People throw that word around so much; they forget what it really means."

I knew what it meant—they ran the school because their families were rich and direct descendants of the five original crime families that founded the Society and this school. I was still fairly new to their world, but the idea of royals had already become part of my vocabulary and way of life.

"What does it mean?"

"One day the weight of the world will fall on our shoulders." His intense blue gaze met mine as he cocked his head to the side. "There are no rules here, Rory. Only survival instincts." He pointed at Santino and Hanna. "Love can get you killed."

They had left the car wash and were headed straight for the clock tower. By the way they looked at each other, I could only assume they were going there to make out. Was that Santino and Hanna's secret place? If it was, no wonder she lost it when she saw me going there. Gosh, did she think I had gone there to meet with Santino?

I glanced over my shoulder, scanning the tent for Enzo, but he hadn't returned yet. Last Friday, he had asked me to meet him in the courtyard. Was the courtyard a hookup place for him too? I bit my bottom lip to suppress a smile. Only a few days ago, Enzo had invited me to meet him there. He wanted to be with me. I wished there was something I could say to make his broody mood go away.

"She's not so bad," I said, when Rex clicked his teeth.

I had to wonder if the only reason why I was defending Hanna was because we were in similar situations. She wasn't a good match for a future don. And neither was I. How did I get here? Just a few days ago, I was strong in my resolve to stay away from Enzo and keep my focus on getting out of dodge as soon as school was over. I touched my fingers to my lips. Now all I could think about was how I wanted to kiss Enzo again. How I wanted those kisses to mean something to him—because they meant something to me.

I still wanted to leave town. That hadn't changed. My marriage to Angelo was still a real threat. The only way to avoid becoming his wife was to disappear. Thing was, I also had this intense, soul-gripping feeling in my chest that screamed why couldn't I have Enzo instead?

"You saw what she did to you because she didn't like you hanging around Santino."

"She said she was sorry."

He crossed his arms over his chest in a way that made him

look so regal and so above all this high school stuff. "Tell me. Did she apologize before or after she found out she was in trouble?"

I rolled my eyes. Did anyone ever win an argument with Rex? I seriously doubted it. "I get your point."

"Do you?" He studied my profile. Rex had a way with words that made my head spin. He was all riddles and puzzles. "You think you know Enzo, but you don't. You don't understand who or what he is. It's better this way."

"What?" My head snapped up at him. "Do you know why he's mad at me? Why he left as soon as I came in?"

"Solid effort, Rex." Donata walked up and planted a kiss on his cheek. "And here I thought your heart wasn't in it. How did you get Enzo to back down?"

"Back down from what?" I asked, but she ignored me.

"This is more than a game, Donata. I'm trying to help her." He pointed at me.

"Of course you are." She smiled at him, then me. For some reason, this entire conversation made her happy. "Rex doesn't believe in love."

"We have a duty to fulfill. Love and duty don't mix well." He inched toward me. It was such a subtle, innocent movement that it didn't even occur to me to back away from him. "Enzo will be king one day. And you'll just be in the way. I'm sorry it's more bad news for you." He reached for a strand of my hair and placed it behind my ear.

The genuine gesture made me think he felt truly sorry for me—sorry I had developed feelings for a future king, sorry I was a nobody in their mafia world, sorry Enzo could never love me back.

"Ease up, Rex. We have plenty of time before any of that happens." Donata put her arm around me. "Santino is right. Trouble can be fun."

"I'm going to get changed." I showed them my new jersey and headed toward the back of the tent.

I slapped the flap out of the way and stepped outside. A part of me had expected to see Enzo standing there, waiting for me. But the small alley between the tents was empty. Just as well, I didn't need another sermon from Rex about duty and survival instincts. That part was very clear to me. Life had dictated very different paths for Enzo and me. There was no 'us' here. I had to get that through my head—just like Enzo had.

At this point, I was sure Rex had had the same conversation with Enzo last night and convinced him to back off, to not see me again. I furrowed my brows as I peeled the cold, wet T-shirt off me. What plans did Enzo have for after graduation? I realized I had no idea what the future dons of a secret society were expected to do after high school. The way Rex put it, it sounded intense—like they were about to become monks or something.

The idea made me smile. Santino a monk? Enzo? I thought of the way he kissed me with so much passion and so much need.

"You seem pleased with yourself." Enzo appeared in my line of sight.

His deep voice startled me, and I dropped both my tops to the ground. When I bent down to pick up the dry one, he did the same. He was faster than me, so he got to it first. A cold breeze brushed my back, while the blast of his body heat hit my front and almost knocked me back on my butt.

He reached for my elbow and steadied me with his free hand. "Pay attention." His gaze swept down my body. I felt it settle on my taut nipples pushing through the silky fabric of my bra. Blood thrashed in my ears, while my heart threatened to crush my ribs. An angry sound, something like a growl and a hiss escaped him. "I can see why Angelo is out there making a fool of himself for you. You are so beautiful."

Was that desire in his eyes? Enzo's words from yesterday flooded my mind instantly.

"I can make you feel so good."

"If you let me."

Problem was, the burn in my chest had now moved to my core and the rest of me. And all I could think about was that Enzo was the only one who could put that fire out. He was the only one I wanted.

"I'm not a klutz. You scared me." I made the mistake of looking straight into his sad eyes. "Why are you mad at me?"

"I'm not." He shrugged and pulled me toward him until my cold skin rested on his soft tee. "I saw you come in with him."

"Is that what this is about? Angelo?"

Shaking his head, he blew out a breath and slid his palm up my chest then wrapped it around my neck. Suddenly, his hand was the only thing supporting me. My eyes fluttered closed. I didn't care that I was standing topless in front of Enzo. Or that we were at school with thirty cheerleaders and a bunch of football players just on the other side of the tent, meaning anyone could come in and see us.

"Such a good girl, aren't you? Saving yourself for him. Because Daddy asked you to."

"I'm not." I gripped his wrist when he tightened his hold on me. "I don't want him."

"There you go again." He surveyed my face. "Messing with my head. Every time you look at me, I can't think."

We stayed like that for a whole minute. And just when I thought he was going to push me away from him, his mouth crashed into mine. He put pressure on my jaw, and I opened for him, letting his tongue explore for a few beats before I attempted to kiss him back. His fingers on my jawline dug into me, commanding me to stop. This was his kiss. He was kissing me, and I wasn't allowed to participate. It was punishment—to have him so close, in my mouth, and not be able to feel him, taste him like I wanted.

My nipples ached from wanting relief. The more he deepened the connection, the more my skin heated with need. But his hand on my throat was all he allowed. He took without giving back.

"You should get dressed before someone sees you," he whispered against my lips. "Angelo was about to blow his load when he saw you all wet. What would he do if he saw you now? God knows, I have a few ideas."

I made to shake my head, but his hold on me was too tight. And I was afraid that if I moved, he might let me go. Slowly, I released his wrist and slid my hands down to his hard stomach. Just as I'd feared, he let go of me with a grimace, as if my touch was repulsive.

With a shaky breath, I took the top he offered and slipped it over my head. Why did I think that talking to Enzo today would resolve anything? I couldn't blame him. If he told me he was engaged to someone else, I'd be furious too. But how could I explain to him that I was just pretending to buy some time with my dad. I wasn't a doting daughter like he made me out to be. I was selfish. I was doing this to save myself.

He stood there with his chest rising and falling, glaring at me—not with anger anymore. Just pain.

I reached for the tent flap and went back inside. At least with Rex and Donata, things made more sense. They spoke of duty and more tangible ideas. Enzo confused me. He made me want things I couldn't have.

"You took long enough." Donata waved me over. "We need a plan."

"For what?" I still hadn't really come back down to Earth from Enzo's searing kiss.

"For wha…" Donata puffed out a breath in frustration. "You're helping us with Angelo, remember?"

"She remembers." Enzo strode in and sat on the tabletop next to Donata. "Just tell her what to do. She'll do it."

I glanced down at my hands. Maybe Rex was right. It was better this way—Enzo acting all cruel and distant was familiar territory.

"That I can do." Donata pulled up a chair and put me in it. "Do you guys ever spend time alone?"

Without meaning to, I shot a glance toward Enzo. He smirked while he waited for my answer. I thought of the times Angelo had come to the house for dinner. Except for one limo ride, my parents were always around.

"He comes to the house to visit. But we're never alone."

"Hmm." She tapped her chin. "That's not gonna work. Do you two ever talk?"

"Not really." Mostly, he liked to watch me, but I didn't think they needed to know that.

"Do you think you could get him alone? You know, so you can ask him questions?"

Enzo shifted his body, clenching his jaw and fists.

"I think so."

"Good. Good. That's something. So now all we need to do is figure out what to ask without making him suspicious." She looked to Rex and Enzo. "Any ideas?"

We were flying blind. There were so many missing pieces to this puzzle, I had no idea where to begin looking. It wasn't like I could straight up ask him, *"Hey, did Don Alfera ask you to kill someone?"*

"I'd like to know what's in the marriage contract." Enzo spoke first. "What is he getting out of it? Other than the obvious." He pointed at me.

"I wonder if he'll talk to you about Don Alfera. The old man doesn't trust anyone. But yesterday, it sounded like he'd given Angelo a big job," Rex said.

"That's true." Donata pointed at him, then reached for my hand. "I'm just going to say it. When Aunt Vittoria said, 'kill a mobster, I don't care,' I thought of your dad."

"Me too." Rex nodded. "But what's the gain there? Stefano Vitali is a nobody." He motioned toward me. "No offense."

Before I knew it, I was being bombarded with questions for Angelo. Bit by bit, I understood that I needed to do this for myself, as much as for them. My family was in trouble. And yeah, I was still planning to leave in a few months, but that didn't mean I was okay leaving them while Dad had a death threat hanging over his head.

Crap. I was going to have to get close to Angelo. Rex was right. Love and duty did not mix. I had to put my feelings aside and focus on what had to be done. And in the process, hopefully, forget about Enzo.

"Do you really have to go?" Donata's soft voice brought me back.

My head snapped, and then I realized she was addressing Enzo. "Where are you going?" I asked.

"Away."

Is This What You Came For?

Enzo

The last three months had been hell. I had not taken Rex's advice to stay away from Aurora because I agreed with his sense of duty. Though I knew he wasn't wrong in that. I walked away because I was losing control. In our world, that was a dangerous thing.

Dad, the great Don Alfera, was a prime example of that. His life with the Society and his position as king were spiraling out of control. All because Mom refused to play his game. She dug her heels in deep and wasn't budging. Dad barely left Brooklyn these days, which was a good thing because that meant I had Manhattan all to myself—that meant peace for me. If I could call it that. Her hands on me, her scent, and her big innocent eyes still haunted me.

I didn't think I'd be able to stay away. But fear was a powerful motivator. The things I felt when Aurora was around scared the shit out of me.

"So why are we here again?" Rex wiped the sweat off his face with his T-shirt and tossed it on the bench.

We'd been playing hoops for the last hour, waiting for Dad at a park near his Brooklyn home. We were tired, but we both needed something to do. I hated sitting on my thumbs, especially when Dad was involved.

"We've been summoned."

"Do you know why?" He passed me the ball.

"He didn't say." I dribbled a couple times, then shot it into the basket. I caught it and passed it back to him. "The old man is losing it."

"I know. Dad mentioned it."

"Is there anything they can do to help him? I can tell you that Mom is never going back to the Upper East Side."

"Dad says they're working on it." Rex shrugged.

"God forbid they fill us in on it." I scoffed. "So, what did I miss this week?"

For the past several weeks, I had stayed home in my high-rise penthouse. I had made arrangements with my teachers to let me do the work from home. One of the perks of being a royal, teachers didn't question me. When I told them I had to go away for a while, they assumed it was mafia related. As long as I kept sending in the assignments, they had no reason to complain or get my parents involved.

Not that my parents would care. Dad hadn't even shown up to any of the football games I played. Last year, he was all over it. But now, it was like I didn't exist.

"You're doing the right thing." Rex slapped my arm.

Since the day of the car wash, Rex had been keeping me in the loop. All I wanted to know was how Donata's new project was going and how Aurora was handling it. According to Rex and Santino, Donata held weekly meetings where she grilled Aurora on her progress. I could show up and find out for myself. But then I'd have to see her. And I knew that wouldn't end well. Had Aurora been able to talk to Angelo? How much time did she have to spend with him to get information? And if he did give her useful intel, what did he ask for in return?

"She hasn't slept with him. The mom watches them like a hawk. And Santino? Well, he's been so distracted by Hanna, I think he forgot about the bet."

"Fuck off." I threw him a hard pass that almost hit his chest.

"Hmmm." He chuckled. "Isn't that why you ask me this question every week?"

He wasn't wrong. When Rex advised me to walk away from Aurora, he knew the only way I'd leave was if Aurora was safe from them. I knew she was into me. But Santino and Rex had their methods when it came to girls. They always got what they wanted. With me stuck at home, I knew they would move in like vultures. Of course Rex saw right through my predicament and offered to forfeit the bet. To him, duty was more important than some stupid game. Santino didn't see it that way. Though it seemed, he'd been too preoccupied with Hanna to care about winning.

"I want to know what Dad is up to. This thing he has going on is taking its toll on him. You'll see what I mean when he gets here."

"I've said it before." He aimed for the basketball hoop. "Love and duty don't mix well."

"So still no progress with Angelo?"

"No." He smirked at me. "Apparently, Aurora's mom is

always around. I get the feeling Lily Vitali doesn't trust Angelo alone with her underage daughter."

"You think?" I smiled.

The image of the two of them with Aurora's mom sitting between them put a big grin on my face. I supposed this was good news, bad news. I didn't want Aurora alone with Angelo. But as long as her mom was in the way, the chances of us getting answers were zero.

"Oh, and get this." He slapped my arm with the back of his hand. "You're gonna love this. Over Thanksgiving break, Brody had a skiing accident, and broke both legs." He grinned. "Anyway, he's off the team. He's not coming back for the rest of the semester."

"Holy shit."

"You think Signoria Vittoria had something to do with it?"

"Her cabin, her plane, her invitation? Hell yes."

"Signoria Vittoria meant it literally when she said revenge was a dish best served cold." I had no proof she was behind the accident. But who else could come up with such a perfectly executed plan? Now Brody was off the team, and for all intents and purposes, suspended from school.

"The Thomases are devastated, and so grateful for Signoria Vittoria's unwavering support." He laughed. "Donata's words, not mine."

"Don't mess with the dragon lady, huh? I'm both impressed and terrified."

"You and me both, brother."

"Enzo," a girl called out from behind me.

"Bells?" I hadn't seen my sister Caterina in months. I almost didn't recognize her.

When I waved at her, she stuffed a candy bar in her mouth

and ran toward me. "Dad said you were here. I didn't believe him. Where have you been?"

"School." I ambled toward the bench and grabbed my tee. "What are you doing here?"

"I wanted to see you. Would you stay for dinner? Mom is making your favorite." She beamed at me, then wiped chocolate off her cheek. She might look grown up now, but she was still a little kid.

Rex tittered behind us. He found the idea of me having dinner with my parents amusing.

"Hey." Caterina waved at him.

"Hey." He winced in disgust. "What the hell are you eating?"

"It's a candy bar." She glanced at him in mock confusion. "Isn't it obvious?"

"That shit will kill you slowly. You should watch what you eat."

"You should mind your own business." She rolled her eyes at him, then took another bite. When she turned to face me, she had this satisfied grin on her face.

"He's right, Bells. Have you seen the ingredients in this thing?" I yanked the chocolate from her hand.

"Oh, come on. Give it back." She made a grab for it.

But I was taller than her and managed to keep it out of reach.

"Don't be a jerk." She pushed me and tried to snatch it again.

"It's for your own good." I tossed the bar to Rex.

He caught it and made a clean dunk into the trash bin. "That's a three-pointer." He laughed.

"Jerk." She glared at Rex. "But that's fine. I have more at home." She shoved me away from her.

"Caterina." Dad's voice rumbled a few feet away. "You saw your brother. Go home. Now."

Caterina took in an exhausted breath and rolled her eyes at Dad. "I'm going."

Like Mom, my little sister had Dad wrapped around her little finger. Anyone else, including me, would've been knocked down to the ground for talking back.

"Dinner tonight? Please." She put her hands together, pleading. "We miss you."

"You're such a brat."

"But you love me." She kissed my cheek. "Come on. I still haven't given you your birthday present. Mom is not happy that you skipped out on the cake she baked for you. It's not every day her oldest son turns eighteen. You suck, you know? It's been a month. You didn't even show up for Thanksgiving last week." She kept going with a long list of all the family events I had skipped.

I hugged her to me to get her to stop. Dad hated it when Mom wasn't happy. When she stopped talking, I whispered in her ear, so Dad wouldn't hear, "Mom knows where I live, Bells. But yes, I'll stay for dinner. Go on now."

"Thank you." She backed away from me. When she spun around, she threw her arms around Dad's neck and kissed his cheek. "See? I told you I could talk him into it."

"Your mother will be pleased. Go on." The gentle tone in his voice made my stomach lurch.

Such a devoted father. I shook my head and joined Rex by the bench. He squeezed my shoulder in solidarity. He, better than anyone else, understood Dad's double life and his two faces—a loving father and husband, and the ruthless king of a mafia underworld.

I waited until Caterina was out of sight to address him. "You wanted to see us."

"Yes." Dad inhaled, while his gaze lingered on the path Caterina had taken home.

Slowly, he turned his attention toward Rex. Rex's eyebrows shot up in surprise. He saw it too. Dad was losing it. Something was eating away at him.

When he finally turned to me, he shook his head. "Some other time, son. Why don't you come home, shower, and eat with us?"

My mouth fell open a bit. For one, because Dad had never used that soft tone with me. And two, because it seemed that Mom had finally won. Dad called his house in Brooklyn his home. After all their fights over how toxic the Upper East Side was, Mom finally got her point across. She got him to see things her way. The problem was, I could see the wheels turning in Dad's eyes. He wasn't a changed man. He was just fucking tired.

"Would you join us?" I asked Rex.

"No, man. I have to get home." He looked to Dad. When Dad nodded, giving his permission, Rex stood and started gathering his things. "Same time next week? Your place this time."

A chuckle escaped my lips. Here I was worried about duty and all the things I was required to do. I gave up on Aurora because of some intangible idea of what the society, and Dad, needed from me. The old man didn't give a shit. All he cared about was himself and this little life he had created for himself in Brooklyn.

If Dad could have his cake and eat it too, why not me?

"I'll see you tomorrow. At school."

"Are you sure?" Rex furrowed his brows at me, then leaned in to whisper, "One family dinner doesn't change shit."

"No, it doesn't. But I'm tired too."

Monday morning, I woke up with a renewed sense of purpose. Like Rex had said, a dinner with the family didn't change much. Though it did give me clarity on what I wanted to do with my life. For one, I couldn't keep hiding from the girl I liked. I couldn't let her have that much power over me. I was in control here.

First period was going to be the toughest. But once I got used to being around Aurora again, I was sure I could focus on school and our plan to get information from Angelo. I shouldered the door open to the Salvatore building and made my way to Chem class.

The rush of adrenaline hit me like a wayward basketball straight in the chest. Aurora was still Aurora, with her long hair, those big eyes, and that innocent look about her that made me want to show her all the things her life was missing. I took in a breath and quickly rushed past her table.

Santino and Donata didn't even look surprised when they saw me, which told me Rex had already talked with them. I was grateful for that. I didn't need a million questions this morning.

Mr. Taylor started his lesson on time, and that gave me the opportunity to regroup and get my emotions in check. Though as much as I tried to keep my attention on the whiteboard, my gaze kept shifting over to Aurora's blonde head. Sometime during class, she had put her hair up in a messy bun. I stared at the nape of her neck and thought of our brief encounter at Tiffany's over the summer.

That day, she'd let me put a necklace on her. The same charge in the air that crackled the moment my fingers brushed her skin filled the air now. As if she could feel it too, she glanced over her shoulder. I didn't bother to look away. I didn't want to.

Our gazes locked. She didn't turn away until the teacher called on her. Then she had to scramble to find the answer in her book. Like me, she hadn't been paying attention to the lesson.

Maybe one class was all I could handle with her today. As soon as the bell rang, I made a bee line for the door. I rushed through the crowded hallways and didn't stop until I reached the courtyard behind the bell tower.

While I was gone, Molly had been in charge of feeding Fluffy during the day. I came to see him every day before and after football practice. Molly used that time to give me a full report on how he was doing. Multiple times, she mentioned she'd seen Aurora in here, playing with the cat.

"You came back."

I slow-blinked and turned to face Aurora. She should not have followed me here. What did she think was going to happen?

"I tried calling."

"I know."

Seeing her name on the screen had made the days bearable.

"Enzo—"

"I didn't come back for you," I lied.

Whatever she wanted to say to me, I didn't need to know. I wasn't ready to be this close to her again. I scanned the courtyard, looking for my cat, but he didn't come out. My heart pumped hard against my chest. I had to get out of here.

"Just stay out of my way." I made to leave, but she stepped in to block my path.

"I don't know why I'm here." She braced her hand on my chest.

That was my undoing. I gripped her hand and turned her around. Her back slammed against my chest, and I held her tighter. "You're not ready for this. I'm not ready for this. Do you understand?"

"No."

I buried my nose in the nook of her neck and shoulder. Then kissed the spot I had spent the last hour staring at. Once I started, I couldn't stop. I sucked and nibbled on her skin, while my hands roamed over her body, her hips, her thighs, and her ass. "Is this what you came for?"

"Enzo. Stop." She faced me, pressing her palm to my heart. "Let me talk. Please."

"Talk?" I chuckled. "After all this time, you want to talk?"

"Please." She smiled up at me with red cheeks. "You left and didn't let me explain."

"Explain what?"

"Why I need to marry Angelo?"

The name on her lips had a sobering effect on me. She was right. We did need to talk. We needed all the cards on the table now. Because I couldn't keep ignoring this thing in my chest. I couldn't keep pretending it wasn't real. I couldn't stay away from her anymore.

"Do you want to get out of here?"

"What? No." She glanced down at her hands.

Was she losing the resolve she had found when she followed me here?

"I have class. I have a math test. I mean, we have a math test."

I kept my gaze on her while she went through all the reasons why we couldn't just leave this place. She was so beautiful.

"Umm..." She ran a hand through her hair. "Okay. Yes, let's get out of here."

"Lunchtime. Meet me at the front gate."

Are We Here to Say Good-Bye?

Aurora

Dazed and confused. That was the state I found myself in, every time I had any sort of interaction with Enzo Alfera. I zigzagged my way through the crowded hallway to get to second period. I had three more classes, three more hours before I could meet with Enzo to talk. I touched my fingers to the nape of my neck where I was sure he'd left a hickey, where he marked me.

"Where did you go?" Penny dumped my backpack on the desk next to hers. "You forgot your stuff."

"Oh, I didn't realize." I moved my bag and sat. "I wanted to talk to Enzo."

"I figured as much." She shook her head in disapproval.

For the past three months since Enzo vanished, I'd been moping around, mindlessly getting to class, and overall, just feeling aimless. Penny had a front row seat to the whole mess. Enzo showing up today just threw me off. I thought he was never coming back. Knowing I'd never see him again gutted me.

"Well, did you talk to him?"

"Sort of." I bit my lower lip. She wasn't gonna like this part. "Um, I'm meeting him for lunch."

"I guess, at some point, you do need to talk. I think he really likes you." She squeezed my shoulder.

"I think so too. Um," I leaned forward, so no one could hear, "we're ditching school."

"Omigod, Rory." She rubbed her temple, furrowing her brows. "That's a bad idea. What do you think is gonna happen? If he was interested in talking, he would do it here. Right now."

"He wants us to be alone."

"And why do you think that is?" She cocked an eyebrow.

I didn't regret telling Penny about my run-ins with Enzo. Of course, she got the PG-13 version of them, with very little details. I didn't tell her how much I saw of him in the bathroom, or how hard he was when he kissed me in the courtyard. But she knew that sex with Enzo was on my mind all the damn time. How could it not be? When he left, he made me realize how much I did want to be with him. Even if we had no future together. Someone like Enzo only came around once in a lifetime. I was prepared to move on after high school and never see him again. But just this once, I wanted more.

"Last I checked, I was an adult. I can do it if I want."

She barked out a laugh. "Seriously? You've been eighteen, for what?" She checked her watch. "Ten hours? And this is how you're choosing to use your brand-new superpower? By making a stupid decision."

"It isn't stupid."

Class started, and I spent the entire hour thinking about Penny's words. Was I jumping into this because I was afraid Enzo would disappear again? I totally was. I rested my folded arms on the desk and buried my face in them. Penny was right. Ditching school to take off with Enzo was a bad idea.

"Hello?" Santino poked my arm.

"She's been like this all day. Hmmm...come to think of it, she's been like this all semester."

I lifted my head and squinted to bring Santino's face into focus. His happy face always put me in a better mood. Somehow, I felt that if I was still close to the royals, I would still have a chance to get back with Enzo.

"Hey."

"Happy birthday." He sat on the desk in front of me.

I scanned the room quickly and realized everyone else had gone. Shit. Did I miss the bell? "Thanks." I glanced down at the box he put in front of me. "What is this?"

"A present. You know? Because it's your birthday?" He winked. "You're officially an adult."

I met Penny's gaze, and she rolled her eyes at me.

"Wow, you didn't have to go through all this trouble."

"I didn't. Pina did. We all pitched in. Go on." He beamed at me.

I took the gift and tore the paper off. Ever since we overheard the Dons talking about their secret plans, Donata, Rex, and Santino had been super nice to me. Mostly because they needed something from me, but I didn't care. A friendship of convenience was better than a mean bully.

I opened the box and removed a pair of odd sunglasses. "Um, thanks?"

"They're night vision goggles. Try them on?" He took

them from me and placed them on my face. After he fiddled with the buttons on the side, the whole room turned green and blurry. "Obviously they work better when it's dark."

"Why would you think she'd need these?" Penny took the goggles from me and tried them on.

"For fun." He exchanged a meaningful look with me.

Shit. This could only mean Donata had a brand-new mission for me. I didn't know why she bothered. Up until now, I had failed all of them. Angelo wasn't an idiot. And Mom had proven that she did care about my well-being. Even when I asked her to let me have a chat with Angelo alone in Dad's home office, she refused. I supposed her ability to lie to herself could only go so far.

"I'll see you later." Santino pushed himself off the chair and took off.

"This is why I told you to stay away from the royals. They're trouble, Rory. Big trouble."

I shrugged and grabbed my bag. I had a full minute to make it to my next class. The closer the hour hand got to twelve, the worse my nerves got. By the time the lunch bell rang, I startled in my seat. Adrenaline rushed through me and washed away any doubts I had about meeting Enzo. We did need to talk. If anything, because I wanted to explain to him why I had gone along with Dad's plan. I didn't do it for Dad; I was doing it for me. I wanted him to know that because it seemed that my marriage to Angelo was inevitable.

I stopped by my locker to drop off all my books. There was no way I would have the energy to do homework tonight. That would have to wait. I followed the crowd of students from the Buratti building to Adaline. Near the entrance to the school, the throng split up into two. I normally went right toward the dining hall, but today, I went in the opposite direction.

As soon as the front gates were in my line of sight, my legs stopped moving. A girl bumped into me and then another.

"Watch it." She glowered at me.

"I'm sorry," I said.

But the rumble of a motorcycle muffled my words. With a huge smile, the girl turned away from me to see who it was. I did the same and my jaw dropped. Why did I think we'd leave the school quietly?

At the outside curb, past the half-moon driveway, Enzo sat on his motorcycle, looking hotter than he had any right to be. He'd changed out of his uniform coat and into his leather jacket. Why? To torture me? He leaned back with his thighs hugging the bike seat and waved me over.

"Oh, sure. He wants to talk." Penny appeared out of nowhere.

"Maybe he couldn't get a car service." I shrugged.

"Go. Before someone else beats you to it." She pursed her lips, suppressing a smile.

I went to adjust my backpack, then remembered I had left it in my locker earlier. I felt naked without it. But I had been waiting for this moment for months. I couldn't back down now. I inhaled deeply and made my way toward Enzo. At first, everyone was too busy ogling Enzo's sexy Ducati with its sleek red panels and shiny handlebars. Though the minute he switched his attention to me, they all did too. Or maybe I just imagined it.

"I don't know what's worse. The limo or the bike?"

"Hop on." His demanding tone made me take a few steps toward him.

I'd never been on a motorcycle. As impressive and powerful as it looked, I didn't trust it. Only Enzo could sit on a machine like that and think he could control it.

"It won't bite. I promise." He handed me a helmet—a smaller version of the one sitting in front of him. "Do you trust me?"

"Everyone's staring." I nodded and stepped forward.

"Do you care?" He put the helmet on me, then patted the small seat behind him, which was just an extension of his.

The only way to get on was to slide my leg behind him and flush my body to him. With all the grace I could muster, I straddled his hips. This position felt so intimate. I wouldn't mind it, except half the school was still looking at us, as if waiting for something big to happen.

He glanced over his shoulder, with a smirk pulling at his lips. "You're going to have to hold on to me."

I tentatively put my arms around his stomach and forgot about the outside world. It was just us now.

"Much tighter than that, Aurora." He took my hands and fastened them closer under his shirt. Then he grabbed both my thighs and hoisted them onto his.

Omigod. Sitting like this was both mortifying and a huge turn-on.

The motor rumbled under my butt as the tires gripped the road and peeled away.

Freedom.

For the past few months, since my family and I arrived in New York City, I had been dreaming of freedom. Up until now, I hadn't really considered what it would feel like. But I was sure it would feel like this—riding fast on a long road, tall buildings rushing by and staying behind while I moved forward with the cold breeze on my face, and a whole new horizon ahead of me painted in light blues and fluffy whites.

After a few minutes, I slid my hands farther up Enzo's torso, feeling every strained muscle on his abs and chest. He hadn't let me touch him before, but it seemed now I was allowed. His laughter filled the air for a second before it rushed past me. My cheeks heated. I was past being embarrassed. I wanted him too much. My whole body ached for him.

I hadn't asked him where we were going, and I didn't care. We turned the corner and a bunch of buildings I recognized came into view. He had rounded the same block at least twice. When we stopped at a red light, he used the time to relax and rub my thigh. His touch ignited a spark in my core—a familiar, and oh so frustrating, sensation.

I curled myself around his back. Before the thought was fully formed in my head, the words came out of my mouth. "Let's go home, Enzo."

The moment I said it, he gripped my leg tighter. "Are you sure?"

"Yes."

He maneuvered the Ducati around the traffic and into a quiet garage. The roaring engine echoed around us as he made his way to the top floor. I was pretty sure we were in his building. My heart picked up the pace as he pulled into a parking spot near the lobby and killed the engine. Silence fell around us. Without the vibrations of the seat, I got the sense that I was floating. He removed his helmet, and I did the same.

"My legs feel like spaghetti." I did my best to comb my hair away from my sweaty face.

He chuckled. "Give it a minute."

He helped me off the bike, then kicked the stand into

place. He moved slower than usual, as if he was having second thoughts about bringing me here. Now that I wasn't so close to him, my brain started working again. Crap, were we really at his home? Where his parents lived?

"Is this your building?"

"It is." He tucked his helmet under his arm, while mine hung from his long fingers.

"Your parents don't mind?"

"They're in Brooklyn playing house." He sneered, then shook his head. He glanced down at me, and his features softened before a brilliant smile appeared on his face. "Would you like a tour?"

"We're already here."

He took my hand in his, and I giggled. Jeez, could I please play it cool just once. "Sorry."

"Don't be nervous. We're just here to talk. Right?"

"Right."

We rode the elevator to the penthouse. When the doors slid open, I wasn't surprised to find that his house was all marble floors, floor-to-ceiling windows, and expensive furniture. The place was immaculate. Did he really live here all by himself?

"It's just us." He ushered me inside. "The maid leaves after lunch. Then comes back to serve dinner. Then she's gone again."

"Do you like being alone?"

"It's fine. Massimo lives here too. But he won't be home for hours."

He left his gear on a bench under the grand staircase, then moved on to remove my uniform jacket. Butterflies inundated my belly when his hot breath brushed the nape of my neck again. I didn't have to look to know he was admiring his handiwork on my skin. The way he ran his fingers across the hickey told me he had done it on purpose. He had meant to mark me—like marking his territory.

"How about a drink?"

"I'll take a water." I puffed out a breath.

"One water coming up." He motioned toward the living area, walked the length of the room, and then disappeared to the left.

I took the time to look around, mostly to ease my nerves. The fancy art on the walls, the massive stone fireplace, and muted colors all over suited Enzo's broody mood. I never thought about what it would be like to be the son of a mafia king. Rex once asked me if I understood what it meant to be a royal. I thought I did. But I was wrong. Enzo lived alone in a fancy penthouse, away from his family and everything else.

"Do you like it?" He pressed a tumbler to my hand, then turned his attention to the large painting over the mantel. The one I'd been eyeing pretty much since I came in. He crossed his arms over his chest, surveying the canvas. "It's my mother."

"It's beautiful. She's beautiful." I sipped my water.

"She hates it. She thinks it's over-the-top ostentatious." He laughed.

"Okay, I can see that." I chuckled. "Enzo." I swallowed the lump in my throat. "Are we here to say good-bye? Or…" I had no idea what we were anymore. We certainly weren't a couple.

"I was hoping for *or*." He cupped my cheek. "I thought I could stay away from you. But I was wrong. What's the point of having all this if I can't have what I really want?"

"What is it you really want?" Adrenaline rushed through me.

It all came down to that one simple fact. I'd had three months to think about what I wanted. More than anything, I wanted this. But did Enzo Alfera, the dark prince with a whole path already prescribed for him, want me?

"You, Aurora. I only want you."

I belong To You

AURORA

"How about you?" Enzo took the glass from me and set it on the side table. "Why did you agree to leave with me? What do you want, Aurora?"

"I don't think I'm allowed to have what I want." I glanced down at my hands.

He released a breath and placed a finger under my chin to make me look at him. The soft wrinkles around his eyes disarmed me. He seemed happy. Not at all angry like before when I followed him into the courtyard behind the clock tower. This version of Enzo was so hard to resist.

"That's not what I asked."

"I want to be with you." I took his hand in both of mine. "I know your life is complicated. The whole future king thing makes you—"

"Lonely?"

I was going to say unattainable. "Is that what you are?"

"It's difficult to form an attachment with anyone when

your future is more or less set in stone." He brought my hands up to his lips. "I never cared about all that. With you, I find myself wanting more."

"More?"

"More." He nodded once and bent down to capture my mouth.

The last time we kissed, he was mad at me because he thought I wanted to marry Angelo. But now, I wondered if maybe he wasn't mad at me, but rather, our circumstances. What did he care if I was engaged to someone else? It wasn't like he was free to choose a girlfriend either. Rex more or less spelled it out for me at the car wash. Enzo was expected to be king, and eventually marry someone who would benefit the Society. I had nothing to bring to the table. I was a nobody.

I deepened the kiss and tunneled my fingers through his hair. When we were alone, it was hard to keep our problems in perspective because all I wanted was to be with him. My heart beat faster every time his tongue swirled around mine. He wrapped his arms around me and cupped my butt cheek. I knew where we were headed. Every time we kissed, we ended right here—at the edge of some precipice I didn't understand. But I wasn't scared anymore. Right now, this moment was all we had. And I didn't want to waste it.

This morning, I woke up with an ache in my chest because I missed Enzo. Because I didn't know when I would see him again, if ever. Today was my eighteenth birthday. And all I could think about was that I wanted to spend it with Enzo—not at some huge party like Mom suggested—I only needed this.

"When I saw you at school, I thought you had come for

me." I met his gaze and chuckled. "I thought you came back because it was my birthday."

"What?" He narrowed his eyes. "I didn't know it was your birthday."

"Oh, I assumed you knew. Donata and the guys got me a gift. Santino said everyone pitched in, I thought he meant you too." I shouldn't be embarrassed about it, but I was. I had no reason to believe my birthday would be important to someone like Enzo.

"You're blushing. I'm the asshole here. I'd been only thinking about seeing you again." He cupped my face and kissed me again. "Happy birthday, Aurora."

"Happy birthday to you too. I sent you a card last month."

"I know." He winced as if it pained him that he didn't call me back, not even to say thank you. "Thank you."

"What happened? Why did you leave?" I'd been so hurt when Rex told me Enzo wasn't coming back. It hurt because I knew he was avoiding me. It hurt because he didn't give me a chance to talk about the whole thing with Angelo. "You didn't let me explain."

"You didn't do anything wrong. I mean, I was, or I still am pissed that you're even considering Angelo. That's not why I left. I thought I was doing the right thing by staying away from you." He pressed his mouth to mine. "Screw the Society and my father. They don't own me."

"No, they don't." I pressed my body to his. "We missed yours, but it's still my birthday. I know how I want to spend it." I slipped my hand under his shirt.

A small part of me had expected him to stop me. Before, when I tried to touch him, he'd pin my hands behind me or over my head. Now, he was letting me explore. I flattened my palm to his hard stomach, while I worked the buttons of his shirt with my free hand.

He watched with intense curiosity. I let his shirt hang open and stood back to see him. He was beautiful. With a half-smile, he reached for my hand and placed it over his chest. The thumping of his heart was hard to miss. I did this to him. The rise and fall of his whole body, his dark eyes and red cheeks—that was all because of me, because he still wanted me. Our time apart hadn't changed that.

"Are you sure?" His voice sounded strained, as if he was using every bit of strength to stand still.

"I'm not scared anymore."

"Show me." His gaze dropped to my top. "Show me you're not afraid of me."

Enzo had seen me in my bra months ago, but that was different. We were in the back of a tent with people not too far away from us. Sex wasn't even on the table. But now, if I did as he asked, there would be no going back, for me anyway. Or maybe the point of no return happened when I left the school perched on the back of Enzo's Ducati. I thought that if Enzo and I ever had sex, I would fall hard for him. I was wrong. Enzo stole my heart a long time ago, long before I even considered the idea of someone like him loving someone like me.

I shrugged out of my uniform coat, then started on the buttons of my blouse. Before I got to the last one, he stepped into my circle and helped me take it off. His hands seared my skin wherever he touched me—my bare shoulder, my waist, and between my breasts.

"I have something for you." He laughed as his gaze roamed my front. "I forgot I had it."

Really? I was about to explode from wanting him so much,

and he had something to give me? I ran my hands up his abs. "Can it wait?"

"No." He moved my hair out of the way to whisper in my ear, "I want to see it on you while I take you."

If he hadn't been supporting most of my weight, I would've fallen on my face. Take me? Ribbons of desire sprung from my core. By now, I knew the feeling well. I also knew that there was only one way to soothe the ache between my legs.

"Okay," I mumbled.

"It's upstairs." He gripped my waist tighter. "In my room."

When I nodded, he stepped back and picked up my clothes. Instead of giving them to me, he tucked them under his arm and offered me his hand. I made to cover the cups of my bra, where my hard nipples poked through. But Enzo and I were way past that point. I wanted him to see me—just me.

He headed toward the stairs, and I followed behind him. He hadn't removed his shirt. With all the buttons undone, the fabric swayed away from him and gave me a spectacular view of his abs. I clung to his hand as if my life depended on it as he ushered me into his suite.

Did I expect the messy room of a teenager? A little bit. But, of course, Enzo's bedroom was as pristine as the rest of his penthouse. The king-size bed in the middle of the room was done in royal blue with velvet pillows and cozy throws. To the far end, he had a desk with what looked like a super fancy computer. Even the art on the walls was neatly done with clean lines in soft grays.

"Wow, your room is so tidy."

"I have a maid for that." He smiled then ambled to his massive walk-in closet. When he returned, he had a Tiffany-blue box in his hand, eyeing it as if he'd never seen it before. "I don't know what compelled me to buy this the day I met you. I wanted to talk to you, but I..." He looked intently into my eyes. "I chickened out."

I laughed. "Why?"

"I don't know. You seemed so innocent and out of place." He touched the pad of his thumb over my lips. "Turn around."

I did as he asked and waited until he opened the box and then placed the necklace on my neck. When I glanced down, I wasn't surprised to find the sapphire pendant he had me try on at Tiffany's. The stone felt cold against my heated skin, but it was as beautiful as I remembered. "Why would you do this?"

"I told you. I thought you should have it." He kissed the nape of my neck. "Get on the bed."

Enzo had these spans of sweet and demanding. I melted for him when he was tender and caring. When he was controlling and ordering me about, he made my whole-body ache for him. I felt raw when his voice changed to a domineering one.

He was the product of his environment, rough and cruel. But I got the sense that, for me, he was trying to be something different. He was trying to be what he thought I needed. The thing was, I needed both—I needed all of him.

I ambled to the bed, turned around to face him, then scooted up. In that time, he'd taken off his shoes and shirt. His belt hung unbuckled along with his trousers. I squirmed on the soft bedding and inched farther up the mattress. He glanced down at his erection, shaking his head.

"Don't be scared."

"I'm not." My gaze dropped to his crotch.

As if he could read my thoughts, he unzipped his pants and pushed them down. And omigod, he was perfect—slim hips, all muscle, and smooth skin. He stood there and let me ogle him for a minute. By the time he moved toward me, his size felt familiar, and I was itching to touch his cock. With a knowing smile, he bent down and picked up my foot to remove my shoe and sock. His lips touched my ankle before he grabbed my other leg. He nibbled his way down and removed the other.

I knew where all of this would end. But not knowing what he planned to do next had my blood pumping harder than normal. I glanced up to the small chandelier in his room. When I woke up this morning, I had no idea I'd end up spread eagle in front of a very naked Enzo Alfera.

"Breathe, Aurora." He braced a knee on the covers, right between my thighs. "Take off your clothes."

My cheeks burned hot, but I did what he ordered. I lifted my butt and fumbled with the zipper. He didn't try to help or even hurry the process. He simply watched me with hunger in his eyes, taking all of me in. He groaned as I slid my underwear off, along with the skirt and shorts I wore underneath. My bra came next. Butterflies fluttered in my stomach when he smiled at me in appreciation. I wanted him to like my body.

"Did you want to know what it felt like to be in Hanna's place?" He brushed the back of his hand over my sex. A rush of raw energy flitted through me when he released a breath over my clit. I didn't want to think about Hanna and Santino right now. But it was too late, he'd already put that image in my head. I thought about how turned on I'd been, how frustrated I'd been that I didn't know what to do about the ache in my chest, and how embarrassed I had been when Rex caught me spying on Santino while he was nestled between Hanna's legs.

All of that came rushing back and it took me to a new level

of turned on. He puffed out another breath, and I squirmed toward him. Was he going to do that to me now?

"Enzo." I called for him, practically begging him to do it already.

"You're so fucking beautiful." He licked along the seam of my pussy.

It was too much. The sensation of his wet tongue right over my aching bud was unbearable. I panted and reached for his hair, pushing him away but also pulling him toward me.

"Show me how you want it."

"I don't know. I didn't see," I mumbled, holding on to the image in my head. Though now it wasn't Santino in my mind's eye. It was Enzo and me. I focused on that and relaxed my hips.

"Such a good girl." He sucked hard on my clit.

Then something else happened—a spark deep inside me. It grew with every nibble and every kiss until I felt like I was on the brink of something, teetering between the edge of the precipice and the hard fall. He buried his face in my pussy and moaned a long, loud groan that pushed me off the ledge. I saw stars. I pressed my thighs to the sides of his face as an orgasm ripped through me. It lingered in my core then burned its way through the rest of me. It did it two more times before I collapsed and let go of Enzo's hair.

"Do you still want to do this?" He pumped his cock a few times, pushing my legs open then taking handfuls of my breasts. "Tell me to go to hell."

"I want this."

"Take a deep breath, and then let it go."

When I exhaled, he plunged into me. I was so wet, he slid right in, but not without effort on his part. He gripped the comforter on either side of my head, and then pushed some more. With another breath out, he thrust again until he bottomed out. I threw my arms around his neck and brought him closer to me. He lay there so still, while I tried to figure out what I felt. It hurt. But the desire I felt deep inside me, the spark fueling my need for him was back.

"Jesus fuck. You're so tight." He breathed heavily into my ear. "Are you in pain?"

"No," I lied. I didn't want him to stop. "I can do it."

He pulled all the way out and glanced down. I did too and got a glimpse of my blood on his erection. It wasn't a lot. But enough to make this moment feel important. I thought about what this meant for a second, about the possible repercussions, then pushed them away. I chose this. This was my decision. The world could go to hell.

His gaze swept up from where his cock lay at my entrance, to my breasts, then the blue stone sitting on my clavicle. He'd said he wanted me to wear the sapphire while he took me. I was ready. I nodded at him, and he smiled.

"I was not expecting this." He pressed his lips to mine in some sort of surrender, then entered me again.

The pain subsided as he began to move again, in and out, with slow and languid strokes. I relaxed, spent from my earlier orgasm and the shock of him ripping my hymen.

"We're not done, Angel." He rocked a little harder, sucking on my nipples. "I want nothing more than to leave my load inside you." He kissed my lips until they were raw, thrusting deeper into me.

"Yes." I labored a breath.

His words and his low-pitched voice in my ear sent me down the rabbit hole again. I still had no clue how to make that happen, but it was coming for me again. The slow burn and then the fall. He increased the pace. A minute later, I was right there with him all over again. The aching sensation exploded, sending waves of pleasure to every inch of my body. There was something else too, something that wrapped itself around my chest and gripped it tightly.

Before my climax was fully spent, he pulled out and flopped his cock on my belly as cum spewed out of the tip. I glanced down at it. Between the mark on my neck, the sapphire, and now this, I realized that, bit by bit, Enzo had branded me as his. Was that what he wanted?

He hovered over me with his intense gaze on mine. "You belong to me. Say it."

"I belong to you."

Let's Talk. But No Clothes

Enzo

Aurora curled her body against mine, while I stared at the ceiling, smiling like an idiot. She lay in my arms, wearing nothing but the sapphire necklace I gave her. I had bought it on impulse months ago. When I realized how stupid it was to buy a gift for someone I didn't even know, I stuffed it in the back of my closet. I had every intention of returning it, but I never got around to it. Maybe this whole time, I'd hoped I'd find my way back to Aurora.

Being here with her surpassed all my expectations. It also confirmed how big of a mistake it was to let my guard down with her. Because now I couldn't lie to myself anymore. I had feelings for her. More than that, I couldn't stand the thought of letting her go.

Apart from Rex, Santino, and Donata, I'd never brought anyone up to the penthouse. Mainly because I didn't want strangers to see my home—how I lived in an ivory tower with an angry parent, who couldn't figure out what he wanted to be.

Dad still struggled with being a good person and being a mobster. Sure, he was king, but at the core of it all, he was just a criminal. My friends were the only ones who understood. I didn't have to pretend with them.

I kissed the top of Aurora's head. Fuck. I wanted her here. I wanted her to see me for what and who I was. Somehow, I knew she'd understand.

"I have to go." She buried her face in the nook of my neck and shoulder.

"School doesn't let out for another hour." I inhaled, holding her tighter. "Stay."

"Really?" She shifted her body to face me, and in the process rubbed her tits all over me.

"Don't sound so surprised." I ran my fingers over her nipples. They puckered in response, and fuck me, if I didn't want to be inside her again. "Did you think I was going to kick you to the curb after I had my way with you?"

"No." She laughed. "Well, a little."

"Oh."

In her defense, I'd been a real asshole to her. Mostly because she scared me. Was it because I saw myself in her? Both our parents thought of us as pawns and had no qualms using us to get ahead. I hadn't forgotten that she was still engaged to Angelo Soprano. I kneaded her breast, smiling at how perfectly it fit in my hand. When I thought of Angelo doing the same, acid built in the pit of my stomach.

I'd never been jealous before. I couldn't stand it.

"I meant it before, Aurora." I gripped her waist and moved her on top of me. "You belong to me."

"Enzo." She blushed.

By now, I knew enough about her to know she wasn't

embarrassed. She was fucking turned on. My cock steeled against her pussy. Too good. She was too good to be true.

"Say it. I want to hear you say it again."

Before, in the throes of her first orgasm, she'd uttered the words on command. Now that the fog had lifted, she couldn't say it. I pushed her off me and sat up. Planting my feet on the area rug below, I made to get up. Why did I think that fucking her would change anything between us? I was still tethered to the king's chair, and she was engaged.

"Wait." She hugged me from behind.

Her hands had barely touched me, but I couldn't move. Not so deep down, I wanted her to say the words, *"Angelo can go to hell."*

"Can we have that talk now?" She reached around me to grab her clothes off the floor.

"No." I grabbed her by the wrist, then pinned her to the bed, caging her with my body. "Let's talk. But no clothes. I want the naked truth. Why are you marrying him? What do your parents have on you?"

"They're not blackmailing me, Enzo." She rolled her eyes.

"They're doing something."

She opened her mouth, but the words didn't come out.

"Fuck. Tell me you don't have feelings for him." I lifted my weight off her, just enough to see her eyes.

"I don't have feelings for him. Of course not. I just don't know how to explain it. Duty is the only word I can think of. When Dad told me he was planning to arrange a marriage, I played along to bide some time. I never had any intention of actually going through with it." She released a breath.

"But now you do?"

"Life in Las Vegas was rough, Enzo. Dad did some stuff that got Mom in trouble. Or rather..." She trailed off.

"What did he do?" I released her and lay down next to her.

She flipped on her side to study my face. "A bad deal. He lost and then stole some money. His boss came after him. When he couldn't pay, he offered up Mom as payment. She agreed. I saw her."

"I'm sorry."

"I knew it was only a matter of time before I had to do the same for him. At first, I didn't want to come to New York. As bad as it was, Las Vegas was home, a place I knew. I figured once I turned eighteen, I could get a job at the casinos and get away from Dad."

From what I knew about her father, Stefano Vitali was a loyal soldier. He had met Dad in Las Vegas during some shooting, where he saved Dad's life. As a reward, Dad offered him a job as his second-in-command, a position Penny's dad had held for many years. I never understood why Dad would kick James Conti out when they were so close. Dad never explained what happened there, other than he now had a new right-hand and that his family was moving to the Upper East Side to join our ranks.

Aurora was here with me because her dad saved my dad's life.

"So New York put a chink in your plans."

"Yes and no. In a way, it made them better. I'd always wanted to go to Columbia, get a degree, and a job that didn't involve serving drinks to drunk, rich men."

"That's a solid plan."

"It was just a dream. Signoria Vittoria used that to get me to sign her NDA and play along, to be a good mafia teen. She offered to get me into Columbia, but now she's backing down. She thinks I should marry Angelo."

"And by she thinks, you mean she ordered you to?"

"Yes."

"So say no."

"Oh, good idea. Exactly how do I do that?" She sat on her heels. "How do I tell Don Salvatore that she's not getting what she wants. You saw what happened to Brody. That guy is never playing football again."

"Good point." I stared at the ceiling. This was one of those good news, bad news situations. The good news was Aurora didn't give a shit what her dad wanted. And she didn't have feelings for Angelo. Bad news was, Signoria Vittoria was involved and that meant Aurora had no way out of this contract. "What's in it for her?"

"What do you mean?"

"What does Signoria Vittoria get out of this marriage? Angelo is a nobody."

"You heard what your dad said. Angelo was Signoria Vittoria's idea."

I glanced at her. She was a vision sitting here in my room, perky tits on display, blonde hair everywhere, and that pendant I gave her making her eyes look even bluer. I shook my head a little. This wasn't the time to get distracted. "Yeah, and you're quite the reward."

"Not anymore." She glanced down at her tight body. "You saw to that."

"Do you regret it?"

"No." She shook her head. "I want only you. I'm just wondering what happens now. What will he do when he finds out I'm not a virgin?"

The only way he'd find out was if they fuck. Anger churned in my stomach at the idea of the two of them together. "You're not his. And you're not going to be." I cupped her cheek and pulled her toward me.

I crashed my mouth to hers and kissed her, wishing I could leave a bigger mark on her. Anything so Angelo would never look at her again. I thought of what he said in Signoria Vittoria's library the day we were eavesdropping on their secret conversation. "I'm keeping the girl." I thought of how he ogled her while she washed his limo, how he could barely contain himself.

I knew the feeling well—wanting Aurora was unbearable. It physically hurt. Her hands slid down to my erection. I nibbled on her bottom lip and groaned as she stroked me. Desire spiraled from below my navel up into my chest. I moved down to kiss her neck and chest, working my way from one mound to the other.

"I used to think of myself as very disciplined. But right now, I'm scraping the bottom of the barrel looking for the last of my self-control, so I won't flip you on your back right now and fuck you seven ways 'til Sunday." I gripped her pussy and squeezed it tight. She was wet for me, but I wasn't sure if she could handle another round. Especially because this time I wasn't planning on going easy or slow. "I need you."

"Do you really like me?" She inched closer to me to give me better access.

"What do you think?" Desire engulfed me like a wildfire. I palmed her with one hand then helped her stroke me with the other—starting at the base and going all the way past the shaft. With a smile, she repeated the process a few more times on her own. Fuck, she was a fast learner. I dipped a finger past her entrance. "Just like that."

"Hmmm...I can do it." She moaned. "Make it feel better."

Who could say no to that?

I thrust my tongue past her lips. She opened for me, letting herself fall on the bed. When I nestled my hips between her thighs, she wrapped her legs around me. Why did I ever think that sex with Aurora would be anything other than intense and all-consuming? Maybe I wanted to believe she'd be a bad lay, so I wouldn't want her so much. But that was impossible. I'd had a hard-on for her since the day she barged into the men's bathroom at school.

For days, I thought of her eager gaze on my cock. I thought of her touching herself thinking about me and what she saw. I dragged the length of me along the seam of her trimmed pussy. A part of me wanted to believe she had done that for me. That she'd gotten herself ready, hoping I'd get to see it today.

"I like this." I wedged a hand between us and rubbed her, feeling her wet folds. "I know you didn't trim for me."

"Hmmm." Her eyes fluttered close as she bucked her hips toward my hand. "The girls in the locker room. They're all shaved. I wanted to try it."

"I fucking love it." I worked her own juices all over it, then I drove into her.

This time, it didn't require as much effort as the first time. It shouldn't matter. But knowing I was her first awoke a feral instinct in me. I wanted to possess her body, be the only one to ever touch her. Her slick walls tightened around me, and I ventured down a spiral of pure bliss. I swelled into her over and over, until I found my own climax. It was as before, an overwhelming heat of ecstasy and pleasure. I dragged out my cock, and my cum slipped out. At the sight of it, I got harder than before. No idea why, I slipped inside her again, pushing all my spunk back in.

When I glanced up, she was looking at me with doe eyes. Her gaze darted between my face and my shaft buried in her folds. There was the usual innocence in them, but something else too. "How many ways are there for you to mark me?" She let out a soft laugh. "I belong to you, Enzo. Do you believe me?"

"Not yet." I sucked hard on her nipple then kissed her mouth. Then it hit me. Fuck, I'd been like a dog marking its territory, I hadn't thought about protection—not from me, I always wore a rubber. But for her. "I came inside you."

"You did."

"Jesus, I'm acting like this is my first time. I'm sorry." I raked a hand through my hair. "There's a drug store at the end of the street. They can help us." I grabbed her clothes off the floor.

When I met her gaze, she smiled. "Slow down."

"What?" I squinted to focus on her face. "You know how babies are made, right?"

"I do. Relax. I'm on the pill."

"Oh, fuck. Jesus, I should've asked." I sat next to her on the bed, then glared at her. Yeah, the thought popped into my head, and I couldn't shake it. She got on the pill for Angelo. Or for the wedding. Whatever, same thing. "Why are you on the pill?"

"Mom's idea. She wanted me to be ready." She stood and wedged herself between my legs. When I didn't meet her gaze, she cupped my face with both hands and made me look at her.

"Don't be mad. It doesn't matter what they want from me. It's just us."

"This entire day has not gone the way I thought it would. I'm not complaining," I added when her smile faded. "It's just that I feel like I'm losing control of everything—my feelings for you, my life, me—especially me. Especially when I'm with you."

"Me too. But is that not what this is about? Letting go. Falling...." She shook her head and glanced down.

"Falling in love?" I lifted her chin upward, then wiped a tear off her smooth cheek.

"Yeah."

"Do you love me?" I didn't mean to laugh, but the giddiness in my chest made that sound for me, and I couldn't keep it inside.

"I think I do." Her eyes welled up with tears. "You don't have to love me back. I understand."

"I think I love you too." I wrapped my arms around her nude body. She felt so good in my arms. "What do we do now? More specifically, how the hell are we going to get rid of your Angelo problem."

"I have no idea." She kissed the top of my head. "Without Signoria Vittoria's help, I don't see how I can undo the marriage contract. Even if I run away at this point, I don't think he'd let me go. He seems like the proud type. He'll see it as an insult."

Run away. That sounded like a great idea. But where would we go? To Dad's house in Ibiza? The Hamptons? Paris? All those places belonged to *him*. Truth was, there wasn't a corner in the world where Dad wouldn't find us. If he had already agreed Aurora was the reward for Angelo, he wasn't going to change his mind—certainly not on my behalf.

"I've been trying to figure it out. The semester is almost over, and I still have nothing."

"Things would be easier if we had Signoria Vittoria's help." I ran my hands down her back. "However, we do have the next best thing."

"Who?"

"Donata."

Trouble Can Be Fun

AURORA

The next day, I zigzagged my way through the crowded hall to get to Chem class. A few students looked me up and down, as if trying to figure out what was so special about me. I could only assume this was about Enzo and me leaving the school in the middle of the day. I didn't care what they thought. I had bigger problems to deal with.

I picked up the pace, even though I still had ten minutes until the bell rang. I was early, but I didn't want to hang out at the steps of Adeline Hall and risk running into Enzo and his friends. Mainly because I didn't know how to act around him anymore. The hours we spent at his penthouse were incredible —a crazy fantasy come true. But now I had to deal with the fallout. I had to deal with my family and with Angelo.

When I left Enzo's place last night, I was still on cloud nine. I didn't think to ask him how things would be at school going forward. The safest bet was to pretend like nothing was going on between us—pretend he wasn't my first, or that I wasn't madly in love with him. How stupid can a person be? I never should've gotten so close. There was no coming back from this.

"Good morning." Penny cocked an eyebrow when I walked into class. "How was the ride?"

"The what?"

"Come on." She rolled her eyes. "The entire school saw you leave yesterday."

"Oh, um." My heart rate spiked, even though we were alone. I wasn't ready to answer questions. "It was good."

"And then what?"

"And then nothing." I sat next to her and took out my chem book. "How was your evening?" Gosh, that sounded so fake.

"The same. Mom was in a terrible mood. She's not getting invited to parties." She shot a glance toward the door, then turned her attention back to the notes in front of her.

My pulse went from one hundred to two hundred beats a minute because the look on her face told me he was here. I swallowed and slowly lifted my head. When Donata smiled at me, I let out a breath.

"So tense today." Donata squeezed my arm. "We're still on after lunch?"

"Um. Yeah. Sure." I plastered on a smile.

For the last three months, I'd been having secret meetings with the royals. Well, all but Enzo. Donata insisted on getting weekly updates on my progress with Angelo, which, as of now, was exactly zero. Mom didn't trust us to be alone. Something I was grateful for because Angelo was getting creepier by the minute. Knowing why he felt like he owned me helped, but it was still crazy weird.

Of course, my parents still hadn't told me about the marriage contract. Though they weren't trying to be covert anymore. For one, all of the other guys Dad wanted me to meet kind of went away. Angelo's visits to the house were almost daily. He'd stop by for planned dinners, random drop-ins, and even brunch on Sundays.

I reported all this to Donata. Something that was super frustrating for her because, in her eyes, I should already know what he knew. But I wasn't her. Talking to Angelo made me feel dirty.

Enzo's signature scent brought me back from my pity party. Butterflies fluttered in my stomach before I even glanced up. This time, I knew for sure he was here. I lifted my gaze, eager to see his hazel eyes again. Sometimes when the light from the window hit the room just right, his irises would turn green. I missed that. I missed his face.

When I glanced up, he laughed at something Santino said, then walked right past me as if he didn't know me, as if we hadn't spent an entire afternoon together in his room. The happy bubbles in my chest popped one by one until I felt empty and sad.

Why did I think things would be different between us? I suppose I should be grateful that he didn't kick me out of his house as soon as we were done having sex. Pursing my lips to keep from crying, I opened my book and started to read about the chemical reactions for a base. I let the numbers replace all the images of Enzo in my head. Though it would take a lot more to erase the feel of his hands and mouth on my skin.

"For a minute there, I thought you were lying to me." Penny leaned over to whisper. "It's better this way, Rory."

My eyes watered. She was right. Enzo was nothing more than a beautiful dream. "Yeah." I had to go back to pretending my heart didn't do cartwheels in my chest every time Enzo walked into the room.

By the time lunchtime rolled around, the buzz about the motorcycle ride had died down. Instead, the gossip was all about Santino kicking the crap out of Ian this morning. I didn't care. I was just glad the glares had stopped.

"Did you hear?" Penny sat next to me at our usual lunch table. "Santino found Ian and Hanna doing it."

"Really?"

"Yeah, I'd never seen him that pissed off. They took Ian to the nurse's office with a busted lip. But apparently, now he's on his way to the hospital with a concussion or something."

Poor Santino. He'd really been into Hanna. "That's crazy. Did he get in trouble?"

"Are you seriously asking me that? They never get in trouble, Rory. This is what I've been trying to tell you." She sipped her water. "Maybe now you'll listen to me and stay away from them?" She dipped her head toward the entrance where Enzo stood scanning the room.

Our gazes met, and all the anger that had been building up in my stomach melted away. He should not have this much influence over me. I started to say hi, but then Donata walked in and ushered him toward their table at the opposite end of the dining hall.

"Yes, you were right about everything." I shot to my feet, pointing to the soda fountain. "I forgot my drink."

I took a glass from the tray and filled it with ice. I went to get a splash of lemonade when Molly, the cook in charge of feeding Enzo's cat, appeared out of nowhere. I'd seen her a couple of times in the courtyard when I went to see Fluffy. She never said hi, but I got the sense that she knew who I was. Even the first time we ran into each other, she wasn't surprised to see me there.

"You got my money, kid?" she asked me.

"What?" I shot a glance behind me and came face to face with Enzo. "Oh."

Molly was talking to him. I stood there like an idiot, frozen in place, as Enzo handed her a thick envelope. The woman was shorter than me, and in that hair net, she shouldn't look so menacing. But she did. She scared me. No wonder Chef kept her in the back of the kitchen, away from the rich, spoiled kids.

"After all this time, you still don't trust me?" Enzo chuckled.

"Not a chance." She sneered at him as she licked her fingers and continued counting the money. "I see you have a thing for strays."

"Hi, Molly." I waved awkwardly. I'd been watching their exchange for a good minute, so I felt compelled to say something.

"Hi, stray." She gave me a half smile then disappeared the same way she'd come in.

"I see you and Molly made friends." Enzo beamed at me.

"Yeah." I blew out a breath, then turned my attention back to the soda fountain.

"Hey." Enzo gripped my elbow.

Goosebumps shot up my arm. He rubbed his thumb over my skin, cocking his head to the side to see my eyes. "Are you mad at me or something?"

"You're the one who's been ignoring me all day." I didn't have to look back to know Penny was glaring at me. I could feel her angry vibes zeroed in on my back. "It doesn't matter." I made to leave, but he held me in place.

"This morning when I walked in, you almost ran out the door. I realized we didn't talk about what we wanted to tell people, so I gave you some space." He stepped into my personal space. "It's been four hours. Are you ready?"

"Ready for what?"

The boyish smile he flashed me made my knees weak. "To tell people."

"Oh." I cleared my throat. What we did last night was going to have consequences. But staying together was the only way to get through it all. Keeping our feelings a secret didn't make sense anymore. "I think so."

"Good." He cradled my cheek. "Because I've been dying to do this all day."

He pressed his lips to mine and tongue-kissed me in front of the whole school. This was a bad idea. The thought flashed in my mind's eye for a second before I gave into the heat building in my core. My eyes fluttered closed, and then I was floating, lost in Enzo's fantasy world.

He pulled away first, breathing heavy in my ear. "I missed you."

The room swayed a few rounds. Then everything came into clear focus. Right, we were still in the dining hall. Suddenly, it wasn't just Penny's glares burning a hole in my back, it was everyone's. When I glanced up, Donata, Santino, and Rex stared back at us. They didn't seem shocked by the news like everyone else. Why? Did Enzo tell them what happened? Heat rushed to my cheeks.

"Did you tell them?" I pointed behind me. "About yesterday?"

"No. That's none of their business." He beamed at me. "Come sit with us."

Sit with the royals? With everyone watching. That sounded like a terrible idea, something Penny most definitely would not approve of—because she knew Signoria Vittoria wouldn't approve. Wasn't that her job? To make sure I did what Signoria Vittoria wanted?

"I can't. I'm sitting with Penny. She's by herself." I pointed behind me.

"Not anymore." He raised a brow.

When I looked back, I caught a quick glimpse of Penny's backpack as she left the dining hall. I was never going to hear the end of this. I had gone and done exactly what she'd warned me not to do.

"I'm in so much trouble." I rubbed my forehead. No doubt she left to call Signoria Vittoria and tell her about Enzo and me.

"Trouble can be fun." He smirked.

"You're starting to sound like Santino." I shook my head, though I couldn't stop smiling.

"He acts like a loose cannon most of the time, but he's not wrong." He brushed his lips against mine. "Come on. I'll get your tray."

I stood there and watched him walk back to my table, grab my things, then make his way back to the other end of the room. I took a big gulp of my drink and ambled over to the royals' table.

As soon as I sat down, Santino dropped his fork on his plate and leaned toward Enzo. "This is against the rules."

"No, it's not." Donata sat back with a Cheshire cat grin on her face.

"She should know. She made up the rules." Rex rolled his eyes.

Enzo's demeanor and overall body language changed in an instant. He sat next to me, ready to throw a punch. I drank from my glass to cover the smile I couldn't contain. Enzo was ready to put his friends in their place. He was ready to be with me.

"So what? That's it?" Santino crossed his arms over his chest. "He won?"

"I think so." Donata reached over and squeezed Santino's bulging bicep. "Don't be a sore loser."

What was his deal? Of all three of them, he was the one I thought would be happy for us. He'd been so nice to me the past few months.

"I'm not a sore loser. I'm pissed that I didn't get a real chance to play my odds. That's cheating. He asked us to put the bet on hold, then he came in the middle of the night and popped her cherry. I didn't even know the game was back on."

"Let it go, Santino." Rex hit Santino's shoulder with his fist. "It's done."

"Yeah, I can see that." He rose to his feet. "Congratulations, you won this year's pop a cherry contest."

"Fuck off." Enzo stood to glare at Santino properly.

Meanwhile, my mind raced with all the things Santino had said. A game? This whole thing with the royals being my friends was a bet? I racked my brain to put all the pieces together. One, they all knew I was a virgin. And two, they placed a bet on who would be my first? Pop a cherry, as

Santino put it. My stomach rolled, and I let go of my glass. It fell to the table and spilled everywhere.

Donata jumped out of the way. "Nice, Santino. Just nice."

I was the stupidest girl in the world. So eager to make a friend, I was willing to look the other way when it was so clear that people like the royals could never be my friends. We came from completely different worlds. Why did I ever think I could cross that line and not get burned?

All these months, they had all pretended to be my friends as a joke. In their own way, Enzo, Santino, and Rex had tried to get close to me, and now I knew why. It was for Donata's amusement. I couldn't even look at her. But I'd bet it hadn't changed from before. The minute she saw Enzo kissing me in front of everyone, she knew it was because he had won—he'd taken my virginity.

I didn't care about that. I cared about the fact that he'd done it knowing what it would mean to my family, to Angelo, and even to Signoria Vittoria. The adults had made a deal that involved me. And the royals thought it would be a fun game to spoil that deal, and in the process, ruin my family. I had played a part in it too, but I did it for love. They did it for sport.

"He cheated." Santino pushed his tray toward the puddle of liquid and splashed both Enzo and me, then stormed off.

And still, they didn't get it. They stood there bickering with each other on whether or not Enzo followed the rules. They didn't care. They didn't get it.

"The holiday season is tough for him since his mom was killed." Rex dropped his napkin on the mess both Santino and I had made. "He'll go back to his cheery self once the Christmas decorations come down."

"So, what?" My gaze darted between Enzo, Donata, and Rex. "Was he lying then? Did he make all that up?"

"No, he was telling the truth." Enzo reached for my elbow, but I yanked it away.

"Don't touch me." I swiped the back of my hand over my cheek. When he tried again, I slapped him hard across the face. "You're not who I thought you were."

Forgive Me

Enzo

I stood outside the Adeline Hall scanning the lawn area for Aurora's face. Fucking Santino couldn't keep his mouth shut about the bet. Who cared how or why Aurora and I had gotten together? What mattered was that we loved each other—that after all these months of being apart, I had finally figured out how I felt about her.

Aurora was mad, and I didn't blame her. But she was dead wrong if she thought I was going to let her end things between us because of some stupid game. I did another quick sweep of the grounds and found Penny glaring at me from one of the picnic tables. I sauntered toward her. As soon as she saw me coming, she began to pack her things. I picked up the pace and caught up to her before she took off too.

"Where is she?"

"How should I know? She was with you last time I checked." She yanked her arm away, and I let her go.

"I need to talk to her."

"She was with you for all of ten minutes and you already broke her heart."

"Did she say that to you?"

"No, but I saw what she looked like. She was obviously hurt." She shook her head at me. "Just let her be. She's got a lot going on at home. She doesn't need this from you."

"Where did she go?" I didn't have time to sit here and explain to Penny that we all had shit going on with our parents. Or that Aurora was better off with me. That now that our feelings were out in the open, I wasn't letting her go. "Tell me now."

She rolled her eyes, crossing her arms over her chest. "Library," she mumbled.

I darted toward the building past Adaline Hall. This time of day almost everyone was either off campus or in the dining hall having lunch. The library was the best place for us to talk. Was that why she'd gone there? The pressure in my chest lifted. Aurora was pissed, but not enough that she wouldn't want to talk to me for days. We'd been apart long enough.

Silence fell as soon as the door shut behind me. I inhaled the scent of books and mahogany and held my breath to get my heart rate to calm down. In this quiet, I could hear my own pulse and loud exhales. I didn't like that Aurora had this kind of effect on me. It put me on edge.

By the time I found her in the Biographies' section, I was somewhere between annoyed and repentant. Her cheeks were dry, but the red in her eyes and nose told me she had been crying. I slowed my gait, so I could watch her put a book back. Yesterday, she'd been happy because of me. Was Penny right? Was I hurting Aurora just by being with her? I refused to believe that. We belonged together. Even if our futures looked bleak right about now, I wasn't ready to give up on us—especially not over some stupid bet.

She froze, then slowly turned to face me. I offered her a smile and imagined myself waving a white flag. She narrowed her eyes at me. I waited for her to tell me off, but instead, she bolted. Fuck. I chased after her, down the long corridor of books. When she was within reach, I pulled her into a bear hug.

"Why are you running?"

"I don't want to be anywhere near you." She squirmed in my arms.

I tightened my hold on her. What surprised me was the tinge of desperation that gripped my chest when she uttered those words. "Don't say that. I know you want to be with me. Let me explain."

"It's pretty self-explanatory. Unless you're here to tell me Santino was lying about the whole thing. Was he?"

"No, he wasn't."

"Did you get a good laugh?" She struggled against my hold, and in the process, her hair covered my face.

She smelled like something sweet, like strawberries. The more she rubbed against my body, the more I noticed her ass on my cock, and my arms over her breasts. I was here to talk, but she was making it damn near impossible to concentrate. She squirmed again right over my erection, and that finally got her attention.

"You can't be serious."

"I meant every word I said to you last night." I released a breath into her neck, then kissed the mark I'd left on her. "I love you."

"You let them watch while I fell for you. Like the stupid

girl I am, I fell for you. And it was all a game. You were toying with me the whole time. Since the beginning when I barged into the boys' bathroom. All the things you said to me, that was all part of your plan." She sniffed.

Her tears pelted my arm. I buried my face in her hair. When she said it like that, we came off as assholes. But that wasn't the whole truth. I hadn't agreed to the bet because I was bored. Or because I was chasing some trophy. I did it because I wanted her. Just her.

"I was an asshole for agreeing to the bet. But I had my reasons. I'm going to let you go. Do you promise to stay and listen?"

Her body felt so good pressed against mine, but she was making it hard to concentrate. And I needed her to hear the truth from me. Not the twisted version Santino dumped on her. He couldn't speak for me because I never told anyone how I truly felt about Aurora.

In the end, I couldn't resist her, I loosened my hold on her just enough, so I could take a handful of her tits. She melted against me, and I released her a bit more. For a long minute, I considered lifting her skirt and burying my cock inside her. If this was the last time we were together, I wanted to make it memorable.

"What else could you say that Santino hasn't already told me? You seduced me knowing I was a virgin. Knowing that I would be in trouble with my family for it. You didn't care if Angelo would retaliate for not getting what he was promised." The sadness in her voice cut me. She sounded defeated, destroyed.

I did that to her.

I thought of what I wanted to say. But there wasn't a single word to explain what I had done and why. So I opted for the naked truth, and started from the beginning. "I was attracted to you since the moment I saw you at Tiffany's. You looked so out of place and innocent."

"An easy target."

"Yeah, that's what I thought. Then I realized that every time I got near you, I fell prey to my own game. The first day of school, I just wanted to mess with you in the bathroom, watch you squirm. But instead, I felt a connection with you. You intrigued me." I panted a breath, while I nibbled on her neck. "Then we kissed, and I realized I was your first. I became obsessed."

"Obsessed?"

"That's when I realized that if I wanted to keep my sanity, I needed to stay away from you. You were more trouble than I first perceived."

She turned to face me. "But you didn't stop."

"No, I didn't. That's when Donata had the bright idea to make you this year's bet. I swear to you. My first reaction was to say no. Then she told us about Angelo. That messed with my head. I told myself it was just a game, but in truth, all I wanted was you. I wanted to make you mine—to mark you in all the ways possible, so he couldn't have you. And no, I didn't give a shit what kind of trouble your father would be in because of it. For that I'm sorry. I'm sorry that I didn't think about how that would make you feel."

She opened her mouth, but the words didn't come out. The good news was that she wasn't crying anymore, and she didn't seem hurt. Confused as fuck, but not in pain. She inhaled and stepped away from me. When I reached for her, she slapped my hand away. "Don't touch me."

Fuck. We were back to that. That was the problem right there. I wasn't ready to take that as her final answer. I needed to touch her, to feel her skin and her body against mine. "If there was ever a punishment to fit the crime, I think it would be this. Aurora, I fell for you. It's more than that." I took in a gulp of air to ease the pressure in my chest. "I'm in love with you. Do you have any idea how I feel knowing that some asshole out there thinks of you as his—that one day, you will be?"

She spun around, eyes big as if she hadn't realized that her marriage to Angelo was a very real possibility. "I don't want him."

"I know that." I stepped closer to her. When she recoiled again, I cupped her cheek. "If we stick together, we can find a way to stop him." I pressed my forehead to hers. "Forgive me."

Her features softened. She wanted to believe me. "Enzo." She slanted a glance away from me. Then did a double take. "Someone's coming."

"Wait." I gripped her elbow and lowered my voice. "We're not leaving until you give me an answer."

Her gaze darted between mine and the couple making their way to the Biographies' section, two rows down from us. She rubbed her temple, then furrowed her brows. I followed her line of sight and turned just in time to see a pair of tits pop out of their bra.

One thing I knew about Aurora was that she liked to watch. She couldn't help it. Her cheeks had already turned a deep red. And she couldn't look away. The couple was so into it and in a hurry, they didn't notice us at all behind two aisles of books.

I walked a circle behind Aurora and wrapped my arm

around her waist. Pressing my lips to her ear, I whispered so only she could hear me, "I bet she's wet for him already."

She nodded.

"I bet he's dying to bury himself inside her."

She leaned back to press her back to my chest. "We. Um. We, we should go." Her words were barely audible.

We should let them have their fun, alone. But I still needed Aurora to tell me she had forgiven me. I still wasn't ready to let her go. I slowly lifted her skirt and wedged my hand into her wet underwear. She covered her mouth as she let out a sigh.

"We are so good together. Don't throw it away because of some bet." I ran my fingers up and down her folds. "Is that where it hurts?" I palmed her clit.

"Yes."

I had no idea what the other couple was doing. But I could guess based on the other girl's moans. Unlike Aurora, the other girl didn't care if she was being loud. And neither did the guy.

"You're almost there, aren't you?" I slipped a finger inside her.

She reached behind her and pulled on my hair in response. The way she gave into it made me want her even more. I love that she trusted me. Even now in the middle of our first fight, she trusted me to take her there, to give her the release she so badly needed.

Her complete surrender made me love her even more. We were the same age. But in my eighteen years, to keep up with Dad, I had seen and done so much more than her. Maybe that was why she wasn't afraid to give so much of herself to me, why she wasn't afraid to fall. She didn't know what this mafia world could do to innocent people like her. She didn't know about all the lies and betrayal that lay beneath the surface. In our world, life was disposable.

I needed to protect her.

"Forgive me." I stilled my hand. "Say the words."

She gripped my wrist and closed her eyes. I chuckled because as angry as she was, she was too far down the path to turn back. Her pussy felt hot in my hand. All I had to do was stroke her a little more and she would come. But I wanted something in return.

"I forgive you."

I placed my free hand on her jaw to bring her mouth to mine. I kissed her hard and desperately while I rubbed her clit. My cock felt like it was about to explode. But this was about her—and what she needed.

"When you come, you have to be very quiet. Do you think you can do that?" I slowed my movements, easing two fingers inside her. Her whole body shivered as she squeezed her thighs together. "Shh." I thrust my tongue past her lips as she found her orgasm.

She melted in my arms as she rocked her hips, gently riding my fingers until her climax was fully spent. She was so fucking perfect. I thought of my confession from a few minutes ago. Aurora knew how obsessed I had become with her. And instead of running away, she let me finger her in the library. As if she understood we were meant to be. To hell with the rest of the world.

"Oh." Aurora's gaze shifted to mine.

The other couple had finished. The girl fixed her skirt, laughing at whatever the guy had told her. In the next beat, she grabbed his hand and pulled him out toward the front entrance of the library. If they noticed us watching them, they didn't show it.

"What is it?" I asked.

"I don't want to give up on us. I mean." She inhaled, still trying to recover from her climax. "If this is real, I don't want it to end."

"It is real." I cradled her cheek. "I can protect you, but we need to stay together. All of us."

A long time ago, Donata, Rex, Santino, and I had made a pact to do exactly that. To stay together and watch each others' backs. Today, I wanted them to know that Aurora needed to be part of that pact too. "Come on. You're late for your weekly meeting with Donata."

She chuckled. "I don't know why she bothers. It's been months. I still don't have anything we can use. I don't even know what I'm looking for."

"I never should've left you. I'm here now. Together, we can figure it out. You're not marrying him." I pressed my lips to hers. I wanted to do way more than that, but we were out of time. My only hope was that we still had time to fix this thing with Angelo Soprano.

"You're joining us today?"

"I am."

We Made a Pact

Aurora

I washed my hands in the bathroom sink, while I stared at my reflection in the mirror. I'd asked Enzo to give me a minute to clean up and recover. My cheeks were still red, and my eyes had that glossy look to them. By now, I knew those were my tells that I was turned on. Omigod, Donata couldn't know what Enzo and I did in the Biographies' section. It would be too embarrassing.

My pulse spiked when I realized that, at some point, they had all sat around and talked about my v-card and the best way to get me to hand it over. Jesus. I had wanted to be mad at Enzo for a little while longer. It was petty, but I liked to see him grovel. The pain in his eyes over losing what we had made me feel in control for the first time since I met him. But then that couple showed up, and Enzo just knew how to use it to his advantage to get me all confused and compliant.

Mind-blowing orgasm aside, I did believe Enzo when he said he was in love with me. That the bet had only been an excuse to get close to me. That he had feelings for me way before then. I also believed him when he said he wanted to protect me from Angelo. Though, in truth, I only needed protection from his dad since he was the one behind it all.

"Aurora." Enzo poked his head in. "Lunch hour is almost over. We need to get going."

"Yeah." I grabbed a paper towel and dried off my hands.

The room where we met every Tuesday was toward the back of the library. It was set up like a teacher's lounge with a large desk, a sitting area, and a credenza with a coffee machine and a fridge. Donata was the only one with a key to it. She mostly used the room for homework and whatever scheming she had going on for the week.

Enzo ushered me through the maze of bookshelves. His hand on my lower back made me feel all warm inside. Was this normal? Ever since we had sex for the first time, I couldn't stop thinking about him or it. Even now, after I had just come, I wanted to do it again.

"Hold that thought," he whispered in my ear and pushed the door open.

I shot a glance at him. The knowing smile he flashed me sobered me up. We had work to do. I couldn't spend what little time we had left before class thinking about Enzo's abs and all the things he could do with his hands.

"Oh, good of you to join us." Donata sat on the long sofa next to Rex. Her gaze lingered on me for a beat, then switched to Enzo. "I'm not even going to ask. Let's just get started." She pointed at the two club chairs in front of her.

"Before we start." Enzo took my hand in his and kissed it. "I wanted to set the record straight."

"Please do." Santino leaned on the threshold. When Enzo

turned to him with a smile, he ambled toward the desk and sat on it. "It's pretty obvious what's going on here. But go ahead."

"Yeah, you guys are not super covert." Donata tucked her ankles under her butt and braced her elbow on the back of the sofa.

My whole body heated with embarrassment. They all knew how I felt about Enzo. And what we were doing. "He explained about the bet, and I believe him."

"I'm in love with her." Enzo dropped the bomb without preamble. "We've been sitting on our thumbs for the past three months. We're not leaving this room until we have a solid plan to get rid of Angelo and his ridiculous marriage contract."

"First of all, I'm so happy for you guys. All's well that ends well." Donata ran her hands through her long hair. "And also, omigod finally. I was starting to think you were never going to get on board. The brooding was getting tiresome."

"For real? This is happening?" Santino leaned forward, pointing a finger at the two of us.

"Yes, for real." Enzo smiled at me.

"Hmm, congratulations, then." Santino shrugged before he turned to me. "Are you sure about this?"

I nodded.

"We need to nail Angelo's ass to the wall." Enzo held me tighter as he addressed the entire room.

"I wasn't able to get into Dad's office." I shrugged, meeting Donata's gaze. "Sorry."

"That's fine. It was a bad idea anyway. I don't think your dad knows what's going on." She patted Rex's shoulder. "Care to share with the group?"

Rex cocked an eyebrow as if this latest news didn't sit well with him. The day Enzo left, he'd given me a whole speech on duty and how there was no room for love. And now here we were telling him to stuff it. But what was the point of anything if we couldn't have love? Looking at Enzo now, I couldn't imagine my life without him. I loved him. And there was nothing Rex could do or say to make that go away.

"Don Alfera paid Dad a visit last night." Rex met my gaze. For a second, his eyes filled with pity for me. "The date has been set."

"The date for what?" I asked since he was still looking at me.

"Your wedding."

"Jesus fuck." Enzo let go of my hand. "When?"

"Before the semester ends. December seventeenth. The day after the school's holiday gala."

"Did your parents say anything to you?" Donata asked. "Or I mean, are they waiting until his dick is inside you to tell you?"

"Sounds like it to me." Santino chuckled.

Enzo glared at them. But before he could tell them to fuck off, Donata raised her hands in mock surrender. "Sorry. It sounded funnier in my head. But you have to agree. They're treating her like cattle." She furrowed her brows at me. "Why haven't you said anything to them? If it were me, I would've given Aunt Vittoria an earful by now."

Leave it to Donata to hit the nail right on the head. She wasn't wrong. I'd become no more than a prized pig. And that was entirely my fault. Since we came to New York, I had been playing along, biding my time, foolishly hoping someone would come and save me. But now a whole semester had gone by, and my situation had gotten worse. I had no way out. God, even Columbia seemed like a faraway dream at this point. None of that could happen without Signoria Vittoria's help.

I'd had my head up my ass because I didn't want to recognize that I was trapped. "Can they really make me marry him? I hoped your aunt would help me get out of it."

"And why would she do that?" Rex asked. "She's not some fairy godmother. You know that, right? You heard her the day the two of you went to her home to get justice for what Brody and Ian did to you. She only cares about what's best for her family. And I don't mean Donata. I mean her empire and the power and money that comes with it."

When he put it like that, he made me sound like a naive little girl. I hated that he made so much sense. "I'm eighteen now. They can't make me sign anything."

"Oh, sweetie, of course they can." Donata placed her hand over her heart. "And don't even bring up the authorities. They're also here to serve themselves."

"That's enough." Enzo put up his hand. "We get it. It's bad news all around. Now we need a plan."

"I thought you'd never ask." Donata rose to her feet, grabbed the whiteboard wedged in the corner by the desk and brought it out with a grin on her face. "I made a few notes." She wheeled the board around to show us.

I stared at her neat writing. She'd made a list of what we knew. Seeing it all together made me realize that maybe we didn't need the play by play of what the adults were planning to do. Who cared why Angelo wanted to marry me? What mattered was that I was his reward. Whatever Don Alfera was going to get out of this grand plan of his also didn't make a difference to me. Because all we had to do was thwart Angelo's big assignment. If we could do that, then Don Alfera and Dad would have no reason to make good on their promise to make me marry Angelo.

That only left Signoria Vittoria. Would she help me run away from this place, if she didn't get what she wanted? Based on Donata's notes, Signoria Vittoria and Don Alfera wanted the same thing.

"I think we need to figure out what Angelo was tasked to do. If we can do that, maybe Dad will listen to what I want." I met Enzo's gaze, and he nodded.

"So, what is Angelo supposed to do?" Enzo tapped at the big question mark Donata had next to Angelo's name. "And how do we find out?"

"Well." Donata grabbed a purple marker and made a line from my name on the board to Angelo's. Then she wrote two new pieces of information, the wedding date and this Saturday's date.

"What's going on this weekend?" I crossed my arms over my chest, feeling lost again. Every time I felt like we were making progress, my parents did something to knock me off axis.

"Your engagement party." Donata glanced up and mouthed, "I'm sorry."

"Don't be." I rubbed the side of my face. "I'm having a serious talk with Mom tonight. How can they be planning all this and not tell me? What are they thinking?" I asked, wishing one of them would tell me that maybe my parents hadn't said anything to me because they were secretly working to make sure the marriage didn't happen. "Seriously, guys. Anything? Feel free to sugar coat it."

"Sugar is bad for you." Enzo braced his arms on his thighs

and offered me a half-smile. Was this him being cute and supportive?

"There's some good news. The engagement party is at Angelo's penthouse. And we're all invited." Rex gestured toward Enzo. "You wanted a plan? Here it is. We break into his office and find out what he has to do to keep Aurora."

"And then we take it away from him." Enzo finished Rex's sentence.

"Exactly."

"I knew those night vision goggles would come in handy." Santino beamed at me.

I got the sense that the three of them knew about the party and the fact that we would have access to Angelo's place. But they waited until Enzo and I were ready to hear the news. They all wanted to help us.

"Why are you helping us?" I met their gazes across the room. "You could get in trouble with your own families."

"We made a pact." Santino shrugged.

"A pact that now includes you, Rory." Donata winked at me. "Don't look so lost. I can't stand it. You need to shake off those big doe eyes and meet Angelo where he is. Beat them all at their own game."

"Easy for you to say. You grew up with all this mafia stuff." I rubbed the goosebumps on my arm.

For a moment I listened to the tiny voice in the back of my head that said I wasn't cut out for this—that I wasn't strong enough. Then I glanced at the whiteboard again and realized that for the first time ever in my life, I wasn't alone. Whatever get-rich-quick scheme my parents had going on didn't matter. I wasn't their stupid pawn anymore. And more importantly, I wasn't alone. I had the royals on my side.

"Sure." Donata raised an eyebrow. "We can sit here and talk about all your shortcomings, or we can talk about how you're going to break into Angelo's office."

"Why her?" Enzo put his arm around my waist. "I can go in there."

"Stop thinking with your dick." Santino drew a big cock and balls on the board, then put an X over it. "If Angelo walks in, Rory can cool off the situation by showing a little cleavage. He's never going to suspect her. Don't look at me like that. You know I'm right."

I thought about Angelo and the way he looked at me when my parents weren't in the room. "I'll do it. But isn't that kind of like bad for business, you know, to have evil plans in writing just lying around?"

"It won't be labeled like that. But I'm sure there's an email or something where Dad outlines his expectations." Enzo rubbed his neck. "There are a million ways to kill a mobster. Dad would want things done his way."

I turned to Donata's notes where she had Signoria Vittoria's words in black, *kill a mobster,* then Dad's name next to it with a question mark. What did Dad do to get on Don Alfera's hit list? I knew Dad's motives were always based on money, but how far did he go this time? He sold me off, and that was bad enough. Now there was a good chance he'd done something else to get himself killed. I wanted to tell the rest of the group about Dad's antics in Las Vegas. But it was too embarrassing. I couldn't tell them about Dad stealing from his boss or what Mom had to do to save all of us.

They didn't need to know anyway. Come Saturday, if I got access to Angelo's computer, I knew exactly where to start looking.

Follow the money.

"Well, I gotta get to class." Donata dug into her back pocket. She dangled the keys in front of Enzo then pressed them to his chest. "Make sure you lock up."

They all made a bee line for the door. A minute later, Enzo and I were alone in a secret library room. A myriad of bad ideas flitted through my mind. Knowing that Donata and the guys now knew what Enzo and I were doing sent a rush of adrenaline through me. It made my skin tingle with anticipation. We were so late to class, but I didn't care.

"How are you doing with all this?" Enzo wrapped his arms around my waist.

"It all sucks." I blew out a breath to calm my rapidly beating pulse. "But I think we're making progress."

"I don't like the idea of serving you up on a silver platter." He kissed my neck then wrapped his fingers around it. "If he touches you—"

"He won't. I can do this." My throat constricted under his grip. "I was thinking. What would Angelo do if he finds out I'm not the virgin he thinks I am? Would he give up on this whole marriage idea?"

"I don't know. It feels like he's gone into the realm of obsession with you. He's a trained assassin, Aurora. We don't want to mess with him. Don't worry. We'll find a way to get him off your back."

He puffed out a breath and walked me back toward the desk. When my butt hit the edge, he picked me up by the waist and sat me on it. I didn't get a chance to think about Saturday night and our plans. Enzo crashed his mouth to mine and kissed me, while his fingers worked on the buttons of my blouse. Oh, wow, he totally meant to have sex with me here.

I thought of the girl from the Biographies' section. She didn't seem to care that people could walk in on them. She had been half naked while her boyfriend fucked her against the bookshelves. Was that what I wanted? My skin heated at the idea of someone barging in on us. I shot a glance toward the closed door as Enzo unbuttoned my blouse. I could tell him to stop. But then, I would have to go to class with this ache between my legs.

His mouth latched on to my taut nipple, and all reason went out the door. I pushed his suit jacket off his shoulders, then pulled his shirt over his head. His body was solid muscle, a work of art—the result of days of training outside and then taking a beating on the football field. His hot skin against mine felt familiar. He felt like mine.

"You're so fucking beautiful." In one fell swoop, he pulled my hips toward him, removed my panties, and thrust into me as if we were out of time—as if he never wanted to say goodbye to me again.

Playing Mobsters

Aurora

"Two weeks left of fall semester." Mom patted my leg to get my attention. "You're practically done with high school."

I peeled my gaze away from the oncoming traffic to face her. "Yeah. It went by fast."

This morning after breakfast, both my parents insisted on driving me to school. Dad sat in the front seat as always, letting Mom carry the conversation. I had tried to wiggle my way out of sharing a car with them, but they insisted. Five minutes into it, and Mom was still talking about the weather and the upcoming semester break. If I could make it for another three miles, I'd be home free. And I could go another day without knowing about the engagement.

"Rory." Mom touched my knee again.

The cool air filled with pity and remorse. Or maybe that was just wishful thinking on my part. I wanted to believe that everything Donata had said about my parents' plans was a lie—

that they would never sell me off to the highest bidder. Or at least, that Mom would try to help me.

"As you know, Dad has been trying to find you a suitable husband. The world is a harsh place. You need someone who can protect you." Mom smiled at me. A sweet gesture that anyone looking in would see as motherly. Maybe she was concerned. Maybe she did love me. "We found someone."

"It wasn't easy." Dad shifted his body to face me. "We wanted the best for you. And we found him."

Gee, I wonder who it could possibly be. Could it be the guy who'd been coming to dinner twice a week for the past three months and looking at me like he owned me?

"She knows that, dear." Mom squeezed my fingers. "Angelo cares about you."

I kept my gaze on the city beyond the car window. *Help.* The word flashed in my head as I tried to focus on the different faces passing by. They were going by so fast, I couldn't look at them long enough to make out their features or remember what they looked like. I supposed it was the same for them. They didn't see me. They couldn't help me. Whatever my parents and Angelo had planned for me, it was happening.

"Say something." Mom patted my hair. "You'll be just fine, Rory."

Donata was right. This whole time, I'd been a coward. From day one, I could've asked my parents about the so-called engagement. I could've begged them not to sign a marriage contract on my behalf. But I was too scared. I buried my head in the sand instead, hoping Mom would do something to save me. But why would she? She finally had everything she worked so hard for. Everything she'd ever wanted.

I inhaled and braced myself for impact. "No, Mom. You say it. You tell me what's happening right here."

Her eyes widened in surprise. We'd been in the car for twenty minutes. We were blocks away from my school and they still hadn't said the words.

"You're marrying Angelo Soprano in a couple of weeks. There's no reason to wait. You're old enough now." Dad shot a quick glance my way as he spoke the words quickly.

"And if I say no? I mean, I still have to finish high school. And then, I have college. And how old is he again?"

"Rory." Mom reached for me again, but I caught her wrist then set her hand down on the leather seat. She didn't get to play the concerned mom anymore.

"What kind of world do you think we live in? Where do you think all this money comes from? Your fancy school and your designer clothes? You don't get a choice in this. None of us do. It's done." He glared at me for an entire block, until the car came to a stop in front of the school.

Finally, Dad had told the truth. And it was everything I'd feared. I had my answers—one, they were doing it for the money. Two, they didn't care about me. And three, the contract couldn't be undone.

"We'll talk more tonight, sweetie." Mom beamed at me. "There's so much to plan. Of course, Signoria Vittoria is helping with all the details, and she's thought of everything. You have nothing to worry about. That's the perk of marrying someone older, with money. Angelo will take good care of you. You'll see."

I scoffed, shaking my head. It didn't matter what I said. Or what I thought. They all had already made up their minds.

"We'll be officially announcing the engagement this Saturday. It would be good for you to spend some time with Angelo. Alone. You know, as a couple in your new home. That's where we're hosting the party." She was bubbly with excitement.

My stomach rolled at the thought of my new home with Angelo. "I gotta get to class."

The driver opened the door for me, and I climbed out. As soon as I did, Enzo's face came into view. Based on the dour look on his face, I could only assume he knew that my parents were breaking the news to me this morning. How did they always know everything before I did?

I walked past him because I knew my parents were still watching. If they found out about Enzo and me, I had a feeling something bad would happen, like they'd move up the wedding date to this weekend instead. Or send Enzo away. Don Alfera and Signoria Vittoria had the power to do that and so much more.

Enzo called after me, but I didn't stop until I got to Chem. Penny was already at our table, looking at me like I was a lamb on the way to the slaughterhouse. So she knew too. When I turned around, Donata and Enzo stood at the threshold. They exchanged a meaningful glance, then shut the door behind them.

"So they finally told you." Donata ambled toward our table. "What did they say?"

"Nothing new." I met Enzo's intense gaze. "The party is this weekend and then the wedding. They've also decided I'm moving into Angelo's penthouse after we're married."

"That makes sense." Donata leaned on the table, surveying Penny's face. "What about you, Penny?"

"What?"

"Come on. I know you've been meeting with Aunt Vittoria

pretty much weekly. It took me a while to figure out it was you. But now I have no doubt." Donata released a breath and carefully placed a lock of blonde hair behind her ear. Her bright blue eyes focused intently on Penny until she squirmed in her seat. "I can make your life at school a living hell. But you already know that."

Penny nodded.

"So, tell us what you know. And what you have told Aunt Vittoria." When Penny opened her mouth, Donata gripped her jaw. "I know you were asked to spy on Rory here. So skip the lies."

"I haven't told her about Enzo. I swear."

"So kind of you." I crossed my arms over my chest. "Really, this whole time, you weren't helping me survive school. You were just what? Gathering intel?"

"Both." Penny's gaze darted between Donata and me. "I'm sorry, Rory. But things are tough at home. We're hanging by a thread. Without Don Alfera's support, Dad's business has been declining. Then Mom's getting snubbed everywhere she goes. I had to do what Signoria Vittoria asked me to do."

"Who cares? Poor you." Donata rolled her eyes as she let Penny go. "What do you know about Angelo?"

"That he's marrying Rory in a couple of weeks. That's it. He's come by the house a few times. He never stays long. When Dad was Don Alfera's right-hand man, Angelo used to look up to him. I think he owes Dad a favor. But I'm not sure."

"Hmm." Donata braced her hands on her hips. "If Don Alfera wanted his old right-hand man dead, he would've taken care of that a long time ago. Right?" she asked Enzo.

"I think so. This doesn't help us." Enzo stepped toward me, but I backed away from him.

I was still trying to process the idea that now I was officially engaged to someone else. Yeah, that had been the case for a while, but now that my parents had said it aloud, it actually felt real. I didn't want anything bad to happen to Enzo because of me. I sat on my counter stool with dread crushing my chest.

The bell rang, and Donata pointed a graceful finger at Penny. "We're not done here. We'll talk more during lunch."

Lunch hour was more of the same. Donata spent her time grilling Penny on what she knew, while I spent my time wondering if Signoria Vittoria or Angelo had another spy in the school. How much did they know about what Enzo and I did every single day?

"Nothing has changed, Aurora." Enzo leaned toward me. "You knew all this yesterday. And the day before." He raised an eyebrow.

Of course Enzo was right. I knew about the engagement when I decided to have sex with him at his penthouse—and yesterday at the library. Yeah, the information we had was the same, but now my parents and Angelo knew I knew. And that made all the difference because now anything Enzo and I did, Angelo would see as cheating. And who knew what that would mean for my family and me—for Enzo.

"I know." I shook my head. "I wasn't thinking before. This thing between us. It's dangerous. We don't live in a normal world."

"Let me ask you this. Did he propose to you?"

"No."

"Did you say yes?"

"Of course not."

"Then you don't owe that asshole shit. You have no moral obligation here. It isn't cheating if that's what you're thinking." He took my hand in his and kissed the inside of my wrist. "Whatever claim he thinks he has on you won't last long. You're not marrying him." He cradled the back of my neck and brought me toward him.

I released a panicky breath because I thought he was going to kiss me with everyone watching. He'd done the same thing the day before. But again, this was different.

"I want to kiss you so badly." He pressed his forehead to mine.

"Before, we could claim ignorance. Now we can't."

"You win." He let go of me, picked up his tray, and stood. "Meet me in the courtyard in five minutes." He bent down, so he could whisper in my ear. "If you don't show, I'll come back for you and kiss you in front of everyone."

I stared at his retreating form with wide eyes. Great. Just great. Rubbing the back of my neck, I quickly scanned our table then the rest of the dining hall. Donata and Penny were still deep in conversation. Rex and Santino grabbed their things and followed Enzo out the door.

For a whole minute, I played with the fruit on my plate. A part of me wanted to chase after Enzo. But the other part, the logical part that didn't want him to get hurt, told me to stay put. Though I knew enough about Enzo to know that he didn't make idle threats. If I didn't meet him, he'd come back and remind everyone that we were together.

"Damn him," I uttered under my breath, rising to my feet.

Before I had fully made the decision to meet him, I was

already on the gravel path that led to the hidden courtyard behind the bell tower. I found him there sitting on the edge of the water fountain playing with Fluffy. The cat had brought him a toy mouse. Enzo wrestled the thing from Fluffy's teeth and then his claws. When he had the stuffed toy in his hand, he threw it across the yard, and Fluffy took off after it.

"Are you playing fetch with a cat?" I laughed.

"He likes it. Watch."

I sat next to him while the cat brought him the bright orange mouse again. When Enzo hurled it toward the stone wall, Fluffy charged like I'd seen wild animals do on TV. "That's funny. I've never seen a cat do that."

"Killing mice is his instinct. He doesn't get to do it for real here. This is the next best thing." Enzo wrapped his arm around my waist. "Kind of like us, don't you think? We come to school every day and play mobsters."

I got up because his hand on my body was already putting all kinds of bad ideas in my head. He walked up behind me and kissed my neck, then my shoulder. A spark ignited in my core, then spread through my whole body. Before I knew it, I was in his arms, kissing him as if I only had a few weeks to live —as if he were my only lifeline.

With a groan, he deepened the kiss, his hand taking handfuls of my ass, while the other cupped my breast over my blouse. My heart thrashed in my ears and silenced all thoughts of doing the right thing. All I cared about was being here with Enzo, tasting him and touching his warm skin. He kissed my neck on his way down to suck on my nipple. Why didn't we meet in Donata's secret room in the library? We could be doing so much more in private. I needed to know that Enzo wasn't giving up on us. I wanted to show him that neither was I.

"They won't win," he muttered, sucking hard on any patch of skin he could find. "You're not his to win."

"This isn't a game, Enzo." I tunneled my fingers through his soft hair. The pain in his eyes cut me, but he had to understand. "Dad's words sounded so final this morning. I don't think he could undo any of it, even if he wanted to. The contract is a very real thing."

"We're real too." He nibbled on my lower lip, then flashed me one of his charming smiles. "Forget about Angelo."

"Sure. Done." I rested my head on his chest. I couldn't just wish it all away, but I could do this. I could make the last five minutes of our lunch break last a little longer.

His chest rumbled with a low chuckle. "There's a holiday gala on the last day of school. It's at my house in the Hamptons. There will be snow and mischief. You should come. As my date."

"What?" I lifted my head to look at his handsome face. "You know I can't do that."

If the fancy party was at the Alferas' beach house, there was a one-hundred percent chance Angelo would be invited too. And I had no doubt he'd expect me to show up with him. Tears streamed down my cheeks. I couldn't spend the rest of my life married to someone I didn't love—watching my only true love from afar, pining over him day in and day out.

"Because of that person we forgot about?" He held me tighter.

"After this Saturday's party, I'll be officially engaged. I can't be seen with you in public." I circled my arms around his waist, taking in his body heat and scent.

"We'll figure out a way to be together. I promise." He kissed the top of my head. "I'm done playing mobsters."

Rory's Phone

Enzo

The last time I stepped foot in Angelo's apartment was last year, when he got his big promotion as boss of one of Dad's crews. Judging by all the new furniture and art in his new penthouse, Angelo was doing well for himself. I didn't care about that. Whatever he had now was no match to what my family had—to what I would be able to offer Aurora one day.

Thinking back to that day, I thought of Dad's other big news. He also announced that James Conti was no longer his right-hand man—and that he had found someone better. His replacement was already working hard and doing great things. He humiliated the Conti family and then cast them off. No one knew what had happened between Dad and James Conti, and no one had a choice; they had to accept the fact that Conti was out.

James was married to Dad's first cousin Bianca. Growing up, we'd spent a great deal of time with the Conti family.

Penny wasn't a royal, but she was in our circle because of her dad's rank within the Society. All of that went away practically overnight. And now Aurora's dad, Stefano, was running the show when Dad wasn't around, which lately was all the damn time. According to my brother, Massimo, who still visited Mom every weekend, Mom and Dad were fighting constantly. So much so that he barely left Brooklyn these days. That gave Stefano carte blanche to run the business as he pleased.

As soon as I sauntered into the living room, a server offered me a glass of champagne. I gulped it down then grabbed another while I scanned the room full of the Society's most prominent members. Even Santino's dad was here. After his wife was killed two years ago, he rarely went out in public. Angelo's engagement party had to be something special. I sipped more of the wine to wash down the bad taste in my mouth. This entire night was ridiculous.

I had arrived late because I didn't want to be here for the big announcement—just my luck that Aurora's family was also not on time.

"Maybe she got cold feet." Santino took the champagne flute out of my hand and replaced it with a short tumbler filled with something more appropriate for the occasion. "Relax, man. This is all just for show. It's not like he's marrying her tonight."

I shot a glance toward him, then drank. "What is this asshole up to? He acts like he's in charge."

"We'll find out tonight." He shifted his gaze toward the front entrance, then grinned. "There she is."

Aurora strolled in, wearing a one-shoulder corset satin dress with a slit that went all the way up to her thigh. She wore the gown for Angelo, but I knew the sapphire pendant resting on her cleavage was for me. Royal blue was her color. It made her big, innocent eyes stand out.

"Jesus fuck."

"She cleans up nicely." Santino patted me on the back, then gripped my shoulder. "You can stop staring now."

I meant to do what he said because he was right: Aurora didn't need me ogling her all night. But then Angelo showed up out of nowhere, his gaze glued to Aurora's tits, which, thanks to that dress, were fully on display. Now that they were engaged, Angelo didn't try to hide his true feelings for her. He stood right there, eye-fucking her in front of everyone.

"This is going to be a long fucking night." I puffed out a breath.

"You don't say."

Angelo didn't waste time. Aurora had barely walked in the door when he grabbed her by the hand and ushered her to the center of the room. "Can I have everyone's attention, please?"

I rolled my eyes at him, already done with this charade. While every person in the room focused on Angelo, Aurora met my gaze. She looked pale, like a lifeless doll. In a way, that was exactly what her parents wanted—a malleable daughter who did as she was told. They seemed pleased with her performance.

"First of all, thank you for coming out tonight." He raised his glass toward Dad, who had shown up alone.

Like me, this was the sort of thing Mom hated the most about the Society—how we used money to cover up the ugly. One hundred people under one roof, and not one person thought to ask why a thirty-year old was marrying a girl who was still in high-school. They all came in dressed in their tuxedos and elaborate gowns to celebrate Angelo's reward because Dad asked them to.

"It means a great deal to me to have all of you here to help me celebrate my engagement to Aurora." Angelo went on and on about himself. Very quickly, his announcement became an acceptance speech that had nothing to do with Aurora.

I tuned out his voice because the asshole got on my nerves. All I wanted to do was walk up to him and punch him. But that wouldn't help Aurora. The best thing to do was to play along and find a way to get into his library and figure out what he'd done to deserve all this.

"To the new couple." Aurora's dad raised his glass as Angelo made a big show of putting a diamond ring on Aurora's finger.

A round of applause broke around the room while Angelo drank eagerly from his glass. When Dad joined him and gave him a heart-felt hug, I weaved my way through the crowd and headed toward the kitchen. I couldn't stand there and watch any more of it.

The staff looked up at me with wide eyes, but other than that, didn't ask me to leave. I dug my hand in the pocket of my tuxedo jacket and fished out a couple hundred-dollar bills.

I handed them to the woman who looked like she was running the show. "Why don't you guys take a fifteen-minute break."

She grabbed the bills as she looked me up and down. "We'll be back in ten."

They exited out the service door. In the next beat, Aurora rushed in with a wild look in her eyes. "I don't have a lot of time. Angelo insists on keeping me by his side." She made a fist with her hand several times.

"Did he hurt you?" I reached for her waist, but she pushed me away.

"No. He just has a firm grip." She looked up at me, and her features softened. "You look good in a tuxedo."

"You." I touched her soft cheek.

"Enzo." She caught my fingers and squeezed, shaking her head.

Right. She was officially engaged and couldn't be seen with me. She was afraid of what Angelo could do to me. But really, what could he do if he saw me talking to his fiancée? Dad might not give a shit about me, but he would care if Angelo went over his head and came after me. I didn't care about Angelo's recent good fortune—I still out-ranked him.

"Oh good, you're here." Donata darted into the kitchen with her mobile in hand. When she looked up, she stopped in her tracks. "Oh, wow, your face. Enzo. Fix it. Right now."

"Fix what?" I braced my hands behind me on the sink counter.

"You look like you're ready to murder someone."

"She's right." Rex strolled in with Santino by his side.

"Can we get on with this?" I gestured toward the service door. "The staff will be back soon."

"My parents are waiting for me." Aurora read something on her phone, then moved to stand closer to the entrance to the kitchen.

"Well, while Angelo was doing his little speech, I quickly went down the hallway to check the rooms. There's a guestroom to the left, and then a powder room. To the right, there's a double door that's locked. My guess is that's his office. I checked the upstairs, but there's only bedrooms up there." She winced. "His room smells like cheap cologne. Why? He certainly has money for something better."

"Some people like the scent of new money. No offense." Santino gestured toward Aurora before he smiled at Donata. "I can pick the lock. That's not an issue."

"Good. Rory, you think you can handle it? No one will suspect you."

"Yeah, I got it."

"Rex, you'll have to keep Angelo entertained. Text me if you lose him." Donata showed him her phone. "I'll linger outside the library and get Rory out of there if we need to."

"What about me?" I stepped toward Donata.

"You stay here and work on your face." She smoothed out her dress and returned to the party.

As soon as Rex, Santino, and Aurora walked off, I received a group text from Donata. She meant to manage all of us from her phone. I sent a thumbs-up and sat at the breakfast table in the corner. The staff returned to the kitchen but didn't complain when they saw I hadn't left yet.

Maybe Donata was right. If I went out there again, I didn't know what I was going to do. I hated seeing Angelo all over Aurora, pressing her to his body like she belonged to him.

The next message to the group came in.

Rex: I got A.

Santino: Going in

I glared at my screen waiting for the next update.

Santino: R, ur up...

Aurora: K

Donata: Coast is clear

The next five minutes felt like an eternity. I could picture Rex carrying on a conversation with Angelo while Santino and Donata lingered in the background to make sure he didn't get away from them. My heart raced when I thought of Aurora in Angelo's office, rummaging through his things. I should be the one in there.

Aurora: No luck on his computer. There's a locked cabinet here though. Santino?

A whole minute went by with no answer.

Aurora: Guys? A little help.

Aurora was asking for help. If Santino didn't get in there, this whole plan would be a bust. I gripped my phone and counted in my head. When I got to ten, I shot to my feet and headed out. She couldn't stay there just waiting for Santino. I could pick a lock just as easily as him.

As I walked through the living room, where most of the guests were gathered, I spotted Donata, Rex, and Santino huddled around Angelo. By the way Donata was flaunting her cleavage, I had to assume Angelo didn't care much for Rex's polite conversation. They weren't even checking their texts.

"Excuse me." I stopped a server. "The restroom?"

"Down the hall to the left." He gestured politely.

"Thank you." I shot another glance at Donata and went in.

What were the odds Angelo had incriminating information on his computer? I would say zero. Now hard documents that could save his ass later if things went to shit, was a different matter. I'd say that locked drawer was our best bet. I pushed open the library door and cursed under my breath. Aurora hadn't even thought to lock it behind her.

I barged in just as she was going through the papers on Angelo's desk. By the desperate look on her face, I'd say she wasn't having any luck. When the door clicked shut, she glanced up at me.

"Omigod. It's you." She darted toward me.

I met her in the middle of the room and kissed her the way I'd been dying to do since she first arrived. She braced a cold hand on my cheek, then buried her face in the nook between my neck and shoulder. Aurora wasn't a criminal. She wasn't like us, who grew up in the middle of it. We'd been playing cops and robbers since we were little.

"There's nothing here. This was a stupid idea. Why would he leave anything lying around?"

"Calm down."

"Really?" She glared at me, pressing a hand to her forehead.

"Wrong choice of word." I kissed her forehead. "Let me try the drawer. Which one is it?"

She rushed to it, then yanked on the handle to prove it was locked. Earlier today, when I'd put my utility knife and cash in my pocket, I'd let my mind go through a quick fantasy where I got to stab Angelo in the chest. I supposed his secret drawer was all I was going to get tonight.

I fiddled with the lock until it gave way. As soon as it popped open, Aurora pushed her way in front of me and started going through the files. The folders were not labeled. Some of them had invoices in them, keys, checkbooks, credit cards, passports. Aurora quickly opened those.

"He's a mobster. Of course he has passports with different names." She pursed her lips. Then her eyes went wide. When she turned to me, she showed me the picture. "This one is mine. Aurora Soprano." I rolled my eyes. "He's assuming I'm taking his name."

"We're taking it." I grabbed it and stuffed it in the inside pocket of my jacket. "What else is in there?"

"A wire transfer for a million dollars to an offshore account," she mumbled as her delicate fingers went through each file in the back. "Lots of invoices for shipments to Africa. He's selling them used cars."

"That's normal. What else?"

"Okay." She looked at me for a beat. "I don't know what any of this stuff means."

"Wait. Go back." I pulled out the manila folder. "He bought a house in the Hamptons. About a block from ours, right on the beach."

"Good for him." She released a breath. "Can we just call it? This whole mission is a bust."

"Not really." I shut the drawer. "Now we know he's planning to take you out of the country after you're married." I purposely didn't use the word honeymoon, but I couldn't help taking a quick glance at her engagement ring. Acid pooled in the bottom of my stomach at the idea of Angelo taking Aurora away from me.

"Enzo." She met my gaze.

"You look so beautiful in that dress." I gripped her waist and walked her toward the desk. When her butt hit the edge, I slipped my hand up the slit along her thigh. "I know you didn't pick it out. Your parents can't be this cynical. Did he buy it for you?"

She nodded.

I crashed my mouth to hers to remind her that she was mine. That this entire party was a complete farce. She moaned softly against my lips. Too many days had gone by since the last time we were together. I needed her. If only for a minute. As if she could read my mind, she hopped on the desk and spread her legs, pulling me toward her and thrusting her tongue past my lips.

By the time I unzipped my pants, my cock was hard as steel. I pushed her dress up, past her hips, and pushed her thong out of the way. There was barely any fabric covering her pussy—and that strengthened my resolve to fuck her right here and now.

I swelled into her, and the entire room came into focus. "Fuck, you feel so good." I planted soft kisses on the mounds barely contained by her corset. The drag of her slick walls against my erection made the anger clutching my insides release their grip. Bit by bit, I melted and molded my body around hers.

"Enzo." She wrapped a leg around my waist.

Her phone vibrated on the desk.

We both stopped and stared into each other's eyes. When I glanced down at the screen, Angelo's name made me see red. "Why is he calling you?"

"He's probably looking for me." She labored to catch her breath. "Before, he told me he didn't want me to leave his side."

"Answer it. Tell him you need a minute."

"What?" She dropped her gaze to where my cock was still buried inside her. "I can't."

Before I had decided what to say, I grabbed the phone and placed it to my ear, glaring at the sapphire on her chest. "Rory's phone."

Aurora's eyes went big like saucers. *Oh, fuck me.* She was

so sexy when she looked at me like that. I thrust into her, then pulled all the way out to the tip before I plunged in again.

"Who the hell is this?" His tone was laced with all kinds of contempt.

"Enzo Alfera."

Run Away with Me

Aurora

I braced my hands behind me while Enzo drove straight into me again. What the hell were we doing? We were in Angelo's library having sex. Not only was Angelo officially my fiancé, but he was also a dangerous mobster. Five minutes alone with him was all I needed to figure that out. He didn't care about me. He cared about his precious virgin prize. And how it made him look in front of the others. He wasn't much different than Dad, doing whatever it took to get what he thought was owed to him. I was his shiny new toy, his payment for something. And he saw me as nothing more.

All night, every time Angelo ran his hands along my arm, I pretended it was Enzo touching me. Enzo had done the right thing and stayed away from me. Though by the look in his eyes, I could see it was killing him, same as me. But when I saw him standing at the threshold, I realized how much I had missed him. How much I didn't want him to stay away or let him go.

Enzo came to help me when I asked, and that put all kinds of bad ideas in my head. Admittedly, this right here—a moan got stuck in my chest as Enzo pressed a hand to my mouth—Enzo fucking me on Angelo's desk was the mother of all bad ideas. And it had to stop. Very soon...

"Don't stop."

His warm hand muffled my words. "She gave it to me." Enzo's strained voice gave me pause. "She had to go outside to get some fresh air. Looked like she wasn't feeling well." He slipped his thumb past my lips. My mouth curled around it, while his hips spread my legs wider. "Maybe she had too much to drink."

What? What? He was really talking to Angelo on the phone. While his dick was inside me?

Omigod.

My eyes went wide in surprise. The crescendo building at my core dissolved into tiny pieces of unfulfilled desire. Because there was no way we could finish what we had started while Angelo paced outside the door looking for me. I wedged my hands between us and pushed at Enzo's chest.

He held me tighter. "You should go look for her outside. She might need help. I'll leave her phone with a server." He ended the call, then let out a groan. "Fuck, you feel so good."

"Enzo, stop." I put my palm over his chest and nudged him.

"You don't owe him anything."

"I know. But he won't see it that way. Do you have a death wish or something?"

"Do you think his mobster act scares me? He's a nobody."

"I love you." I cupped his cheeks. "But we can't do this anymore. I mean, why would you answer his call?"

"Because I'm dying to tell him that you're mine. That this whole farce of a party is just that, a fucking lie." He puffed out a breath and stepped back, leaving me exposed and feeling so empty.

I let my shaky legs drop to the floor and squeezed my thighs together while I fixed my dress and underwear. My sensitive clit ached in protest, sending raw waves of desire across my belly—a last attempt to try and get back the unobtained orgasm. Gosh, it hurt.

I grabbed my phone and checked the messages to see if Donata and the guys knew where Angelo was. We couldn't just walk out of the library and risk being caught. When I clicked on the group chat, twenty messages flurried up the screen.

Rex: I can help.

Santino: Shit. Romeo is going in.

Donata: oh no, no, no. Enzo. Stop. Do not go in there.

Santino: He went in.

Rex: Jesus fuck, Enzo.

Donata: Guys, I lost A.

The thread went on and on while Rex, Santino, and Donata freaked out over Enzo coming over to help me. They had spent the last ten minutes looking for Angelo, while we were in here playing Russian roulette. I started to type sorry, but then a new message came in from Donata.

Donata: I just spilled red wine on a very expensive Turkish rug. You better get out of there now. R, go straight to the bathroom, I'll meet you there.

Enzo: I sent A. outside.

Santino: Checking

"Enzo, come on." I rushed to the door and cracked it just

enough so I could see if the hallway was empty.

"Go." He waved his hand, while he stood over the cabinet. He took a few seconds to straighten out the desk, and then, darted toward me. "Bathroom." He took my phone, pointing behind me as he headed in the opposite direction.

I stood there, ogling Enzo's retreating form while my heart pumped so hard, I could feel it in my throat. For a minute, I forgot where I needed to go and what I needed to do next. I was not cut out for this.

Gripping the tight bodice of my dress, I took several gulps of air to calm down. If Mom saw me like this, she would know something was up. That was the thing with her. She could always tell how I felt by just looking at my face. Of course, she knew I was repulsed by Angelo. But she chose not to see that.

I spun around to find the powder room and ran straight into Angelo. Crap. The space between his brows was wrinkled as he looked me up and down. My guilty conscience immediately went back to Enzo. Could Angelo tell I was having sex a few minutes ago? Was that why he was so mad right now?

"When I call, I expect you to answer your goddamn phone." He gripped my elbow. "Where were you?"

My throat closed, and suddenly I couldn't breathe. "Outside. I needed some fresh air." I racked my brain, trying to remember what Enzo had told him on the phone. "I wanted to get some air. It's so stuffy here. I thought I was going to throw up."

Crap. Was that too much? I was the worst liar.

"Have you been drinking?" He leaned in to smell my breath.

I recoiled because he smelled like stale beer. "No. All these people. It made me feel sick. It's too much for me. I'm not used to parties. I feel like I'm gonna throw up." The feeling sick part was no longer a lie.

I hated having him this close, manhandling me like I was some rag doll. "I want to go home. Have you seen my parents?"

"They're in the living room with our guests. Where you should be." He circled his arm around my waist. "We're going to be married in a couple of weeks. How about we stop pretending now?" He charged for my mouth, but I turned away in time. He didn't seem to notice as he latched on to my neck instead. "I thought this dress would look good on you. But I was wrong. You look absolutely fuckable in it."

"Thanks." I squirmed away from him.

"Stay." He pulled me toward him and dropped his gaze to my cleavage. "I have been plenty patient with you. You owe me this." His erection pressed to my hip at the same time he moved his hand to my ass. I winced as he rubbed against me with a smug look on his face, as if his gyrating was supposed to make me crazy with desire.

Did he not get how disgusted I was right now?

"I should find my parents. They're probably looking for me."

"They won't care if they know you're with me."

Anger pooled in my chest. No, of course my parents wouldn't care. What did they get? A wire transfer into their offshore account for one million dollars? I supposed I should feel grateful that anyone would be willing to pay that much money for me—and my v-card. I hated that Dad put me in this position. And that Mom did nothing to help me.

"Please stop. No." I shoved him as hard as I could with both my hands. "I said no."

Angelo was drunk enough that he lost his balance and

stumbled backward. "You're not allowed to say no," he said through gritted teeth, gripping my elbow. Pursing his lips, he lifted his other hand and slapped me lightly on the cheek. For a split second, I wondered if he'd even done it. "Do you understand?"

Understand what? That this situation could get worse for me?

"Angelo." Enzo's voice boomed in the hallway. The cacophony of voices and music in the living room sounded so far away. "I see you found our girl."

"What do you want? This is a private conversation."

"I came to return Rory's phone." His gaze dropped to my arm where Angelo had a vise-like grip on it. "You have a few missed calls." He took my hand and placed the phone in it.

I wanted to close my hand and feel his warmth, but Angelo was already in a pissed-off mood. I didn't want to make things worse than I already had. Tonight had been filled with a bunch of wishful thinking on my part. Angelo didn't get to where he was as Don Alfera's most-trusted man by being stupid or careless. We all took a huge risk tonight that didn't pan out. And now I had a feeling Angelo was going to make me pay for my transgression. He had wanted me to hang from his arm, so he could parade me around the room in front of his friends. He had specifically asked me not to leave his side tonight, and I disobeyed.

Now I knew what to expect if we got married. Angelo wanted a young, obedient wife.

"There she is." Donata strutted down the hallway with a big glass of wine in her hand. "I haven't said congratulations to you." Her gaze quickly darted between Angelo's grip on my elbow, and Enzo's hand holding mine. "Give us a hug."

She tugged me toward her with the kind of strength she couldn't have if she was as drunk as she pretended to be. Enzo and Angelo had no choice but to let me go. "Thank you." I hugged her tight, swallowing the lump in my throat.

"Yeah, well we need to debrief." She broke away first. "Angelo, Don Alfera is looking for you. He wants to say goodbye."

The name drop had a sobering effect on Angelo. He fixed his hair and tuxedo jacket and headed out without another glance in my direction.

"You almost ruined this entire operation." She pointed a finger at Enzo. "What the hell were you thinking?"

"That Aurora needed help. That's what I was thinking."

"He got the drawer open." I pushed strands of loose hair away from my face. "But didn't find anything. Tonight was a bust."

"No, it wasn't." Enzo beamed at me. "We found out Angelo plans to leave the country with Aurora."

"Oh yeah?" Donata's face lit up. "What did you find?"

"A passport for Aurora Soprano."

"Oh, sweetie." She rubbed my arm. "I can't imagine spending any amount of time with that Neanderthal."

"She won't have to." He opened his jacket and showed Donata a bit of the passport.

"Nice. Good work." She released a breath. "But we're back to square one. The wedding is practically here, and we still don't know how we can undo the contract."

"Do we know for sure that there is one?" I asked. "I feel like if he had a copy of it, it would've been in that drawer."

"I'm so stupid." Donata hit her forehead with the heel of her palm. "Of course there's a contract. It's how we do things.

But they're not going to give it to that schmuck. The executor of it, the witness, gets to keep it."

"What do you mean? An executor, like a will?"

"Yes." Her eyes darted from one end of the hallway to the other.

I could see her mind going a hundred miles an hour. What did we miss? We'd been looking for incriminating evidence that Angelo was hired to kill someone. His payment was me, and possibly one million dollars. That would be assuming that the receipt we found in his secret drawer of a wire transfer was payment for this upcoming job. Who knew what else he was doing for Don Alfera?

"An executrix, to be exact." She bit her bottom lip. "Aunt Vittoria didn't get to be where she is by letting the men run the show. When you guys came to see me, she was very explicit on that point. There's something she wants, and she's about to get it. Angelo is part of that equation. Why else would she even let him set foot in our house?"

"That makes sense." Enzo chuckled. "Your aunt has that contract."

"And I bet you, it's been right under my nose this whole time." Donata fisted her hands in frustration. "But that's fine. I can fix this tonight."

"What are you going to do?"

"Break into Aunt Vittoria's library. Tonight. Let's meet in the lounge room, so we can make a new plan."

I nodded like an idiot because no matter how hard I tried to think of what to do to get out of this marriage, I always came back empty. Right now, Donata's plans were the only ones we had.

"See you Monday." She walked off with a special strut in her step.

Based on tonight's shitshow, I didn't know how much longer Enzo was going to put up with the idea of Angelo and me getting married. That whole sex on Angelo's desk thing was about Enzo making a point. I belonged to him and only him. Marrying anyone else would be a living death.

I thought of the Shakespearean play we had to read for our language class. Romeo and Juliet constructed a whole plan to get away from the man her parents had chosen for her, so she could marry her true love. In the end, all their plans went to hell, and they ended up dead. That couldn't be us. I refused to die to pay for Dad's mistakes. Mom's lifeless eyes while Dad's boss was fucking her in our motel room flashed in my mind's eyes. No, Dad couldn't do this to me. If anyone had to die for his actions, it had to be Angelo.

We were not in some sixteenth-century drama. We had choices. We could run away together. If Donata's plan didn't work. Enzo and I could disappear, start fresh somewhere else. I met his gaze. He offered me a kind smile as he placed his hand over his heart and my passport.

I glanced up and Mom waved in my direction. She mouthed something that looked like "we're leaving." I nodded in response and headed toward her. I didn't want to risk being seen alone with Enzo again. The less my parents knew about my relationship with Enzo, the better. Right now, they had no reason to suspect that the royals and I were doing everything we could to break the marriage contract.

As I ambled past Enzo, he leaned toward me and whispered, "Run away with me."

This Boy Was Trouble

AURORA

"Make sure you eat all your breakfast." Dad added another strip of bacon to my plate of eggs, bacon and fruit. "You're too skinny."

In my head, I picked up the food and dumped it on his head. But when he continued to stare, waiting for me to do as he said, I took a forkful of cantaloupe and bit into it. I made myself swallow and then smile sweetly. Yeah, the wedding was next week, and my only plan was to continue to play along until I found a way out. So pathetic.

"Rory, say hi to the twins." Mom strolled in from the kitchen and sat next to me. "Boys, show her the new clothes I sent you." She beamed at me. "I swear they've grown half a foot since school started."

"Hey, guys." I waved at them. "When are you coming home?"

Mom furrowed her brows and took the phone away from

me. "We haven't talked about that yet. But don't worry they'll be here in time for your big day."

"My big day?"

"Yeah, you know." She got up again and walked away. "Can you show me the back of your pants? I want to see how they fit."

"I guess she's not ready to tell them about the wedding."

"They'll find out when they get here." Dad shrugged. "Angelo wants to see you tonight. Make sure you come home right after school."

"Why?" I ate more of the bacon, then drank black coffee to wash down the bad taste in my mouth. Every time I thought of Angelo and his hands all over me, I wanted to puke on his Italian leather shoes.

"He's your fiancé. He wants to see you. It's been a week."

I'd used the end of semester exams as an excuse not to see Angelo. But obviously, I'd run out of time. At school, I had also avoided seeing Enzo. And that was killing me, but what choice did I have? Our feelings for each other were a ticking bomb. Every time Enzo talked to me or even looked my way, we ran the risk of someone seeing the truth in our eyes and then running off to tell Signoria Vittoria. For now, Donata had put the fear in Penny, so she would keep our secret. But even the royals couldn't get the entire school under their control.

"Angelo is worried about you. He said you got sick during the party. Is that true?"

I didn't know what was worse, when Dad pretended I didn't exist or when he played the concerned father. "No, I just needed some fresh air. I'm fine."

"Rory." Mom called from the other room. "The car service is here. Go. Don't be late for school."

"We'll see you tonight." Dad switched his attention to his phone.

"Yeah." I grabbed my backpack and headed out.

Living with my parents had become truly unbearable. I hated how they went about their lives as if they hadn't sold me off as some sort of consolation prize to a man much older than me, one who was both ruthless and violent. I rubbed the side of my face. Angelo hit me at the engagement party. Not hard, but he slapped me like it was nothing. Was he so drunk that he didn't care what my parents thought of him mistreating me? Or did he know for a fact that my parents wouldn't mind if he put a hand on me?

Run away with me.

Enzo's words flashed in my mind. The thought put a smile on my face. I would love nothing more than to get away from this place and spend all my time with him. I hadn't seen him since last Saturday night, and I missed him like crazy. We had two classes together but sitting in the same room as him wasn't enough. I wanted to touch him—kiss him.

I made it all the way to the curb to the limo parked in front of my building when I realized I didn't know the guy holding the car door. He'd looked familiar, but now that I was this close to him, I was sure I didn't know him.

"I'm sorry. I thought you were here for me."

"Ms. Vitali?"

"Yes."

"I'm covering for Zack this morning." He gestured for me to get in.

"Oh, okay." I climbed inside the car and settled in.

I'd gotten pretty good at spacing out during the car ride to school. The store fronts and all the people rushing down the avenue had become white noise these past few months. I watched it all go by without paying attention. As the car weaved through traffic, it jostled me forward, so I had to put out my hand to keep from planting face-first on the floor. The honking right next to me brought me out of my reverie.

When I glanced out the window, I realized we were not headed in the right direction. "Excuse me." I switched to the bench seat under the window and knocked on the tinted partition. "Where are you taking me?"

He didn't respond. And that shot my heart rate into overdrive. What the hell? I banged on the glass. But again, there was no answer. He was not driving me to school. I scooted over to the right to open the door, but it was locked. Crap. I had never considered how limos were death traps. I could kick and scream, and no one would hear me. The driver could take me wherever he wanted. I had no way out.

Was this Angelo's doing? Did he decide he didn't want to wait until after school to see me? My stomach rolled. I thought of the way he looked at me at the party, how he rubbed his crotch against me, and grabbed my ass. I had assumed he would wait until after the wedding to have sex with me, but really, there was nothing stopping him. He'd said it himself Saturday night. *"You're not allowed to say no."*

Was this his way of proving his point? He wanted to show me he was in control. Now that we were engaged, he could do whatever he wanted with me. I tried not to think about what he would make me do once he had me in his apartment all alone. But I was in full panic mode now. The adrenaline kicked in and I couldn't stop the tears. I couldn't stop the images flitting through my mind.

After another minute, I wiped my cheeks and took a deep

breath to calm down. Maybe this had nothing to do with Angelo. But then who else would want to kidnap me like this? I fished my phone out of the front pocket of my backpack. My fingers hovered over the screen as I considered who to call and what to say. If this was Angelo's doing, my parents wouldn't care. I scrolled to Enzo's name on my contacts list when the limo rolled to a stop. A few seconds later, the door swung open.

"Don't be mad." Enzo's shirtless body moved into my line of sight.

"Are you insane?" I climbed out and hit him square in the chest. "You scared me half to death."

"I wanted to see you." He put up his hands in surrender. Then turned to the driver standing by the limo. "Thanks, Arthur. I can take it from here."

"He's your driver?"

"Yes. You met him before. Didn't you?"

"No." I raked a hand through my hair. Or maybe I had once. But I honestly didn't remember. "You can't summon me whenever you feel like it. I have school. They're gonna call my parents if I don't show."

"Donata has that covered." He wrapped his arms around my waist and kissed me. "I didn't want to see you from a distance at school or that stuffy lounge. We can spend the day here, like last time."

Butterflies fluttered in my belly when I thought of what we did when he brought me to his home the first time. Gosh, that day felt like it'd happened months ago, not just weeks. "You could've told me you were planning this."

"Yes, but you're a terrible liar. I didn't want your parents to get suspicious."

He took my hand and pulled me toward the private lobby.

We rode the elevator car up to the penthouse in complete silence. Mostly because I was still trying to sort out my feelings. I had been so scared on the way here. Now that I was alone with Enzo, all I wanted was to be with him.

"I'm still mad at you." I strolled into his living room as the last of the lingering adrenaline faded away.

"Let me make it up to you then." He pressed his chest to my back and kissed my neck. "I meant what I said at Angelo's party."

I turned around to look him in the eyes. "Run away? That would never work. You know that."

"You belong with me." He pressed his lips to mine and walked me toward the grand staircase.

At the bottom of the steps, he flashed me a sexy smile and went up. Of course he knew I would follow. In truth, I would follow him to the ends of the earth, if it meant being with him one more time. Bracing my hand on the banister, I fell in step next to him. The planes and valleys of his abs were a major distraction.

Suddenly, I didn't care how I'd gotten here. I didn't care that I was missing school again because of Enzo. What did it matter anyway? Our parents had already decided our futures. Columbia was never going to happen. But at least, I had Enzo. For a few more days, I still had him.

As soon as I stepped foot inside his suite, he began to unbutton my blouse. The last time we were together, we had to stop before either one of us finished. It'd hurt so much to leave him that night. "I missed you." I met his gaze as he slid my bra straps off my shoulders.

"I know." He wedged his hand inside my panties and palmed my pussy. "You're so wet already."

He had that effect on me. He knew what he was doing when he decided to meet me in the garage without a shirt on. I ran my hands all over him, doing my best to memorize every inch of him—the dust of hair on his chest, the tight muscles, and that V going into the waistband of his boxer briefs.

When he ran his finger up and down my folds, my eyes fluttered closed. As much as I wanted to watch him, the sensation was too much. In the next beat, I was floating in a sea of wanton desire, waiting for the sweet release I knew he could give me. He drew circles around my aching clit, then bent down to suck on my nipple. The shock of pure bliss to my core made my knees weak. I gripped his shoulder, pushing him toward the bed.

Shaking his head, he grabbed my wrist and pinned it behind me, letting his fingers brush the curve of my butt cheek. "Stay exactly where you are. Don't move."

Don't move?

My legs were about to give out from under me, but I widened my stance, anyway, to give him better access. With a knowing smile, he moved down to kiss my belly and hips. My whole body trembled with the new sensation of his lips and tongue on my sensitive skin. And just when I thought I'd fall from the intense heat shooting down to my toes, he moved his face between my thighs and closed his mouth around my overly stimulated bud.

He open mouth kissed me there, while he inserted a finger inside me. "That's right. Stay just like that." He puffed several hot breaths onto my pussy, then resumed his sucking and nibbling. I did as he asked because I didn't want him to stop. Though it was getting harder and harder not to let myself drop to the floor. He continued to work my G-spot, bringing me closer to the edge with every stroke and kiss. "Hmmm." The word vibrated inside me. "You're such a fucking good girl."

"I'm not." My eyes flew open immediately and landed on the full-length mirror hanging over his door. Did he put it there for me?

"Tell me what you see." He glanced up at me with dark eyes. "Tell me how good you look."

I shook my head but didn't look away from our erotic reflection. I stood there, naked in the middle of his room, and watched him bury his face between my thighs again. And then it happened, finally, the release I had been obsessing over since last Saturday. It exploded deep inside me and worked its way outward, down my legs and into my chest. The heat spiraled over and over, while Enzo worked relentlessly to wrench another orgasm out of me.

"Omigod. Enzo." My knees gave out, but he was there to catch me.

He wrapped his arms around my waist and carried me to the bed. I fell on my butt. When I made to lie down, he gripped my hips and flipped me over. "My turn." He panted a breath.

My brain had barely registered his words when he thrust inside me from behind. He pumped several times until he found his own climax. I moaned into the covers and let his scent wash over me. When it was over, I couldn't move. My legs and my whole body were just spent.

"I don't have a frame of reference, but I can't imagine this getting any better."

"I'm definitely willing to give it a shot." He let some of his weight fall on my back while he breathed heavily into my ear. "Every day could be like this. If you wanted."

I would love nothing more than to wake up next to Enzo every morning—spend our days in bed having sex. But that was an impossible dream—nothing more than a fantasy. Wasn't it?

He rolled off me and braced his head on his hand to look at me. "Run away with me."

"Stop saying that." I inched closer to him and kissed him. "Where would we go?"

"Ibiza. I have a boat there." He cradled my cheek and pressed his salty lips to mine, brushing them softly and slowly before he whispered, as if he were telling me a secret. "We could sail the Balearic Sea. Just us."

"I don't even know where that is." I laughed. "Wait. You have a boat?"

"A yacht." He beamed at me. "A present for my eighteenth birthday.

"Oh wow, all I got was a pair of leather boots."

"Here, I'll show you where it is." He sat up to draw on my sweaty back with his finger. "This right here is Spain." He drew a shape over my shoulder blade that was sort of like a square. Then he traced a long, winding path on the opposite side that went all the way to my waist. I squirmed a little, and he chuckled. "This is Italy. There are a handful of islands between the two countries." He touched a spot closer to Spain. "Ibiza is right here."

"Hmmm." I rested my head on the sheets, letting his soft touch soothe me. "You can be my geography tutor any time."

"I'd like to take you there."

I bit my lower lip and let myself consider the idea of going with Enzo to an island far away from here. What a beautifully, divine dream. Every time he talked about running away, he made it sound so doable. As if we could just agree to meet at the airport and fly into the sunset. I wanted that dream. I wanted to run away with him. I wanted to never have to think about Angelo and his stupid marriage contract again.

"I think I would go anywhere with you."

"Prove it." He raised an eyebrow, flashing me a sexy smile.

Trouble. This boy was trouble.

Dreams For Plans

Enzo

"Prove it?" She laughed. "How? Are you going to carve your initials on my butt?"

"Don't tempt me." I fixed a lock of hair behind her ear. Her tits stood proud, testing my resolve to stay focused and finish telling her my plan before we got lost in another round of sex. "Last Saturday, I realized that Angelo is not going to let you go. Whatever his reasons, he's sure he gets to keep you. The only way to stop him is if you and I disappear."

"Omigod, you're serious?"

I sat up on the bed and let my back rest on the upholstered headboard, while her gaze brushed up and down my naked body. She made it impossible to concentrate. But we were running out of time. By some miracle, Angelo didn't know Aurora and I were an item. We had the element of surprise on our side. Though that window was closing fast. If I wanted a life with Aurora, I couldn't afford to have dreams for plans.

"Like a heart attack." I ran a thumb over the line of my jaw, trying to sort out all the ideas in my head. I spent all week thinking about what our next steps should be. "The school's holiday gala is on the last day of school for the semester. Everyone we know will be busy getting it all together up until that night. I'll meet you at the party and we can go from there."

"Angelo won't be able to say no if it's a school thing." She glanced down at her hands, furrowing her brows. By now, I knew that was Aurora's tell. She was seriously considering my proposal. More than that, she was about to say yes.

"So you're in?"

"Of course I am." She scooted closer to me. "I don't want to spend a single day with Angelo. Now that the engagement is official, he acts like he owns me."

"I know. I was there."

When I saw Angelo gripping her arm, ready to strike her, I wanted to kill him with my bare hands. But killing Angelo would not solve anything. Her parents would just find a new guy to sell their daughter to. The only way around this mess was for Aurora and me to go somewhere new, like Ibiza. Aurora and I had a shot at something real. If I didn't act now, I knew in my gut that I would lose her forever.

"I know the locals in Ibiza. I promise you Angelo will not find us there. You'll be safe. The ocean is a big place."

"A week is going to feel like a very long time. But I can do it. I'll wait for you. I promise."

I pulled her toward me until her head rested on my chest. In an ideal world, Aurora and I could stay like this forever and not worry about mobster evil plans and arranged marriages. But the reality was that we lived in a mafia world, where the innocent paid for the sins of the wicked.

Aurora was scared. I felt it in the way she clung to me. But I was still the dark prince. As much as I hated the title Donata gave me, today it gave me the confidence I needed to know that I could protect Aurora from Angelo and her parents. After all, I was the future king of the Society. That carried weight with anyone who understood how our organization worked. When the wheel turned again, and Dad was no longer able to fulfill his duties as the head of the board, it would be my turn to step up.

According to the by-laws, when an ascent to power happened, be it king or don, anyone loyal to the old leader had to be executed. Like a game of chess, certain pieces had to be removed to protect the king. Angelo Soprano was at the very top of that list for me. One day, Dad would be gone. And I'd finally be able to wipe Angelo's smirk off his face. But, the old man had many years ahead of him. For now, Aurora and I would have to hide and bide our time.

I sat up and let my feet drop to the soft rug beneath the bed.

"What's wrong?" she asked.

"I'm sorry. Earlier when I had the brilliant idea of sending Arthur to get you, I didn't think about how it would look to our parents." I raked a hand through my hair. I caved into my need to see her, and we might lose the only thing we had going for us—the element of surprise. "They can't know about us until we're long gone."

"We're fine. I didn't realize what was going on until we were far away from my building. I didn't call anyone." She wrapped her arms around my shoulders. "Really. The only person I thought to call was you. I knew you'd be the only one who would care."

"Still. We should go to school. Catch a few classes before the end of the day."

"Hmmm." She pressed her heavy tits to my back and kissed my neck. "Okay. You're right. We should play it safe." She released a hot breath that quickly spread down my spine like warm water. "What happened here?" She traced a finger over the raw skin over my shoulder blades and lower back.

"Dad." I simply said. With Aurora, I didn't need to hide the ugly parts that made up my life. "It started a couple of years ago when Mom moved to Brooklyn. She doesn't like his mobster side."

"He gets angry at her and takes it out on you." She hugged me tight. "Why do they get to treat us like our lives belong to them? It isn't fair."

"Life is pain." I shifted my body to face her. "I think that's what he's been trying to teach me. The only way to win is to strike back."

"Yeah." She straddled my hips, brushing her lips to mine. "I keep waiting for Dad to do the right thing. But he's never going to be the man we need him to be. He's done this before. To Mom."

"Which part?"

"He got into trouble with his old boss. Then got Mom to have sex with that old dude to save himself."

"And now he's doing it again. But with you."

She nodded.

I ran my hands up her thighs and the curve of her waist—she was all smooth skin and sweet perfume. I planted a kiss on her shoulder then moved inward toward her tits. I couldn't stop touching her. My life didn't seem so gloomy when she was near. I didn't feel so lonely when she looked at me like I was the only person in the world.

"Maybe we don't have to leave right this second." I buried my face in her hair.

The grinding of her pussy steeled my cock. Suddenly, being inside her was all I could think about. I needed her like I needed air. In a fluid motion, I pushed to my feet then laid her on the bed. I took in the scent of her arousal and the sight of her sprawled on my sheets, waiting for me.

"Do you know what you do to me?" I ran my index and middle finger up and down her slit. She was so wet; her folds gave way with the smallest pressure. I played with her pussy lips, palming her, pulling, and pinching, just to watch her squirm. "Answer me." Shaking her head, no, she bucked her hips upward, then spread her legs wider for me. "I think you do. You drive me mad, wanting you so much."

I nudged her entrance with my shaft, rubbing it up and down her pussy to show her how much I wanted her. I was so hard for her; it hurt. I bent down to suck on her pink nipple and thrusted into her. The grip of her tight walls around me pulled at something below my navel. And just like that I was lost in the ride. Her body felt so perfect beneath mine—soft and toned at the same time.

"You're mine." I shoved her legs wider and rammed into her. "Do you feel that?"

"Yes." She called for me, biting her lip and running her hands all over my torso.

She lay there, taking everything I had to give her. I fell into a rhythm, where I would bottom out, drag my steel cock out, then plunge back in. Seeing her take it like that was such a turn-on. The more I gave her, the harder I got. I kept at it, until the raw charge crackling at my navel shot out, as if trying to find a way out of my body and into hers.

"Enzo." Her slick walls gripped me tightly as she climaxed.

Seeing her come, all red cheeks and panted breaths, was my undoing. I hooked her leg over my shoulder, pressing my hips against her ass. I wanted my cum deep inside her. I wanted her to keep every drop. I wanted to leave my mark on her forever. My whole body tensed on top of hers while the last of my orgasm fluttered through me.

Fuck. I was so far gone. And so in love with her.

"I never knew my body could feel like this." She wrapped her arms around my neck. "I didn't know sex could be like this."

"Like how?" I kissed her mouth.

"How do you even know what to do?" She slipped her tongue past my teeth.

"Maybe that's a conversation for some other time." I chuckled, letting some of my weight fall on her. "You know, when my dick isn't still inside you."

"I was just curious."

With a loud exhale, I rolled off her to lay on my back next to her. "I started early, I guess is the answer. Pretty much, the minute I thought about having sex, women showed up. Because of who I am. A few of those times, I was sure Dad sent them. Believe me, it doesn't always feel like this. What we have is special." I stared at the chandelier hanging in the middle of the room.

"I'm sorry." She kissed my cheek. "I have to stop assuming that you've lived a charmed life just because you're one of the royals."

I flipped on my side to face her. "It's been quite the opposite. For all of us."

"I love you." She smiled at me. What I saw in her eyes warmed me to my core. It wasn't pity. It was pure and utter empathy because she understood—because our lives were equally fucked up.

"Me too."

I brushed her lips with mine. And the now familiar surge inside me ignited again. Would I ever not want her this much? Because right now, my cock was game for another round. But a tentative knock on the door stopped me in my tracks.

"Enzo?" Maggie's timid voice was laced with warning.

Shit.

"Yeah. Don't come in. What is it?" I climbed out of bed and started to collect our clothes from around the room.

"Arthur just called. Your father is on the way up."

Fuck. Fuck. Fuck.

"Thanks," I called to Maggie, then grabbed Aurora off the bed. "I'm so sorry, but you're gonna have to hide. He can't see you here."

Her eyes went wide in surprise. "Oh."

"Not oh. You have to move." I placed her clothes in her hands and pushed her toward the bathroom door.

"Wait. Who was that?"

"Maggie. Our maid. My maid." I nudged her again. "Go. Don't come out until I say."

She nodded. After another beat, she took a step and then another until she was in full-escape mode. I picked up my boxer briefs off the floor and put them on. As soon as I spun around to get my jeans, Dad swung the door open. Forget knocking or giving me privacy. Those things were meaningless to the king of the Society.

"You skipped school this morning." His gaze darted across the room as he slowly put two and two together. I'd brought a girl home.

"I wasn't feeling well." I took my time donning my pants, shoes, and tee.

"I can see you're better now." He focused on the bra under my desk chair. Crap. Slowly, he walked to my bathroom door. He was a predator hunting its prey, following its scent, sensing its fear. "Get rid of your whore and meet me in my office downstairs."

I opened my mouth to say, "yes, sir," but he cut me off.

"Now, Enzo." With a look of disgust in his eyes, he turned on his heels and walked out.

What the hell happened to put him in this kind of mood? As of late, he'd been pissy and volatile. But this was something new. He seemed deranged.

I rushed to the door and poked my head into the hallway. When I didn't see him, I returned to the bathroom to let Aurora out. "Did you catch any of that?"

"Omigod." She placed a hand over her forehead. "I thought he was here for me."

"He's not. He came for me." I tossed my covers to the floor and then rummaged through the sheets until I found my phone. I texted Arthur and asked him to get ready. "Dad's in his office. You're gonna have to make a run for it. Come on." I took her hand in mine and pulled her behind me. I bolted down the corridor and the staircase. When I was sure Dad wasn't in the living area, I darted toward the elevator door.

"Take it to the garage level. Arthur will take you to school." I cupped her face and kissed her. "I'm so sorry."

"No, don't be. I'll see you tomorrow."

"Yeah, tomorrow." I hated saying good-bye. I hated not knowing that if I'd see her tomorrow. Because this thing with Dad felt big and not good at all. "Go."

I released a long breath to get my heart rate down to a normal pace. Gripping my phone in my hand, I paused outside Dad's office. As much as I didn't like the idea of dragging my friends through my own mess, my gut told me I couldn't do this alone. Not today. Aurora's future, our future, was on the line.

I messaged Rex. *Dad's in a mood. Text me later?*

He responded almost immediately.

Rex: Will do. Something happened. We need to talk in person.

In the same beat, Santino and Donata's names appeared on my screen.

Donata: How are you doing? Call me.

Santino: I'm coming over to your place. Pick up your damn phone.

Had they been calling me? I checked my missed calls. And, sure as fuck, I had ten missed calls from them. What the hell happened? I could only assume that whatever it was, it pissed Dad off. It couldn't be that he had found out about Aurora and me. He would've barged into my bathroom, where he was sure I was hiding a girl. So if this wasn't about Aurora, what then?

I knocked on his door.

"Come in." He practically barked the words.

Fuck my life.

Go Home, Brother

Enzo

I tentatively shouldered open the door. Dad's office was so quiet, I thought maybe he'd left again. But no, he sat at his desk, shuffling through some papers, clicking on the keyboard as if he were matching data from the hard copy in front of him to his screen. Not too long ago, before the beatings started, I had loved this version of Dad—the king of the Society, a leader, and a beloved father.

But then Mom left, and it all turned to shit. By the messages my friends had sent, I had a feeling that shit was about to change again. Though Dad didn't seem perturbed anymore. If anything, he looked like before, when we used to talk about the man he wanted me to become—the leader the Society needed me to be. These days, I was no more than a guarantee that when he died, the highest seat within our crime organization would stay with the Alfera Family, as it had been for the past four generations.

"Is everything alright?" I tentatively stepped closer to him.

When he glanced up, his eyebrows shot up in surprise, as though he hadn't expected to see me here. Ten minutes ago, he barged into my bedroom, looking like he'd lost his mind, asked me to send *my whore* away, and then took off. Now he was looking at me like he didn't even know I existed.

"Enzo." He beamed at me. "I'm glad you're here. Sit." He gestured to the chair across from him.

This was a new level of fucked up. Did he have a lobotomy after he left my suite?

"Dad, what happened? Earlier, you seemed out of sorts. Worried." I chose my words carefully. Calling him deranged might set him off again. Though dealing with a super fatherly version of Dad was creeping me out because it wasn't any better than the violent version of him.

"What? No." With a chuckle, he gestured toward the upstairs, a reference to our exchange earlier. "I was in a hurry. Are you ready to leave?"

Shit.

"Sure." I leaned forward to glance at the invoice in front of him. "Where are we going?"

"A shipment came in. I thought you might want to join your old man. Like old times." He offered me a kind smile that made me miss the way things used to be between us before Mom went and fucked it all up.

"Let's do it." I pushed to my feet, then stepped back to let him lead the way.

He grabbed a set of keys, then patted his pockets looking for something. When he came back empty, he shrugged then strode out of his office with me close behind him. I quickly texted Arthur to see if he was already on his way back from dropping off Aurora. He texted back in full sentences to basically say yes. At least she was safe. Unfortunately, the only way to find out what happened to make Rex, Donata, and Santino freak out was to go on this father-son joy ride.

"Enzo." He gripped my shoulder when the elevator door closed shut.

His hand on me startled me and made my whole-body tense. "Are we headed to the docks?"

"Yes." He patted my shoulder. "When we get there, stay close to me. Pay attention. But don't get involved. Let me handle things. Got it?"

"Yeah. Got it."

When we reached the parking garage, Arthur had already switched from a limo to a black SUV. He nodded at me as if saying, *She's safe.*

"Arthur, my old friend." Dad squeezed his shoulder, the way he had done with me a few minutes ago. "Let's make this one count."

Arthur had been our driver for so long, I didn't remember the guy who came before him. As our driver, he was privy to a lot of confidential information. Some of the shit he knew about me could land me in jail right now—or juvy, a few months back. But Arthur was loyal. He was family. I was glad to see that no matter how much of an asshole Dad could be, he at least remembered who his friends were.

"Always, sir." Arthur smiled politely, then stepped forward to open the door for him.

I went around the back of the SUV and climbed in from the other side. Now that I wasn't alone in the penthouse with Dad, I felt more at ease about this run to the docks. The import and export of cars wasn't illegal. Though, with the volume Dad moved in and out of the country every year, he didn't think he should be required to pay taxes. He spent the money where it was needed most—with the people who worked at the docks. He was appreciated for it.

That had always been one of our main mandates. The Society got started at a time when our government couldn't help us. In Dad's mind, not much had changed in the last century. Our purpose hadn't changed.

Fac Fortia et Patere—do brave deeds and endure.

We all lived by that code. We were the protectors. We were order.

Arthur pulled into the parking lot, drove around the main building, and continued on to the area where the shipping containers were stored. The place was empty. I had to assume Dad's crew had cleared out the docks for Dad's arrival. The SUV came to a stop. As soon as his door opened, he motioned for me to go with him.

I did as he asked. Partly because I was curious to find out what this was all about. The last time I went on a run with him was two years ago. A lot had changed since then. I still couldn't decide if Dad's invitation was a good thing or a bad thing.

We walked farther into the shipyard to a container that matched the number on Dad's invoice. This was an easy drop off. All Dad had to do was verify the delivery and sign off.

"Don Alfera." A short stocky guy shook Dad's hand. "We were not expecting you today."

"Change of plans." Dad made a show of scanning the area, which was empty. "Where's the rest of your crew?"

"They're coming." The man eyed me up and down.

Since Dad hadn't bothered to introduce us, I decided to let it be. I was here to watch and pay attention. I crossed my arms over my chest, seemingly at ease. But in truth, my body was so wound up, I was ready to pop someone. Dad and the man continued to talk about the shipment and the agreed upon payment. In the next beat, Dad gripped the man's shirt by the collar and squeezed, choking him.

He talked fast in the man's ear, but I couldn't catch any of his words. The man struggled under Dad's hold for another minute before Dad released him. Then Dad turned to me with that wild look in his eyes. The one he'd had when he first barged into my bedroom earlier today.

Fuck.

I put my hands up in the air as he reached in the inside pocket of his suit jacket, retrieved a utility knife, and cut the man's throat in a swift backward motion. Blood gushed out of the man's neck as he fell to his knees.

"What happened?" I stepped forward slightly but kept my distance. "You killed him."

"He was a rat."

The minute he uttered the word, the rest of his men showed up. There were five of them and two of us. How the hell was I supposed to stay close, but not get involved like he'd asked? The docks' crew advanced, looking at us with murderous intent. But other than that, they didn't lift a finger. They were afraid of Dad and of retaliation from the other Dons. Civilians didn't know exactly how the Society worked or how it was organized. Though everyone was clear on the kind of support Dad had from the other families and their crews.

Whatever their Spidey senses told them, it was right. They couldn't mess with Dad, even though he had just killed one of their own in broad daylight.

"Tony." He pointed at the man lying in a pool of his own

blood. "Put me in a tough position today." He walked to one of the guys with the blade still in his hands. "I hate rats. I hate them even more when they make friends with pigs."

"Don Alfera." The guy brought his hands together to form a steeple.

Like before, Dad's movements were like a reflex, muscle memory. He was fast and precise. The second guy fell to the ground, choking on his own blood, legs kicking out like he was trying to get away from Dad. By now, the other four men got a clue. At least I hoped they did. Because Dad was here for all of them.

He punched the next guy in the gut. Sheer fear and a smidge of hope kept the man on the ground—fear of retaliation if he fought back, and hope that maybe Dad was done killing, that he might be the one to survive the assault. The man stayed on his knees while his friends ran off in different directions.

"Don Alfera." The man spoke when Dad gripped him by the hair to look at his face. "I didn't rat on you. I swear it on my mother's grave."

"Just like old times." Dad patted the man's cheek, smearing blood all over him.

The chill in the air wasn't enough to keep the stench of blood away. It rose in heaps off the concrete and mingled with the salty breeze until the smell of death was everywhere. I covered my nose and mouth with the back of my sleeve, keeping my eyes on Dad. In the back of my mind, the same question swirled over and over.

And then panic set in. Was this what my friends were worried about? Was I as stupid as the guy kneeling in front of Dad, thinking he'd be the one Dad would spare?

I shot a glance behind me and spotted Angelo. He was

here with ten other men, who I recognized as the cleaning crew. The crew everyone called when a murder clean-up was needed. I knew Angelo had been recently promoted. But I hadn't bothered to ask what his new role was, simply because I didn't give a shit about his life. I should've asked when I had the chance. The realization came too late. He was the new boss of the cleaning crew.

Now the question was, had Dad brought me here to learn a lesson or to kill me? The fucked-up thing about it was that Dad's mood could go either way. I tore my gaze away from Angelo just in time to see Dad plunge a blade through another man's Adam's apple. He turned around and waited as Angelo's guys brought in the remaining crew.

I watched the man who I'd seen read to my little sister at night, teach Massimo how to catch, and kiss Mom like she was the only woman in the world, brutally kill the remaining three. The adage of *shooting fish in a barrel* came to mind. The man never stood a chance.

When it was done, Dad was out of breath. His chest swelled with every inhale and exhale as he combed a hand through the strands of wet hair plastered to the side of his face. The seagulls whined somewhere in the distance. They were the only ones who dared make a sound.

With the breeze blowing in my face, I stood there and waited for Dad to do his worst. Dark prince or not, I was in the same boat as the other men. If Dad wanted me gone, there was nothing I could do to stop him.

Was this about Aurora? I glared at Angelo, who slowly walked around me to join Dad and the pile of bloody bodies in front him. I opened my mouth to tell them to get on with it. If this was about who and what I took from Angelo, so be it.

"When the time comes," Dad broke the silence, "I expect you to do what's right for your family, Enzo. Do you understand?"

I didn't.

"Life is pain. You showed me that."

"Yes, it is. But family is all that matters. We need you now more than ever. Come." He gestured for me to join him.

I fell in step next to him as we made our way back to our SUV, where all the four Dons stood waiting for us. The tension in my body gave way as soon as I spotted Rex next to Don Valentino and Don Gallo. Santino next to Don Buratti. And Donata next to her aunt Don Salvatore. My friends released a breath at the same time when they saw me, which told me they too thought Dad had brought me here to kill me.

Why didn't he? Because I was family?

"Jesus Christ. Look at him." Signoria Vittoria glared at Dad in disgust. "You had to make a show of it."

"You wanted blood. There it is. Have at it." He put out his palm, but Signoria Vittoria recoiled. "There's more back there. Buckets of it."

"Enough, Michael." Don Valentino stepped in. "Go home, brother. And never come back."

Donata snuck behind Rex and pulled me toward her. When I turned to face her, she mouthed, *Let's go.*

Standing here was like coming in at the end of a movie. Something big happened today. Hours had gone by, and Dad still was speaking in riddles, telling me nothing. I was done waiting for answers. Whatever he had going on, I didn't care to be part of it.

"I'm going too," I said to Dad, then spun around.

I saw Arthur sitting in the driver seat of our SUV. Oddly

enough, his presence here made me feel safe. He was trained to protect us, and no matter what, bring us home.

"Enzo, wait," both Don Valentino and Signoria Vittoria said in unison.

I started to ask what for? But in the next beat, a loud boom echoed across the marina. It sounded so far away, though I knew the explosion had happened fifty feet away because now our SUV was upside down and up in flames. The heat licked my face and my clothes felt like they had caught fire. I made to run toward the SUV, but Rex and Santino stopped me.

Shifting my body to look for Dad, I found him walking in the opposite direction with Angelo by his side. The old man had brought Arthur here to die.

"What the fucking fuck?" I fought against the hold my friends had on me.

"He didn't tell you, did he?" Santino asked.

"Tell me what?" My gaze darted between Santino and Rex.

"Your dad is leaving the Society. He stepped down as king and don of the Alfera family." Rex spoke softly.

"Come on." Donata tugged at the front of my shirt. "Let's go, Enzo. We have so much to tell you."

'Til Death Do You Part, huh?

Enzo

Rex shouldered open the door to his parents' penthouse on the forty-fourth floor of the Crucible. Years ago, Dad had sold them the property. Something we all thought was out of character for him—to give up a piece of himself that was so deeply connected to the crown. The King of the Society owned the Crucible since the inception of the Society. And yet, Dad allowed the Valentino family to take over.

Or maybe he hadn't allowed shit. How long ago did Dad abdicate? It sure as hell didn't happen today. Dad had been working toward this goal for a very long time. How about that? When he promised that we would soon not have to lie to Mom, he meant it. Of course, I figured he was thinking he'd get Mom to reconsider her stance when it came to Dad's mafia life. None of that mattered anymore.

Dad was no longer king.

I repeated those words in my head. It was so hard to believe. If Rex had told me earlier that Dad had been killed in some alley, I would've believed that immediately. But this? Abdication? It couldn't be. Though Dad's decision felt real when I factored Mom into the equation.

What the hell would happen now?

"Say something." Rex shut the door behind him.

"He did it for her. For Mom." I glanced up at him, then switched my attention to Donata and Santino.

They all stared at me as if I were some wounded wild animal, bound to snap at any moment. My mind looped through the same piece of information a few more times—Dad is no longer King. Piece by piece, the whole chess board came into view. I sifted through what I knew of Dad and the Society by-laws as I tried to figure out what the Dons would do next.

Looking at my friends with their wide, expectant eyes, I could only assume they had already figured it out. They were waiting for me to connect the dots.

"The changing of the guard," I whispered.

"The changing of the guard." Rex nodded. "Dad took over."

"I got that." I gestured to the lavish penthouse, feeling like an idiot for not seeing any of this coming. But it all made sense now—Dad's recent behavior, the secret meetings between the Dons, Penny's family being cast off. It was all because he knew this day would come. Rex was now next in line to be king. And I was…collateral damage. "What are you going to do, brother?" I scoffed. "Kill me?"

The spot between Rex's brows furrowed. "Of course not."

"Of course not," I said, relieved. Not that I thought Rex wanted to harm me. But the Society meant everything to him.

Dad was a cold-blooded killer, a ruthless monster, but despite all that, family meant everything to him. He showed me that today. The father-son joyride to the docks was about him proving how much our family meant to him. As much as I hated Dad these days, I had to be grateful. He did me a kindness by lifting this responsibility off my shoulders. A smile pulled at my lips.

Now I was free to marry Aurora.

"Wipe that grin off your face, Enzo." Donata gripped my shoulder. "This isn't good news for you."

"It is." I met her gaze. "Now Dad won't care if I run away with Aurora."

"What did I say?" Santino rubbed his cheek in exasperation. "Stop thinking with your dick, and look at the bigger picture here. Donata, show him the contract."

"Screw the contract." I braced my hands on my hips. "Now I can marry Aurora if I want. There's nothing tying me to this Society anymore, to the so-called crown."

"Angelo is the one making room for the new king, Enzo." Rex's voice boomed in the foyer. We hadn't even made it to the living room before we started our conversation. "Do you think he'll let her leave? He's obsessed with her."

"He's obsessed with the idea of having a virgin wife." I let out a breath. "I can handle Angelo."

"When you were the future king? Sure. But now, you're just another soldier. Do you understand?" Rex gripped my shoulder. "You don't get to leave the Society. Only Michael. You, Massimo, and Caterina." He swallowed. "You belong to us."

That was it? The big secret Signoria Vittoria and Dad were arguing about months ago. Dad was leaving the Society. My siblings and I were the payment in exchange for this ultimate favor of letting him go. That only left one thing to do.

Angelo was promoted to crew boss because he was in charge of killing everyone in Dad's inner circle. And now it made sense why Dad cast off his previous right-hand man. He did it to save them, because the Contis were family.

The Vitali family was not.

They were the replacements.

The Society required blood to seal this deal. Dad brought them Stefano Vitali, the guy who saved his life last summer.

I lifted my head to meet Rex's gaze. "Aurora. He's going to kill her."

"No." Donata grabbed my hand and pulled me into the living room. She dropped a manila folder on the coffee table and gestured toward it. "Thanks to Aunt Vittoria, Aurora gets to live." She cleared her throat. "As Angelo's wife."

"Over my dead body." I snatched the papers.

"That's kind of the point, Enzo." Santino walked to the bar cart and poured whiskey into four tumblers. He pushed one into my hand. "Read."

The first page outlined what Aurora was required to bring to the table. Mainly, her virginity, along with the ability to produce five children. Did she even want kids? Angelo hadn't even bothered to ask if she wanted to marry him. I doubted he'd bothered to ask if she wanted to be a mother.

To his credit, he was generous in his offerings. Provided she was pure, Aurora would receive a million dollars in an offshore bank account. That explained why he had that receipt in his cabinet. She'd get a house in the Hamptons and a full ride to Columbia.

"Fuck. This is everything she'd ever wanted."

"It's not a bad deal." Donata winced. "You know, if she's willing to…"

I was glad Donata let the end of the sentence linger in the air. Though it was too late. The image of the two of them together was already tattooed on my mind. Angelo wanted a life with Aurora. No, he wanted more than that. He wanted to make use of her soul and her body. And he was willing to pay for it. Everything we found in Angelo's locked cabinet was meant for Aurora as a fucked-up wedding gift.

"It doesn't matter what he wants or what this contract says." I rose to my feet. "Aurora no longer fits his definition of pure." I cocked my eyebrow. "And she's a terrible liar. She would never be able to dupe him. I don't think she wants to either. She wants to be with me."

"I get that." Rex cleared his throat, which usually meant he was about to say something we didn't like. "But with you, she's guaranteed a very short life. Is that what you want?"

"Enzo." Donata's voice was barely above a whisper. When she spoke, her tone was soft, as if she was speaking to a child. "You have to consider the fact that she might be better off without you. Sure, she won't have you. But she'll have everything she wants. She'll be free of her parents; she'll go to college. She'll even have a home by the beach. And all you have to do is let her go."

"If she got over the fact that her husband killed her parents, she could be happy." Santino shrugged.

Aurora would never love someone like Angelo. Someone who bought her simply because he saw her one day and came up with a bunch of crazy ideas about who she was. He didn't love her. He couldn't make her happy. She would live a half-life. That was worse than dying.

"You don't know that. You can't possibly know what would make her happy because you don't know her like I do. I can't let her go." I inhaled, trying to sort out all the ideas floating in my head.

Every thread I followed through to its conclusion, circled back to the same place. If we ran away together, Angelo would find us. Dad would help him, of course. Who knew what kind of punishment he'd conjure up for her. He would hurt her out of revenge and then kill her. If she stayed, and Angelo found out she'd been with me, his reaction would be the same. If I married her, would Dad change his mind?

"Did you read?" Rex's voice brought me back. "Angelo is obsessed with her. Or rather, the idea of her. What do you think will happen if she runs off with you?"

"Yeah." I raked a hand through my hair. "The same thing that will happen if he sleeps with her. Do I have to spell it out for you? She's not a virgin. This contract is null and void. Unless I do something, she'll die along with her family." I pinched the bridge of my nose to keep the tears at bay. "My father saw to that. She's here because of him."

"Enzo." Donata threw her arms around my neck. "Angelo has a long list of people to kill in the next few days. And her parents are on it. We don't know when any of that will happen. What we do know is that if Angelo finds out about you two, he'll add Aurora to that list. Do you understand?"

"I do." I smirked at her. "We do know one more thing. Angelo will not kill the Vitalis before the wedding. That means we have until the seventeenth to come up with a plan that doesn't include serving up Aurora as a sex slave."

"That's this weekend." Santino knocked back his drink. "So what's the plan?"

"Any chance we can appeal to Don Valentino's romantic

side?" Donata peered at Rex. "He cares about Enzo and his family."

"Dad needs Angelo. His hands are tied." Rex blew out a breath. "Everyone is bending over backwards because they're all getting what they want."

"Just like Aunt Vittoria said." Donata nodded. "The ruthless king is no more, and now they get to run things the way they've always wanted. They need Angelo to clear the way."

"Exactly." Rex crossed his arms over his chest as if he had more to say. His gaze bored into mine. After another beat, he shook his head and ambled to the bar cart.

In his own fucked-up way, Dad cared about me. He could've walked off and left me to the wolves, but he chose not to because it was as he had said: family is all that matters. Even his cousin was spared because of him. Penny would get to finish high school and have a long life because Dad considered her family. What of Aurora? What would it take for Dad to extend his goodwill to Aurora?

Signoria Vittoria was right. A marriage contract was the best way to keep her protegee safe. But she chose the wrong guy. Aurora belonged with me and not Angelo. She wanted me.

"What about Signoria Vittoria's romantic sensibilities?" I asked Donata. "If I told her the truth, that I want to marry Aurora. Would she help us? If she's married to me, she's family, right?"

"Oh Enzo, I don't know." Tears brimmed her eyes. "Aunt Vittoria never does anything for free. And certainly not out of the kindness of her heart. I wouldn't count on her help. Or I don't know. We've got nothing to lose, I suppose. I could ask."

Except we had everything to lose. Right now, Aurora and I

had the element of surprise on our side. We could get married tomorrow and be gone before anyone noticed we skipped school. But if we asked Signoria Vittoria for help and she said no? She would ruin all our plans for sure.

"You love her that much?" Rex narrowed his eyes at me. As if the idea of giving up everything to love someone was completely foreign to him. I supposed it was. He'd never met someone like Aurora—been with someone like her. He didn't know true love. "What you're planning could kill you."

"She's worth the effort. She's worth everything."

"She can't know." Donata took the folder from me. "In fact, no one outside of this circle can know about the abdication. The adults have a plan to handle that. It's out of our control. Until I speak with Aunt Vittoria, Aurora can't know about her parents or that you're not a royal anymore."

"I don't care about that." I glared at Rex. "Rex wants to be the dark prince. He can have it."

"It wasn't like I had a choice." He pursed his lips.

"Except you did." Santino gripped Rex's shoulder. "You could've said no."

"And let the great Don Alfera wreak havoc until the end of times? At the rate he was going, I didn't think his heir could survive his reign anymore." Rex put up his hands when I leveled him with a stare. Then he moved to sit on his chenille sofa with his legs out in front of him. When his eyes fluttered closed, he spoke again as if merely spewing facts that had nothing to do with life or death. "Without your title, you're unprotected."

He looked beyond exhausted. Unfortunately, I didn't have time to think about what all this bullshit with Dad meant to him. If he had a choice or not, it didn't matter. Choice was more of a figure of speech in our world. Either way, Rex was about to find out just how heavy the crown was.

"Then promise me something." I sat across from him, bracing my arms on my knees.

"Anything for you, brother."

"Promise me you'll protect her. No matter what happens, promise me you'll be there for her."

He nodded. "I promise."

"We made a pact, Enzo." Donata smiled at me. "Aurora is now one of us. We'll keep her safe."

"You're really getting married, huh?" Santino put a fresh tumbler in my hand. "This whole thing feels extreme. You're eighteen. And no offense, there are a lot of fish in the ocean. Not to mention, women are tricky. I mean, does Rory even want to marry you?"

I was banking a lot on that fact. Aurora had already agreed to run away with me. Getting married was the next logical step. My chest expanded as air rushed into my lungs. For the first time since I saw her leave the apartment earlier today, I felt lighter, like I could breathe again. Aurora as my wife seemed like an impossible dream. But I was willing to die trying if she was. We only had this one shot at being together.

"You had to ruin the moment." Donata wedged herself between me and Santino, then shoved his shoulder. "Not all women are Hanna. What Enzo and Aurora have is real. We have to help them."

"Yeah, sure. I'm here to help." Santino placed a hand over his chest, looking at me with pity in his eyes. "'Til death do you part, huh?"

"That's the idea."

Life Is Pain

Aurora

The entire day I had a crushing feeling in my chest. As if something bad had happened to Enzo. I'd texted him like a hundred times, but he was ignoring me. A few times, I'd seen the three dots flutter on my screen. I held my breath for several beats, waiting for his response that never came. What was so bad that he couldn't tell me?

I'd stayed at school for as long as I could. But Angelo wouldn't wait for me any longer, so he sent his driver to fetch me. I didn't want to make a scene at the school gates, so I got in the car. I was glad for the traffic because I wasn't in the mood for Angelo's creepiness. It had been a whole week since our engagement party, but I couldn't avoid him forever. Especially when our wedding was in five days.

I wasn't ready to give up on Enzo and me. We still had time to run away together like he wanted. I glanced at my phone in my lap every other minute. Did he still want that? Or did his dad make him change his mind? He had been so intense when he barged into Enzo's room this morning. My whole-body shuddered at the memory. If Don Alfera had found me in Enzo's bathroom, half-naked, I'd probably be dead right now. Either Angelo or Don Alfera would've seen to that.

"Miss." Angelo's driver met my gaze in the rearview mirror. "We're here."

With a nod, the diver pulled over. The doorman was already at the curb, waiting to get the door for me. I relaxed a bit when I saw him. Meeting Angelo at home felt safer than his place. At least here, he had to keep his hands to himself. Many times, in the past week, I'd thought about our exchange in the hallway—the slap on the face, the way he rubbed his erection against me, and his hands all over my ass—anger washed over me every single time. I hated that he thought he was allowed to treat me like that.

I climbed out and steeled myself for whatever Angelo had in store for me—in my own home no less.

"Rory. You're home." Mom met me at the door. "Look who's here to see you."

I rolled my eyes. Did she not know Angelo had sent for me? "I see him, Mom." I waved at him. And I didn't even care if he could tell I was annoyed with him. I was never the best liar. The disgust I felt for him was painted all over my face.

His gaze swept up and down my body. "You look radiant." He watched me for a few more beats before he turned to Mom. "I'd like to see her in private."

I clenched my jaw, then turned to Mom, expecting her to say no like she'd done many times before. Except this time, she didn't deny him. "Of course. You can use Stefano's office. You'll be more comfortable there." She gestured upstairs.

"Mom?" I glared at her.

"I need to get ready. Angelo is treating us to dinner tonight. We're going to that fancy place your father likes." She beamed at me, then headed down the hallway toward the kitchen.

I opened my mouth to tell her she was going the wrong way but figured there was no point. She'd been like this since the beginning. I was on my own when it came to Angelo. With a deep sigh, I adjusted my backpack on my shoulder and climbed the steps up to Dad's office. The whole way, I could feel Angelo staring at my ass.

"Have a seat." He shut the door behind him and gestured toward the leather sofa along the wall, facing Dad's big desk. "I have something for you. I would've given it to you sooner, but you've been so busy this week."

"Yeah, end of semester stuff."

He reached inside the pocket of his suit jacket and retrieved an envelope. "I want you to know that I'm very much looking forward to getting to know you. I want to be a good husband to you." He placed a manila folder on my lap and sat next to me.

I recognized the papers he showed me. I'd seen them in his cabinet last week when Enzo and I went snooping in his office. My eyebrows shut up in surprise—not because of what it was, but because it dawned on me that this was a wedding gift—a house in the Hamptons, a million dollars, a full-ride to Columbia. It was all for me.

My eyes blurred as I stared at all the things I'd always wanted. I'd assumed that once I had my own place, money, and a top-notch education, I'd be free from my parents and this life. It seemed every time I solved one problem, a bigger one took its place. To get what I wanted, I had to accept Angelo's contract.

I had to give up Enzo. I had to sell my body and soul to a ruthless mobster.

Enzo was right. *Life is pain.*

"Life with me can be very easy for you. I can give you anything you want." His soft tone made his words sound like a confession of sorts, as if he actually loved me. But how could he? He didn't even know me. Up until now, I didn't think he could even see past my tits. He cleared his throat, then brushed the back of his fingers along my bare thigh. "If you let me."

"This is all happening too fast."

"I know. I wanted to tell you about our plans months ago. But your parents wanted you to get used to the idea first. You know, get to know each other first." He inched closer to me. "We'll have the wedding here at city hall. Something small. Just our circle of friends. Then we'll spend a few days in the Hamptons. It's cold there this time of year, but I plan to spend all our time indoors." He chuckled.

I squirmed away from him. Suddenly, my lungs refused to breathe the stale air. If he planned to spend our so-called honeymoon at the beach, why did he get a passport for me? If Donata were here, she'd know exactly how to get more information out of him. Me, I couldn't stand his hot breath on my face anymore.

"I know you're a virgin." He seemed so pleased with himself.

I would do anything to wipe that smug smile off his face. He couldn't buy me like I was some shiny trinket. On instinct, I shot to my feet. "I think getting to know each other first is a good idea."

"And we will do that." His gaze moved down to my chest. "I can't wait to eat that cherry."

"Here." I gave him back the papers, though what I really wanted to do was punch him in the face. I didn't have some fruit stuffed up my vagina. What the hell was wrong with him?

As much as I had tried to keep a poker face, I couldn't do it anymore. I couldn't hide my disgust for him. When he reached for my cheek, I recoiled, pursing my lips. That was the wrong move because that made him drop the loving husband act.

"Isn't this what you wanted?" He fisted one hand as he placed the folder on the coffee table. "I thought you'd be happy with my wedding gift to you. I had expected a different reaction." His gaze darkened.

I'd seen that look on his face before, in the limo when he asked me to wash his car, then at the engagement party when he rubbed himself all over me. My heart raced as the hairs on the back of my neck prickled. I turned away from him to hide my emotions. In the next breath, his hands gripped my waist, and he shoved his nose in my hair, taking in a long whiff.

"Please. Not here." I pushed down on his wrists as his fingers dug into my hip bone.

"Then where? I've been patient with you. You owe me this." He shifted my body, so I would look at him.

I wanted to say that I never promised him anything, that I never asked for him. But he was convinced that whatever deal he made with Dad, I was required to deliver on it. He was wrong. I never said yes to him.

When he moved in to kiss me, I was ready. I twisted away from him and shoved him as hard as I could. That stunt had worked on him before because he'd been drunk. But he was sober tonight. He stood his ground, glaring at me with so much contempt in his eyes. I wounded his ego, again. I made to get away from him, but he held me in a bear hug. Before I realized what he meant to do, he walked me to Dad's desk and jostled me over it, face down. He couldn't possibly want to have sex with me here—in Dad's office.

"Fuck. Your ass." He wedged his elbow into my lower back as he lifted my skirt with his free hand to take a handful of my butt cheek.

"I-I thought you wanted a traditional wedding," I said through gritted teeth. Mom had mentioned that she'd picked out a white dress for me to wear this weekend because Angelo wanted to do things right. It was her way of saying he had agreed to wait until our wedding night to take my virginity. I wracked my brain for the right words to get him to stop. My rejection had set him off. I couldn't take it back. "I'm not ready for this."

"I can make this as hard or as easy as you want. I was sure you'd pick easy. That if I showered you with gifts, you'd be nice to me. You'd give me what was promised. But now I'm thinking maybe you're not as sweet-tempered as you look. Was it all an act? Are you a fucking liar like all the others?"

"What?" I glanced over my shoulder to meet his gaze. "I didn't ask for this."

He didn't look at me. Rather, he focused on my back while he stuffed his hand under my skirt to find the swell of my ass. "Which one are you, Rory? Are you a good girl or a slut?"

The sound of his belt unbuckling and then his fly unzipping sent my heart rate into overdrive. I tried to get away, but he pinned me harder to the desk. When he thrust from behind, his cock rubbed all over my outer thigh. I squeezed my eyes shut because I didn't want to see any part of him. He'd undone his pants and was now fisting his cock. Whatever he planned to do—fuck me or just put the fear in me—there was nothing I could do to stop it. If I screamed, no one would come to help me.

I gripped the edge of the desk and did my best to block out the grunts he made every time his erection rubbed my skin. My eyes flew open when I finally understood what was happening. He was jerking off—to my ass—like I wasn't even here. A groan escaped his lips as he stepped closer to me, jabbing his elbow deeper into my spine to hold me in place.

I had no doubt in my mind that this was Angelo's idea of doing the right thing. But it was humiliating. Did he not see that? For a second, I thought about what would happen if my parents barged in on him right now. But then I realized that would never happen. Mom sent us up here, for him to do this. She fucking knew. And of course, Dad knew too. Why else would he be out of the house right now?

The wet, lewd noises his hand made every time he pumped himself increased in tempo. He kept at it, using me for support, more than anything else at this point—like some fucking piece of furniture.

I figured if I stayed very still, he wouldn't try to put it in. In truth, I was so stunned by the turn of events, I couldn't move anyway. With my mouth open, I stared at our family picture on Dad's desk while I waited for Angelo to finish. I didn't remember where the photo was taken. We all seemed so much younger, so it had to be before we lost our house in Las Vegas. Before Mom had to save us by letting Dad's boss fuck her in the motel where we lived for months. I hated the look on my face—so naive and full of hope.

The girl in that picture was long gone. I was never going to get out from under Dad's thumb and his bad business deals. Though, he'd done well for himself this time. He'd gotten fifteen thousand dollars for Mom in Vegas. For me, he'd gotten a million. That was how much his daughter was worth.

"Ah." I winced, pursing my lips to keep quiet as Angelo jostled me against the desk again.

"Oh fuck." He used his free hand to lift my skirt even higher and move my underwear out of the way.

Strings of something wet and warm painted my butt cheek as Angelo made guttural sounds, riding out his orgasm. He panted a breath and stepped back. I could only imagine he was admiring his handiwork. Was it over? My lip trembled once. And then my whole body began to shake.

"You don't have to be afraid of me." He grabbed my elbow and pulled me to stand. "Go get ready for dinner. We leave in fifteen minutes."

I couldn't look at him. I didn't want to see the satisfaction in his eyes. I didn't want to hear kind words from him. When I stepped away from him, I was surprised my legs could move again. Tears brimmed my eyes, and then I bolted. As I ran down the hallway to my room, the cool air brushed my bare ass and reminded me of the cum he'd left on me—like a dog marking his territory.

When I got to my suite, I locked the door behind me and went straight to the shower. I ran the hot water and got in before it was warm enough, before I even thought to take off my school uniform. All I wanted to do was wash his stench off me.

I stood under the spray for a good five minutes. When I stopped shaking, I slowly began to remove my clothes. I used a lot of body wash and scrubbed my backside until my skin felt raw. I hated Dad and Mom for doing this to me—for bringing someone like Angelo into my life.

How the hell was I supposed to spend my life with someone I didn't love, someone I couldn't stand—someone who wasn't Enzo?

"*Life is pain.*" Enzo's words echoed in my head. "*I think that's what he's been trying to teach me. The only way to win is to strike back.*"

Then Marry Me Instead

Aurora

Dad met us at the restaurant. With only five days until the wedding, Mom and Dad were in a hurry to finalize the contract. They wanted to make sure the money and the house were in my name and that the transfer had happened. The purpose of the dinner date was to get all the paperwork finished. Sure, we could've gone to the law firm office, but I was sure that made Dad uncomfortable. That was the thing with all things illegal. If you dressed them up fancy, they didn't seem so shitty.

The caviar and champagne at our table made everyone overlook the fact that I was getting a million dollars and a house to marry a guy I barely knew—that he was willing to pay that much to, as he put it, eat my cherry.

I glanced down at my phone nestled in my lap, hidden in the flowy fabric of my cocktail dress. Still no text from Enzo. At this point, I was one hundred percent sure he was ignoring me. Though in the back of my head, I wanted to believe that he was busy with his dad, that his silence had nothing to do with us.

"Ms. Vitali, if you would, please." The fancy lawyer Angelo had introduced me to when we arrived gestured toward the papers in front of me.

I inhaled and peered at Mom. I'd spaced out for the last five minutes and missed a big chunk of their conversation. But I didn't care why we were here. I wasn't the virgin Angelo wanted. And I sure as hell had no plans to go through with this ridiculous wedding. Even if Enzo didn't want to run away with me anymore, I wasn't staying.

Earlier today, I got a good idea of what my life with Angelo would be like once we were married. I would rather die than spend a single day with him. Mom also proved she didn't care about my well-being. She left me alone with Angelo, knowing what he could do to me. She allowed it to happen because it served her plans. If Don Alfera went after my parents because I didn't hold up my end of the deal, that would be on them—not me. I owed them nothing.

"Rory, they need you to sign. To show you understand." Mom smiled politely at the lawyer.

I thought of the contract I signed over the summer when we moved to the Upper East Side. Signoria Vittoria made me sign a non-disclosure agreement. She was clear on the fact that the terms were non-negotiable and could not be broken.

"There isn't a place in the world where our organization won't find you or your family, if any one of you chooses to betray us."

She owned me. And now Angelo would too.

I flipped the page and smiled. For months, Donata and I had been trying to get our hands on the wedding contract.

What I would give to show it to her right now, to get her take on it, to tell me that it was all going to be all right. I skimmed through the legalese until I got to the page where it clearly stated what Angelo expected of me. Yeah, he wanted a virgin wife. That much we knew. But he also wanted children.

My head snapped up to look at Mom, but she didn't even acknowledge me while she spread caviar on a piece of toast. I turned to Dad next. He was busy talking to Angelo. Why did I keep trying to reach out to them? They were never going to change their minds.

I shifted my gaze toward the door, and my belly did a somersault. Enzo. What in the world was he doing here? I quickly scanned the people at the table before I peeked in Enzo's direction again. He winked and sauntered toward the bar, where a tall blonde waited for him.

I beamed.

Enzo hadn't been ignoring me. He still wanted me. He was here for me.

I cleared my throat. "I need to freshen up."

"Of course, dear." Mom shot a glance to the contract. Her smile faded when she noticed I hadn't yet signed it. Why did they need my signature? They were already planning to force this marriage on me. What did it matter? Was it to ease their conscience? "Take your time."

I nodded and slowly rose to my feet. When Angelo didn't stop me, I practically bolted to the bathroom. With my heart pumping hard, I ambled past the bar where Enzo and Donata sat enthralled in conversation. I wished I had their flare for this kind of thing. Angelo was a ruthless mobster. Even if Donata and Enzo were royals, they could still get hurt. They had to know that, and yet, they didn't care.

They sat there like two superheroes who couldn't be touched.

The bathroom door slowly shut behind me. I exhaled loudly while I searched every stall to make sure I was alone. The place was ideal for a clandestine meeting with its low lights, hues of red behind the mirrors, and cozy lounge area near the entrance. I focused on the fancy art and soft music while I paced up and down. On the third round, I spotted Enzo's reflection in the mirror.

For a moment, I froze because I wasn't sure if it was really him. Or just an illusion. He was impossibly beautiful. And he was mine. Like I was his.

Releasing a breath, I turned around, fully expecting him to disappear. "You're really here."

"I followed you." He took a single step toward me. "I stopped by your apartment as you were leaving." He winced.

No doubt he saw how Angelo had had his hands all over me while he ushered me into his SUV.

"Enzo."

"It doesn't matter." He closed the space between us and kissed me. "I just need a few more days. I promise." He whispered in between kisses.

"I have so much to tell you." I slipped my hand under his shirt, feeling his toned abs and smooth skin.

"Me too." He cradled my face and thrust his tongue past my lips.

We'd been together this morning, but right now, it felt like our time in his bedroom happened months ago. I needed him. I needed to be with him. "I want you." I tunneled my fingers through his hair, hoping he understood my meaning.

"Here?" He chuckled, kissing my cheek. "We can't risk

being seen together. It's the only thing we have in our favor right now."

"Yeah, I know." I shook my head to clear my thoughts and focus. "Um."

"What is it?" He searched my eyes. The lines between his eyebrows deepened with concern. "Did he?"

His question lingered in the air. Why would he go there? Because I was thinking about what Angelo did in Dad's office? Was it written all over my face—the shame, the anger, the sense of powerlessness? I couldn't tell him. There was nothing Enzo could do about that now.

"No." I raked a hand through my hair, avoiding his gaze. Technically, I wasn't lying. Angelo hadn't forced himself on me. He just used me to get off. "I just mean, Angelo has plans for this weekend."

"What is he planning? Did you find out where he's taking you after the wedding?"

"Yeah, the Hamptons. He bought me a house there. Do you remember the deed we saw in his office? The money? That was all for me."

"I know." He pulled me toward him until my head rested on his chest. "Donata got a copy of the contract. So no honeymoon?"

"Well, not right away, anyway." I glanced up at him. "If he has a passport for me, why not leave the country right away and start this so-called marriage? Why is he waiting a few days in the Hamptons of all places? Isn't it cold there?"

"Yeah, they might get snow this weekend. Hmm. What is he planning to do? I mean, other than the obvious." He kissed my forehead, holding me tight. "If I were marrying you, I would want to get to the consummation part as soon as possible."

"I don't want to marry him, Enzo. Please."

"Then marry me instead."

"What?" I stumbled backward. "You can't be serious."

"Does it look like I'm not being serious?" The intensity in his dark eyes made me take another step away from him.

In a flash, a life as Enzo's wife went through my mind. I saw myself in his home, in his bed, and in his arms. Always. My eyes watered because those were the kind of fantasies I never allowed myself to have. For one, we were too young to get married. But also, because he was Enzo Alfera, the future king. I was a nobody.

I shook my head.

"He can't marry you, if you're married to me." His features softened as if the thought of a life with me pleased him.

How was this even possible? "You love me that much?"

"More than you know." He exhaled loudly, then said through gritted teeth, "I can't stand the thought of you being his. The idea that he's out there eating caviar, drinking champagne, thinking of you as his, is killing me."

"Rory, go wash your hands." Donata barged into the bathroom and grabbed Enzo's arm. "He's on his way here."

"Fuck." Enzo made for the door.

"No, we don't have time for that." She pulled him into one of the stalls.

I stood there in the middle of the room, looking for a way out. In the end, I did as Donata said. I darted to the sink and ran the water. The coolness of it calmed my nerves a bit. By the time Angelo appeared in the threshold, I wasn't shaking anymore.

"What the hell is taking so long? Your meal is getting cold." He snapped his fingers at me. "Let's go."

I rushed to him mainly because I didn't want him to say anything else—anything that might set off Enzo. We were both at the very edge as it were. As I walked past Angelo, he gripped my elbow then took another second to scan the stalls and lounging area.

My heart raced again. I plastered on a smile, hoping that would ease the intense pumping in my chest enough, so he wouldn't feel my pulse, so he wouldn't see how scared I was. When he finally let the door shut, I released a breath.

"I'm not feeling well." And that was the truth. The whole night I felt like puking.

"Dinner isn't over yet." He escorted me to my seat.

Dad glanced up at me with his fork halfway to his mouth. "Make sure you finish your steak. You're getting too skinny."

I gritted my teeth. I opened my mouth to tell him what he could do with his fatherly concerns, but then, I spotted a blonde head making her way toward the front door and all my anger went away. We didn't get to discuss our getaway plan. But knowing that Enzo and his friends were out there looking out for me made this entire dinner less shitty.

"It looks delicious, Dad."

"She doesn't need to eat all of it." Angelo reached over the table to caress my cheek. "Her body looks fine to me."

For the rest of the meal, I sat there and pretended to listen to their conversation. Mom, more or less, did the same. She spoke up a few times to thank Angelo for his generosity and to tell him how happy she was that we were all one big family now.

Mom's words prompted the lawyer to ask about the

contract again. I didn't fuss about it anymore because it didn't matter. I could sign a million contracts, and they would still not stop me from running away with Enzo.

"One big happy family." I grabbed the pen in front of me and signed.

As soon as I did, the lawyer grabbed the papers, stuffed them in his portfolio, and then excused himself. If I'd known the dinner would be over as soon as I signed, I would've done it much earlier than this.

"I enjoyed myself tonight." Angelo gave me a meaningful glance as if we now shared secrets like a real couple. "But I have a lot to do tomorrow. Work." He raised his hand to get the server's attention and then asked for the check.

On the ride back home, Angelo let me sit between Mom and Dad. I was glad for it because I couldn't stand being near him for another second. Though, once the SUV pulled up to our building, he climbed out, opened my door, and fetched me out of the car. His fingers dug into my hip as he held me close to his body.

"Such a gentleman." Mom beamed at me, then glanced up at Angelo, like he was some big hero for walking us to the lobby. "Thank you again for dinner. Rory had a lovely time."

"It was my pleasure." He nodded, keeping his gaze on me. "I will see you tomorrow."

"Why?" I cleared my throat. "I mean, I have a school project due. I have to stay late."

"We also have to go shopping. The holiday gala is this Friday," Mom added.

Angelo glared at me, as if trying to decide what to do. The wedding was only a few days away. Was he planning on jerking off with me in the room until then? The blue in his eyes thinned out as his pupils dilated. I got the feeling he was thinking about it.

"Join us for a nightcap?" Dad asked.

"I can be patient a little longer." Angelo leveled Dad with a stare, then stormed off.

I turned on my heel and ran to the elevator bay. Mom and Dad stayed in the lobby. Their bickering was the last thing I heard as the doors slid shut. Numb, I made my way upstairs and straight to my bathroom. I didn't know how many showers it would take to wash Angelo's touch off my skin—more than two for sure. I ran the hot water, stripped off my dress, then stepped in.

My tense muscles relaxed under the warm spray. And then the tears came. At this point, I didn't have a specific event in my mind to cry over—the sobbing just felt good. I scrubbed my whole body again, then washed my hair.

When I couldn't smell Angelo's cologne on me anymore, I shut off the water and grabbed a towel. My bathrobe wasn't where I had left it earlier, hanging behind the door. Had I left it on the bed and forgot?

A rush of cold air hit my nude body as soon as I opened the door. With a shudder, I ambled out of the bathroom. The lights were off in my room, though I distinctly remembered turning them on when I came in. My pulse quickened when I made out a shadow in the corner. Had Angelo decided to come up for a nightcap after all? I bolted toward the door. Two steps in, the stranger in my room clamped a hand over my mouth, while holding me by the waist with the other. I slammed against his front while I fought him frantically.

"Shh."

We'll Make It

Enzo

"Shh," I repeated against her ear. "Don't scream. It's me."

She stopped fighting me, and in the next beat, she melted against my chest. "Omigod." She spun around to face me. "You scared me half to death. I thought..."

"That I was him?"

She shook her head. I got the sense that Angelo did something to her. Back at the restaurant, she seemed desperate to be away from him. I hadn't forgotten how pale she turned when Donata came in to tell us Angelo was on his way to the bathroom. Fuck, the next few days were going to be hell for the two of us.

"What are you doing here?" She padded to the door and flipped the lock. "How?"

"How did I get in? Santino's dad owns this building. The doorman let me in."

"Just like that?"

"Turns out, he was short on cash. I made his night." I winked at her.

Getting in was a bit more involved than that, but Aurora didn't need to know. Until we were married and away from New York, she couldn't know how much danger she was in. Would she hate me for not trying to save her parents? Probably, but my hope was that one day she'd see that her dad brought this on himself. And there was nothing anyone could do to save him. Getting in bed with the mob never ended well for anyone. Stefano was just another pawn on Dad's chess board.

My gaze swept up and down her body. "Do you always walk around your bedroom naked?"

"Oh." She went to grab her bathrobe off the bed.

"No, leave it." I grabbed her by the waist and pulled her to me. "I like you like this."

I cupped her breast and pulled her nipple into a peak. When I had the bright idea to sneak into her suite, so we could finish our talk from before, I didn't think about how difficult it would be to be alone with her and not do anything. That was the thing about Aurora. I had zero self-restraint when she was near. Right now, I wanted to send all our plans to hell and bury my cock deep inside her.

She raised her blue gaze to meet mine. And, fuck me, if she wasn't as turned on as I was. I captured her mouth and kissed her hard, holding her tight against me. "Your parents are downstairs." I wedged my hand between us to find her pussy. "You're already wet."

She blushed. "I did everything they asked me to do today. They're feeling guilty about it."

"They won't come knocking?" I buried my fingers in her folds, drawing circles around her clit.

"No, they won't," she whispered, letting her head fall on my chest.

I was addicted to her surrender, her scent, and the little sounds she made when she was close to coming. She was at the very edge right now, and I fucking loved it. I rubbed her a little harder before I slipped two fingers inside her to tease her G-spot. We had a lot to talk about—plans to make for this Friday. But in this moment, I had the odd sense that I'd never see her again. There were too many days until we could be together forever. If this was all we had, I wanted to make it count.

"Come for me." I spoke into her ear, taking a handful of her ass to keep her in place while I worked her wet pussy. "Let it go, Angel."

"Enzo." She gripped the lapel of my leather jacket as she thrusted into my palm.

"Did you ever do this here?" I panted a breath. She looked so good like this. "Did you ever play with yourself in this room?"

She nodded.

Her skin turned to silk with red blotches everywhere. She was so close. I kissed the pulsing vein on her neck. I loved that I could make her feel like this. That she was a wanton puddle because of me. "Did you think of me? While you played with your pretty pussy. Did you think of me?"

She curled her heated body against mine, squeezing her eyes shut. "Yes. Yes." She clung to me.

"I can see you, Angel. All pretty in your bed, legs spread for me, pretending I'm here while you played with yourself. Is that how it was?"

She blinked quickly, as if she could see the image I had just painted clearly in her mind. Aurora liked to watch. But if she could see herself right now, she'd understand why I was so in love with her. Every time she was with me, her surrender was absolute. I'd never met anyone like her. No one ever made me feel this important. She needed me.

I dragged my fingers all the way out, then plunged in again. Gripping the nape of her neck, I brought her mouth up to meet mine. It was just in time for me to muffle her moans. Her juices dripped down her leg as she came hard on my hand. She was so beautiful and perfect when she orgasmed—when she trusted me enough to get her there.

After several beats, she took my wrist and pushed my palm away from her. "Oh." Her gaze stayed fixed on the mess her juices had made on the floor. "I didn't know that could happen."

"I've never seen it happen in person." I chuckled. "And that's making me really hard."

I walked her toward the bed. When the back of her knees hit the edge of the mattress, I picked her up by the waist and dropped her on the covers. She giggled as she watched me take off my clothes. It was a true miracle that I had lasted this long. If I didn't find release soon, I was going to explode.

Pushing her knees down, I nestled my hips between her thighs and swelled into her. "Fuck." The drag of her slick walls on my cock made me groan.

"Shh." She cupped my cheeks, then pressed her lips to mine.

I pumped into her, memorizing the feel of her body beneath mine, her soft skin, and her hands all over me. I wanted this for us. Forever. In a few days' time, she would be all mine. That thought alone pushed me past the edge. The usual spark ignited at my navel and then there was nothing I could do to stop it. Raw energy fluttered through me as I thrusted into her pussy, filling her with my cum. Suddenly, the lights were too bright and my panting was too loud. I rode her hard until every bit of my climax was spent.

She held onto me with her legs around my waist, giving me all of her, as her labored breaths brushed my ear. It had a soothing and calming effect on me. I rolled off her and settled next to her. "So much for being quiet."

"I don't think they noticed. They had a whole bottle of wine at dinner." She laughed.

I laid there for a minute, staring at the ceiling. Now that I'd come down from cloud nine, I remembered I had a very specific reason for sneaking into Aurora's bedroom tonight. "I didn't get my answer earlier."

She released a breath. "An answer to what?"

"My proposal."

"Wait." She sat up. "What? You're serious."

Her wet hair was plastered to her cheek while her breasts were covered in a thin sheen of sweat. Fuck, I had to focus. "About marrying you? Yes. It's the only way to keep you safe." I took her hand and brought it to my lips. "Desperate times call for desperate measures." I pressed her palm to my chest, right over my heart. "And I am desperately in love with you."

Her eyes watered.

"Aurora, would you marry me?" I beamed at her. "And don't ask if I'm serious. Yes or no. Those are the only two words you can say to me right now."

"Yes." She leaned forward and kissed me. "Of course I want to marry you."

"It didn't sound like it before." I peeled strands of wet hair off her temple.

"I was in shock." She kissed me again. "This is all happening too fast."

"I know. Unfortunately, we're not calling the shots here. Angelo is. All we can do is beat him to the punch."

"By getting married before my wedding to Angelo on Saturday?" She sat on her ankles.

"Exactly."

We already had plans to run away together this Friday. Getting married only added one more stop to our exit plan. "We'll meet at the holiday gala. And go from there. Santino is working on finding someone to officiate the marriage. Then we'll drive out of the country and catch a plane in Canada."

"Wow, sounds like you've worked it all out."

"I've had all week to think about it. Your answer was the last thing I needed."

"And now you have it." She bit her lip then glanced down to my hands. "Angelo seems like the type who would take this as a personal insult. I don't think he'll let us be."

"You're right, but we can deal with him. I'm still the dark prince." That last part was a lie. I had been demoted to a mere soldier because of Dad's recent abdication. But I still had Rex's support. I trusted my friends. "We'll make it. I promise."

She snuggled next to me. "I thought about asking Signoria Vittoria for help. She seems to care about me."

"It's how she works, Aurora. Don't fall for it. She can make you think she's your protector. But all she wants is to control you. Just look at what she did."

"What do you mean?"

"Do you really think your dad has the smarts to strike a

deal with Angelo?" I shook my head, pinching the bridge of my nose.

For a minute there, I did think Signoria Vittoria wanted to help Aurora's family. Maybe kindness had finally afflicted her in her old age. But no, that wasn't what Signoria Vittoria was after. From the beginning, she saw Aurora as an asset. Through her, she managed to control Angelo. And all because she wanted Dad out of the picture. The day we overheard their conversation at Donata's apartment, Dad treated Signoria Vittoria like his little bitch. I was shocked that she had put up with it. Even if Dad was King, Signoria Vittoria had zero tolerance for that kind of insolence. But she bit her tongue in the name of the greater good.

Dad was forever out of the society. Angelo was here to make room for the new king. Signoria Vittoria used Aurora to control Angelo. I didn't know how or what Signoria Vittoria wanted from Angelo, but Aurora was the key. This whole marriage contract wasn't Stefano Vitali's bright idea at all. The dragon lady had been pulling his strings since the beginning.

"Are you saying she helped?"

"There's a lot more at stake here, Aurora."

"Tell me."

"I will tell you everything." I brought her closer to me. "When we're away from this place. I'll tell you everything."

"Why not now?"

"Because you're a terrible liar." I attempted a laugh.

I didn't want her scared, knowing the kind of danger we were in. And if I was being honest, I didn't want her to know how far I'd fallen. My friendship to Rex was the only thing keeping me alive. If he hadn't vouched for me, Don Valentino would've come for me. And no one would blame him for it. Right now, I was the only person standing in the way of his ascension. But Rex knew I didn't want to start a war between the families to claim my rightful place at the head of the table. Dad threw it all away. And I was fine with that.

I only wanted her—my angel.

"I'm perfectly capable of telling a lie." She shifted her weight in my arms, rubbing her tits all over my side.

"Oh yeah? Let me ask you this. Did Angelo fuck you today? Did he try?"

Her face blanched, and that was my answer. The asshole did do something to her today.

"No, he didn't." She swallowed hard and squirmed to get away from me.

"Did he put his dick inside you?"

"No," she said with real conviction in her voice.

"Then what was it?" I brushed her cheek with my fingers. "You can tell me."

"He jerked off in front of me."

"That fucking asshole," I said through gritted teeth and pressed my lips to her forehead. "In a few days, you will never have to see him again."

"I believe you."

I stayed in her bed until her breathing slowed down, and she loosened her hold on me. Rex, Santino, and Donata were waiting downstairs. I'd asked them to give me an hour with Aurora, so I could ease her nerves and find out what Angelo had done to her. Unfortunately, because of his standing with Don Valentino and his role in the change of the guard, I couldn't touch him.

With a heavy weight on my chest, I swung my legs off the

bed and sat. Leaving Aurora was getting harder each time. But I had to play it smart.

"Where are you going?" She reached for me. "Stay."

"I can't." I shifted my weight to face her. "The guys are waiting downstairs. But I'll see you Friday, yeah?"

She nodded. Then blushed.

The pink in her cheeks was a dead giveaway that she was thinking about sex—that she was turned on for some reason. I'd bet she was already wet. Desire swelled through me like an avalanche. When I thought about how many days we had before we could be together again, I couldn't find a reason to leave now. Even when I knew my friends were waiting downstairs.

"It turns you on, doesn't it? To know that our friends know what we're doing right this minute." I reached out and fondled her breast, playing with her nipple the way she liked it.

"What? No." She let out a bated breath.

"You're such a terrible liar." I chuckled and prowled toward her to kiss her lips.

Cradling her neck, I deepened the kiss and brought her down with me, hooking her right leg over my hip. We landed on the pillows with her straddling me. My cock steeled at the sight of her like this—tits swaying in front of me, wet pussy rubbing on my balls. Fuck, I wanted her again.

I gripped her hips, lifting her so I could enter her. She opened for me, letting me slide in. Her blue eyes went big in surprise. For the longest minute, she sat still as if she had no idea how we got here—as if she didn't know what to do next. I cupped her butt cheeks and guided her to move up and down my shaft. She smiled and kept going, even after I let her go. Her chest turned different shades of red as she watched my erection go in and out of her. When I rubbed her clit, she dug her nails into my chest, but her gaze stayed on our connection.

"You look gorgeous riding my cock like that. Did you know that?" I wrapped my fingers around her delicate neck. Her lips parted. Then I moved my thumb from her folds to her mouth. She latched on to it like it was the most delicious thing in the world. When she had sucked it clean, I slid it down to her pussy again. "Soon. Every night will be like tonight."

"Promise me." She dragged her hips into me, making me see stars.

"I promise, Angel."

He Knows

Aurora

"You look beautiful, Rory." Mom's eyes filled up with happy tears. "Angelo is so generous. And thoughtful."

"Yeah, my sugar daddy has good taste." I smoothed out the blue velvet dress Angelo had sent over this morning. I had managed to avoid him all week with pretend projects and busy schedules. But our wedding was tomorrow. He wanted to make sure I knew he hadn't gone away.

"Be grateful." Mom smoothed out a few strands of hair in my updo. "He cares about you."

I stood there and watched Mom fuss over the gown, the hair, and the makeup. As much as we didn't agree on a lot of things, she was still my mom. Even if running away with Enzo was what I wanted, I knew I'd miss her. I hated that I couldn't have everything—my family, school, and Enzo. But their choices drove me to this decision.

"I love you, Mom." I hugged her, taking in her sweet perfume and her small frame. Maybe one day, she would see things my way. Maybe one day, I'd get my family back. "I gotta go."

"Yeah, of course, sweetie." She dabbed the corner of her eye. "The car's been waiting on you."

"I wanted to see Dad before I left."

"He's working late. You'll see him in the morning." She glanced around. "Do you have everything you need?"

"Yeah. I think so."

Monday night when Enzo came to see me in my room, we agreed not to bring luggage. He took a bag with him that had the essentials, a getaway outfit for tonight and an extra change of clothes. He had his car packed and ready to go. My chest swelled with giddiness. Enzo and I were getting married in just a few hours. Donata had secured the venue and even decorated it. She sent me pictures of the lounge room in the back of the library, done in white flowers and an aisle runner filled with petals. Santino had also confirmed he had someone fully licensed to perform a quick ceremony. Rex was the best man, and Donata my maid of honor. We were as ready as we would ever be.

I still couldn't believe this was happening though. A few months ago, I didn't want to leave my home in Las Vegas. Now I was leaving again to start a new life with the man I loved.

Mom took a million pictures of me on the elevator ride down, and then in the lobby, which was all decked out in Christmas lights and huge poinsettias. Beyond the tall glass double-doors, the snow flurries swirling around made Fifth Avenue look like a Christmas card. With a sigh, I turned to Mom and gave her one last hug.

"See you soon, Mom." I meant it. I did want to see her

again someday. Once Enzo became King, he'd figure out a way to bring us home.

"Don't stay up too late." She waved.

"Miss Vitali." Our driver opened the door for me with a polite smile.

I didn't know why I thought this part of our getaway plan would be more complicated. Enzo was right. The element of surprise was on our side. By the time anyone thought to look for us, we'd be long gone. I'd never been to Canada. A road trip with Enzo sounded like a dream come true.

The ride to the school grounds was longer than normal. Or maybe my nerves were getting the best of me. But once we arrived, and Donata came out to greet me, I knew we'd be alright.

"There you are." Donata took my hand, then leaned in. "We're all set. We'll wait for the dancing to be in full swing in the Adeline Hall before we make our way to the library. For now, go have fun. Enzo's already inside."

"Where are you going?" I asked once we entered the dining hall, which looked like a winter wonderland.

"To check on the food. You think all this happens magically? I'll see you in a bit." She winked at me then made her way toward the kitchen.

I stood at the threshold, admiring the incredible decor—the shimmering lights, the fake snow falling from the ceiling, and all the garlands covered in white flowers. Across the way, at the royals' table, I spotted Enzo, Rex and Santino. The tables in the middle of the hall had been removed to make room for dancing. It was no coincidence that the royals table was exactly as it always was. Donata arranged the room around it.

My gaze zeroed in on Enzo. It should be illegal to look so

hot in a tuxedo. He flashed me a smile that melted my heart. In the next beat, he pushed off the table and came to meet me halfway. The minute he was at arms' length, the live band started to play a slow tune.

"You look beautiful." He reached for my waist and pulled me to him.

"Everyone's watching." I ran my hands into his hair.

"We'll be gone in a few minutes. It doesn't matter anymore." He pressed his nose to my neck and inhaled. "I missed you."

Yeah, four days was a long time to be away from Enzo. But it had been worth it. My parents and Angelo didn't suspect our plans at all because I stayed home or at school the entire time.

"Me too."

"So as soon as the dance floor is crowded, we can make our way to the library." He turned me a few times, then settled into an easy step I could follow. Of course Enzo was a good dancer. He was everything to me. "You're not getting cold feet, are you?"

"Never. I just can't believe we're really doing this."

"They left us no choice."

"I know."

Five minutes into the song, couples made their way to the dance floor. Before I knew it, we were dancing in a sea of bodies. And that was the whole point. We needed to become invisible—something that was a little impossible given Enzo's status. But the low lights and music made everyone forget about us.

"You ready?" Enzo kissed my hand.

"Yeah." I nodded, seemingly calm. Though I had a thousand butterflies fluttering inside my belly. "Let's go."

Enzo took my hand and zigzagged his way through the crowd, toward the front entrance. As soon as we reached the edge of the dance floor, my heart dropped to my stomach like a brick. The adrenaline kicked in, and I pulled Enzo back into the safety of the throng.

"Angelo's here." I said into his ear. "He can't see me."

"He won't. Let's go through the kitchen." He pointed in the opposite direction where Angelo stood. Two steps in, he stopped in his tracks. "The fuck?"

I followed his line of sight toward Angelo. "Why is he talking to Brody? Why is Brody here? Wasn't he in rehab, recovering from a skiing accident?"

At the beginning of the semester, Brody and his friend Ian had assaulted me in the courtyard behind the bell tower. Brody didn't get in trouble for it, but Signoria Vittoria made sure he kept his mouth shut about what happened with me. She'd helped me keep my reputation intact at school because she didn't want the marriage contract with Angelo to fall through. I was stupid for thinking she helped me because she cared.

But now the question was, would Brody keep quiet? He had to know that his skiing accident wasn't an accident—that Signoria Vittoria had done that to teach him a lesson. Of course he didn't need to tell Angelo about how he almost made me suck him off. All he would have to do to ruin things for me was to tell Angelo that Enzo and I had been seeing each other and even kissed in front of the whole school a few weeks ago.

I didn't even want to think what Angelo would do if he found out about Enzo and me. He would definitely stop tonight's wedding. And then what? What would he do to me? To Enzo?

"I guess he's fully recovered." Enzo glanced back to the

royals' table. Rex and Santino were still there. "Go through the kitchen. I'll meet you in the library."

"I'll stay with you."

"No, if Angelo sees you, he won't let you go. Go. We'll make sure Brody keeps his mouth shut." He escorted me past the soda fountain and then to the small corridor that led to the kitchen. "Find Mollie. She'll help you find your way."

"I love you." I kissed his lips.

"Me too." He opened the door and ushered me in.

The place was chaos with the dinner preparations, which was a good thing, because no one batted an eye when they saw me rushing through the line of stoves and prep stations. With my heart pumping hard, I followed the exit signs. When I reached the back end of the building, I shouldered open the door and found Mollie taking a smoke break. I didn't need help finding my way anymore. But I stopped to talk to her anyway, in case Enzo came through looking for me.

"Hi, Mollie." I glanced around to make sure we were alone.

"Hey, Stray." She took a long pull from her cigarette, then puffed out a white cloud of smoke.

"If Enzo comes looking for me, could you tell him I'm waiting for him in the library?"

"Sure thing." She shrugged.

"Thank you." I made a run for it.

In heels, I couldn't go that fast, but it was something. Before I reached the steps, I got a text. With shaky hands, I stopped to fish my phone from the pocket of my dress.

Enzo: he knows
Me: what now?
Enzo: wait for me in the lounge

Me: hurry

I entered the library and darted toward the back room. My eyes filled with tears. Donata had done a beautiful job turning the place into a mini-wedding chapel. My only hope now was that Enzo would be able to get away soon. Of course, my brain conjured a bunch of scenarios where Enzo and Angelo got into a fight. What if Angelo brought a gun? Why would he though—if he was here for a school dance, to spy on me?

"Come on, Enzo. Where are you? Where's everybody?" I paced the length of the room, gripping my phone tight, waiting for news.

After what felt like an eternity, the door swung open. When I spun, I came face to face with Angelo. He was alone. Did that mean Enzo was safe? Or was he hurt somewhere on the school grounds? I opened my mouth to ask what he'd done. But I figured that would make things worse for me.

"What's going on?"

"Whore." He practically spat the word, then slammed the door shut. "At first, I thought your friend Brody was lying because he was jealous—because I found a virgin. I can see he wants you. But now I understand. He was telling the truth." He gestured toward the flowers and the aisle runner. "You're marrying the Alfera kid. Did you really think you could make a fool of me like that?"

"I can explain." The words spilled out but that was it. I had nothing else to say. Everything he had said was the truth.

He stepped closer as he unbuckled his belt. "I wanted to treat you right, but you're just like the others. Sleeping around like a whore. He's nothing. Don't you know that?"

In the next breath, he pulled on the buckle. He was so fast I didn't have time to think about what he was doing. He shoved me against the desk and struck me across the back. The shock of the assault froze me in place. It hurt, but the velvet fabric provided some protection. He hit me again, then twice more.

When he tossed the belt to the side, I released a breath. Deep down, I hoped that was the end of his rant. But I knew something worse was coming. Then I heard it, his zipper came down and then his pants. A few days ago, one thing had stopped him from taking what he thought was his. Angelo had this idea that he wanted to do right by me. Thanks to Brody, all that was gone.

I bolted to the door, but he grabbed me by the hair then shoved me face down on the sofa. With his knee on my lower back, he yanked my dress up. My brain was slow to catch on. Maybe I was in shock, or maybe I still refused to believe that men could be this evil. In his mind, I owed him sex. That was his plan right now. Before, I didn't fight him when we were in Dad's office, because keeping my relationship with Enzo a secret was more important. But now, all the cards were finally on the table. And I didn't have to pretend in front of him anymore.

As he positioned himself between my legs, I grabbed the vase of flowers on the side table, twisted my body, and struck his head. The glass didn't break. So I hit him again. His eyes had already gone blank, like he'd passed out, but his body hadn't caught on yet. I knew I should stop, but I couldn't. Even with all the blood everywhere, I couldn't make myself stop. I slammed the vase on his head again, and then, the whole thing shattered to pieces.

When Enzo and his friends barged in, Angelo was on the sofa unconscious and covered in shards. I was on the other side of the room, with Angelo's blood smeared on my dress. "He attacked me," I blurted out as they stepped inside. Their eyes opened wide like they were afraid of me, or were afraid I had lost my mind.

"Of course he did." Enzo rushed to my side and helped me up. "I'm so sorry I didn't get here sooner. Brody started a fight with me. I didn't realize it was all a distraction, so Angelo could get to you until Mollie messaged me to say Angelo was after you."

"How did he even know where I was?"

"He followed you. Mollie saw him. That's why she texted." Enzo's gaze fell on the belt on the floor then touched his fingers to raw spots on the nape of my neck. "Did he hurt you?"

"It doesn't matter now. Get me out of here."

"That's a great idea." Rex strode to Angelo to take his pulse. "Fuck. Of course he's alive. Should we tie him up? It might buy us some time."

"With what?" Santino braced his hands on his hips. "We're wasting time. His men will be here soon. I'm sure."

"Yeah, let's go." Enzo pulled me to him and headed out.

Outside, the chill in the air made my shivering worse. Though the bitter cold on my skin was better than Angelo's hands or the bite of his belt on me. What he almost did was the least of my worries right now. I had to think about what his next move would be. Because there was no way he was going to let me off the hook that easy.

"Aurora." Enzo turned to me when we reached the front gate. He cupped my face. The look in his eyes sent a chill down my spine. "You're going to have to go with Rex."

"No. Why? I don't want to go without you."

Where No One Can Find You

AURORA

"What did I miss?" Donata rushed to our group while Rex and Enzo talked on their phones, trying to find their drivers. "I went to the lounge room in the library. Please tell me that wasn't your blood." She surveyed my face and clothes.

"The short of it?" Santino pulled her toward the wall where it was dark. "Angelo found out about the love birds. He tried to get payment from Aurora, but she nailed him in the head with one of your vases."

"Oh no, that was good crystal."

"Did you see Angelo?" My heart rate spiked.

"No, there was no one there." Donata pressed a hand to her forehead.

This was not good.

"Then where is he?" I asked.

"Probably not awake yet. Otherwise, he'd be here." Santino shrugged, putting on a nonchalant facade. But by the way his neck muscles strained under his collared shirt, I could tell he was as wired and as ready to fight as Enzo. "Anyway." He motioned toward the street. "We're waiting on Rex's car. And also, Enzo was about to tell Aurora everything. But I think it's better if we wait until she's on the move."

"That's right now." Enzo wrapped his arm around my waist. "Rex will explain everything. I'm sorry I didn't do it before. I really am." Tears brimmed his eyes as he leaned in to press his mouth to mine. "Do you trust me?"

"I do." I chuckled at the words.

"Then please, go with Rex. He'll explain everything."

"I love you." I threw my arms around his neck and kissed him again.

"I love you too." He smiled. "I'll see you on the other side."

I hugged Donata and Santino as Rex impatiently waited for me by his car. I held on to Enzo's hand until he stepped away and let go. My only motivation to get in the SUV with Rex was to find out what things Enzo was keeping from me, and why his eyes watered when he apologized for not telling me before.

I climbed in the back seat. In the next breath, the tires screeched as they peeled away from the curb. With shaky hands, I grabbed the seat belt and fumbled with the buckle.

"Here." Rex reached over to help, but I swatted his arm away.

"I can do it."

He arched his brows as he watched me intently, waiting for me to get it right. When I failed over and over, he scooted over and buckled me in. His body next to mine felt so comforting and it reminded me so much of Enzo. Before I could stop them, tears streamed down my cheeks.

"Shh."

The minute he wrapped his arm around my shoulders, I let go and started bawling. Yeah, I was in Rex Valentino's shiny car, crying my eyes out. Every plan we had for tonight had gone wrong. Worst part was, Angelo knew I wasn't the virgin he'd bought. And he was pissed. He was more than pissed. He was on a warpath.

"Will he go after my parents because of me?" I asked in between sniffles.

Rex reached into the front seat and grabbed a pack of tissues. He started to give me one, then decided to let me have the whole thing. "He was going to do that anyway."

"What do you mean?"

"Are you sure you want to know?" He glanced up at the road ahead of us. "We have about thirty minutes to talk."

"I am." I blinked to clear my vision, inhaling deeply to calm down. This wasn't the time to lose my shit. "Please don't hold back. I need to know what's going on."

"Yes, you do." He inhaled. "Michael Alfera abdicated the throne." He gestured toward himself. "My dad has taken over."

"I didn't know you could do that."

"It's not ideal, and certainly not common. But all year, this is what the adults have been working toward. To find a way to get the old Don Alfera to step down. Angelo was handpicked by the board to clear obstacles for the new king—my father."

I stared at him with wide eyes, mouth slightly opened. My mind was going a million miles an hour as I tried to connect the dots. Though I kept going back to a single detail. "Enzo is no longer the dark prince."

"No. In fact, he's been demoted to a soldier. When the news spreads, his privileges will be gone."

"That's what he couldn't tell me?" I puffed out a breath.

"He was afraid I wouldn't want to be with him anymore. Is that why I'm here with you?"

"Honestly, I'm sure that's part of the reason. Enzo can be a real idiot sometimes. He thinks women like him for what he is or was, rather than for who he is. He wanted me to tell you that if you want to go on your own, you can."

"Idiot is too nice of a word."

"He really loves you. Can I assume you don't care about that stuff, that he's not the dark prince?"

"I never cared that he was a royal."

If Enzo were here, I would give him a piece of my mind. How could he think that I would stop loving him just because he wasn't the future king of a secret society? Hadn't I proven myself to him? I left my family and all my dreams behind just to be with him. That should count for something. It should count for everything.

"What's the other part?" I wiped my nose with a tissue. "Why am I here with you?"

"Because Angelo can't touch me."

"Because you're the new future king."

"Right. You're safe with me. We're on our way to Teterboro airport. I have a private plane there waiting for us. We'll fly to Canada and wait a few days for Enzo to meet us there. From there, you can go anywhere you want. Get married. Be happy." He touched my chin to make me look at him. "He deserves to be happy."

"You're flying with me? Won't your dad be looking for you?"

"No, he trusts me. Enzo is like a brother to me. I owe him." He shifted his gaze toward the windshield.

If I didn't know any better, I'd say Rex was feeling guilty.

As if he'd stolen something from Enzo. I didn't know much about their rules and the dynamics between the five original crime families. But it didn't seem like Rex and Enzo had a choice in any of this. Just like I wasn't given a choice to marry Angelo. To our parents, we were just pawns on their demented chess board.

Wait. What did he say about my parents before? *"He was going to do that anyway."*

"What did you mean by that? He was going to do that anyway." Tears stung my eyes again because I had a pretty good idea. But I wanted him to say it aloud. I wanted to hear the words. "Angelo. He was handpicked?"

He nodded as if waiting for me to do the math. When I couldn't say the words, he finished for me. "When an ascension takes place, the inner circle of the old don, or king in this case, has to be eliminated. That's your family. It would've been you too. Except, you were given to Angelo as a gift. They enticed him with the idea of a virgin bride."

"No." I scooted forward and tapped on the driver. "Turn around. I want to go home."

The driver ignored me because he was here to do Rex's bidding, not mine. He met Rex's gaze. When Rex shook his head once, the driver stayed in his lane.

"Rex, please. I didn't know my parents were in this kind of danger. If I had known..."

I trailed off because I didn't know what I would've done if from day one Dad had explained to me that my marriage to Angelo meant my whole family got to live. "Why didn't they tell me? Turn around." I yelled at the driver. "Turn around now."

I slammed my hand on the back of the driver's seat. When

I made to climb over to the front, Rex grabbed me by the waist. The car swerved a few lanes when I pulled on the driver's sleeve. He yanked his arm away and continued driving, as if he didn't have some crazy girl going ape shit in his car.

"Stop, Rory. Getting us in an accident is not going to change anything." He held me in a tight bear hug. I kicked and screamed some more. Only because that was all I could do. He was right. I couldn't help my family. Their fates were sealed the day Dad agreed to move to New York. Rex exhaled loudly in my ear. "They didn't tell you because they didn't know. They got money for you and that was it. They were going to die no matter what. Haven't you done the math yet? Your family was brought to the Upper East Side to die."

"Why?" I sobbed into the sleeve of his tuxedo jacket.

"To save Penny's family. Her dad used to be the old king's right-hand man. He's married to Michael's cousin. In a fucked-up way, this was Michael Alfera's way of keeping his extended family safe."

"And sacrificed mine in the process." My voice sounded so far away.

"But Signoria Vittoria found a way to save you."

Now it all made sense. Why when I asked her for help with Brody's situation, she jumped in and made it all go away. She knew that if my reputation was tarnished, Angelo wouldn't want me anymore. And she needed him to want me. Because, otherwise, if he didn't marry me, he would have to kill me. I ruined her plans.

"He's going to kill me too, isn't he?"

"No, he's not." Rex loosened his tight hold on me but didn't let me go. "I promised my brother I would do anything in my power to help you. And that's exactly what I'm going to do."

"How?" I shifted my body to face him.

"You're safe as long as you're with me. We fly to Canada. Wait for Enzo there."

"Then you go where no one can find you. Away from all this."

Before, when Enzo and I had made plans to run away together, I assumed we would hide for just a little while. A few years, until the whole fiasco blew over. I had it all wrong. This was never going to end for us. Angelo had orders to kill my parents, and who knew who else. And now, I was on his hit list.

I never paid much attention to anything he said to me. But I still managed to learn a few things about him. One, the world was black and white for him. Do or don't. Live or die. He was meticulous. And he was smart. The rage I saw in his eyes after Brody told him I was with Enzo and possibly not a virgin anymore flashed in my mind's eye. A cold shiver ran up my spine as I realized that Angelo would never let me go. He would never forgive me for giving my virginity to Enzo.

"He's never going to stop looking for us, is he?"

"No." He swiped his thumb across my cheek. "Which is why you need to think long and hard before you get on that plane with me."

Thanks to Rex, Enzo and I had a solid plan B: to run away together. Was that what I wanted for him? A life on the run? If we left tonight, we could never come home again. But then what was the alternative? A life with Angelo? Assuming I could convince him that I was still a virgin, could I spend the rest of my days like that—loving Enzo from afar?

"I'm being selfish."

"Yes, you are. But so is Enzo. Maybe two wrongs can make a right." He shrugged.

"I'm confused. You think what we're doing is the wrong thing to do, but you still want us to run away together?"

"Like I said, Enzo is like my brother. He deserves to be happy. Even if it's away from us. Not to mention, I promised him I would keep you safe."

"How about you? What do you want, Rex? Are you okay with all this being dumped on you now? I saw what it did to Enzo, carrying the weight of the world on his shoulders just because one day he had to take over for his dad."

"I didn't get a choice. Not really." He chuckled. "We never do. I hope you understand that now."

"That's why we're leaving." I glanced down at my hands. "Do you want to be king? Because I don't think Enzo ever wanted it."

"His dad was so concerned with keeping his two worlds from collapsing, he forgot to teach Enzo what we are to the Society."

"And do you know?"

"I do. I believe we can do great things." He cocked his head to look me in the eyes. "So, what's it gonna be, Angel?" He put emphasis on the word *Angel*—Enzo's term of endearment for me.

I was no angel. Or a good girl like Enzo thought. Because anyone else in my position would be thinking about doing the right thing.

I wasn't. I didn't want to think about the right thing.

I didn't want to think about my parents, sitting at home, not knowing something terrible was coming for them. I didn't want to think about what Enzo could have if he stayed here. Even as a soldier, he could still have a good life. The future king considered him a brother. That had to count for something.

So instead, I focused on the one thing I could see clearly in my head. Our future together—sailing the Balearic Sea on his yacht, like he wanted.

"I want Enzo."

The moment I uttered the words, the driver met my gaze in the rearview mirror. He put on his blinker and slowed down. With a loud rumble, the wheels veered into the rumble strips, while I tried to figure out what was happening. The road we were on was dark and empty. But as soon as he shut off the engine, two other cars pulled up—one in front of us and one behind us.

"Fuck." Rex's voice rumbled in the car.

I followed his line of sight to where Angelo stood in the circular glow cast by the headlights. One by one, he was joined by his men. I stopped counting once I got to ten. What did it matter? It wasn't like we could fight them all off. We were outnumbered.

Rex's driver climbed out and opened my door. "I'm sorry, Mr. Rex. King's orders."

"You betrayed me." Rex fisted his hands.

"The king is trying to keep the friends he has." The driver frowned as if letting Rex down pained him. "He's going to need them."

"Rory." Rex cupped my cheek. "I'll find a way. You and Enzo will be together. I promised him. And now I'm promising you."

"Take care of him, Rex." I hugged him.

Angelo reached in and gripped my elbow. I thought about running. But what would be the point? It was as Signoria Vittoria had said, there wasn't a place in this world where her people wouldn't find me. That included Angelo, and his mandate to make room for the new king.

The King is Dead

Enzo

Where the hell were they? Aurora had left the school with Rex over half an hour ago. He should've texted by now to let me know they had made it to Teterboro. We had agreed to keep communication to a minimum, so Angelo wouldn't suspect Rex was helping us. But how long did it take to type a quick message to say, "she's safe."

In the blink of an eye, our plans had gone to shit. But I had to admit, plan B was solid, even if it meant being away from Aurora for now. As much as I hated the idea of Rex playing her hero, he was right. Thanks to Dad, I was no more than a soldier. And now that Angelo knew the truth about Aurora and me, he would use any excuse to kill me.

With Rex, she had a shot at making it to Canada.

If I traveled alone with Donata, I could make it there too. New York was no longer safe for me.

Rex hadn't spelled it out for me, but I wasn't an idiot. Don

Valentino had shown my family mercy by letting us live. Beyond that gesture, he wasn't required to do much else.

The new king would sleep better at night if I wasn't alive. If Dad or I ever did anything to jeopardize his seat at the head of the table, Don Valentino would have no qualms calling for our heads.

My gaze darted to the clock on the mantle and then the screen on my laptop, while I paced the length of the living room. Fuck. Five days without seeing Aurora were going to be hell. I had hoped to be married to her by now. But as long as she was out of the country tonight, she wouldn't have to see Angelo ever again—let alone marry him tomorrow.

By this time next week, we would be man and wife. Sure, we would be on the run, hiding, but I didn't care. I only wanted to be with her. Oddly enough, after all this time, I couldn't even say I would miss this place. Ever since Mom left, my life here had been filled with pain.

I sat on the sofa and checked the security feed on my screen. The men who followed me home were still keeping guard downstairs. I had no doubt they were here on Angelo's orders. Dad was no longer king. He didn't have a crew at his disposal anymore, which meant he couldn't have me followed.

Dad still hadn't taken the time to explain to me how he had managed to convince the other Dons to let him walk away. Or why he had decided to leave the Society—why he had strung me along, making me believe I'd be king one day.

Mom hated this mafia world, and what it did to Dad. Was it possible that he was doing this for her? That had been my initial thought. But if that was his only motivation for abdicating, it would mean Dad was a halfway-decent husband. And I knew for a fact he wasn't. Whatever his reason, it didn't matter anymore because I was as good as gone.

Another five minutes went by. I couldn't stay here and wait for news. I fished my phone from the inside pocket of my jacket and called Rex. The phone rang and rang—no voicemail and no Rex. What the fuck?

I shot to my feet. When I turned, I came face to face with Dad. He had that same crazed look in his eyes he had the day he killed an entire crew in front of me. It was as if he didn't recognize me. I sure as fuck didn't recognize this version of him. Dad had officially lost his mind.

The blood caked in between his fingers made me take a couple of steps back. I thought of the day at the docks. After he killed those men, he had left with Angelo, no doubt to fulfill his part of whatever bargain he made with the new king. Dad and Angelo were on a dark mission to kill everyone in Dad's inner circle. That was the price he had agreed to pay to keep the rest of us alive.

"Where's Mom?" I asked, not only to get him to snap out of it, but to remind him he still had a family to look after.

"Home."

"What are you doing here?"

"I came for you." He ran a hand through his hair. "Get your things. You're moving to Brooklyn with us."

The hell I was.

"No." I stood my ground. "I'm not going anywhere with you."

"This was always the plan. Do you not get it? You were never going to be king." He had to make it sound like it was all my fault, but he couldn't pin this one on me. I was done being his punching bag. He met my gaze. "Your mother wants a normal family. And that's exactly what she's going to get. She wants you home for the holidays."

I winced because I hadn't thought about how Mom would feel if I didn't come home for Christmas, but she had to understand that this thing she had with Dad wasn't real. He wasn't a devoted father and doting husband. Even if he wasn't a mobster anymore, he was still a criminal, a killer—it was who he was.

"Did you really leave the Society for Mom?"

"Yes, I made a promise to her. So many years ago. This is me keeping that promise."

I swallowed hard and tried not to think about Aurora and her family. There was a good chance the blood on Dad's hands belonged to her parents. Did Mom have any idea how many people had to die because he made her a promise?

He squeezed his eyes shut and wiped his cheek. When he opened them again, he unbuckled his belt. This was Dad's cycle—he would spend time playing the good husband. Only to succumb to his need to be this monster. Then the guilt would set in because he really wanted to be a better man for Mom. It killed him to know that she couldn't accept him for who and what he was.

Anger flashed in his eyes. He hated that Mom made him do this. So now he needed me. He needed the relief—a place to dump all his rage.

"You didn't come here because you wanted to bring me home. You're mad at her." I pointed my chin at his bloody hands, gripping his belt tight.

He raised it high over his head and brought it down across my chest.

"I said no." I caught the end of the strap.

He shot me a leveling glare and tugged at the buckle. I towered over him and looped the leather once around my fist. Then I yanked it so hard, he had no choice but to let it go. He knew that if he fought me, he would lose. All this time, I let him use me because he was our king. Because he was the most powerful man I knew. Now, he was no one. We were the same.

"This is not what Mom wanted from you. She's as blind as you are. Everyone can see you will never be the kind of man she thinks you can be."

"How dare you,"

"Look at yourself." I raised my voice. Adrenaline rushed through me as I tried to tamp down the pain and frustration rushing to the surface. "You're nothing if you're not a criminal."

I tossed the belt aside and headed for the door. If I stayed, if I stooped to his level, I would be no better than him. Because all I wanted to do was to strike back and ease this pressure in my chest, to find relief.

"Don't you dare turn your back on me, boy."

His footsteps moved swiftly across the floor. I turned around in time to meet the lick of his belt. Red spots floated in front of me as the pain seared across my cheek. I punched him once, then again and again. The surprise in his eyes had to match my own. I hadn't meant to crack his jaw. I hadn't meant to hit him at all. But now that I had started, I couldn't find a reason to stop.

He fell backward and landed with a loud thud. His busted lip and nose bled profusely and added a layer of fresh blood to his hands. That right there made me pause. To see him so vulnerable, looking up at me with actual fear in his eyes.

The king is dead.

"Go home, Dad. We're done here."

I headed downstairs as my mind flashed more images of Dad, bloody and defeated. It didn't matter if Angelo's men followed me. All I wanted to do was ride my motorcycle and forget about Dad.

In the garage, I hopped on my bike and careened out of the parking deck. The cold air did nothing to defuse the rush of adrenaline sweeping through me. A part of me wanted to go back and finish what I started. What would our lives be like without Dad?

"I'm not him." I repeated the words aloud over and over.

In the side mirrors, I spotted Angelo's men. For a moment, I thought about facing them too. But the last thing I needed tonight was to leave a trail of bodies. I couldn't give Angelo a reason to come after me. I needed my freedom to see Aurora again.

So instead, I maneuvered through traffic. After I ran a few red lights and cut a corner, I was able to shake them. Oddly enough, the short chase helped me calm the fuck down. I pulled over and killed the engine when I reached the end of a dark alley. I had plans to stay in the city for a few more days, but now I couldn't do that. I had to get on the road tonight.

I tried calling Rex again. I needed to know Aurora was safe.

"Enzo." He picked up on the first ring. "Jesus Christ, where the hell have you been? I've been trying to reach you."

"Something came up. Is it done?"

"I'm sorry." He exhaled loudly into the speaker. "Angelo took her. I couldn't stop him. My driver betrayed me. I don't know where Angelo's taking her."

"Fuck." I gripped the phone. "They could be anywhere right now."

My mobile buzzed with a new call from Donata. I added her to our call and let Rex explain the situation. I did my best to stay focused on what we had to do. But my mind kept flitting through different scenarios, all of which had to do with Angelo and Aurora alone. What would he do to her?

Aurora had been right in thinking that Angelo would feel cheated if he ever found out I was her first—that she wasn't the virgin he had bought. Would he still want her? Or was this all about revenge? How far was he willing to go to appease his sense of pride.

"That's why I was calling, guys."

"What do you mean?" I realized I hadn't been keeping up with the conversation. "Do you know where he took her?"

"Um." She cleared her throat. "Promise me you won't judge."

"We don't have time for this." My heart pumped hard. The serenity I felt when I entered the alley was now gone, replaced by sheer agony and utter fear for Aurora. "Since when do you care what we think?"

"I had plans to meet Luca tonight," she blurted out then paused for effect. When neither Rex nor I commented, she continued, "Good. I'm glad that's out of the way. I sent Giuseppina to our beach house last night. You know, to get things set up for us."

"And?" I asked.

We could deal with the Luca situation later.

"As she was leaving the house earlier, she spotted one of Angelo's guys moving a couple of gas containers into a beach house five houses down. She recognized the guy because he'd been to our penthouse a few times. Anyway, she called me because she knew we had a certain operation scheduled for tonight." Donata gave us a second to digest this new information. "Pina's gut is never wrong. So I sent Luca to check things out. Didn't you say he bought her a house in the Hamptons?"

"What is Angelo up to?" I asked.

"Luca called back a minute ago. Aurora's parents are there. He said it didn't look like they were guests. Guys, if Angelo took Aurora, do you think he means to marry her tonight?"

"Or, if he already had orders to kill Aurora's family. What's one more?" Rex let the question linger in the air.

I thought of Angelo and the way he kept Aurora close to him at the engagement party, the way he looked at her like she belonged to him. The more I tried to read into everything he did and said that night, I couldn't figure out what his next move would be. How much did he want her? Enough to forgive the fact that she'd slept with me?

If it were me, I wouldn't care because I loved her. Did he love her? He couldn't. He didn't even know her.

Best case scenario, Angelo would marry Aurora tonight and take her away from me forever. Worst case, he would kill her along with her parents. I swallowed the lump in my throat. Either way, he was taking her away from me. And I had no way to get to her in time.

"Rex, can we still use your plane?" I needed to get to the Hamptons. Aurora didn't have much time.

"No, we can't. Dad found out I was leaving the country with Aurora. He asked me to stand down, Enzo." He lowered his voice as if he were talking to a wounded animal. "Angelo knows about you and Aurora. Even if you get her back and manage to escape, he will find you. You have to consider the idea that the only way to keep her alive is to let her marry Angelo."

"Before you said he meant to kill her. Now he's the good guy who wants to marry her? Which one is it?"

"I don't know, Enzo. That's the whole point. You're flying blind."

The element of surprise was all we had. And now we didn't even have that. Things had gone from bad to worse, yes, but I wasn't ready to give up on Aurora—to give up on us. I promised her we would run away together. I promised her she would be safe with me.

"I don't give a shit what your dad and Angelo think or want. Aurora wants to be with me."

"Wait." Donata's voice went up a few octaves. "Are you thinking about going to the Hamptons to look for her? You don't know for sure Angelo is taking her there. If you go there, and she's not there. Then what?"

"Then it's over."

I had no idea where Angelo was taking Aurora. But the Hamptons was our best bet—our only bet really. I was going purely on a hunch, but what other option did I have? I couldn't stand here and waste any more time.

"Donata, I can be at your place in five. Can you be ready to go? I can't go home."

"Yeah, I'm ready right now."

Such A Beautiful Liar

Aurora

"Where are you taking me?" I glanced back at the bright headlights and Rex's dark silhouette. "My parents will be looking for me."

Angelo scoffed. The gravel crunched under his shoes, then the wind got knocked out of me as he slammed me against the side of the SUV. I squeezed my eyes shut and refused to look in Rex's direction. It didn't matter. He couldn't help. Even if he was next in line to be king, no one could stop Angelo.

I gasped for air while Angelo jammed his forearm just below my chin. His breath laced with whiskey puffed into my face. He didn't move again until Rex's car peeled away and got lost in the distance.

"Is that what you think?" he asked through gritted teeth.

I wanted to beg for Enzo's life, for my family. But the sheer anger I found in Angelo's eyes told me that groveling wouldn't help our case. The worst had happened. Angelo knew the truth. And even though he never asked me if I wanted to be with him, he still considered my actions a betrayal.

"Answer me." He gripped my jaw and forced me to meet his gaze. "Do you think your parents are at home worrying about you? You're wrong. I'm the only one looking out for you. But you're too dumb to see it."

"See what exactly?" I winced when his fingers dug into my cheeks. "That you paid a million dollars for a virgin?"

"I offered you more than money." His gaze searched mine. After several beats, his features softened, but he didn't loosen his hold on me. "I was willing to save your life, and make you my queen." He pressed his forehead to mine. "Such a beautiful liar." He said mostly to himself.

My heart thrashed in my ears. Angelo was showing he cared about me, though he seemed conflicted about something. Then the realization of his dichotomy washed over me like a bucket of ice water. He didn't want to kill me, but he had to. That was his job—to kill my parents. Now that our contract was null and void, he had to kill me too. And possibly the twins. Were they part of the equation too?

As much as I hated the idea of touching him, I reached for his hand gripping my cheek. Enzo was right. I was the worst liar. But right now, lying was the only thing that could save me and my family. Was that even possible? To save us all? I wracked my brain for the right words, the perfect lie. Anything to make him change his mind. He had to change his mind. I was being selfish before—thinking I could run away with Enzo and live happily ever after with him.

It was just a dream.

Angelo was real. He was the only choice.

"Brody assaulted me at the beginning of the semester.

Enzo came in just in time before he could do any real damage." I rambled out the words, not really knowing where I was going with it. I inhaled, and my throat tightened some more. It felt so dry and raw, even breathing hurt. "He hated me since then. He lied about me and Enzo. I barely know Enzo."

"You barely know Enzo." He stepped back. "Are you trying to tell me you're still a virgin?"

"Yes." Tears streamed down my cheeks. "If you spare my family, I'll go with you. Anywhere you want. I promise."

He stood there with his arms crossed over his chest as his gaze swept up and down my body. Apart from the headlights shining ahead of us, the side of the road was dark. I doubted he could see much of me. This wasn't about what he could see, but what he wanted to do next. I dropped my hands to my sides and let him explore—a sign that I was a willing partner from here on out.

My parents didn't deserve my sacrifice, but Jesus Christ, no one deserved to die like this. No matter what they had done, this was too cruel. My brothers were also in danger. Signoria Vittoria knew exactly where to find them because she sent them to that boarding school. They were innocent. If staying with Angelo meant saving the twins, I had to at least try.

"Can I go home? To get my things." I asked after what felt like hours.

"Get in the car."

As soon as he uttered the words, his driver climbed out of the SUV and opened the door for us. I got in and scooted all the way to the end. Did he believe me? Was this his way of saying he was accepting my offer? In the back of my mind, I was hoping Mom and Dad would have a way to fix the mess I created. But how could they, if they didn't understand they had come to New York to die at the hands of a trained assassin.

"Drive," Angelo mumbled when his driver sat behind the wheel.

"Are we going home?" The mousy tone in my voice made my stomach roll. But this was the choice I had made. I had to learn to live with it. "Please."

"Face the window." He reached into the inside pocket of his suit jacket.

I shifted my body away from him. Maybe he didn't want me to see who he was calling. Or maybe this was a test to see how pliable I was willing to be going forward. Whatever it was, I bit my lip and stayed facing the distorted reflection on the window. I stared at the mascara smeared on my cheeks and the patches of wet strands of hair stuck to my temples. Could he tell I was lying?

"I don't give a shit about the plan. It must happen tonight. Tomorrow will be too late."

Did he mean our wedding? Were we getting married tonight? I braced my hands on the seat and took in a long breath. When I turned to face him to ask what his plan was, he stuck a needle in my neck then shoved me against the door. The inside of the car went dark. I could hear Angelo talking to his driver, though I couldn't make out what they were saying. Their words sounded like we were under water, muffled and warped. The worst part was, I couldn't move—I was semi-conscious and unable to move.

After a while, I dozed off and even had dreams. Though most of them were really memories of the short time I had spent with Enzo. They ran out of sequence and on a loop—over and over, I saw him kissing me for the first time. Then I saw him calling plays on the football field. I saw him staring at me from his lab table in the back of Chem class. I clung to the images as if my life depended on it. Because, from now on, this was all I could have of him. Memories were all Enzo and I had left of each other.

I hugged my belly and focused on his beautiful face. "Give me my sin again," he whispered in my ear.

Who knew how long I was asleep? But when the car stopped, it jostled me forward, and I face-planted on the front seat. I was awake, but I still couldn't move.

"What did you give me?" I mumbled the words, though I wasn't sure he heard me.

"Get her inside." Angelo pulled me back toward the seat and then climbed out of the car.

For a moment, I couldn't tell if I was dreaming still or if this was really happening. Though the cold air and the snow flurries brushing my face felt too real. Big arms fished me out of the SUV like I was a ragdoll. I closed my eyes and focused on what was happening. Doors opened and closed. Then I heard Mom crying, calling for me.

"Mom," I called for her.

The guy carrying me dumped me on a sofa. We were in a house, but this didn't feel like our apartment. Where the hell were we?

"Get her up," Angelo towered over me, "I want her to see the place."

Two guys propped me up. My legs felt like jelly still, so I let them hold me in place. "Where are we?" I sighed in relief because I didn't sound like a drunk anymore. "Where's Mom?"

"Rory. We're here."

The men turned me to face them. They were both tied to

dining room chairs. Dad had a gag on. Not that it mattered, he couldn't even look at me. Like before, when he got in trouble in Las Vegas, he never said a word either. Didn't apologize or try to tell us it would be all right. He just sat there and assumed Mom would fix everything for him.

"Mom, he's going to kill us." By now, I had figured out Angelo hadn't bought my lie about being a virgin. Not only that, but he had also decided about me.

"Angelo," Mom pleaded with tears in her eyes, "Let her go. She's too young."

"I bought this beach house for you." Angelo stood in front of me.

With a smirk, he gestured toward the dining room, which was done in a coastal cottage style with beige and tan colors. The quintessential chandelier made of seashells hung over my parents' heads. The room was beautiful. Even though they were tied down, I bet they could still pretend Angelo was their friend.

To my relief, the twins weren't here.

"We're in the Hamptons?"

When Enzo and I rummaged through Angelo's things the night of the engagement party, we found the deed to a beach house. Enzo had mentioned it wasn't far from his own home. My pulse spiked. Then I shook my head to clear the stupid thought that popped into it. Enzo had no way of knowing that Angelo would bring me here tonight.

I couldn't think about Enzo coming to save me. Because he wasn't. If Rex loved him like he said, he would keep him away from Angelo and away from me. If only to keep him alive.

"This house could've been a safe haven for you." Angelo brushed his fingers down my cheek. "Now it's the place where you'll die." He flashed me a creepy smile. "My apologies, but I couldn't get your brothers here on time. You see, this was all supposed to happen after our wedding."

"Please don't do this. I'll do whatever you want."

"I only asked one thing from you." He stepped closer, while his men held me in place. "Tell me the truth, did you sleep with the Alfera kid?"

"No." I swallowed. "I swear."

"She's telling the truth," Mom called from the other side of the sofa, struggling with the rope tying her to the chair. "She would never do that to you."

"You thought you could play me." He glared at me while Mom spoke fast in the background, begging him to give us a second chance.

To her credit, she wasn't asking him to let her go, she only wanted her children to be safe. So, all this time, Mom wasn't pretending things were fine because she loved the glitz and glamour of this world. She honestly believed she was doing it for us. She believed all this money and our new social status would keep us safe.

"Shut her up." Angelo pointed to the man standing closest to Mom.

He quickly stepped in and gave her a shot in the neck, similar to the one Angelo had given me in the car. Her eyes went wide in surprise as she tried to rub the pricked spot against her shoulder. A few seconds later, her gaze bounced between Angelo and me.

"Listen to me, please." She swallowed, but the drug was already taking effect. It only took but a minute before her words were jumbled, and then, she couldn't talk at all.

She glanced up at Dad, as if asking for help. But he didn't

even move. And now I wondered if he was dosed too. What kind of drug was that? Had he given us an overdose of Valium? That was the only point of reference I had when it came to drugs.

When we were in Las Vegas, and I got kicked off the cheer team, Mom had given Valium to calm me down. This dreamlike state felt like that but multiplied by ten. Dad's gaze turned to me. It was as if he could see me but didn't know me. Why would Angelo drug us? What did he want?

I scanned the space, looking for exits. There was one on the other side of the dining room. Past the area where Mom and Dad sat, there was a long hallway that led to the kitchen, where I could see another door with a glass window. The snow continued to fall against the dark frame of the glass. My gaze shifted back and forth.

Even though my brain was still fuzzy, I kept trying to understand the clues. When the guy holding me chuckled, I turned to face him. "What are you going to do to us?"

"Isn't it obvious?" Angelo answered for him. "It'll be a tragic accident for sure."

"Please." I wasn't sure what I was asking for anymore.

The word please played on repeat in my head. Even though I knew I couldn't change his mind—I couldn't stop begging. I checked the doors and then noticed the red containers of gasoline. If he was planning to burn the place up with us inside, the police would know. Then again, if he was doing this for the new king, chances were, the police were already writing a report that showed it was all an accident—a gas leak.

We didn't even have the mobility to walk out the door.

"Go get everything ready," he told the men holding me.

When they let me go, Angelo guided me onto the sofa. The fabric smelled of gasoline or maybe the stench was already all over the house. I took in a deep breath and ordered my legs to move. But nothing happened. Not even a twitch.

"Such a beautiful liar." He smoothed out my hair, then kissed my lips. "One of you had to pay for making a fool of me. Do you understand what you did? You stood there at our engagement party, mocking me. All the while you were sleeping around with Enzo and God knows who else. I bet you have a long list."

I shook my head. "Please."

He pushed to his feet. When he turned to leave, panic rushed through me. I hurled myself toward him. This time, my arm swung out, and I fell to the hardwood floor with a thud. He stopped for a moment to look at me, then strolled out of my line of sight. The front door clicked open, and a gust of frigid air fluttered through the floor beneath me.

Then the house got quiet—too quiet—that for a moment, I thought maybe he had taken my parents with him. But he hadn't. They were calmly sedated just a few feet away from me.

I exhaled, and then, the house exploded with a thundering bang. The cold turned to hot in an instant. And I still couldn't get my legs to move.

The Descent

Enzo

"Do you know which house? I haven't been able to get a hold of Luca or Pina." Donata typed furiously into her phone.

"It's on my street." I took the sharp turn off Main Street and headed home. "I saw the address the day Aurora and I broke into Angelo's home office."

I'd done this drive to the Hamptons so many times. But tonight, everything seemed to be moving at a slower pace. Fuck, I should be there already. Every minute I wasn't there for Aurora felt like an eternity. Worst part was, I couldn't shake this feeling that I was too late, that I had already lost her.

As soon as our beach house was in my line of sight, I killed the headlights and pulled into the driveway. I had spent the past ninety minutes devising the perfect plan to break into Angelo's place unnoticed, find Aurora, and get out. But now that we were here, all I could see in my mind's eye was Angelo's face as I punched it repeatedly.

"Enzo, wait," Donata called after me when I climbed out of the car. "Let's wait for Luca. You can't go in there alone."

She chased me down the street. But I couldn't wait. I needed to see Aurora. I needed to know she was safe. My hopes deflated as I got closer to the house. It was dark and empty. Did we get it wrong? Had Angelo taken Aurora somewhere else? I had expected to, at least, see her parents here, more cars, more movement.

"Maybe it's already done?" Donata fell in step next to me. "They're gone."

Whatever else she said, I didn't catch it. The house exploded, and her words got muffled by the blast. When the shock wave hit me, I grabbed Donata and brought her down with me. I shielded her with my body, but the worst had already happened. Long licks of fire extended outward from the upper windows and the attic. In an instant, the entire house was alive with light and smoke. From this angle, I could make out a woman in the dining room. I squinted at the silhouette, while I swallowed hard to make the ringing in my ears go away.

Was that Aurora? Or was I seeing things?

"Was she in there?" Donata echoed my words as she shoved me off her.

"I don't know." I pushed to my feet, feeling nauseous from the heavy fumes in the air. "Stay down. And dial 911," I called over my shoulder then bolted for the front door.

"You know I can't do that," she whisper-yelled, "the police will help him."

Maybe I wasn't too late. Maybe Aurora wasn't even here. Maybe she survived the explosion.

The minute I reached the lawn, another detonation went

off inside the house. Not as loud as the first one, but enough to break more windows and blast off another wave of hot air in my direction. The flames engulfed the house with long arms that refused to let go.

Behind me, the street was empty and quiet. No one was coming to help. If Angelo wanted to make an entire family disappear, this would be the ideal place. There were a million ways to dispose of a body. All he required was a house away from prying eyes.

I followed the path to the right of the house and trudged up the driveway. When I reached the side of the house, Angelo and five of his guys came out of the gate, as if they had been waiting in the backyard. My heart raced because Angelo's presence here could only mean one thing—Aurora was here.

"I'm pretty sure Daddy told you to go home." He chuckled, while his eyes held all kinds of contempt for me.

Before, I wanted the chance to punch him in the face. Now, all I cared about was getting to Aurora. If she was inside, she didn't have much time. "I'm not here for you. Get the hell out of my way." I headed toward the yard gate, but he shoved me back.

When his crew didn't intervene, I figured he meant to take me on himself. The asshole had a bone to pick with me? I wasn't the one who paid for an underage wife. I didn't force myself on Aurora. She chose me. Not him.

"The world no longer lies at your feet. You're nothing without your daddy." He eyed me up and down. "How does it feel? Huh? You lose."

"It doesn't matter what happens to me. She will never love you. You know why? Because she's in love with me."

The pressure in my chest lifted from saying those words

out loud. Aurora and I were no longer a dirty little secret. We were real. Our love was real. And Angelo couldn't take that away from us. Angelo had to live with the fact that Aurora would never marry him.

"You took something that didn't belong to you." He gritted his teeth. "You don't get to keep her."

"That's not up to you, asshole."

At this point, we were beyond words. Angelo knew what he needed to know. Aurora belonged with me. Forever.

I clocked him square in the face.

His nose made a satisfying crunch before it spat blood on his neatly pressed button-down shirt. The same images flitted through my mind as I pounded on his face with everything I had. I thought of all the times his gaze swept up and down Aurora's body, the way he held her all night at the engagement party, and the time he jerked off to her.

When his guys finally decided to step in, Angelo was in a heap on the ground, cowering from my punches. As they lifted me off him, I managed to kick him in the mouth for good measure.

"Enzo, this doesn't help matters." Luca stepped between Angelo and me. It was overkill since two men already had me in a vise-like grip.

"It feels like it does," I argued.

The red droplets explained why my jaw felt achy and thick. Luca turned to glare at me as if this was a fight on school grounds. Did he not get it? This was about life and death. Aurora needed our help.

"He brought her here to die. Don't you see? You can't take his side."

"There are no sides here, Enzo. He's with us. We're all in this together."

I shot a glance to the burning house. It was too quiet. Near the front, the wall had already crumbled. And still, she wasn't asking for help. She should be screaming. She had to know I was coming for her.

"Aurora wasn't part of the deal. He's pissed off because she chose me. This has nothing to do with the new king." I struggled against the men holding me. "Luca, she has to live."

Angelo rose to his feet, fixed his hair, then turned to meet my gaze. A smug smile pulled at his lips, and I fisted my hands. My raw knuckles screamed in protest, but I didn't care. I was ready for another round with that asshole. To hell with his mandate and what the new king wanted.

"I can handle him." Angelo pointed his gun at me.

"Hang on a minute." Luca raised his hands and stepped closer to shield me.

Angelo shifted his stance and adjusted his aim. A trained assassin like him could make that shot. By the determined look in his eyes, I could see he had already decided I needed to die tonight. "You saw him. He tried to undo what I started here. This task is the most important one. Don Valentino's ascension can't be complete until Alfera's right-hand man is dead."

"Angelo." The warning in Luca's voice told me he saw the same resolution in Angelo's gaze.

"If he's not with us, then he's against us." Angelo projected his voice. Yeah, he needed witnesses if he wanted to be pardoned for my murder.

"Luca." Donata called from somewhere behind me.

"Donata, this is not the time to play the hero. Go home." He glanced over his shoulder to look at her.

Angelo nodded.

Adrenaline rushed through me as his guys let go of me. By the time I met Angelo's gaze, his gun had already gone off, and my stomach was bleeding. I toppled over, hugging my belly. The burning house shifted and rumbled as more of it crashed to the ground, blasting us with yet another shock wave of debris and hot air that made it impossible to breathe.

"Enzo. Stay with me." Donata's sobbing sounded so far away.

My head hit the cement as bright timbers floated up into the sky and mingled with the snow flurries rushing through the treetops. I focused on the roaring fire to my left, listening for Aurora's cries. Why was she so quiet?

"We need to apply pressure." Donata talked fast as she hovered over me. "Where the hell is the clean-up crew?"

"That would be Angelo's crew." Luca removed his jacket and shoved it into her hands.

"Then call your people. Do something." Donata's voice pierced my left ear.

It hurt.

It all hurt.

Everything felt like it was on fire, starting with the hot poker stuck to my side. I made to touch the wound, but Donata laced her fingers through mine, making a shh sound to soothe me.

Get it out. It burns.

"Aurora." My voice didn't sound like my own. My body didn't feel like my own. No matter how hard I tried, it refused to move—to get up and save Aurora. "Find her."

"Shh. Don't move." Donata used her entire body to apply more pressure to my stomach. "Rex is here. Santino went after

Angelo. Help is here, Enzo. You're going to be all right. Just hang on. Please."

Was I? Was I ever going to be fine if Aurora didn't make it out of the burning house? I didn't think I could live without her. She was the only light in my life. She was the only person I cared about. It took me a long time to figure it out, but I knew now.

She was the beginning of something beautiful for me.

She made this mafia world tolerable.

The faces around me blurred, while the voices muted into echoes, then whispers, and finally, a deep silence. When I blinked, the starry sky came into focus. The snow falling cooled my face and my hands, until the burn on my flesh subsided. I'd assumed dying would be more painful than this numbness—this sense of being somewhere between falling and floating.

In a matter of days, I had lost everything.

Aurora's beautiful face and bright blue eyes swam in and out of focus. When her image was clear, I could see the flurries playing with her hair. I blinked, and then, she was gone.

Anger and despair ate away at my memories of her—her smile, her touch, her soft skin—it all vanished with the rising smoke, until there was nothing left, only madness.

If she was the beginning...

Her house burning was the end.

The descent into darkness.

Epilogue

Rex

Weeks later...

"You let her die." Santino pursed his lips, accusing me of something he knew nothing about.

Though, the fury in his eyes was justified. A long time ago, we made a pact. I failed to protect them—to have their backs. But keeping Enzo alive was more important. I didn't make it to the Hamptons on time. Now, I would have to live with that and the choice I had to make. That was the thing in our world, choice was just a figure of speech.

"Aurora and Enzo together were never going to survive Angelo." I glanced at Enzo's unconscious body on the hospital bed. "I tried to help him. I volunteered to stay with her in Canada. You can't say that I didn't try hard enough."

"The all-powerful Rex comes to the rescue." Santino made a flitting gesture toward Enzo. "The only thing I can say for sure is that you were in a hurry to get Enzo out of the country.

Away from your family and away from the throne. Don't pretend this was about anything else other than you."

I turned to Donata for help. I got that Santino was hurting. Our childhood friend's life hung in the balance, and I was to blame. Because if I hadn't offered my help, Enzo would've given up on Aurora the day of the Holiday Gala when Angelo found out Enzo and Aurora were in love and planning to run away together. I was the one who offered them a second way out.

"I read your father's contract, Rex." Donata arranged Enzo's pillow out of habit.

Enzo didn't care about his sheets, or the water she kept by his side table every day. He'd been barely alive for weeks. At this point, I was sure the only one who could bring him back was Aurora. But she couldn't be here. I promised her I would do anything to keep Enzo alive. This was me keeping that promise.

"Santino's not wrong." She shrugged. "It's probably better if he's not here when you take everything that was his."

I glanced up, taking a deep breath. "If you see a different way out, please by all means, show me the way."

"Fuck off, Rex." Santino grabbed his coat off the foot of the bed. With a smirk of disgust on his face, he waved good-bye on his way out. "Heavy is the crown as they say."

"I'll come back later." Donata made to follow Santino out the door, but I gripped her elbow to get her to look at me.

I wasn't sure what I needed to hear anymore. "He's going to hate me. Isn't he? When he wakes up and she's not here, he's going to hate me."

She glanced down at my hand, where my hold had tightened around her arm. "Heavy is the crown."

I wanted to hang on to Donata. It felt as though she was the only friend I had left. Ever since Dad told me about the deal he'd made with Michael Alfera, my life slowly began to slip through my fingers. I stood there and watched my best friends walk out on me for something I had no control over. Or at least, not in the way they needed me to.

What I wanted no longer mattered. I promised Aurora I'd keep Enzo alive. And that was exactly what I planned to do. Even if, in the end, he hated me for it, Enzo could never know the truth.

THANK you so much for reading Fallen Raven (Raven Duet #1). I hope you enjoyed Enzo and Aurora star-crossed lovers story. Their epic romance concludes in Fallen Raven (Raven Duet #2), where Aurora lands on a submissive auction block, and Enzo has to risk it all to get her back. I've included the first chapter here.

Aurora
I should've stayed dead.
I should've run when he challenged the winning bid.
I should've said no to his contract.

But the ruthless **Don Enzo Alfera** gets what he wants.
He wants revenge.

More than anything, he wants me.

Download FALLEN RAVEN (Raven Duet, #2) Today!

Fallen Raven

BOOK TWO

Never Again

Enzo

11 years later, New York City

"Take off her dress." I projected my voice, so the two brunettes kissing on my bed could hear me over the sensual music playing in the suite.

I sat back on the sofa, facing them, and extended my long legs out in front of me. With the dim lights in the master suite casting a soft glow on their smooth skin and the white sheets, the scene was set. The four-poster bed was the stage. Aurora and I were the eager spectators.

Next to me, Aurora adjusted her top, shifting her body closer to mine. Her gaze darted between the two women putting on a show for us and me. God, I loved it when she squirmed like that. Aurora loved to watch. But she had yet to admit that to herself.

Earlier tonight, Ruby and Sage had offered to come home with me. After hours at the Crucible, drinking whiskey to numb the pain that resurfaced every summer, I couldn't find a reason to say no to them. The game was always the same—make Aurora watch to the point of madness. My reward was to see her come on my hand, my tongue, my dick. I lived for this moment when she unraveled just for me.

Right now, she was all that mattered. I inhaled deeply, expecting for breath in my chest to catch, to squeeze my heart, to hurt. But it didn't. I exhaled easily, getting lost in Aurora's blue gaze. She was all the air I needed. Her soft cheeks turned a bright red as she kept watching, while her fingers inched under her panties. She was so close, but for now, I stayed on my side of the sofa with my arms braced on my knees. When Ruby's dress dropped to the marble floor and her huge tits were finally freed, Aurora let out a tiny gasp.

"Do you like that, Angel?" I asked, brushing strands of hair away from her face.

She nodded, licking her lips.

Ruby sat on her heels and met my gaze, silently begging me to tell her what to do next. By the way her chest heaved in anticipation, I was certain she was desperate for relief. Her taut nipples looked painfully aroused. Sage had thoroughly kissed her for the past fifteen minutes, and now Ruby was ready for more. But I wasn't ready for our game to end.

I wanted Aurora to surrender to it. To tell me what she wanted to see next.

"What do you think, Angel?" I leaned toward Aurora and whispered in her ear. "What do you think she needs?"

Aurora shook her head, kneading her own breasts over the silky fabric of her top. "I don't know."

"I think you do." I wrapped my fingers around her throat and turned her to face the women ready to fuck each other senseless. I kissed the soft spot behind her ear before I turned to Ruby. "Kiss her."

"Fuck yeah." Sage crawled toward Ruby.

Her mouth descended on Ruby's tight peak, sucking hard while she played with the other mound. They fell into a heap of legs and arms, tearing off each other's underwear. Sage shot a quick glance my way. When I nodded once, she kissed her way down Ruby's belly and settled between her legs.

Eleven years ago, Aurora found one of my friends doing a similar move on his girlfriend. Instead of doing what most people would do, Aurora stayed and watched until my other friend caught her in the act. She'd been so turned on by the scene, she couldn't make herself walk away from it. I smiled at the memory from so long ago. That summer before senior year, I had no idea I had met the woman I would love for the rest of my life.

"Enzo," Aurora called for me, sliding her hands into my hair, right before her lips found mine in a heated kiss.

I squeezed my eyes closed and let her voice seep through me. How was it possible to love someone this much? After all this time, how could she still make my blood stir so easily?

Cupping her face, I moved on from her mouth to nibble on her neck and the mounds pressing against her top. Desire fluttered in my stomach and quickly made its way into my chest. The longing I felt for Aurora made me lose myself completely, along with the sense of time. Out of breath, and at the edge of insanity, I tore off her clothes and covered every inch of her with kisses, starting with her gorgeous tits, then moving down to her pussy. She was so wet for me, so ready.

"Do you want to feel what she feels?" I rubbed the stubble on my cheek along the inside of her thigh.

"Yes." She fisted my hair, pulling me toward her needy pussy.

Goosebumps spread over her thighs as she bucked her hips to give me better access. I slid two fingers past her entrance while I unbuckled my belt with my free hand. She mumbled a string of demands that mostly had to do with how much she wanted me to be inside her already.

Who was I to deny Aurora?

I picked her up by the waist and carried her to the bed, where Ruby and Sage converged on me as soon as I let go of her. They ran their hands all over me as they worked together to get me out of my shirt and pants. Aurora sat up on the bed as her gaze swept up and down my torso before it settled on my erection.

I could stay like this forever—with Aurora looking at me like I was the only person in the world.

"Take it." I gripped the nape of her neck and guided her.

Her lips around my cock were the biggest turn-on. She sucked me off with so much eagerness, I could barely hold it together. Somehow, I managed to fuck her pretty mouth with relentless thrusts. I kept at it, feeling the tip of my shaft sliding down her tongue until it reached the back of her throat and her eyes watered. When her gag reflex kicked in, I eased up to let her recover. She smiled up at me, and I slid past her teeth again. Fuck, she was so perfect.

My Aurora.

When I was sure I was going to blow if I didn't stop, I brought her up to meet my mouth for a searing kiss. I kissed her mouth hard, tasting my pre-cum on her tongue. Her moans had me at the edge. I couldn't wait any longer. I needed to be inside her now. I pushed her onto the mattress, then flipped her over. She landed on her belly with a sexy laugh that made my cock twitch painfully.

"Enzo, please." She raised her perky ass in the air.

"I know, Angel." I gripped her hips and swelled into her.

Sage and Ruby's hands fell away from me. In this moment, it was just us. I fucked her hard and without mercy, without pause.

Aurora was mine.

She was always meant to be mine.

"Omigod, Enzo. Don't stop." She fisted the duvet cover, lifting her hips to meet my quick thrusts one for one.

Fuck, I loved how she took all of me. Placing my hand over hers on the bed, I gave her everything I had. She was already there. All she needed was a little push. I pressed my chest to her back, gripping her hair into a ponytail, so she could get a better view of Sage, who'd been watching us fuck from the top of the pillows, while she rubbed her pussy.

"Look at her. She's so close just like you." I panted in her ear.

My cock steeled with every pass.

Aurora nodded, her eyes big and wide as she focused on Sage's short strokes over her clit. I dug my fingers along Aurora's jawbone and made her turn to me. I searched her gaze until I found a glimpse of all the things we were so many years ago. Aurora and I were still us. It was painted in her eyes, her lips, her skin. I clung to that image, kissing her long and hard while I pumped into her like my life depended on it.

"You feel so good, Angel. Fuck."

"Don't stop." She yelped, reaching out to squeeze my fingers.

We were connected in every way possible. In the next

breath, her slick walls clenched around my cock. She tensed under my weight. The moans she made when she orgasmed were my undoing.

I let go, pumping my cum deep inside her.

Then I was free-falling into an abyss where only Aurora and I existed. Ribbons of adrenaline sprung painfully below my navel and rushed to the rest of me. I tried to focus on Aurora's climax, but it was so hard not to get lost in my own release and the intense pleasure I'd only ever felt with her.

I surrendered to it.

Her moans were muffled by my own heart thrashing in my ears. Then the room was quiet and dark. Tomorrow, I would have to let go of this impossible fantasy, but for now, I wanted to feel Aurora's soft body under mine. I wanted to revel in this space where the pain of losing her didn't exist. I leaned forward until our sweaty bodies were pressed together, and I could kiss the salty sheen on her upper lip. I nibbled on her shoulder, and my cock got hard again while I was still inside her.

I wanted her one more time. One more time and then...

It would never be enough.

Ten years was not enough.

I would never get over her.

The next morning, I woke up with the mother of all hangovers. My head felt like a jackhammer was drilling right behind my left eye. How much did I drink last night? I rubbed the side of my temple and let my legs drop to the side of the bed. I sat up and winced when the room swayed a few rounds.

"Good morning." A small and groggy voice filtered through my painful daze.

I turned to face the other side of the bed. Fuck me. The

three strangers glanced up at me with expectant smiles. And then, all the events of last night came rushing back. A quick memory of meeting Sage and her friends flashed in my mind. I glanced down at her blonde friend.

When she reached out to touch my shoulder, my body jerked in response. "Don't touch me."

"Why? I thought we could—"

"You thought wrong." I scanned the room before my gaze settled on hers again.

In the bright light and without the whiskey in my system, it was impossible to pretend—impossible not to see she wasn't my Aurora.

"Who's Aurora?" she asked with a sexy smile, as if trying to drag me back into last night's fucked-up game.

I glared at her with disgust brewing in my chest. Not for her. For me. For letting myself fall prey to this fantasy again. The one I had sworn would never happen again. I took in a shallow breath that made my whole body ache for Aurora. The reprieve was over. In the light of day, her absence was stamped everywhere.

"My housekeeper will call a car service for you. Be gone when I'm done with my shower." I strode across the bedroom toward the en-suite bathroom.

Behind me, Sage's friend huffed and puffed as she collected her clothes that were strewn all over the floor and sofa. I shut the door behind me and ran the water. While I waited for the steam to fill the room and ease my pounding headache, I texted my housekeeper.

Me: *My guests need a car service.*
Mollie: *I'm not here to clean up your messes.*
Me: *Just get rid of them.*

I tossed the phone on the vanity. The screen lit up again with her response—a rolling eyes emote. Two seconds later, she barged into the bedroom.

"Out you go. Show's over." She clapped several times. "Come on. Your car is waiting, but it won't wait long."

"Who's Aurora?" The stranger's words echoed in my head.

I stepped into the shower and let the hot water ease the tension in my shoulders. If only it could wash away the pain in my heart. If only it could erase all my memories of her. I tried to fight the movie that began to play in my head. But it was too late—the explosion and the house burning with Aurora in it had already flashed in my mind's eye. It was all there, clear as day, the moment Rex told me he couldn't save her. That he had been too late.

"I'm sorry, brother. She's gone." Rex had stood by my hospital bed, looking at me with pity in his eyes, like I was some lost puppy. *"I swear I tried."*

"You let her die." I'd screamed at him in anger, yanking at the needle in my arm to remove all the tubes holding captive. I swung at him sluggishly. I had no idea how long I'd been unconscious. All my strength was gone. Though to me, it felt like the murders in the Hamptons happened only yesterday.

I had been in a coma for six months. After that, a whole month had gone by where I was in and out, loaded up on drugs. Someone didn't want me to come back to the land of the living. But then, Rex came to see me. I literally woke up to the news that our plans to save Aurora had gone to shit. I was the lucky one. The one who survived.

Angelo, the asshole who had bought and paid for Aurora's virginity, made good on his promise. When he found out Aurora and I had plans to get married and run away together, he killed her—burned his beach house to the ground with Aurora and her parents in it. Then he shot me and left me for dead.

For years, I told myself the clean-up crew could not have done such a good job making all the bodies disappear the next day. Maybe she was still alive. I searched for her. But in the end, I came to the realization that it was all just wishful thinking. That I was only looking for a ghost.

Aurora had been dead for ten years. And there was nothing I could do to get her back. Fucking three strangers in a drunken stupor only made things worse. I missed her now more than ever.

I braced my hands on the shower tile and hung my head.

Never again.

Made in the USA
Las Vegas, NV
17 October 2023